Praise for the r

"A compelling novel tha
The exciting plot is edg
suspenseful twists leading
ending. Mofina is at the top of his game."

—*FreshFiction* on *Whirlwind*

"With the exciting plot and a conclusion that is a true surprise to one and all, this is one book that has to be seen ASAP."

—*Suspense Magazine* on *Into the Dark*

"Mofina is one of the best thriller writers in the business."

—*Library Journal* (starred review) on *They Disappeared*

"Rick Mofina's tense, taut writing makes every thriller he writes an adrenaline-packed ride."

—Tess Gerritsen, *New York Times* bestselling author, on *The Burning Edge*

"A blisteringly paced story that cuts to the bone. It left me ripping through pages deep into the night."

—James Rollins, *New York Times* bestselling author, on *In Desperation*

"Taut pacing, rough action and jagged dialogue feed a relentless pace. *The Panic Zone* is written with sizzling intent."

—*Hamilton Spectator*

"*Vengeance Road* is a thriller with no speed limit! It's a great read!"

—Michael Connelly,
New York Times bestselling author

"*Six Seconds* should be Rick Mofina's breakout thriller. It moves like a tornado."

—James Patterson,
New York Times bestselling author

Also from Rick Mofina and MIRA Books

WHIRLWIND
INTO THE DARK
THEY DISAPPEARED
THE BURNING EDGE
IN DESPERATION
THE PANIC ZONE
VENGEANCE ROAD
SIX SECONDS

Other books by Rick Mofina

A PERFECT GRAVE
EVERY FEAR
THE DYING HOUR
BE MINE
NO WAY BACK
BLOOD OF OTHERS
COLD FEAR
IF ANGELS FALL

And look for Rick Mofina's next thriller
featuring investigative reporter Kate Page
EVERY SECOND
coming soon from MIRA Books!

RICK MOFINA

FULL TILT

Recycling programs for this product may not exist in your area.

ISBN-13: 978-0-7783-1745-6

Full Tilt

www.MIRABooks.com

Printed in U.S.A.

This book is for you, the reader

FULL TILT

He healeth the broken in heart,
and bindeth up their wounds.
—*Psalms* 147:3

1

Rampart, New York

The old burial grounds.

Nobody ever goes out there.

Chrissie was uneasy about her boyfriend's birthday wish to "do it" there.

"That place gives me the creeps, Robbie."

"Come on, babe. Think of it as your first time with an eighteen-year-old man, and our first time in a graveyard. How cool is that?" Robbie sucked the last of his soda through his straw, then belched. "Besides, we've done it everywhere else in this dog-ass town."

Sad but true. There was not much else to do here.

Rampart was a tired little city in Riverview County, at the northern border of New York. It was home to small-town America—flag-on-the-porch patriots, fading mom-and-pop shops, a call center for a big credit card company, a small Amish community and a prison.

The way Chrissie saw it, all people in Rampart did was work, get drunk, have sex, bitch about life and dream of leaving town.

Except maybe the Amish, she thought—they seemed content.

Chrissie and Robbie had been together for two-and-a-half years. Now, as they sat in his father's Ford Taurus waiting for the light, she contemplated the dilemma facing them.

She'd been accepted at a college in Florida. Robbie didn't want her to go. He was getting a job at the prison and was talking about marriage. Chrissie loved Robbie but told him she was not going to stay and be a Rampart prison guard's wife, working at the mall, driving her kids everywhere while trying not to hit the Amish buggies.

Chrissie wouldn't be leaving for a couple of months, but Robbie avoided talking about it. He lived in the moment. That was fine, but sooner or later she would have to end it with him.

But not tonight. Not on his birthday.

The light changed and they rolled by the Riverview Mall. Its vast parking lot was deserted and dark.

"So, are you up for the boneyard, babe?"

Robbie was already guiding the Taurus along the highway out of town. The white lines rushed under them and she made a suggestion.

"Why don't we go to Rose Hill?"

"Naw, we go there all the time."

Chrissie felt Robbie's hand on her leg.

"Come on. It's my birthday."

"But it's so freakin' creepy. Nobody goes out there."

"That's what makes it fun." He rubbed her inner thigh. "I got the sleeping bag in the trunk."

Chrissie sighed and looked out her window at the summer night.

"Okay."

The headlights reached into the darkness as they drove beyond town. The Ford's high beams captured the luminescent eyes of animals watching from the forests along the lonely drive.

After several miles, Robbie slowed to a stop and turned off the road onto an overgrown pathway. It was marked with an old weather-beaten sign that was easy to miss and bore two words: Burial Grounds.

The car swayed and dipped as he drove slowly over worn ruts until they stopped at a no-trespassing sign wired to a gate that was secured with a chain and lock.

"There, see." Chrissie pointed. "We can't get in."

Robbie slipped the transmission into Park.

"Yes we can."

He got out and went to the gate, his T-shirt glowing against the blackness. Moths fluttered around the headlights as he worked on the lock, and the only sound was the chorus of crickets.

Chrissie knew the area's history. She'd written about it for a ninth-grade paper.

In the late 1800s, the state built a large insane asylum in Rampart. It had its own cemetery because locals didn't want patients buried next to their loved ones. When the asylum was closed down forty years ago, all the headstones had been removed and grave sites kept secret to protect the families' privacy. There was nothing there now but a stretch of green grass bordered by lush woods.

Robbie unlocked the lock, the chain jingling as he removed it and opened the gate. After edging the car through, he closed it.

"How did you open that lock?"

"Trev's dad works with DOT and he told me that if you give that old lock the right twist, it'll open."

Robbie drove slowly along the wooded border of the graveyard, cut the engine and killed the lights.

Stars blazed above.

Guided by the light of Robbie's phone, they walked to a remote section where the grass was like thick carpet. They unrolled the sleeping bag.

"Nothing around but the crazy dead under us."

"Shh, birthday boy."

Robbie slipped his hands around Chrissie's waist then under her shirt and jeans. They kissed and as her fingers found his zipper she froze, pulled away and looked into the pitch-black forest.

"What is it?"

"Something's out there!"

Robbie followed her gaze to flames, flickering deep in the woods.

"What's that?" Chrissie held Robbie tighter.

"I don't know. There's nothing there for acres."

"There's an old barn the asylum used years ago, but—"

A faint, distant scream—a woman's scream—carried from the fire.

"Oh, God, Robbie!"

"What the hell?"

More screaming, this time louder, pierced the night, raising gooseflesh on Chrissie's skin.

"Help me! Please! Help me!"

Robbie grabbed Chrissie's hand and started for the woods leading to the fire—but she yanked him back.

"Let's take the car!"

"I don't know if we can get through!"

"We'll be safer in the car, Robbie!"

They ran to the car, dragging the sleeping bag.

Robbie fumbled for his keys, turned the ignition and headed the car down the path that seemed to vanish into the woods ahead.

The flames were growing.

Chrissie called 911.

"I want to report a fire and a woman screaming for help!"

As they followed the trail, knifing into a thick wall of trees and undergrowth, Chrissie guessed they were about one hundred yards from the fire. She gave the dispatcher directions and was assured that fire, paramedics and police were on the way.

Leafy branches continued scraping and slapping at the car. Robbie drove carefully over the rugged road.

"My old man will kill me if I scratch the Taurus!"

Underbrush and stones smacked at the undercarriage as they came to a clearing, gasping at the sight before them.

The old barn was engulfed in flames, the fire raging against the night sky.

A woman ran from it shrieking, trailing smoke and sparks. The flames that were devouring her entire body flapped like horrific flags as she staggered and collapsed into a burning heap in front of the car.

Chrissie screamed.

Robbie grabbed the sleeping bag, rushed to the woman and smothered the flames. While the inferno of the barn crackled and roared, Chrissie's screams were soon overtaken by the approaching sirens.

The woman groaned in agony.

As Robbie tried to take her hand, which was now a blackened hook, they saw charred ropes tied to her wrists.

2

Rampart, New York

Oxygen flowed in a soft, calibrated rhythm through the ventilator tube connected to the burn victim in the intensive-care unit of Rampart General.

The small screen above her bed monitored her heart, her blood pressure and her other vital signs.

An IV pole with a drip stood beside her bed.

She was wrapped from her head to her ankles in gauze and was heavily sedated to alleviate the excruciating pain of third-degree burns to over 85 percent of her body.

She'd lost her hair, ears, face, nearly all of her skin.

Her feet were charred stumps, her hands charred claws.

Her injuries were fatal. She would not live through the night, the doctor had told Detective Ed Brennan of Rampart Police Department.

Since then Brennan had waited with the ICU nurse by the woman's bedside, never leaving it.

He'd been home when he got the call.

His wife had put their son to bed. He'd made popcorn and they were watching the end of *The Searchers*, when his cell phone rang.

"White female, mid-twenties," Officer Martin had told him over blaring sirens. "Found her near the old burial grounds. Burned bad. They're taking her to the General—they don't think she'll make it. Looks like she was tied up, Ed."

Brennan rushed to the hospital in the hopes of obtaining a dying declaration from the victim.

The doctor took Brennan aside after emergency staff had done what they could for her.

"There's no guarantee she'll regain consciousness."

Brennan needed her to help him solve what would soon be her murder.

In the hours he waited, he'd gotten used to the room's smell. They had no ID for her. There was no chance of fingerprints and no indication she'd had any clothing or jewelry. If so, it had been burned away. They'd have to review local, state and national missing persons cases.

The most disturbing aspect was the ropes.

Again, Brennan looked at the pictures on his phone that Martin had sent from the scene.

Again, he winced.

Then he concentrated on the charred ropes.

She appeared to have been be bound by ropes.

The fire could've allowed her to escape from the building.

Escape from what and from whom?

Once they doused the fire and things cooled off they needed to get the forensic people in there.

"Detective?" the nurse said.

The charred remnants of what was once the woman's right hand moved.

The nurse pressed a button above the bed and the doctor arrived, checked the monitor and bent over the woman.

"She's regaining consciousness," the doctor said. "We'll remove the airway so she can talk, but remember, her throat and lungs are damaged."

Brennan understood.

This may be his only shot.

Once the tube was removed, the monitor started beeping as the woman gasped. They took a moment to tend to her and the beeping slowed. Then the doctor nodded to Brennan, who stepped close and prepared to make a video recording with his phone.

"Ma'am, I'm Detective Ed Brennan. Can you tell me your name?"

A long moment of silence passed punctuated with a gurgle.

Brennan took a breath and looked at the doctor before he continued.

"Ma'am, can you tell me a name, or tell me where you live?"

A rasping sigh sounded, then nothing.

"Ma'am, is there anything you can tell me?"

A liquidy, coarse utterance began to form a word.

"Share— R…"

"I'm sorry, ma'am. Try again."

"There…are…"

Brennan glanced at the doctor and nurse, blinking to concentrate as the woman tried to raise her blackened hand as if she wanted to pull Brennan to her.

"There are…there are others…"

The woman lowered her arm.

The monitors sounded alerts and the tracking lines flattened.

3

Rampart, New York

Brennan whirled his unmarked Impala out of the McDonald's drive-through and headed for the scene.

He gulped his black coffee but only managed a small bite of the blueberry muffin. His stomach was still tense from the hospital, the victim and her dying words: *There are others.*

What're we facing here?

He'd alerted his sergeant and lieutenant. They definitely had a suspicious death. Confirming the victim's ID would be critical. A forensic odontologist from Syracuse was en route to make the victim's dental chart. They'd submit and compare everything—height, weight, approximate age, X-rays, DNA—with all the regional and state databases, missing persons cases, and check her teeth with dental associations and with the New York State Police.

Sooner or later we'll get an ID on her. Then I'll have to tell her family the worst news they're ever going to hear.

He hated that part of the job.

As Brennan drove along the highway he focused on his case. They'd need to pull in Rampart's other detectives to help. The sun was climbing, which was good because they had to scour that scene. He figured the state police Forensic Identification Unit would be there by now.

Rampart PD often drew on the resources of the New York State Police or the FBI because, as a small jurisdiction, Rampart didn't get many homicides, maybe five or six a year.

You need challenging cases to make you a better detective. Brennan considered the forest rolling by. *Like my life.*

He was thirty-four and had been with the department for ten years, the past five as a detective with the investigative unit.

At times he yearned to be with the FBI, the DEA or Homeland, something bigger. But his wife, Marie, a teacher, loved their small-town life, saying it was good for Cody. Their son was five and prone to seizures if he got a fever or was overly stressed.

It didn't happen often, but when it did, it was frightening.

The other day when they were all shopping together at Walmart, Brennan realized that what he had here was good. But when he considered that his last major case was bingo fraud, small-town life got to him. Especially after the weekend call from his high school buddy who was with the Secret Service.

How's it going there, Ed? I'm protecting the vice president in Paris next week. Are you still chasing the Amish in Ram Town?

Brennan knew that Cody needed the quiet of a small town, but that call had left him reflective.

A cluster of local media vehicles had gathered at the entrance to the burial grounds, which was blocked by a state patrol car. Recognizing Brennan, the trooper waved him through. Brennan ignored questions reporters tossed at his window.

His Chevy rolled alongside the cemetery, then dipped and swayed when he cut into the forest on the old path, which had widened from the increasing traffic. As he reached the scene, the air smelled of burned wood. Smoke curled from the ruins, floating over the clearing in clouds that pulsed with emergency lights from the fire and police units at the site. Brennan parked and went to Paul Dickson, a Rampart detective, and Rob Martin, the first officer to respond. They were huddled with the state guys and firefighters. Brennan, who had the lead on this case, knew most of them and did a round of handshakes.

"Hey, Ed," Dickson said. "We heard she didn't make it."

"No," Brennan said before shifting to work. "What do we have so far?"

Consulting their notes, Dickson and Martin brought him up to speed. The fire had cooled enough for the forensic guys to suit up. At the same time, Brennan heard a yip and saw the cadaver dog, and its handler in white coveralls and shoe covers, head carefully into the destruction while, overhead, a small plane circled. The state police were taking aerial photos of the scene and mapping it.

"The teens who found her are asleep in my car, waiting to talk to you," Martin told Brennan.

"Okay, I'll get to them in a bit for formal statements."

The barn was state property built in 1901 as part of the farm that grew food for the asylum before it was shut down in 1975 and abandoned.

Brennan took in the piles of rubble, the stone foundation and watched Trooper Dan Larco with Sheba, a German shepherd, probing the scene. As she poked her snout here and there in the blackened debris, her tail wagged in happy juxtaposition to the grim task.

Sheba barked and disappeared into a tangle of wood at one corner. Larco moved after her, lowering himself to inspect her discovery.

"Hey, Ed!" he called. "We got something! Better take a look!"

Brennan pulled on coveralls and shoe covers, then waded cautiously into the wreckage.

The charred victim was positioned on its back beneath a web of burned timber. Most of the skin and clothing were gone. The arms were drawn up in the "pugilistic attitude." The face was burned off, exposing teeth in a death's head grin. From the remnants of jeans and boots on the lower body, it appeared the victim was male.

Brennan made notes, sketched the scene and took pictures. The forensic unit would process everything more thoroughly. Maybe they'd yield a lead on identification. In any event, there would be another autopsy.

Now we have two deaths. Is this what the first victim meant when she'd said, "There are others"?

Larco's radio crackled with a transmission from the spotter in the plane.

"There's a vehicle in the bush about fifty to sixty

yards northeast of the site. A pickup truck, you guys got that?"

A quick round of checks determined that no one on the ground was aware of the vehicle. Two state patrol cars moved to block it. Brennan, Dickson, Martin and some of the troopers approached the vehicle. They took up positions around it with weapons drawn and called out for anyone inside to exit with hands raised.

There was no response.

They ran the plate. The pickup was a late-model Ford F-150, registered to Carl Nelson of Rampart. There were no warrants, or wants for him. A quick, cautious check confirmed the truck was empty. Brennan noticed the rear window bore a parking decal for the MRKT DataFlow Call Center.

He pulled on latex gloves and tried the driver's door.

It opened.

A folded single sheet of paper waited on the seat.

Brennan read it:

I only wanted someone to love in my life.
It's better to end everyone's pain.
God forgive me for what I've done.
Carl Nelson

4

Rampart, New York

"Yeah, that's Carl's truck. What's wrong?"

Robert Vander's eyes flicked up from the pictures Brennan showed him on his phone and he snapped his gum.

"Carl's been off sick, why're you asking about him?"

Vander glanced quickly at his computer monitor, a reflex to the pinging of new messages. He was the IT chief at the MRKT DataFlow Call Center, which handled millions of accounts for several credit card companies. With five hundred people on the payroll, it was Rampart's largest employer.

Vander was Carl Nelson's supervisor.

"What's this about?" Vander looked at Brennan, who sat across from his desk, then at Paul Dickson, who was beside Brennan, taking notes.

"We're checking on his welfare," Brennan said.

Vander halted his gum chewing.

"His welfare? He called in sick two days ago, said he had some kind of bug. What's going on?"

Brennan let a few moments pass without answering.

"Mr. Vander, can you tell us about Mr. Nelson? What he does here, his character?"

"His character? You're making me nervous."

"Can you help us?"

"Carl's been with MRKT about ten years. He's a senior systems technician, a genius with computers. He helped design the upgrade for our security programs. He's an excellent employee, very quiet and keeps to himself. I got nothing but good things to say about him. I'm getting a little worried."

"Has he been under any stress lately?"

"No, nothing beyond the usual workload demands."

"What's his relationship status? Married, divorced, girlfriend, boyfriend?"

"He's not married. I don't think he has a girlfriend, or partner, whatever."

Vander repositioned himself in his chair.

"Do you know if he has any outstanding debts?"

"No, I wouldn't know."

"Does he gamble? Use drugs or have any addictions?"

"No. I don't think— You know, I'm not comfortable with this."

"Would you volunteer a copy of his file to us?"

"Not before I check with our human resources and legal people." Vander's mouse clicked. "I think you need a warrant."

"That's fine. Thank you for your help."

Brennan and Dickson got up to leave.

"Wait," Vander stood, his face whitened. "Would this have something to do with that story about the fire killing two people at the old cemetery?"

Brennan let a moment pass.

"Mr. Vander, we can't confirm anything and we strongly urge you to keep our inquiries confidential."

Later, as Dickson drove them from the center, he was frustrated at where things stood in the thirty-six hours since the fire was discovered.

They'd talked to Robbie and Chrissie, the two teens who'd called it in, and got repetitions of what they already knew.

"We've still got nothing on our Jane Doe. Nothing more on our John Doe—slash Carl Nelson. We've got his note, his truck. There's no activity at his residence and he's not at work. We know it's him. This is a clear murder-suicide, Ed. When're we going to get warrants and search his place for something to help identify the woman and clear this one?"

Brennan was checking his phone for messages.

"We'll get warrants once we confirm his identity. Let's go to the hospital. Morten wants to see us, maybe he's got something."

Morten Compton, Rampart's pathologist, was a large man with a Vandyke who was partial to suspenders and bow ties.

He was pulling on his jacket when Brennan and Dickson arrived. His basement office in the hospital smelled of antiseptic and formaldehyde.

"Sorry, fellas, I got to get to Ogdensburg." Compton tossed files into his briefcase. "I'm assisting the county with the triple bar shooting there and I got the double fatal with the church van and the semi in Potsdam."

"So why call us over, Mort?" Brennan asked. "Have you made any progress with either victim in my case?"

"Some, but first you have to appreciate that confirming positive IDs will take time, given the condition of the bodies and the backlog my office is facing. My assistant is in Vermont attending a funeral. I'm arranging for help from Watertown."

"So where are we on my double?"

"We've submitted dental charts for the female and male to local and regional dentists and dental associations. Toxicology has gone to Syracuse and we've submitted DNA to the FBI's databank."

"That's it?"

"Well, I don't think the male died in the fire."

"That's new. What's the cause for him?"

"Possibly a gunshot wound to the head. I just recovered a round, looks like a nine millimeter. You need to find a gun at the scene, Ed."

As they drove to the scene, Dickson raised more questions.

"So how does a dead man start a fire, Ed?"

"Maybe he didn't start it. Or, maybe he tied her up, started it, then shot himself in front of her, leaving her to burn to death."

"If he wanted to end things, like the note suggests, why not shoot the woman first? Make sure she's dead?"

"Maybe he did and missed and we haven't recovered the rounds yet. My gut tells me we're just scratching the surface here, Paul."

As Dickson shook his head in puzzlement, Brennan returned to the woman's dying words.

There are others.

The bright yellow plastic tape surrounding the blackened remnants of the barn bounced in the midday breeze. Techs from Troop B's forensic unit, clad in white-hooded coveralls and facial masks, continued their painstaking processing of the ruins.

Mitch Komerick, the senior investigator who headed the squad, brushed ash from his cheek as he pulled down his mask to meet Brennan and Dickson at the southwest corner of the line.

"Got your message on the update, Ed," Komerick said.

"Find a gun?"

Komerick wiped the sweaty soot streaks from his face, then shook his head.

"No weapon and no rounds, or casings, so far."

Brennan nodded and looked off in frustration.

"There are deep fissures where we found the male," Komerick said, "big enough to easily swallow a gun. My money says that's where it is. We're going to put a drainpipe camera down there. We're far from done."

"All right."

"My people have gridded the scene, and we'll sift through every square inch of the property. We've sent the pickup down to the lab in Ray Brook for processing. The arson team says an accelerant, probably unleaded fuel, was used, so the fire was intentional."

"Okay."

"But we've got something to show you, something disturbing. Suit up."

After Brennan pulled on coveralls, he followed Komerick and his instructions on where to step as he led him into the destruction. The smell of charred lumber and scorched earth was heavy. Some of the singed beams had been removed and stacked neatly to the side, revealing sections that had been processed. There was a heap of small machinery, now charred metal. Komerick pointed to the wreckage. "Look, these were livestock stalls that someone converted to small rooms, confinement cells."

"How can you tell? It's such a mess."

"We found heavy doors with locks, metal shackles and hardware anchored in the walls and floors, remains of mattresses, at least half-a-dozen cells so far. Somebody was definitely using the place, possibly for porno movies, for bondage, for torture. God only knows, Ed."

Brennan felt the hairs on the back of his neck rising.

"Mitch, over here!"

One of the forensic technicians was on his knees delicately brushing the ground with the care of an archaeologist. Another technician was recording it.

"Look," the technician said while clearing the small object, "we can run this through missing persons databases and ViCAP."

Rising from the grave of sooty earth and ash was a fine chain and a stylized charm of a guardian angel.

5

New York City

Kate Page, a reporter with Newslead, the global news service, blinked back tears as she consoled the anguished father, who she'd reached on his phone in Oregon.

The man on the line was Sam Rutlidge. His eleven-year-old son, Jordan, had vanished six years ago while walking to the corner store, two blocks from his home in Eugene, Oregon. Kate was writing a feature on missing persons across the country, on the toll cold cases exact on the families.

"I accept that he's gone," Sam said, "and before cancer took my wife, she told me she'd accepted it, too, that she'd see our boy in heaven. But I need to know what happened to him. Not knowing hurts every day, like an open wound that won't heal, you know?"

Kate knew.

She underlined his words in her notebook, the quotes she'd use in her story. Her heart ached for Sam, a haunted trucker. She asked him a few more questions before thanking him for the interview.

After hanging up, Kate cupped her face in her hands and let out a long breath. Then she walked from her desk across the newsroom to the floor-to-ceiling windows where she looked at the skyline of midtown Manhattan.

It never gets any easier.

A part of her died each time she talked to a grieving mom or dad. It always resurrected her own pain. When Kate was seven years old her mother and father had died in a hotel fire. After the tragedy, Kate and her little sister, Vanessa, lived with relatives, then in foster homes. Two years after their parents' deaths, Kate and Vanessa's foster parents took them on a vacation. They were driving in the Canadian Rockies when their car flipped over and crashed into a river.

The images—hell, that moment in her life—were fused into her DNA.

The car sinking...everything moving in slow motion...the windows breaking open...the freezing water...grabbing Vanessa's hand...pulling her out...nearing the surface...the icy current numbing her...her fingers loosening...Vanessa slipping away...disappearing... Why couldn't I hold you? I'm so sorry, so sorry.

Kate was the only one who'd survived.

Her sister's body had never been found. Searchers reasoned that it got wedged in the rocks downriver. Still, in her heart, Kate never gave up believing that Vanessa had somehow gotten out of the river.

Over the years, Kate had age-progressed photos of Vanessa made and submitted them with details to missing persons groups. She drew on her contacts with them, with police and the press, and she looked into open cases. But any leads always dead-ended.

It had become her private obsession.

Why was I the only one of my family to survive?

Wherever Kate went, she secretly looked into the faces of strangers who might now resemble her sister. For twenty years, Kate's life had been a search for forgiveness.

I know it's irrational, I know it's crazy and I should just let it go.

But she couldn't. It's the reason she'd become a reporter.

"Kate, are we going to see your feature today?"

She turned to see Reeka Beck, Newslead's deputy features editor, and her immediate boss, standing behind her.

Reeka was twenty-six years old, razor-sharp with degrees from Harvard and Yale. A rising star, she'd worked in Newslead's Boston bureau and was part of the team whose collective work was a finalist for a Pulitzer.

Her thumbs blurred as she finished typing a text message on her phone, then she stared at Kate. Reeka's cover-girl face was cool and businesslike while she waited for Kate to answer.

"Yes. It'll be done today."

"It's not on the budget list."

"It is. I put it on yesterday."

"Has it got a news angle?"

"It's a feature. We talked about this with—"

"I know we talked about it, but we'd get better pickup with a news peg."

"I'm adding the latest justice figures on unsolv—"

"Maybe you could find a case police are close to solving."

"I know how to write news—"

"Did you remember to arrange art for your story?"

Kate let the tense silence that passed between them scream her offense at Reeka's condescending tone. She was forever curt, blunt and just plain rude, cutting reporters off when they answered her or dismissing their questions. Every interaction with her bordered on a confrontation, not because Reeka was ambitious and convinced she had superior news skills but rather, as the night editors held, because one of Newslead's executives was her uncle and she could get away with it. Every newsroom Kate had ever worked in had at least one insufferable editor.

"Yes, Reeka, there's art. The story's on the budget. I'll file it today, as noted in the budget, and I'll insert the new justice stats."

"Thank you." Reeka pivoted while texting and left with Kate's eyes drilling into the back of her head.

Be careful with her. This is not the time to make enemies. Kate walked back to her desk amid the newsroom's cluttered low-walled cubicles. A number of those desks were empty, grim reminders that staff had been cut in recent years as the news industry continued bleeding revenues.

It was rumored Newslead would introduce a process to measure how many stories reporters produced and subscriber pickup rates of their work, against that of competitors like the AP, Reuters or Bloomberg.

Bring it on. Kate could go toe-to-toe with anyone. She had proved that a year ago in a brutal job competition at Newslead's Dallas bureau where she broke a story about a baby missing during a killer tornado. It's why Chuck Laneer, a senior editor in Dallas, later offered her a job at Newslead's world headquarters after he was transferred here to Manhattan.

Since then, Kate had led Newslead's reporting, often beating the competition on coverage of serial killings, mall shootings, corruption, kidnappings, every kind of chaos that unfolded across the country or around the world.

Reporting was in Kate's blood.

And for as long as she remembered she'd always battled the odds.

Her life had been a continual struggle for survival. She'd bounced through foster homes, spent her teen years on the street, taking any job she could get to put herself through college. She'd worked in newsrooms across the country and had a baby by a man who'd lied to her and written her off. Now here she was: a single mother who'd just turned thirty, and a national correspondent at one of the world's largest news organizations.

Settling back into her desk, Kate's heart warmed as she looked at Grace, her seven-year-old daughter, smiling from the framed photograph next to her monitor.

We've come a long way, baby. We're survivors.

Less than an hour later, she finished her feature and sent it to the desk.

As she collected her things to leave, her phone rang.

"Newslead, Kate Page."

"Kate, this is Anne Kelly, with the New York office of the Children's Searchlight Network. Do you have a second?"

"Sure."

"Fred Byfield, one of our investigators, said I should

call. You'd asked that we alert you to any queries we get that may relate to your sister's file, no matter how tenuous?"

Kate's pulse quickened. "Yes, go ahead."

"We wanted to give you a heads-up about a query we recently received from law enforcement."

It sounded like the woman was reading from a message.

"All right," Kate said.

"We were asked to check our files for a piece of jewelry concerning missing white women in their twenties."

"But that's routine."

"It is, but in this case, Fred said that they're asking about a necklace with a guardian angel charm."

Kate froze.

Shortly before her death, Kate's mother had given her and Vanessa each a necklace bearing a guardian angel charm. Kate had described the necklace in the file she'd submitted with missing persons organizations.

"Does it say anything about engraving or an inscription?"

"No."

"Can you give me more details, Anne?"

"I can have someone call you."

"Okay, but can you tell me anything more right now?"

"Well, we just got a message that the query went to our national office in Washington to run a search on the item, and, Kate, I'm sorry but it concerns a homicide."

Kate slid down into her chair.

6

New York City

Kate's express train barreled north out of Penn Station.

As she stared into the darkness, her mind raced, absorbing the call about the necklace.

Could it be Vanessa's?

Contending with the ramifications and questions, she felt a knocking in her heart that turned into apprehension.

Stop it.

Vanessa's dead. She died twenty years ago. Why do I put myself through this? Why do I cling to the hope that she survived? And now this: a homicide.

The subway platforms blurred by until Kate reached her stop. That's when her phone rang. It was Nancy Clark, her neighbor, who watched her daughter.

"Hi, Kate, is this a bad time?"

"No. I'm just about home. Everything okay?"

"Oh, yes, Grace really wanted to talk to you."

"All right, put her on."

The sound of the phone being passed to Grace was followed by "Hi, Mom?"

"Hi hon. What's up?"

"Mom, can I get my own phone?"

"Oh, sweetie."

"But all my friends have phones."

"I'll think about it. I'll be home soon. We'll talk about it then."

"Okay, Mom, love you."

"Love you, too."

Kate touched her phone to her lips and smiled.

What a kid.

Grace was her sun, her moon and the stars in her life. She'd taken to New York City like she was born here. She loved her school, her new friends, Central Park, the museums, everything about the city.

Kate treasured her job with Newslead, given her long road to get to this point. It had taken a little luck and a lot of hard work, but she'd turned a corner professionally and financially.

We've got a good life here. They lived in Morningside Heights in a Victorian-era building where she'd sublet an affordable two-bedroom apartment from a Columbia University professor who'd taken a sabbatical in Europe. While walking the few blocks home from the station, Kate checked for any updates from Anne Kelly at the Children's Searchlight Network.

Nothing.

Kate picked up her mail in the lobby, the place where she and Grace first met Nancy Clark, a retired and widowed nurse who lived alone on the floor above them.

She was so kind and warm she had practically adopted Kate and Grace. They had each other over for coffee and Nancy quickly insisted she look after Grace whenever Kate worked or traveled. Now, outside Nancy's apartment, Kate noticed the aroma of fresh baking before Grace opened the door.

"Hi, Mom! We made cookies!" Grace hugged Kate then went back to the kitchen table and collected a small tin and her backpack. "Nancy says I can take them home."

"Okay," Kate said. "Thanks for this, Nancy."

"Anytime. We had fun. I'll see you guys tomorrow."

At home Kate and Grace each had a cookie while settling in before supper. As usual, Grace emptied her school backpack on the coffee table. Kate set aside the mail, fired up her laptop to review emails, then changed into jeans to prepare chicken tacos, rice and salad. Before setting the table, Kate checked her phone again.

Nothing from the Searchlight Network.

"Mom, did you think some more about my phone?" Grace asked while biting into her taco.

"Still thinking on it, hon."

"Maybe we could look on your computer for a good one?"

"Not so fast, kiddo." Kate smiled.

After supper, Kate helped Grace with her book report on *Horton Hears a Who!*

"Mom, who do you like better, the Cat in the Hat or Horton the Elephant?"

"Well, the Cat creates a lot of mischief whereas Horton tries to help people, so I guess Horton, for that reason."

"The Cat's a lot of fun, though."

"Yes, but he leaves a big mess."

Later, when Kate got Grace into the tub for her bath, Kate's phone rang. The number was blocked. Kate left the bathroom door open and kept an eye on Grace, who was singing to herself as she splashed. Kate moved down the hall to take the call out of earshot.

"Hello?"

"Kate Page?"

She didn't recognize the man's voice.

"Yes, who's calling?"

"Detective Ed Brennan, Rampart Police, Rampart, New York. I got your name and number from the flyer you'd submitted to the Children's Searchlight Network."

Kate caught her breath and tightened her grip on her phone.

"Yes."

"My call concerns your listing of a necklace your six-year-old sister was in possession of when she was presumed to have drowned after an auto accident in Canada, twenty years ago."

"Yes."

"Could you go over the details of the necklace for me?"

"Now?"

"Yes."

Kate cleared her throat.

"A month before our mother died, she gave Vanessa and me each a tiny guardian angel necklace with our names engraved on the charms. Vanessa wanted to trade them, so she wore the one with my name on it and I kept the angel bearing her name."

"So, except for the engraving, they're identical?"

"Yes."

"Do you still have the other necklace?"

"Yes, I do."

"I understand you live in New York City."

"That's right."

Brennan paused as if to choose his words carefully.

"I know this would be very difficult, and I apologize for the imposition, but would you be willing to bring the necklace to Rampart to show us? It might help with an ongoing investigation."

"Couldn't I just send you a picture?"

"We'd prefer to see the actual necklace—we might have other questions."

Kate's stomach began tightening.

"Can you tell me more about the case, Detective?"

A few moments passed.

"This is confidential," Brennan said.

"Of course."

"We've found a necklace at a crime scene that fits with the description you gave. However, the engraving is unclear at this point. It'll need further analysis because it was badly charred."

"Charred?"

"Unfortunately, it was discovered in the remains of a fire at the scene of what appears to be a murder-suicide. We have a white female in her twenties deceased, who was burned beyond recognition. We're doing all we can to confirm her identity."

Kate put her hand to her mouth, then glimpsed her daughter happily playing in the tub.

"You say it's a murder-suicide, what—what else can you tell me?"

"The male's identity is also unconfirmed. We've not released many details to the public at this point. I am very sorry to put you through this. But we wouldn't have imposed if we didn't have reason to believe your cooperation might assist us. Will you be able to bring the necklace to Rampart?"

"Yes. Yes, I'll be there with the necklace tomorrow."

After hanging up, Kate got Grace to bed, then called Chuck Laneer's cell phone. Although Reeka Beck was her immediate boss, and going over her head would create tension, Kate preferred to talk to Chuck about this. They had a good relationship going back to Dallas when she'd told him about Vanessa's tragedy.

"That's an incredible development for you, Kate," he said when she filled him in. "I don't see a problem with you taking a few days off to follow up. But to steer clear of any potential conflict, you're not going up there as a Newslead reporter."

"Right."

"You're going on your own cost and time, to follow up on a private matter. I'll let Reeka know you're off for a few personal days."

"Thank you."

"Good luck with this, Kate. It can't be easy."

Kate then made arrangements with Nancy to watch Grace. She used her points to book a flight and car and started packing.

Then she went to her jewelry box and took out the necklace bearing the tiny guardian angel with the name "Vanessa" engraved on it. She held it in the palm of her hand until tears rolled down her face.

I tried to hold you. I tried so hard.

7

Rampart, New York

The calm *clip-clop* of a passing Amish horse and buggy carried through the window of the Rampart Police Department, belying Kate Page's unease.

After her plane had landed in Syracuse, she'd made the two-hour drive in a rented Chevrolet Cruze. Mile after mile her knuckles were white on the wheel, until she'd reached the edge of town where Rampart's sign welcomed her to the Home of the Battle of the High School Bands.

Following the GPS, she went straight downtown to the limestone building housing police headquarters. A receptionist directed her to a creaky hardback bench where she waited for Detective Brennan. Still anxious from her trip, Kate checked local coverage on her tablet.

Mystery Surrounds Double Death. The headline in the *Rampart Examiner* stretched over a sweeping aerial photo of the crime scene. The charred blotch of the obliterated barn was branded on the lush woods like a wound.

Is this where my sister died?

For much of her life Kate had cleaved to the remote hope Vanessa was alive, and, now, to learn that she might've died here was overwhelming. But Kate held on to her composure by concentrating on news reports.

A new one posted on a radio station's site said police still hadn't identified the victims. However, sources had told the station that the male was believed to be Carl Nelson, an IT technician at the MRKT DataFlow Call Center. They described him as a shy, "near-reclusive" man, whose truck was found near the burial grounds, the site of the fire. Mystery continued to swirl around rumors that a note was left in the apparent murder-suicide. Police remained tight-lipped about the investigation, the report said.

Kate saved the story with others she'd collected.

As she wondered about Carl Nelson, she looked up when someone said her name.

Two men in sport jackets stood before her.

"I'm Ed Brennan, this is Paul Dickson. We appreciate you coming all this way. How was your trip?"

"It was all right."

"Good. We'll go in here to talk."

They went into a windowless meeting room, where Brennan offered Kate something to drink.

"Thank you, water would be fine."

"I understand you're a reporter in New York with Newslead, the wire service."

"Yes."

A shadow of concern passed over Brennan's face and Dickson shot him a subtle glance.

"But you're not here to report on this case. This is a personal matter."

"Yes."

"What we discuss here must remain confidential, do you understand?"

"I do."

"Good."

Brennan positioned a chair for Kate and gave her a bottle of water. She sipped some, reached into her bag for the angel necklace and put it on the table. Brennan looked at it then opened his notebook to a clean page.

"For our benefit, Kate, would you please give us an overview of your family's background?"

Kate recounted the history of the necklace again.

"Would you be willing to volunteer your necklace for us to process for comparison?" Brennan asked.

"Of course. May I see the one you found?"

Brennan was silent for a moment.

"No, I'm sorry, that's physical evidence. But we'll show you this."

He slid a file folder to Kate. She caught her breath at the crisp, enlarged color photograph of an angel necklace. It was battered; the engraving was illegible. It was blackened, set against a white backdrop, next to an evidence tag and photo-document ruler to show scale.

"They are similar," Brennan said. "We'll pass yours to the forensic unit."

Absorbing the charred necklace in the picture, Kate's thoughts rocketed to Vanessa, the barn fire, the agony she must've suffered.

"I just don't understand," Kate said.

"What?"

She lifted her head from the photo. "If this is my

sister's necklace, then how did it get from our accident in Canada to here?"

"If it's hers, there're a number of possibilities. It could've washed onto the shore. An animal could have carried it off. Someone may have found it. Then, over the years, it made its way through flea markets, yard sales and jewelry stores, pawn shops, who knows, back into the world, as it were. We have a lot of theories and questions."

"So you're discounting the possibility that my sister survived and somehow turned up here?"

"We haven't confirmed anything, so we're not discounting anything. In fact we've made some inquiries with the Royal Canadian Mounted Police."

"Into my sister's case?"

"Listen, we'd rather not go into detail, but there are other aspects."

"What aspects? I'd like to know."

"I know how this sounds but we can't discuss our investigation."

"I read that there was a suicide note—what did it say?"

"We'd rather not discuss any other aspects."

"Well, I'd like to see her, the woman who was killed."

Brennan exchanged a look with Dickson and shifted in his chair.

"Given the condition, I don't think it would be beneficial."

Kate sat there not knowing what to think or say as a long silence passed.

"We're doing everything we can to confirm identification," Brennan finally said. "I hate to ask this, but is there any chance that you would still have your sister's hairbrush or access to her dental records?"

Kate stared at him.

"No, I don't."

Kate looked away for a moment.

"Kate, would you be willing to volunteer a DNA sample?"

"Of course, if it helps."

"It would," he said. "We'll get someone from the state forensic unit to do a cheek swab once we're done."

As the time passed, Brennan consulted his notes and asked Kate more about her family history, if she recalled any connection to Rampart, or Carl Nelson.

"No, there's none. I've never been here until today."

"Does this man register with you in any way, Kate?"

Brennan showed her an enlarged color photocopy taken from a New York State driver's license. Icy eyes glared from the face of a fully bearded man, in his late forties, who evoked a cross between the Unabomber and Charles Manson. A chill climbed up Kate's spine as she sensed something seething just beneath the surface.

Is this the last face Vanessa saw?

Kate memorized his address, 57 Knox Lane, Rampart.

"No, I've never seen him before. He's not familiar to me in any way," she said. "Is this the man who died in the fire?"

"We're confident it is, but we're awaiting positive confirmation from the pathologist."

"What do you think the relationship was between

Carl Nelson and my sis—the woman who died in the fire?"

"That's under investigation."

After the detectives ended the interview, they watched as a technician from the forensic unit used a cotton-tipped swab to scrape Kate's inner cheek. Then Kate signed papers concerning her DNA sample and the necklace. Before leaving, she asked the detectives to direct her to the scene.

"It's still being processed," Brennan said.

"So?"

"We'd prefer you didn't go there—you can't see anything from the highway."

"Can you take me out there?"

Kate looked both detectives in the eyes.

"We're sorry, we can't do that," Brennan said.

"Why not? Haven't I helped you?"

"We need to protect the integrity of the investigation and we ask that you keep our discussion confidential. We trust you understand."

"Sure, I get it. You wanted me up here just to help you."

"No, it's not like that. We know how difficult this must be for you, but as a reporter you understand that we have to be careful with how things proceed."

"I get it." Kate gathered her bag and exchanged cards with Brennan and Dickson. "How long before you can confirm the identity of the woman?"

"There's no telling," Dickson said. "The challenge is the condition and the fact the pathologist's office is backlogged with other cases."

"Kate," Brennan said. "Go home. We appreciate your help, and what you're going through."

"I don't think you do, Ed. Either my sister died twenty years ago, or lived two decades without me knowing before she died two days ago. That's what I'm going through."

8

Rampart, New York

Kate used the aerial news photo and the Chevy's GPS to get her bearings for the burial grounds at the edge of town.

She *needed* to see the crime scene.

She'd deserved that much from Brennan and Dickson.

But she should never have expected it.

From her years of reporting Kate knew that detectives were fiercely protective of their investigations. They had to be so that cases didn't fall apart when they got to court.

But this is my life.

Brennan could've taken her to the scene. She'd helped him and he could've done the same for her. She'd paid for the right to know what had happened to her sister—she'd paid for it the moment her hand had slipped from hers in that cold mountain river.

Screw Brennan.

Kate had endured too much and come too far not to find the truth, especially now when she was this close to it. She'd keep digging on her own, just like she'd done most of her life. She owed it to Vanessa and she owed it to herself. All Brennan and Dickson had wanted was for Kate to give them the necklace and her DNA, then go home.

She glanced at aerial crime scene photos on her tablet on the passenger seat.

We'd prefer you didn't go there.

Just try and stop me. She guided her rental along an empty stretch of highway that curved through dark, wooded countryside. After a few miles she came upon a New York State patrol car blocking the overgrown entrance to the burial grounds. A strip of yellow crime scene tape was extended across the gate.

Kate had an idea.

She parked nearby, got out and approached the lone trooper sitting at the wheel. He gave her a cool appraisal, watching her hands as she reached into her bag.

"Hi," she said. "Kate Page, I'm a reporter with Newslead." She showed him her plastic ID. "How're you doing?"

"Just fine. Can I help you?"

"Can you show me where the press can access the crime scene?"

"This is as far as you go," he said.

"Really?"

"Yeah, the others were here this morning. You can get updates from Rampart PD. I can give you a number."

"I need to take pictures of the scene—can I get closer?"

"This is as far as I can let you go. They're still working on it. The scene hasn't been released yet."

Kate tapped her notebook against her leg. So much for that idea. There wasn't much more she could do here. She was already on thin ice for using her job with Newslead the way she did and against Chuck's caution.

"Okay, thanks." Kate returned to her car.

She drove away feeling defeated.

How could she just leave? It was like she was losing Vanessa again. She had to do something.

What? What can I do?

As she struggled to find a solution, the answer came around the next curve in the shape of a roadside rest area. Kate pulled in and parked at the extreme edge, nearly out of sight. She checked her phone. There was still service here; the signal was good. She consulted her map, the aerial photo, then coordinated things with the compass app on her phone. The crime scene was less than a quarter of mile northeast through dense forest.

Kate locked her car, adjusted her bag so it rested on her back, found a straight branch to use as a hiking stick and set off into the woods. The terrain was treacherous. She was glad she was wearing flat shoes today. Thick underbrush concealed the uneven ground. Leafy low-lying branches tugged and pulled at her. She sought deadfall to cross a creek. Several times she was convinced she was going the wrong way but stayed true to the northeast direction of her compass.

Some thirty minutes after she'd set out, Kate heard distant voices carrying into the forest and spotted flashes of yellow and white through the woods. Then she reached the clearing and the blackened ruins of the barn. The scene was ringed with yellow tape. Technicians in white coveralls were probing it, sifting the debris.

A number of vehicles from Rampart PD, Rampart Fire and county and state police were parked at the far side. Keeping to the edge of the woods, Kate moved toward them, where she was able to get closer without anyone noticing her.

The air carried the smell of charcoal and the memory of death.

As the forensic people worked with funereal care the reality hit Kate full force.

Did Vanessa die here?

Anguish swelled in Kate's throat as an image came to her:

Vanessa is young and they're crossing the street. Kate's taking her hand; the earth shakes as a huge rig thunders by. Fear rises on Vanessa's little face, but she trusts her big sister, loves her, worships her, as her little fingers tighten around Kate's.

Needing to be closer to the ruins, Kate reached into her bag for her compact digital camera. It had a high-quality lens and she zoomed in on the jagged black tangles of planks and trestles. With each picture Kate stepped closer, and with each photo her heart broke a little more. Moving in, she scoured the burned rubble, her camera offering more detail the nearer she got. She focused on a series of charred beams jutting from the aftermath. They were tagged, indicating they'd been processed. On patches of the wood that were not burned, Kate saw crude markings scratched into the surface. To see them better she needed to get closer—she needed to do the unthinkable.

Kate lifted the tape to step into the scene but hesitated.

She'd be breaking the law.

But this could be the last thing my sister touched.

Her heart raced.

She might never be this close again.

Kate stepped into the scene, taking more photos. Moving in deeper, she looked beyond the beams, noticing pockets within the devastation that appeared to be gridded, cleared and tagged. She concentrated on those areas, zooming in, taking—

"Hey!" Keys jingled as a uniformed officer trotted from one of the vehicles. "Step out of there now! You're under arrest!"

9

Rampart, New York

Kate could hear her pulse thudding in her ears.

Over that, she heard the police radio dispatches.

She was in the backseat of Rampart Officer Len Reddick's patrol car. He was in the front verifying her Newslead ID, which he held in his hand. She could smell his cologne and peppermint gum. His jaw muscles pumped away, letting her know that he was still pissed.

"That's right, Kate Page," Reddick chawed into his microphone. "Page. Poppa Alpha Golf Echo. Employee number seven-two-six-six."

Kate's wrists throbbed against the metal handcuffs. The cuffs were an overreaction because Reddick was angry that he'd failed to spot her. She'd seen the *Sports Illustrated Swimsuit Edition* splayed on the front seat when he put her in his car.

He'd seized her camera, her phone and her bag, then read Kate her rights.

As his radio crackled, she looked out the window.

This morning she'd kissed Grace goodbye; now

she was handcuffed and facing charges. She knew that it was wrong to step into a crime scene, but she was compelled by a raw feeling that her sister had been here.

I can feel it, I can just feel it.

As Reddick pawed through her things she endured the sting of humiliation and, when he found Detective Brennan's card, braced for what was to come.

Reddick's inquiries to his dispatcher had launched a train of trouble. Calls were made to Newslead to alert her editors. Brennan was called and was en route. He'd insisted on questioning her, as it was his scene. Reddick meantime had waved over one of the forensic technicians to examine Kate's camera and phone to review the pictures Kate had taken.

Kate's heart was racing. So far, Reddick hadn't patted her down.

She'd taken precautions to save her photos. The instant Reddick had discovered her inside the crime scene, she immediately removed her camera's stamp-sized memory card, slid it into her sock, then, moving as fast as she could, installed a new card and resumed taking more photos. If the police didn't find her hidden card, she could look at the images later.

At that moment, Reddick's cell phone rang.

"Your people in New York."

Kate raised her cuffed hands and Reddick passed his phone to her. He stepped out of the car to show the technician Kate's phone, allowing her some privacy.

"It's Reeka. What's happened?"

Kate's stomach tensed.

"I think I should talk to Chuck, Reeka."

"He had to go to an emergency meeting in Chicago. I'm your supervisor, talk to me."

"Didn't Chuck tell you why I'm here?"

"He told me nothing. You should've advised me if you were assigned something on your day off. Why are you under arrest in Rampart?"

Kate explained everything to Reeka, exposing the fact she'd gone over her head to Chuck.

"So, from what the police just told me," the temperature of Reeka's voice plummeted to a prosecutorial level, "and from what you're telling me, you go up there on your time for personal reasons, then present yourself as a Newslead reporter to try to gain access to a crime scene, are refused, then you later breach the scene and are now facing charges."

Kate admitted that was correct.

"You're aware of Newslead's policy on how our reporters are to represent the organization and conduct themselves, especially at crime scenes? You're aware of that, Kate?"

"Of course."

"Yet, you've clearly violated it."

Kate said nothing.

"I'll be discussing your situation with senior management. Until then, I suggest you get yourself an attorney."

The call ended.

This was Kate's fault and she chastised herself when she thought of Grace. What would happen to her if she was jailed? Would social services be called?

Why didn't I think this through?

She scanned the scene again, unable to deny its

emotional pull. Decades of guilt, of being haunted by Vanessa's ghost, had clouded her judgment.

Brennan had arrived and was near the car with Reddick and the technician, huddled over Kate's camera and phone, while Reddick continued searching the contents of her bag. Occasionally Reddick pointed to the scene, with the technician nodding, before Brennan approached the car and helped Kate out.

"I asked you not to come here, Kate. You know full well we have to protect this scene. Anything and everything is considered evidence." He shook his head. "You misrepresented yourself to the state trooper, you breached our scene and tromped though it, contaminating it, or, possibly planting evidence. You're facing possible interference and criminal trespass charges. I can't understand why you did this."

"Why?" Adrenaline and fury coursed through her and she let go. "I can't believe you have to ask me that! You found my sister's necklace out there in that—that killing ground and she's—"

"We haven't confirmed it's hers yet."

"You know and I know it's hers!"

"No, we don't. Kate, everything we have to this point is circumstantial. Nothing's conclusive."

"You found her necklace out there! My God, she was supposed to have drowned twenty years ago in Canada! So you tell me how did it get there?"

"We don't know and we don't know that it's your sister's. You of all people should understand the huge emotional and legal consequences of making assumptions that result in misidentification."

"Then tell me why you have contacted Canadian police."

"I'm not discussing this case with you."

"Yeah. Remember, Ed, you called me to help you! That's why I'm here. I've lived with this for twenty years! I deserve to know the truth! That's why I did what I did!"

A few tense seconds passed.

"Did you take, touch or leave anything, Kate?"

"No, all I took were some pictures with my camera. That's all."

Brennan returned to the others for another long discussion, then returned with her things and Reddick, who removed her handcuffs.

"The technician found no pictures on your phone, so we're returning it."

"I told you, I didn't take any pictures with my phone."

"We're keeping the memory card from your camera and the additional memory cards we found in your bag. The technician tells me that your camera had wireless connectivity but that you didn't send any images anywhere."

"I didn't. Are we done? Or are you going to go full-bore cop and strip-search me?"

Brennan let her comment pass.

"No. I don't have a female officer on duty, for one. I'm going to make a judgment call here, but I think we've covered this given the circumstances and the situation."

"So I can go?"

"Not yet. Now, you're going to show us your path into the scene so we can mark it," Brennan said. "Then we're going to need impressions of your shoes and take your fingerprints. When we're done, Officer Reddick will drive you to your car."

"Am I being charged?"

"No, but if you interfere again, we'll bring the charges back. Understood?"

Kate met Brennan's stare and she nodded.

"I appreciate your help," he said, "and what you're going through. Go home, Kate, and let us do our job."

10

Rampart, New York

The grill of Reddick's patrol car filled Kate's rearview mirror for several miles after she'd left the rest stop.

Driving to town, she bit back on her tears and her anger at Rampart police but mostly at herself. She was churning with rage and an underlying ache, because she'd never been this close to Vanessa.

I've got to think clearly.

Kate looked at the time.

Even with the drive to Syracuse she had a few hours before her early evening return flight. Enough time to check into the other part of the case.

Carl Nelson.

She'd become so consumed by the necklace that she'd overlooked his role. She knew nothing about him, the man the local press had named as the second fatality in the fire, the reclusive computer expert. Remembering his long hair and beard from the driver's license photo Brennan had showed her, Kate thought Nelson fit the image of a creepy eccentric. What part did he play in this? What was Vanessa's relationship to him? And what about the rumors of a suicide note?

Kate needed to talk to Nelson's family, neighbors and coworkers.

Stopped at a traffic light, she was glad to see Reddick had backed off. Kate concentrated on her GPS and entered Carl Nelson's address, 57 Knox Lane, which she'd memorized from his driver's license.

Is going there a smart move after what happened at the scene?

This is a democracy, and people have a right to talk to other people, she thought, searching her mirror for any sign that Reddick was still tailing her.

Nothing.

She headed for Nelson's neighborhood and came upon his home, a modest ranch-style house with a neat yard and a detached garage.

And a Rampart police car parked out front.

Kate cursed to herself and let out a long breath.

She wanted to knock on the door, talk to anyone who was there, and Nelson's neighbors. She wanted to do her own digging for answers, but not with a cop sitting there eyeing the quiet street.

Kate bit her lip, taking in the house as she drove by slowly, knowing the cop was likely recording her plate. No, this wasn't going to work. Kate rolled down the street for a few blocks, coming to a gas station.

Maybe somebody at the station can tell me about Nelson and point me to people he worked with at the call center.

When Kate stopped and signaled at the intersection, she spotted another Rampart patrol car parked on the street.

Reddick again.

He'd been watching her.

Un-freaking-believable. Okay. She got the message.

Kate headed for the interstate and Syracuse.

As she put Rampart behind her she refused to be knocked off her feet. There were other ways she could pursue this. It took about sixty miles for her to calm down. She stopped in Watertown at a Sunoco to fill up then went to a Burger King for a coffee and a muffin. She sent Reeka and Chuck a message.

Worked it out with Rampart PD. Not going to be charged. Heading home.

After sending it, Kate looked at Grace's face, the background image on her phone, and checked the time. She should be home with Nancy.

Kate pressed her number.

"Hi, Nancy, it's Kate."

"Hi, how're things going up there? Did you have success?"

Nancy was aware of Kate's tragedy and her lifelong search for answers.

"A bit, but it's complicated. I'll tell you about it when I get back."

"Would you like to talk to Grace—she's right here?"

"Yes, thanks. And, Nancy, thank you for doing this."

"No need to thank me, here she is."

"Hi, Mom!"

"Hi, sweetie, how did school go today?"

"It was fun. We learned about butterflies, it was so cool."

Kate cut a lonely figure in the corner of the restaurant. Listening to her daughter tell her about her day was a balm, briefly pulling her mind from Rampart, the death scene and the questions that troubled her.

The flight to La Guardia was delayed.

Kate waited in pre-boarding, too tired to think or do much else but look at her phone and older photos of herself with Vanessa when they were children. There they were, sisters, hugging at Christmas. There was Vanessa on the sofa, looking so small and smiling so big. Her new angel necklace glinted in the flash. Kate blinked at the memories before closing the images.

Later, as the jet finally lifted off, Kate contended with the aftershocks of self-reproach for messing up. Then she considered Brennan and his reluctance to escort her to the scene.

Why wouldn't he do it?

Seasoned detectives she'd known would've had no trouble with her request, which indicated to her that Brennan was either a rookie or being overly cautious, or that something more was going on.

Well, there's no way I'm letting this go.

When the plane leveled she shut her eyes for a few tranquil minutes.

When Kate got home, Grace was asleep in Nancy's guest room, which smelled of lavender and loneliness.

"You can let her spend the night, if you like."

"Thank you, Nancy, but we've imposed all day."

Kate caressed Grace's cheek, kissed her softly. She stirred and groaned, "Hi, Mommy...love you," as Kate hefted her into her arms.

"Oh, you're getting so heavy."

Nancy got the door, carrying Grace's backpack, and followed Kate back to their apartment. After Kate put Grace into bed, she returned to her living room and put five crumpled twenties into Nancy's hand.

"What're you doing, Kate? I can't take money from you."

"You're always helping. Take it. Please."

"Now, listen to me." Nancy put the money into Kate's hand, closed it and held her hands firmly around it. "Ever since my Burt died, I lost my way. We have no children, no family, well—you know. You and Grace arrived in my life like an answered prayer. I'm here to help you whenever you need it. You mean more to me than you'll ever know."

Kate found a depth of warmth and love in Nancy's kind face that came as close to a mother figure as she'd ever known. Kate hugged the older woman, holding on for a moment.

"Thank you. I'd be lost, too, without you."

"Okay, good night. Now you get some rest and let me know if I can help with anything."

Kate took a hot shower and made a cup of raspberry tea, glad that she'd have another day off to recover. Still, something was niggling at her.

I'm forgetting something.

Before going to bed, she went through her unopened emails. Most were routine and could wait. Then she came to one from Reeka, sent only minutes before.

Be in the office tomorrow for an important meeting at 10 a.m.

11

New York City

Newslead's world headquarters took up an entire floor near the top of a fifty-story office tower on Manhattan's far West Side.

Kate waited alone in a corner meeting room. It offered sweeping views of midtown, the Empire State and Chrysler buildings, but Kate only saw trouble in front of her. Being summoned as she was after what had happened upstate was not a good sign, especially on a day off.

At least she had gotten Grace to school before coming in.

The large room was cold. Kate used her phone for a quick check for updates out of Rampart. *Nothing.* She listened to traffic on the streets below and the hum of the ventilation system until the door clicked open.

Three people filed in.

First, Chuck. His tie was already loosened, his shirt sleeves rolled up and his hair mussed. He dropped a folder on the table and sat without looking at Kate.

Next was Morris Chambers, from Human Resources. He was the antithesis to Chuck. He wore a suit, button-down shirt and bow tie. He opened a leather-bound executive notebook and clicked his pen.

Reeka followed, dressed to kill in a dark power blazer that would've worked for a funeral. Her face was in her phone, thumbs pausing when she shut the door and started the inquisition.

"Kate, this meeting is a result of what happened yesterday."

Kate threw a questioning look to each of them. She thought this had been resolved, that Reeka had updated Chuck upon his return.

"I admit that what I did was stupid, but I was not charged."

"This goes to your breach of Newslead policy."

"But I worked it out with Rampart PD—this was a personal matter."

"Yes, Chuck informed us of your sister's tragedy. It's heartbreaking. Still, it doesn't excuse the violation, Kate."

Reeka turned to Morris, cuing him to step in.

"Yes..." Morris cleared his throat. "The policy forbids Newslead staff from using their position for any form of personal gain."

"But I didn't gain anything."

"You went to Rampart on a personal, private matter," Morris read from his notebook. "But you represented yourself as a Newslead reporter on assignment, to New York trooper Len Reddick in an attempt to gain access to a crime scene. After you were refused access, you trespassed."

"That led to possible charges." Reeka stared at her.

Sensing a noose being tightened, Kate turned to

Chuck, who was just sitting there. She couldn't believe it. She and Chuck had been through hell together. He'd begged her to come to New York and work for him at Newslead. He knew about her sister and had been supportive. He was the most powerful manager in the room and, she thought, her friend. But there he was staring at the skyline. Leaving Kate alone.

"Quite frankly, Kate," Reeka said, examining her own glossed nails. "I fail to comprehend why you went up there and did what you did."

"What?"

"My read on this is that it's a regional story, a rural domestic, a murder-suicide. Didn't you lose your sister in western Canada?"

"What the hell do you—"

"Kate," Chuck intervened.

"I was called by Rampart police," Kate said. "They requested my help and I cooperated. There are strong indications my sister, who's been feared dead for twenty years, was a victim!"

"Kate, take it down," Chuck cautioned.

"But identities in Rampart have not been confirmed, have they?" Reeka lifted her eyebrows to punctuate her point.

"What? Reeka, how can you sit there and—"

"Kate, hold off," Chuck said. "This is a difficult, complicated situation. It's put you under stress and strained your judgment. The best action here is for you to take two weeks off, Kate, starting now."

"Are you suspending me?"

"No, you're taking time off with pay. I've approved it."

Chuck signaled an end to the meeting.

"We have counseling services available, if you need it." Morris clicked his pen and closed his notebook.

"I suggest you look into that, Kate. It's for the best," Reeka said.

They walked out of the room, leaving Kate alone with Chuck.

Several beats after the door had closed she turned to him.

"What happened?"

"You lost control in Rampart, Kate. The organization will not tolerate that. I cautioned you before you went there to avoid any conflict. You were on your own and could not represent yourself as a Newslead reporter."

"Yes, but the indication my sister had been there was so strong."

"You've followed similar leads over the years and unfortunately each one has dead-ended. Didn't you tell me that yourself, Kate?"

"I know, Chuck, but this time it's different."

"I appreciate what you're going through. Take time off, for your own peace of mind. See how your Rampart lead plays out, but if you pursue this, for God's sake, do it on your own. Is that understood?"

Kate nodded.

"Listen," Chuck added, "the rumors of more layoffs looming may come true. We're not breaking big stories. We're losing subscribers. Everyone's on edge." He ran a hand over his face. "Kate, you're a good reporter, an asset to the company."

"Thank you."

"Morris had your termination papers in his notebook. Reeka wanted you fired. I put a stop to that."

12

New York City

Kate was still reeling when she returned to her empty apartment.

She splashed warm water on her face, then buried it into a towel as a million thoughts swirled through her mind.

I was that close to being fired.

She shut her eyes tight, then opened them.

Thank God, Chuck had my back.

And the rumors of layoffs were true.

If I'd lost my job... Calm down.

She had a nest egg, built from the freelance pieces she'd done, like the big one for *Vanity Fair* on the Dallas story. And, because of her sublet deal and having gotten rid of her car, she'd saved more money.

Grace and I have been through hard times before—we'll make it.

Eclipsing everything was the reality that Kate had never been this close to finding out what had happened to her sister. She had to use these next two weeks to go full throttle in her search for the truth.

I'm forgetting something. What am I forgetting?

Her phone started ringing. She went to her bedroom and answered it.

"Kate, Ed Brennan in Rampart."

Her anger rose before she could think.

"I want my necklace back, Ed. And when you're done with my sister's necklace I want it, too."

"Hold on there—everything's still under investigation. I'm calling to update you because you should be among the first to know."

"First to know what?"

"We've confirmed the identity of the deceased female."

Kate's stomach tensed and she gripped the phone tighter.

"Is it Vanessa?"

"No. I'm sorry. The victim's name is Bethany Ann Wynn from Hartford, Connecticut. Identification was confirmed through dental records. She'd been missing for three years. Her age at death was twenty-two."

Vanessa would've been twenty-six.

For a long moment Kate didn't know what to say.

"I'm sorry for Bethany Wynn's family. Do they know?"

"They've been informed and we've just posted a news release."

"What does this mean for the situation with my sister?"

"I can't answer that at this time."

"But how did Bethany come to be at that barn, Ed?"

"I'm not going to answer that or speculate."

"And how did my sister's necklace get to the scene?"

"We still haven't confirmed if the necklace belonged to your sister."

"Come on."

"It's being processed. Look, we still have a lot of work to do."

"Well, who's Carl Nelson?"

"We still haven't confirmed the identity of the deceased male."

"What do you think went on at that barn?"

"Kate."

"What about the cause of the fire? Was it intentional?"

"Kate, I'm not getting into any of this. I've told you, respectfully, to back off and let us do our job. Because you've helped us, I'll update you on a need-to-know basis, that's it. I have to go."

Kate sat on the corner of her bed.

Her eyes went around her room as she processed the development. She was saddened by the news, heartbroken for the victim's family, but what had happened only raised more questions.

Who was Bethany Ann Wynn and how did she get from Hartford, Connecticut, to Upstate New York? Moreover, who was Carl Nelson?

The best thing she could do now was get to work.

Kate switched on her tablet, went to the Rampart PD site for the press release. It was brief and she latched on to the key facts about Bethany.

> At the age of nineteen, she was reported missing from the Tumbling Hills Mall in the Hartford suburb of Upper North Meadows, after completing her evening shift as a part-time manager at

The New England Cookie Emporium. At the time of her disappearance she was last seen leaving the mall to take a bus home.

Kate collected those facts, then, like a prospector, she mined the internet for more information on Bethany's background.

Scrutinizing older news stories and anniversary features, Bethany Ann's short life emerged. She was the daughter of James and Rachel Wynn. James was the owner of a tow-truck company. Rachel was a school nurse. Bethany was a junior at Albert River College, studying veterinarian medicine. She had a younger sister, Polly, and at the time of her disappearance, a German shepherd named Tex.

Bethany had had a happy, stable life with a loving family. No indication of depression, drug use, bullying, boyfriend trouble, or any other reason to run off. No mention of Carl Nelson or a connection to Rampart. There was speculation of abduction, although security cameras at the stop Bethany took were not working and no witnesses had stepped forward.

Photos of Bethany showed a pretty girl with a bright smile and hope in her eyes. Kate scrutinized each picture for any jewelry she wore but found nothing resembling the angel necklace.

Kate thought for a moment, then found a home telephone number for the Wynn family.

Maybe Rampart or the local police had told the Wynns something about the case? Maybe they knew something about Carl Nelson, the necklace, her sister? Kate reached for her phone. She was in full-bore reporter mode as she dialed the number, reasoning that since the press release was public, the family would surely be getting calls from reporters. As the line rang, Kate envisioned TV trucks rolling up to the Wynns' suburban home.

She hated calling. It was part of her job she loathed, intruding on people at the worst times of their lives. Over the years people had cursed her, hung up or slammed doors on her. Still, the majority struggled to talk about their loss. In most cases, through choking sobs, they would pay tribute to the father, mother, daughter, son, husband, wife, sister, brother or friend. Or they'd send Kate a heart-wrenching email, or pass her a tearstained note. If she went to their home, they showed her the rooms of the dead and the last things they'd touched.

It tore her up each time and she hated it.

But it was part of the job.

She never took their reactions personally. In that situation people had every right to lash out. Kate strove to be the most professional, respectful, compassionate person she could be in each case.

The families deserved no less.

As the line clicked, Kate steeled herself.

A man answered. His voice was deep, but soft.

"Hello."

"Is this the home of James and Rachel Wynn, Bethany's parents?"

"Yes."

"My apologies for calling at this time and my condolences."

"Thank you."

"Sir, my name's Kate Page and I'm a—" Kate stopped herself cold. She was on the brink of identifying herself as a reporter from Newslead, a reflexive act that was now a firing offense. She was not on the job right now. "I'm sorry. My name's Kate Page and I'm calling with respect to the press release that Rampart police in New York just posted online about Bethany Ann Wynn's case?"

"Yes."

"I was wondering if I could speak to her mother or father. Are you her father?"

"No, Beth's dad passed away last year. Cancer. I'm her uncle—Rachel's my sister-in-law. She's out right now, at the funeral home making arrangements. I'm here receiving people at the house until she gets back."

"Oh, I see."

"What did you need to talk about?"

Kate considered the propriety and her own anguish. The uncle seemed steady, receptive and kind, so she seized the opportunity.

"My little sister, Vanessa Page, has been missing for a long time and I've got reason to believe her case is somehow connected to Bethany's. Is that name familiar to the family?"

"Vanessa Page? No, it's not. I'm sorry."

"Did Bethany ever own a necklace with a guardian angel charm?"

"Goodness, I wouldn't know. Her mother would know that."

"Sorry to ask so many questions."

"It's all right."

"I was just wondering if Bethany's family knew much more about what happened in Rampart."

"All we'd heard from police here was that this Carl Nelson was some kind of computer expert and a reclusive nut and that he left a note…that maybe it was a murder-suicide. We figured he must've been the one who took Beth three years ago, kept her prisoner before he—"

"Did the police tell you much more?"

"No, I'm sorry. It all happened pretty fast. I think it was the other day, a detective here told Rachel the police in New York were checking Beth's dental records. It gave us hope that maybe they found her and—" His voice broke. "And that somehow maybe she was alive. But, deep down, we knew. I'm sorry. I'm not thinking too clearly. It's been real hard on all of us. God, I remember holding her when she was a baby. I'm her godfather. This family's seen a lot of pain these past few years, a lot of pain."

"Sir, I'm so sorry to intrude. I'll let you take care of things."

"Wait, there's something. I do remember Rachel saying that one of our detectives here who'd been working on Beth's case said the guys in Rampart were fearful there may be other victims."

"Other victims?"

"Yes, and that maybe they just hadn't found them all yet."

13

New York City

Kate stood in her kitchen feeling horrible for having intruded on Bethany's grieving family.

But she'd had to make that call. So much was at stake.

As tendrils of steam rose from her kettle she searched them for answers. Bethany's uncle—*Lord, I never got his name*—had been kind to her and she weighed what he'd revealed about the case.

There may be other victims...they just hadn't found them all yet.

Other victims.

It changed everything.

Kate had thought there was only one female victim. This helped explain why Brennan was so guarded. His case was more than a murder-suicide.

What really happened at that barn by the cemetery? Who was Carl Nelson?

The kettle's whistle pierced the air like a scream.

Kate made raspberry tea, returned to her desk and her online digging, intent on finding more on Nelson. She regretted that she'd missed the chance to talk to people in Rampart about him and considered going back.

Maybe she'd do some phone work?

First she'd check Rampart news sites for any updates. The *Rampart Examiner*'s latest item was short, naming Bethany Ann Wynn as the female victim but offering no confirmation of the deceased male. The investigation was continuing. The region's TV news and radio stations were reporting the same, as were news sites in Hartford.

Kate then checked her email.

She'd set up an alert for anything posted online on the case to be sent to her. She'd received more stories from Rampart and Hartford, but they contained nothing she didn't already know.

I'm forgetting something—what is it? Wait—it's the pictures!

Suddenly she'd remembered how she'd slid the tiny memory card with photos from the Rampart crime scene into her sock. Kate rushed to the hamper in the bathroom, rifled through the clothes, finding the socks she'd worn, shaking them until the little square fell to the floor.

How did I forget this?

Kate returned to the kitchen, inserted the card in her camera then connected the cable to her computer, downloaded the images and opened them. They showed the jumble of charred lumber, an array of protruding trestles and beams. On sections that were not burned she noticed markings, like messages cut into the wood.

Kate enlarged the image but the area was blurred.

She opened another photo, one that was crisper. As she zoomed in, carved words swam into focus and she read "I am Tara Dawn Mae. My name used to be—"

It ended there.

What is that?

After studying the words for several moments, she wrote them down in her notebook. Had they been scratched in the wood earlier, prior to the deaths by somebody joking around, like some sort of graffiti? But it was not the usual obscenity or put-down.

Was it evidence?

It had been tagged for processing by the forensic cops.

I am Tara Dawn Mae. My name used to be—

Was this an unfinished message from one of the victims?

Kate immediately searched the name online.

In seconds, the results matching her query appeared, offering pages of headlines and excerpts that stunned her:

Canada's Cold Case files…
Tara Dawn Mae was last seen at a truck stop…
never seen again…

Royal Canadian Mounted Police—MISSING…
Tara Dawn Mae was 10 years old when she vanished from…

Brooks Prairie Journal—Mystery Disappearance Haunts…
It has been twelve years since the disappearance

of Tara Dawn Mae, and neighbors in the tiny farming community try to remember…

FIND THE MISSING KIDS
Tara Dawn Mae. Age at time of disappearance: 10. Eyes: Brown…

Kate continued searching, finding a police summary of the case.

Tara Dawn MAE Cold Case Files
Location: Brooks, Alberta, Canada

On July 7, 2000, Tara Dawn MAE was ten years of age and living with her parents, Barton Mae and Fiona Mae, on their farm near Brooks, Alberta. After shopping for groceries in Brooks, the family stopped at the Grand Horizon Plaza, a large and busy truck stop along the Trans-Canada Highway.

While Barton purchased gas for the family pickup truck, Fiona and Tara entered the facility to use the restroom. While browsing the food court and gift shop, Tara got separated from her mother and was never seen again.

An exhaustive investigation has failed to yield any leads as to Tara Dawn MAE's location or details as to her disappearance.

Kate then found a webpage showing several photographs of Tara. There she was smiling in a full-face shot. Next, a formal head-and-shoulders school portrait, and then Tara with a puppy and laughing.

Tara looks so much like Vanessa.

Deep in a corner of Kate's heart, something cracked, a thin ray of hope emerged and she blinked back her tears. She needed to know more about this case and how it was connected to Rampart.

Kate reached for her phone and called Anne Kelly, with the New York office of the Children's Searchlight Network. Anne alerted Fred Byfield, one of the group's investigators.

"I'll get in touch with our sister networks in Canada," Fred said after listening to Kate. "I'll get back to you as soon as I can."

Kate continued researching. Again and again she came back to the pictures, haunted by the little girl's sweet, shy smile, her dark eyes, shining like falling stars.

Could this be Vanessa?

Kate used maps and made some calculations. Their accident happened about ten miles east of Golden, British Columbia, when their car left the highway and crashed into the Kicking Horse River. That was some 270 miles west of Brooks, Alberta, a five-hour drive across the prairie and through the Rocky Mountains.

Vanessa would have been twenty-six now. If Tara Dawn Mae is still alive, as the message in Rampart suggests, she'd be around twenty-five or twenty-six now, as well.

Was it all coincidence?

Kate went back to the crime scene photos.

My name used to be—

What was her other name?

Was Tara Dawn the Maes' biological child or an adopted child? Kate couldn't find any divorce records on public sites. Maybe Tara Dawn was a street kid who'd run away and changed her name? It was not uncommon. Kate knew that, from her time on the street. Kids were always running from something.

As she continued working throughout the day she came across an in-depth article done on the third anniversary of the case that stopped her cold. It said that Barton and Fiona Mae had adopted Tara Dawn about three or four years before her disappearance.

Adopted?

Kate's mind raced.

She tried searching for court records, knowing that they weren't usually made public, a fact confirmed when she called the clerk's office for Alberta's family courts in Edmonton, the capital. Kate was thinking of hiring a Canadian private investigator to help her dig deeper into the case when she realized the time.

She had to pick up Grace from school.

They'd passed the remainder of the afternoon with Grace coloring a project about the world's oceans and chatting about her day while Kate got supper ready. Whenever she could, Kate thought about the case. That evening while they were watching *The Wizard of Oz*, Fred Byfield called.

"Kate, I talked with our people in Calgary affiliated with our network and I don't have a lot more to add."

"I'll take anything, even advice."

Kate patted Grace's leg and left the sofa to take the call in the kitchen.

"Canadian police still have it listed as a cold case."

"Yes."

"No real leads, nothing at all, and both of the parents have since passed away."

"I didn't know that about the parents. How'd they die?"

"Accidents, maybe, we're not sure but did you know that Tara Dawn was adopted?"

"Yeah, I found a magazine piece that mentioned it. Any details on that?"

"I don't know, and our source in Calgary didn't know."

Kate considered the information.

"So what do you make of these factors? Is it Vanessa, Fred?"

"When you add them up—the necklace at the scene, the carved message from Tara Dawn Mae, the dates, ages and the fact they never found Vanessa's body—they do present a compelling argument that your sister was at the Rampart crime scene."

"But? I detect a 'but' in your tone."

"But, you know as well as anyone, real life is not like mystery books and thriller movies where it all ties together nicely. Real life is complicated and missing persons cases can be complex. Simple factors that appear to be connected often have explanations proving there is no link whatsoever."

"Yes, I know."

"And there's no DNA from Tara Dawn's case to compare to yours, at least none that we know of. And we don't know what Rampart police know, or what they may be telling the RCMP in Alberta about their case. Now you've got to decide what you're going to do next. I think this warrants further investigation and we'll help you as much as we can."

"Thanks, Fred."

Kate returned to the movie, sitting next to Grace.

As Dorothy followed the yellow brick road in her quest to get back to Kansas, Kate searched for the right path she needed to take.

"You were talking about Aunt Vanessa on the phone," Grace said. "I could hear you say her name."

"Yes, I was."

"Is that why you went away the other day, to look for her again?"

Kate looked at her and smiled. Grace was a smart little girl. Last year when she'd turned six, the same age as Vanessa at the time she went missing, Kate had told Grace about the crash, how she'd lost her hold of Vanessa's hand, how they'd never found her and how she still looked for her everywhere. Grace understood, or seemed to, and Kate was okay talking about it with her.

"Yes, honey, that's why I went away the other day."

After the movie, as Kate got her into bed, Grace asked her a question.

"Are you going to go away again to look for Aunt Vanessa, Mom?"

"I'm not sure. I have some time off from work right now, so I'm not sure."

"Maybe one day you'll find her, Mom, just like Dorothy found her way back home to Kansas."

Kate smiled.

"Maybe."

Later that night, as Kate continued researching, she couldn't help but think how her pursuit of the truth about Vanessa had turned into her own yellow brick road of doubt and defeat by dead-end leads. Kate was a reporter and, like a cop, needed facts. What she had now were puzzle pieces, and what she needed to do was keep digging for more to see if they all fit. Kate found herself on airline sites checking flights to Calgary.

Kate called Nancy.

After telling her everything, after explaining her situation, Kate was still unsure about leaving Grace, about the whole idea of going to Canada, with her job situation and everything else.

"There's no question you have to go," Nancy said. "This is part of the fabric of your life, of who you are. How would you live with yourself if, after all that's happened, you never did all you could to find the truth about your sister because you'd left a big stone unturned? Go. I'll take care of Grace."

Five minutes later Kate booked a flight to Calgary.

14

Rampart, New York

Pathologist Morten Compton sat at his desk in his basement office at Rampart General and reviewed his notes on the two deaths at the old burial grounds.

We've got to nail down the ID on the male. And the cause of death.

It was late and as Compton worked he started wheezing again. His wife had warned him to cut back on the meatball sub lunches at Sally's Diner and to drop a few pounds. The job stress didn't help.

Compton's temporary assistant, Marsha Fisher, who'd gone for the day, had left him a summary.

> Detective Brennan's extremely anxious for updates.
>
> As you know Dr. Hunt made dental charts, which we've circulated with no results so far. If the male victim had a dentist, it appears he didn't visit one recently or locally.
>
> One potentially positive new aspect: the forensic unit at the scene recovered a military dog

> tag in the vicinity of where the male was found. I've attached a photo of it. I've submitted it to the military's National Personnel Records Center in St. Louis with an urgent request for comparison of our dental chart with the dog tag info. You should be hearing back anytime now.

Compton clicked on the image.

The dog tag was charred and twisted metal, but the information was clear to read. The name was: Pollard, J.C., blood type was O positive, followed by the Social Security number, and other information.

Compton stroked his Vandyke.

Were there more victims?

The blood type was the same as the presumed victim, Carl Nelson, but O positive was very common. The dog tag could have already been at the site and have no bearing on the victim. Then again, it could be a key piece of evidence.

Identifying a body this severely burned was always challenging. The face was gone, so identification by a relative or friend would not be possible. The hands were gone, so fingerprints were not possible.

Clothing was destroyed. No distinctive jewelry for the male had been recovered.

Compton had taken X-rays of the remains, hoping to find any medical implants or screws for a broken leg and such. He'd circulated them with doctors in the region. So far to no avail. And as far as the DNA went, he was unsure if, given the extensive damage to the body, the tissue sample he'd submitted to various databases, including CODIS, the FBI's national DNA database, was viable.

That brought him to the cause, which had all the indications of a self-inflicted gunshot wound. The entrance was the right temple. The wound track was right to left and slightly forward to the left temple, where he'd recovered the 9mm round, but there was also a significant skull fracture from blunt trauma. The injury could've been a result of being struck by debris, such as a large beam, falling from the burning building. The problem for Compton was that given the severity of the damage to the body, he couldn't conclusively determine the order of events. He was leaning to concluding that death was the result of a self-inflicted gunshot wound, and the skull fracture was postmortem, given the other supporting factors of Carl Nelson's suicide note, his vehicle and his absence from his job.

The phone rang.

"Pathologist, Compton."

"Dr. Compton, this is Major Robert Ellis with the office of the chief of dental services with the United States Army. I'm calling in response to your request, concerning the dental records of Sergeant Pollard."

"Yes, Major, thanks for calling." Compton reached for a pen.

"We can confirm that the chart you sent for comparison is the chart of Sergeant John Charles Pollard formerly of the US Army Special Forces. He toured Iraq and Afghanistan and was honorably discharged seven years ago."

"You're positive on the chart?"

"Yes, sir. It's clear regarding the patterns and wear of several large amalgams."

"This is one hell of a game changer."

"We've arranged to expedite written confirmation and can provide you with scanned and physical copies of Sergeant Pollard's full military records and photographs to assist your investigation."

"Thank you, Major Ellis."

Compton hung up.

His breathing had quickened.

He stared at his computer's monitor and the charred, twisted dog tag that belonged to the former US Army sergeant. Before Compton made another note, before he called Brennan, he absorbed the new information.

If the body is Pollard, then where is Carl Nelson?

And why would Nelson leave a suicide note seeking forgiveness for what he'd done?

What the hell have we got here?

15

Buffalo, New York

Yellowing tape held meal schedules to the walls of the dining hall of the mission in downtown Buffalo.

The rules were up there, too: "No weapons, no drugs, no booze and no fighting. We offer: Love, respect, understanding and healing." After reading them Dickson shook his head.

"It sickens me that any veteran, after sacrificing everything for our country, comes home to this."

Ed flipped through his notes. The two Rampart detectives were at a table waiting for the mission crew to finish up with breakfast so they could interview people about former Sergeant John Charles Pollard.

That Pollard, not Carl Nelson, had been identified as the male victim took this thing to a whole new level. They needed to determine his connection to Nelson, to Bethany Ann Wynn, to any aspect of the case.

After the pathologist had alerted them yesterday to Pollard's ID, Brennan and Dickson pored over his military records, made calls and tracked his last known location to Buffalo.

Pollard, aged thirty-nine, was from Toledo, Ohio, and had enlisted as an artillery man in the US Army in 1998. He was assigned to the 3rd Battalion, 319th Airborne Field Artillery Regiment and had several deployments to Iraq and then Afghanistan. By 2009, he was with the US Special Forces in Kandahar's Zhari District. Later, at a Forward Operating Base in Paktia province, his unit was pinned down in a firefight that lasted a week. Pollard witnessed the deaths of most of his squad members.

He came home to Toledo, suffering post-traumatic stress and became addicted to alcohol and other drugs. He lost his job as a truck driver, his wife left him. He fell into debt, then drifted across the country, ending up on the streets and finally in this homeless shelter.

Brennan was grateful to Buffalo PD, which had made initial inquiries with local shelters. It cleared the way for him to get up at four this morning and make the four-hour drive to Buffalo with Dickson to continue their investigation. They hadn't released Pollard's name yet. They were working with the military to locate his family.

"Doesn't it make you sick that vets end up homeless when they should be treated like heroes?"

"It's a disgrace." Brennan sipped his coffee and over the rim saw Tim Scott, the shelter's director, wiping his hands with a towel as he approached them.

"Thanks for waiting." Scott joined them at the table, then waved to staff members behind the counter. "Sure we can't get you fellas something to eat after your long drive?"

"We're good with the coffee. Thanks," Brennan

said. "What can you tell us about John Charles Pollard?"

"I can't believe he's dead. In a fire…maybe he took shelter in the barn?"

"Maybe."

"It always hurts when we lose a client." Scott shook his head. "People come to us broken. We give them a meal, a bed and hope in the way of counseling and services. J.C. had been with us for five months and was showing promise. He'd gotten clean and sober. He'd gotten his license again and was ready to apply for driving jobs."

"So things were looking up?"

"Yes, despite all he'd faced, he was slowly getting back on his feet. But some guys have their setbacks and they disappear. That's what I thought might've happened."

"That he'd had a setback?"

"That's what I was thinking. The other guys who knew him best had been asking about him because he hadn't been around for a week or so. Reggie and Delmar. They bunked with him for a time and were probably the closest he had to friends. They're right here."

The first man was in his thirties. His clothes hung loose on his skinny frame. His face bore fresh scrapes, as if he'd collided with the sidewalk.

"Is it true? J.C.'s dead?" The man called Reggie sniffed and sat down.

"I'm afraid so. My condolences."

Reggie nodded sadly.

"May I ask what happened?" Brennan indicated the man's cuts.

"Was drunk, fell on the street."

"Reggie, may I get your last name, date of birth and could you show me your Social Security card? It's routine."

Brennan cleared a page in his notebook, took down Reggie's information then did the same for Delmar, the taller of the two. Delmar had a full, scraggly Moses beard dotted with crumbs.

Brennan thanked them and said, "We ask that you keep our inquiries confidential. It's critical to our investigation."

"So he got killed in a fire in Rampart?" Delmar looked around the table.

"Something like that. Guys, can you recall if John—"

"Oh, we call him J.C., nobody called him John," Reggie said.

"Sorry. Can you recall if J.C. had any connection to Rampart?"

The three men shook their heads.

"Ohio, mostly, that's where he came from," Reggie said.

"Do the names Carl Nelson or Bethany Ann Wynn mean anything to you in relation to J.C.?"

"Don't think so." Delmar looked to the others, who agreed.

"What about Canada? Did he ever talk about it?"

More shaking of heads.

Dickson cued up photos on his tablet.

"Do you recognize anything in these pictures, any connection at all?"

The first were several photos of Bethany Ann Wynn.

None of the photos registered with the men.

Next were photos of Tara Dawn Mae, from her missing persons file from Alberta.

Again, nothing.

Then they showed them enlarged photos of the necklace with the guardian angel charm.

Nothing.

"What's this really about?" Scott was clearly troubled. "I get the feeling there's something more serious going on. Do you think J.C. had something to do with these people?"

"At this point, we're not sure what to think," Brennan admitted.

Then came photos of Carl Nelson.

"That guy." Delmar tapped his finger on Nelson's face.

"He used to come around, talk to J.C.," Reggie said, nodding.

"When did he start coming around?" Brennan stared hard at the men.

"It started a month or so back, maybe two months," Reggie said. "We were in the park, passing a bottle of Thunderbird. J.C. wouldn't take none, he was on the program doin' fine without preachin' to us. That's when this guy—" Reggie pointed at Nelson "—came up and just gave us money. Fifty bucks each. Said he remembered when his family had hard times. We get that sometimes."

"Did he give you his name?"

"Jones, Adam Jones, I think," Reggie said.

"Then the guy came around more," Delmar said. "Bought us lunches and took an interest in J.C., his military time, telling J.C. how thankful and honored he was." Delmar jabbed his forefinger into the table.

"I tell you, sir, that meant the goddamn world to J.C. because he was still carrying the ghosts of the men he lost."

Reggie nodded.

"J.C. was a true-blue soldier. You know, he still had his dog tags. Put them in his boot so no one would yank them from his neck if he got jumped. I think we were the only ones he told."

"Can you recall any other details about the man's interest in J.C.?"

"He started bringing him clothes, pants, boots, jackets, stuff he said he no longer needed, or never wore," Delmar said.

"Yeah," Reggie said. "Good stuff, because they were practically the same height, build, age, the same everything. The guy told J.C. the clothes were his and he didn't need them anymore."

Brennan and Dickson exchanged a glance.

"Do you recall anything else?"

"They were getting chummy," Delmar said. "I remember, about two weeks before we last saw J.C., he was saying that he might have a lead on a good job but it was across the state."

"In Rampart?" Brennan asked.

Delmar shook his head. "Didn't say, but he sure was feeling good about things, you just saw it on his face and stuff."

"Then that was it," Reggie said. "We never saw J.C. after that."

Brennan and Dickson shared their theories on the case on the long drive back to Rampart.

"What do you think, Ed? Nelson was making bondage, porn movies at the barn, maybe invited Pollard to take part?"

"Maybe, but look again at what his note said."

Dickson read it aloud. "'I only wanted someone to love in my life. It's better to end everyone's pain. God forgive me for what I've done. Carl Nelson.' Okay, so something else was going on. Where does Pollard fit?"

"We need to get warrants on Nelson's house, his bank records, credit card and his computer."

"Wait, how did Nelson use Pollard?"

"Look at their physical particulars, both are white males, both are six feet tall. Nelson's in his forties and Pollard's thirty-nine, almost the same age and both have the same body type."

"So what are you saying?"

"I think Nelson selected Pollard to stage his own suicide."

16

Calgary, Alberta

The Southern Alberta District headquarters for the RCMP's K Division in northeast Calgary was housed in a glass-and-brick building overlooking Deerfoot Trail, the city's major expressway.

Thankfully, it was also near the airport, Kate thought as she wheeled her rented Toyota into the parking lot.

Kate had arranged to meet a Corporal Jared Fortin at 9:00 a.m. to discuss Tara Dawn Mae's disappearance and Vanessa's case.

She had ten minutes before her meeting and checked her phone for messages. Nothing new. Smiling at her daughter's face, she remembered what Grace had said before giving her a million hugs goodbye yesterday.

"I hope you find out what happened to Aunt Vanessa, Mom."

Kate entered the building and went to the front desk.

"I'm Kate Page. I have an appointment with Corporal Jared Fortin, who I believe is with Major Crimes."

"Yes, one moment, please."

As the receptionist's keyboard clicked, Kate looked at the wall map behind her. The Southern Alberta District had more than thirty detachments and covered everything in the southern region of the province west of Calgary to British Columbia, east to Saskatchewan and south to Montana, an area larger than most states.

The receptionist stopped and looked at Kate.

"Kate Page, from New York City?"

"Yes."

"Did Corporal Fortin not contact you about today?"

"No. Is there a problem?"

The woman resumed concentrating on her monitor, then, finding something, her expression changed, indicating all was well.

"No, it's fine. Sorry." She then requested Kate exchange two pieces of photo ID for a visitor's badge and her signature on a sign-in sheet. "Thank you. Please have a seat. Someone will be right with you."

Kate went to the waiting area, wondering if the receptionist had inadvertently signaled a problem. She sat in a chair and glanced at the spread of magazines on the table. Something was up. She took out her phone. She hadn't received any new messages. She scrolled through news sites out of Rampart, scanning stories for any updates.

She'd found nothing new.

"Ms. Page?"

A man in a dark blue suit had materialized. He was about six feet tall with a solid build, short brown hair and thick mustache. He looked to be in his late forties.

"Staff Sergeant Ian Owen." He extended his hand. "I'm Corporal Fortin's supervisor. Right this way."

He led her to his office. Through the large windows

Kate saw jets approaching the airport. Sergeant Owen directed her to a chair before his desk.

"Can I get you a coffee or anything?"

"No, thank you. I'm fine."

Owen sat, took up his pen and leaned forward, staring at it for a moment.

"Ms. Page, I'll come to the point. I know why you're here. Unfortunately, there's not much we can do to help you."

"But Corporal Fortin assured me he was willing to discuss my sister's case and the cold case of Tara Dawn Mae."

"He explained your call to me. All I can say is that we're supporting an active investigation in another jurisdiction."

"But the case in Rampart, New York, and the case in Brooks, Alberta, are linked and there's every possibility they're linked to my sister."

"I understand, and I can only imagine how terrible this sounds to you, especially after you've traveled here from New York."

As Kate's heart sank, she grew angry. Angry at herself for believing police here would help her when, in the back of her mind, she knew cops were all the same. As her resentment rose she realized what had happened.

"You've been talking to Ed Brennan about me, haven't you?"

"As I said, we're supporting another jurisdiction in an ongoing investigation."

"I got that. Forgive me for being blunt, Staff Sergeant, but I'm not an idiot. Let me give you some context, which I'm sure you know from talking to

Rampart. Ed Brennan called me, requesting my help. He asked me to bring my necklace to him so he could compare it to one found at his scene, which resembles my sister's necklace."

Owen said nothing, letting Kate continue.

"At the same time, there's evidence at the Rampart scene that's tied to the disappearance of Tara Dawn Mae, which is in your yard. Now, here we sit, some one hundred and fifty miles from where I lost my sister in the Kicking Horse River."

"That was twenty years ago near Golden, BC. That's E Division's jurisdiction."

"Stop, stop this bureaucratic police bull, please! I was underwater in that river when our car crashed into it. I held my sister's hand—"

"Ms. Page, I understand but—"

"No, I'm sorry, you don't understand. For twenty years I've lived with being told my sister was dead. But her body was never found and I've refused to give up hoping that she'd somehow survived. And now her necklace surfaces at a murder scene in New York with a link to the cold case of a missing girl from your jurisdiction. I've cooperated with you guys. I've given you my necklace, my DNA, yet you, just like Brennan, throw up your hands with the *I can't discuss the case, it's an ongoing investigation* when we all know that it's the ghost of my sister that's tying this all together for you!"

Owen repositioned his pen as his jawline pulsed.

"Since we're being blunt, allow me to give *you* a little context, Ms. Page. It's my understanding that you have charges pending against you in Rampart for trespassing on a crime scene, possibly tampering or planting evidence?"

"Oh, for God's sake, I did not tamper or plant evidence."

Owen leaned forward.

"That may be, but given your personal stake, a good defense attorney could easily create the perception in court that you did, and destroy a case, allowing someone guilty to go free. Now how do you think that would sit with the family of Bethany Ann Wynn?"

Kate let out a long, tense breath and glanced at the 747 approaching the airport.

"Ms. Page, I'm sure you can appreciate that it's critical for investigators not to risk weakening an iota of the case so that it will remain solid when it comes to prosecuting it."

Kate said nothing, letting a few moments pass.

"I think it'd be best if you let us do our job." Owen stood to conclude the meeting. "Give me your contact information and if there are any developments that I can share with you, I give you my word, I will."

Kate reached into her bag for her wallet and handed him one of her business cards. Owen then escorted her to the reception desk, where she traded her visitor's pass for her identification.

"Safe travels, Ms. Page." Owen shook her hand.

In her car, Kate was still simmering from the exchange.

Before she'd left New York for Alberta, she'd made other calls. She paged through her notes for other people who'd agreed to talk to her.

Sheri Young was a neighbor of Barton and Fiona Mae at the time of Tara Dawn's disappearance. Then there were Eileen and Norbert Ingram, who now owned the Maes' former house. And the Children's Searchlight Network was working on finding her people familiar with the Mae case. She roared out of the lot. As she glanced at the RCMP building in her rearview mirror an image burned across her mind.

A tiny hand rising from the cold dark water...

Kate squeezed the wheel. No way was she backing off.

Not now.

Not ever.

17

Tilley, Alberta

Kate drove toward the horizon undaunted.

The Trans-Canada Highway east from Calgary cut across gentle hills that soon flattened for as far as she could see. Still smarting from her meeting with the RCMP, she was now counting on the people of Southern Alberta to help her.

"Certainly, we'll talk to you," Eileen Ingram had told her earlier when Kate had called. Eileen and her husband, Norbert, were the current owners of the Maes' house.

Two hours after leaving Calgary, Kate had reached Brooks, a small prairie city known for agriculture, gas, oil and meat processing. Staying on the Trans-Canada, she passed the Grand Horizon Plaza.

The truck stop where Tara Dawn Mae was last seen fifteen years ago.

Kate continued east to the hamlet of Tilley then followed a ribbon of highway south for another fifteen minutes or so before coming to the remote property amid the eternal rolling treeless plain. It was a modest two-story frame house, set back from the road. Gravel crunched under her tires when she rolled along the driveway to the house. Two women and a man stepped onto the porch to greet her.

"I'm Eileen, this is my husband, Norbert, and this is our neighbor, Sheri Young. She used to babysit Tara Dawn for Fiona and Barton."

"You made good time," Norbert said as Kate shook everyone's hand, noticing that Norbert held an unlit pipe.

"Thank you for agreeing to see me."

The house smelled of soap and fresh soil. They led her to the kitchen and a table covered with a checkered tablecloth. Everyone sat while Eileen made tea and coffee, then set down a plate of cookies.

"Eileen told us about your accident in BC, when you were a child." Norbert looked into the bowl of his unlit pipe. "What a terrible thing."

"You really think that Tara Dawn's disappearance is connected to your sister's case?" Sheri spooned sugar into her coffee.

"Yes, a lot of new factors have surfaced with a recent murder and suicide in New York State."

"What sort of factors?" Eileen passed Kate a mug.

Kate gave them an account of what was found at the Rampart site and how, along with dates, it all aligned with Vanessa and Tara Dawn's cases.

"That sounds unsettling, for sure," Eileen said.

"Could be there's something to it." Norbert nodded.

"I'm not sure how much we can help, though," Eileen said. "We never knew the Mae family. We're from Manitoba and bought this place ten years ago this spring after Norbert retired from the railroad. Sheri knew the family better than anyone."

"I did," Sheri said. "What would you like to know?"

"Tell me what you can about the Maes, about Tara Dawn's adoption and her disappearance."

"Well..." Sheri reached back over the years. "Barton and Fiona didn't mix with other people. They were private, deeply devout. You only saw them at church, or at the store. They just worked on their farm. Then Fiona had a baby, a girl, but she died after a year."

"What happened?"

"Nobody in town really knew. One day we saw the ambulance and the Mountie cars out at the place. Later, it got around that their baby had died. My mom figured it was SIDS or some sickness. Then my dad said there was a rumor that Barton had dropped her. But no one knew the truth."

"How long ago was that?"

"Oh, that was over twenty-two, twenty-three years, back. Anyway, they both took it hard, as you can imagine. People saw even less of them. It was like Barton and Fiona were haunted by it. Then two or three years later, they started coming to church with Tara Dawn, who was about five or six. At first people thought she was a niece who was visiting. Then it got around that Tara Dawn was their adopted daughter."

Kate showed Sheri a picture of Vanessa on her cell phone.

"Did she look like that?"

Sheri studied the photo for a few seconds.

"It was a long time ago, but I'd say she looked a lot like that."

"Tell me more about her."

"Eventually, we'd heard that Tara was adopted from a distant relative in the United States and that was that. Not too long after, my mom said that Fiona asked if I would babysit occasionally. It didn't happen often, but sometimes Barton and Fiona would go to Hanna, or Medicine Hat, for some deal on a tractor, or something. I don't know why they didn't take Tara with them, but I liked watching her."

"What was she like?"

"Very quiet, shy. I remember one time I tried asking her about where she used to live, what had happened, and all she did was cry. I gave her a hug then we went to the barn to play with the kittens. That cheered her up. But I felt so bad I never asked her about that kind of thing again, because she didn't want to talk about it. Some days I would look across the field from our place and see Tara playing by herself with her dog. She looked lonely but she seemed happy. She always smiled at me and said hi if I saw her with Fiona in the store.

"Then, a few years later, she was stolen away at the truck stop. Oh, it was horrible. The whole town was shocked. I never saw so many police cars. They had dogs, helicopters, searchers, roadblocks. It was in all the news. People prayed in the churches for a miracle, for a happy ending. Reporters came from everywhere. It was a big story, but as time went by, things seemed to slow down and it wasn't in the news as much.

"Barton and Fiona were devastated. Nobody saw them...they stopped coming to church. They were like ghosts. About a year after Tara Dawn went missing, Barton's tractor rolled on him. He was in a coma for a week before he died. A year or so after that, two women from the church went to check on Fiona and found her dead in her bedroom. She'd overdosed on sleeping pills."

Eileen passed tissues to Sheri, who dabbed her eyes.

"There were some anniversary stories about Tara Dawn's disappearance, but her story faded until it was practically forgotten. Of course, the place went up for sale," Sheri said.

"We knew the history," Norbert said. "So did a lot of other people, but they weren't interested, so we bought at a good price and parceled some of the land to rent."

Eileen looked pensively out the window at the expanse of flat land. "Every morning when I get up I say a little prayer to their memory." She turned back to Kate. "We can show you Tara's room, if you like?"

Kate gripped the banister and the stairs creaked as she climbed them behind Eileen, with Sheri and Norbert behind them. A double bed and mirrored dresser took up most of the room, which smelled of pine and moth balls. White-on-white-striped paper covered the walls.

A curtained window opened to the eternal sky.

Kate traced her fingers along the frame envisioning Tara Dawn—*or Vanessa*—standing in this very spot searching the horizon.

So alone.

"We use it as a guest room when our son and his kids come to visit," Eileen said. "I redid the walls, and the furniture is ours. I'm sorry, there's nothing here from the Maes. It all got auctioned."

As Kate's eyes swept the room, Norbert, who was leaning against the doorway, stood as if a memory had prodded him to attention.

"Wait, we still got those trunks from Doug Clovis's son."

"What trunks?"

"Last year, Eileen. You were in Calgary that day." Norbert turned to Kate. "Doug Clovis sold his auction business and his son found two trunks in their warehouse left over from the Mae auction. They were supposed to go to charity but they dropped them here. I said, might as well leave them here. Our son could go through them first." Norbert pointed somewhere with his pipe. "They're in the barn if you want to look."

The barn was a rusting metal Quonset hut some distance behind the house. The old building had been subdivided into pens and stalls that had once been used for livestock.

"We don't keep any animals. We use it for storage," Norbert said.

The air was still strong, stale and musty. Dust swirled in the light, shooting through the line of ceiling vents. They went to an area holding a small tractor, wheelbarrows and other equipment. Norbert pulled back a heavy canvas tarp, sending dust mites spinning as he revealed two time-worn, flat-top steamer trunks. They were dark green with leather handles and hinges that creaked as he opened them.

Each trunk was jammed with clothes, cardboard boxes and various items. Kate, Eileen and Sheri sifted through plaid work shirts, jeans, socks, women's clothes, underwear, coats, boots, shoes, hats, scarves, gloves and mittens.

Eileen covered her mouth with her hand when she found baby items, bibs, shoes, little jumpers.

They came across plates wrapped in newspapers, a tea set, a lamp, candleholders and a clock.

"What exactly are we looking for?" Sheri held up a framed picture of a tropical sunset.

"I don't know." Kate set aside a shoe box of papers, mostly invoices. "Adoption records, any evidence that might connect Tara to my sister."

"Look." Eileen held up a photo album, opened it and pointed to a color photo of a woman with a baby. "Me and Charlotte" was written under it.

"That's Fiona with her baby daughter," Sheri said.

The album pages crackled as Eileen turned to more photos: Barton next to his tractor, Barton fixing a truck, Barton laughing with Charlotte on his knee.

Those pictures were followed by album pages of nothing. Eileen kept flipping the crackling pages until new photos appeared. "Our Miracle, Tara Dawn" was written under the first picture.

Kate felt the air rush from her gut.

She spasmed as a cadenza of sound shrieked through her mind, burning across years of loss, years of guilt, years of senseless hopes and prayers. Years of never believing, yet refusing to not believe; years of battling every reason to abandon the irrational, unable to let go.

"Are you all right, Kate?" Eileen touched her shoulder.

"That's my sister, Vanessa!"

"You're sure?" Eileen passed the album to her so she could take a closer look.

"Yes!" Kate flipped pages, her voice breaking. "I don't understand how she could've got here." Kate came to a shot of girl showing a timid smile. She was wearing a necklace.

Tenderly Kate ran her fingertips over the picture.

I found you! I found you!

Fighting her tears, her hand shaking, Kate reached for her phone and quickly cued up a photograph of her necklace, the matching one she'd shared with Detective Brennan in Rampart.

"See, it has the same guardian angel charm, see? It's the necklace our mother gave to each of us!"

"Oh, my God, it is!" Sheri said.

"This is a helluva thing!" Norbert was shaking his head. "Just a helluva thing!"

At that moment the light on Kate's phone flashed and it rang.

"Kate Page."

"Hi, Kate, this is Carmen Pearson in Calgary. I'm a private investigator. I do volunteer work for the Children's Searchlight Network. They gave me your number."

"Oh, yes."

"Fred Byfield said I should call you directly if I came across anything that might help you in Alberta."

"Yes, okay."

"I've located Elliott Searle and he's agreed to talk to you about Tara Dawn Mae's case."

"Elliott Searle? Who's he?"

Sheri's eyes widened with recognition as Carmen

answered, "He's a retired RCMP inspector. Kate, he's the Mountie who headed the investigation into Tara Dawn's disappearance."

18

Bragg Creek, Alberta

Is Vanessa alive?

It was one of a million questions Kate agonized over while driving to meet the retired officer who'd run the investigation into Tara Dawn's disappearance.

Maybe I'm wrong?

Maybe I'm giving too much credence to coincidences and resemblances? Maybe I've become blind to reason over the years?

Kate found the Sweet Pines Café, a small log building in Bragg Creek, a postcard-perfect community at Calgary's southwestern edge, tucked in the thick forests in the foothills of the Rocky Mountains.

Retired inspector Elliott Searle was right where he said he'd be: in a corner booth reading a newspaper.

"Inspector Searle?"

"Yes." He stood.

"Kate Page. Thanks for meeting me, sir."

"Call me Elliott. It's no problem." He shook her hand. "Have a seat."

He was an imposing figure in faded jeans and a

navy shirt that accentuated his short, silver-white hair and piercing eyes. He had a gravelly voice befitting a capable man accustomed to being in charge.

"I work with missing persons groups," Elliott said. "They told me about your case. I'm aware of the current activity and your involvement. Police circles are tight, Kate, and no cop would do anything to damage a case. I'm sure you already know that."

"I'm well aware."

They both ordered coffee. Before it came, Kate got to the point.

"I think Tara Dawn Mae is my sister."

The old Mountie's poker face betrayed nothing as Kate related the whole story. She reached into her bag and pulled out the Mae family albums, which the Ingrams insisted she have. She flipped through the photographs, then showed Elliott pictures of the necklace as she raised question after question about her crash in BC, Tara Dawn and the case in Upstate New York.

"The adoption records were incomplete," Elliott said.

"Incomplete? I don't understand."

"Before our meeting I reviewed my personal notes to refresh my memory. When Tara Dawn vanished, part of our investigation was to examine the family history, their background. That's when we found that the adoption records were incomplete. The Maes had said a distant relative, a cousin, who was a heroin addict and had been charged in a robbery and was jailed in South Dakota, was Tara Dawn's mother. She lost custody of the girl and begged social services to give her to a family member.

"We pursued that account and found that a relative

of Barton's had in fact committed suicide in a South Dakota jail. But if there was any sort of adoption, there was no record of it. A courthouse fire had destroyed a lot of state court records, so anything pertaining to any adoption would've been lost. The family court in Alberta acknowledged the fire and that records were incomplete but still allowed the adoption."

"Why?"

"They accepted the account given by the Maes' lawyer and because no party had come forward to challenge it."

"What do you think of that, in light of what we know now?"

"The adoption story's questionable, but when it came to the disappearance, the Maes struck me as honest people."

"Why do you say that?"

"We polygraphed each of them twice, once with our examiner and once with a Calgary police examiner. The tests concluded that the Maes were being truthful about Tara Dawn's disappearance. We were confident of their account of what happened at the truck stop. We had supporting witness statements, and we used credit card records and receipts to track down as many people as we could who were there at the time. Unfortunately, only one security camera was working properly so we did not get all the plates."

"Did you have suspects?"

"There were two ex-cons on parole passing through, but we cleared them off the top. There was also a church group charter bus of children. We thought Tara may have somehow got taken onto that bus in error, but we tracked the bus and cleared it."

"So no one, really?"

"No. It was very busy at the time. A lot of traffic but, no, nothing emerged. We believe she was abducted and our action and investigation was exhaustive. When it happened we moved fast and took no chances. We set up roadblocks to inspect vehicles and alerted the border crossings, but we didn't have the resources to cover every point immediately."

"But what about the adoption—you say it's questionable?"

"Either it happened the way the Maes said it did, or it didn't."

"If it didn't, how did the Maes come to have Tara Dawn? And how did she get to Rampart and leave a cryptic message fifteen years later?"

"Only one person knows the answers to those questions, Kate, and that's Tara Dawn."

Searle declined the waiter's offer of more coffee, indicating their time together was nearing an end. Kate reviewed her notes.

"In my research I read a couple of articles that said you'd received more than one-hundred-and-fifty tips. Did anything come of them?"

"We followed all of them for leads. They yielded nothing."

After letting a long moment pass, Kate unfolded a photocopy of a newspaper clipping from the *Medicine Hat News*.

"What about this? I dug this old news story up."

Elliott looked at the old article, which said that on the day before Tara Dawn went missing, Medicine Hat City police received a report of a man trying to lure a girl into his van.

"Medicine Hat's about a hundred kilometers, or sixty miles east of the truck stop, right?" Kate said.

"That's right." Elliott tapped the clipping. "This is one incident that continues to eat at me to this day."

"Was there something to it?"

"We followed it up with Medicine Hat police. It seems kids nearby got a plate, but they weren't sure if it was an Alberta plate, or Saskatchewan, North Dakota, BC or Montana."

"So, if you got the plate number that's only about sixty possibilities to run down?"

"Well, then the kids weren't certain on the sequence. Then another kid said the stranger was only asking for directions, that it was not a lure or abduction attempt. Still, that one haunted me because the Medicine Hat van was generally similar to one that was seen at the truck stop at the time of the abduction. We pursued that lead but it led nowhere."

"Would you give me the license number?"

"I'm off the case, that plate is not mine to give you, Kate."

"I see."

She closed her notebook and put it in her bag.

"I wish it were different," Elliott said.

"It's okay, I understand. You've been very helpful."

19

Rampart, New York

Faces of the dead and missing.

Enlarged photographs of Carl Nelson, John Charles Pollard, Bethany Ann Wynn and Tara Dawn Mae stared from the corkboard at the men and women who'd gathered at Rampart police headquarters.

Investigators from the Riverview County Sheriff's Office, the New York State Police and the FBI were now helping on the case.

In all, two dozen law enforcement people were seated around the board table studying the three-page summary Ed had prepared.

He tested his remote control for his laptop, which was connected to the large screen at the end of the room, and took a hit of coffee.

"Okay, let's get started." Brennan cleared his throat. "The purpose of this meeting is to bring you up to speed on what we know, what we've done, what we're doing and what we need to do. Then we'll take your feedback."

While displaying images of the key players, the

crime scene and evidence, Brennan said that the investigation adhered to the following scenario: that Carl Nelson, of Rampart, a man with no prior record, abducted and held Bethany Ann Wynn, of Hartford, Connecticut, captive in an abandoned barn for three years. After that time, he intended to kill her and stage his own suicide in a ruse that involved burning the barn after murdering former sergeant John Charles Pollard, whom he lured or abducted to the site from a Buffalo homeless shelter.

Given the severity of fire damage to Pollard's body, autopsy results were inconclusive but showed a 9mm round was recovered from Pollard's skull. Ballistics confirmed it was fired from a Glock 17, registered to Nelson and recovered at the scene. However, the autopsy also found a significant skull fracture from blunt trauma.

"We believe that Nelson killed Pollard then set fire to the barn intending to kill Bethany Ann Wynn, who was bound with rope in a confinement area. We believe the fire loosened her bindings, allowing her to escape at the final moment."

Brennan explained that Nelson left a note in a Ford F-150 pickup truck, registered to him and found near the scene. "The note was printed on a laser printer, consistent with one recovered this morning at Nelson's residence. Search warrants were executed earlier this morning for Nelson's residence and place of employment as a senior systems technician at the MRKT DataFlow Call Center.

"Nelson had called in sick two days before the fire, prior to a weekend, which would have given him ample time to prepare." Brennan clicked to a picture of Bethany Ann Wynn smiling. "Prior to her death from her injuries, Bethany Ann Wynn indicated that there were 'others.'" Brennan clicked back to the barn's charred ruins. "Troop B's forensic unit continues processing the site as we speak, but has indicated evidence in the barn shows the crude construction of confinement rooms, the installation of a generator and a sophisticated use of a coil to steal small amounts of electricity undetected from power lines running nearby. This way Nelson kept a small part of the structure heated in winter."

Brennan felt his phone vibrate in his pocket. Ignoring the call, he clicked on a photograph of Tara Dawn Mae and gave a summary of her fifteen-year-old case out of Brooks, Alberta, Canada.

"Among the evidence at the scene—this message carved into a wooden beam." Brennan clicked on an enlargement of the carving. "And this item." He clicked on the necklace. "A couple of things. One, the necklace has been submitted for analysis. We understand that there may have been a million of these charms sold some years ago. We're working with the FBI and the manufacturer to determine more information on an identity of the owner. It was found at the scene, damaged in the fire. We may have a lead, but the engraving is illegible."

Brennan continued.

"Two, we're also working with the RCMP on this aspect of the investigation. If Nelson abducted Tara Dawn Mae, it means he may have held her captive for over fifteen years. Other case histories show that perpetrators have kept their victims for even longer periods, so we don't know what we're dealing with here, but what's emerging is chilling."

Investigators had a lot of work ahead of them, including processing the scene and looking deeper into Carl Nelson's background.

"After executing the warrants, we're combing through Nelson's credit cards, bank, phone, internet and every other record. No leads have surfaced so far," Brennan said. "Now, we'll open this up to questions and feedback."

"Sounds to me, Ed—" Vern Schilling, a veteran New York State Police investigator, legendary for having one of the NYSP's highest clearance rates and being a prick to other detectives, adjusted his glasses "—that given Nelson's professional expertise, he's a guy who could outsmart you and disappear."

"Except that we know what he did and I don't think that was his intention."

"What do Nelson's friends and neighbors have to say about him?"

"Not much. We talked to his employer. We know Nelson's lived in the community for some ten years and that he was quiet, practically socially isolated."

"Hard to do that in a small town," Schilling said. "Somebody's got to know more about him. You need to push harder."

Brennan caught a look of unease from his lieutenant.

"Did you look into the history of the burial grounds and the old insane asylum?" one of the Riverview County deputies asked. "Maybe Nelson has a connection to it?"

"That's on our list."

"What about online, maybe Nelson's part of a porn production network?"

"The FBI's helping with that."

"Ed, why wouldn't he just shoot the girl, Bethany? Why would he risk her getting free to disclose his activities?" a Rampart detective asked.

"Maybe he did and missed, maybe he was confident the fire would kill her? We don't know the answer to that one."

Brennan's cell phone vibrated again, and again he ignored it, taking more questions before Vern Schilling looked up from his notes.

"Tell me something," Schilling said. "If Nelson set this up, then vanished, how did he get in and out? Did he have another vehicle? Did he have help, because this is a long way to walk?"

"It's a good question. We're checking for other access points and for evidence of other vehicles."

Brennan went around the table for final questions.

"Your summary here mentions a public appeal for information, as in news conference. When are you planning to do that?" Wade Banner, the FBI agent from Plattsburgh asked.

"Within the next day or so," Brennan said. "Okay, thank you, everyone."

"Hold on," Schilling said. "I'm curious why you didn't obtain warrants sooner on Nelson's residence and job?"

"We needed to confirm the male victim's identification."

"You're kidding. With all the circumstantial evidence—his truck, the note and ballistics confirm his gun used. Come on, Ed. With that much time lost, you allowed for the potential of people going in and out of Nelson's residence, possibly removing or destroying evidence."

"We had a patrol sitting on the house, Vern."

"Like you did at the scene? I heard about a woman walking all over it and taking pictures."

"That was very brief. We addressed it and believe no harm was done to the scene."

"Let's go back to Nelson. If he's a technician at MRKT DataFlow and had access to accounts, isn't it possible that he selected the victim through her account?"

"That's possible, but she didn't have an account that they processed."

"Well, on another angle, given his access, he could easily have stolen identities, right?"

"That's under investigation."

"And, with his expertise, there's a strong chance he'd have the skill to destroy evidence remotely. Did you think of that?"

"Vern." Brennan inhaled, let out a long, slow breath and rubbed the back of his neck. "We thought of that. But let me say with the greatest respect—no one knows better than you—that each case has challenges. Second-guessing doesn't help."

"Whoa." Vern held up his palms. "I'm only offering my feedback, as requested."

Brennan caught his captain's reaction as he subtly telegraphed to Brennan to let it go. He did.

"Thank you, Vern."

At that moment, Beverly, the office manager for the investigative unit, knocked on the door as the meeting broke up.

"Ed, I am so sorry to interrupt, but Mitch Komerick has been trying to reach you. He's at the scene and says it's important."

"Thanks, Bev." Brennan took his phone from his pocket and saw several missed calls from Komerick. He called back without listening to the messages.

"Mitch, this is Brennan. Sorry, I've been in a meeting. What's up?"

"Ed, we've found something," Komerick's voice conveyed a sense of urgency. "You'd better come out."

20

Rampart, New York

At the crime scene, New York State Police trooper Dan Larco watched his canine partner, Sheba, sniffing the ground far off in the distance.

During the time they'd been assigned to help find human remains in the ruins of the barn, Larco had been thorough.

After Sheba had probed the burned wreckage, Larco had her search the fields and brush of the surrounding area in a widening grid pattern. They'd started north, moved west, then south, then east. Now, Sheba was in the northeast sector, some seventy to eighty yards away.

If there's anything out there, she'll find it.

Sheba could smell a small tooth in a football stadium, which was pretty good for a dog that started life fated to be put down.

She'd been abandoned, found eating garbage in alleys in Queens, put in the pound, then rescued by an animal welfare charity and offered to the state police canine team to train at Cooperstown. Now, the three-year-old was one of the best cadaver detection dogs in the state. She'd also played a key role in finding people in several search-and-rescue operations.

So far, at this site, she'd found only the deceased male in the barn.

A few of the other scene investigators had quietly indicated they were ready to sign off. But Larco was confident that if more human remains were here, Sheba would locate them.

The dog was able to detect human scent at any stage of decomposition, even if the remains were buried several feet under the surface. The scent radiated and weather conditions, like wind, humidity and temperature affected it. Sheba was trained to alert Larco whenever she detected any type of human decomposition by sitting down at the site. She was also trained not to dig up a site, so as not to disturb the evidence.

But Larco knew how her eager-to-please personality got the best of her sometimes. He watched her in the distance, snout to the ground, poking and probing, tail wagging, getting herself all worked up.

She ended searching abruptly, immediately sat and barked.

Had she found something?

Larco didn't think so for, at times, sitting also meant a false alert—Sheba's way of saying she was frustrated.

Pissed off, might be the truth.

She barked again, insistent this time.

"All right, I'm coming, I'm coming."

Larco was about twenty-five yards out when Sheba ceased waiting and began pawing at the earth under some bramble.

"Hey there!"

Larco chided her because she knew not to do that.

What's got her so excited?

At first he thought she was pulling branches and sticks in order to get at whatever had her excited. Then she came at him, as if to prove that what was clamped in her jaws was not brush.

It was a leg bone with a decomposing human foot attached to it.

"Damn!"

Larco reached for his radio.

21

Banff, Alberta

Driving west through Banff National Park amid the grandeur of the towering snow-crowned Rockies filled Kate with an overwhelming ache.

She missed her daughter.

She pulled over at a rest stop and called home.

Service in the mountains was spotty, but the line rang through to Nancy's voice mail. Kate left a message for Grace, then sought consolation in her daughter's picture on her screen.

Taking in the majestic landscape as she got back on the road, Kate realized that she'd been climbing mountains all her life in search of the truth. How fitting her search would lead her back to the same highway she'd traveled twenty years ago when everything changed, leaving her the lone survivor of her family, haunted by not knowing what had really happened to her sister.

The new information she'd unearthed these past few days was so startling she'd started doubting it herself. Yet a voice, an unyielding emotional force deep inside, impelled her to hold on to the faint hope that Vanessa had actually been alive all these years.

Don't let go of it. You can't let go.

She passed Lake Louise, then entered British Columbia. The thick sweeping forests and jade rivers pulled her back through her life and the memories rushed by her.

Kate's mother was a supermarket cashier and Kate's father worked in a factory that made military truck parts. She remembered how her mother smelled like roses, how she felt safe in her father's big strong hands whenever he lifted her up and said, *How's my Katie?* She remembered how Vanessa's eyes twinkled when she laughed and how happy they were in their little house near Washington, DC.

Then came the night when Kate and Vanessa were home together with their babysitter, Mrs. Kawolski, and police came to the door. Kate's parents had been at a wedding in Boston. Fear had clouded Mrs. Kawolski's face as the officers filled the kitchen, their utility belts making leathery squeaks as they cleared their throats, the policewoman giving Kate and Vanessa little stuffed bears to hold. "There was a terrible fire at the hotel. I'm so very sorry, your mommy and daddy won't be coming home. They're with the angels now."

Kate was seven and Vanessa was four.

In the month before her death, Kate's mother had given her and Vanessa each a tiny guardian angel necklace with their names engraved. Vanessa wanted to trade them so she wore the one with her big sister's name on it and Kate had the angel bearing Vanessa's name.

They cherished those necklaces.

After their parents died, Kate and Vanessa pin-balled through a succession of homes belonging to increasingly distant relatives. Ultimately, they lived with strangers. All Kate remembered from that time was how they were forever moving, city to city, state to state, but lucky to stay together. They were with new foster parents from Chicago when the crash happened.

Not many miles from here.

Kate glanced at her GPS, then at the map folded on the seat, and adjusted her grip on the wheel as the images loomed*...the car sinking...everything moving in slow motion... They never found Vanessa's body...*

No.

She couldn't think about it now.

After the accident, Kate lived in a never-ending chain of foster homes. Some were good, some weren't. As soon as she was old enough, she ran away and survived on the streets. She panhandled, lied about her age and took any job she could, but she never stole, used drugs or got drunk. She never prostituted herself.

Somehow Kate managed to follow an internal moral compass, which she believed—no, knew—she'd inherited from her parents.

During that time, Kate couldn't help dreaming that Vanessa might be alive somewhere. She kept reading news stories about people finding long-lost relatives after enduring years of pain. Those stories and the reporters who wrote them gave Kate hope, gave her direction.

She would become a journalist. She would search for the truth.

At age seventeen, Kate was living in a Chicago

group home and taking night classes. She wrote an essay about her yearning to know what really happened, *to be forgiven for*, the night Vanessa's little hand slipped from hers. Her teacher showed it to an editor friend at the *Chicago Tribune*. Impressed, the editor gave her a part-time news job. From there, Kate went to community college, then on to reporter jobs across the country.

All the while she was quietly searching for Vanessa. She'd sent age-progressed photos to missing persons groups and chased down Jane Doe cases, always in vain.

She was working at the *San Francisco Star* when she fell in love with a cop. After she got pregnant she learned that he'd been lying about his divorce and was married and had two sons. She left California for a job with the *Repository* in Canton, Ohio, where she had Grace at age twenty-three.

Kate thrived at the paper where, through relentless digging, she'd tracked down a fugitive killer. While her work was shut out for a Pulitzer, she won a state award for excellence. But after several years she'd fallen victim to downsizing and was laid off. Things got dire. Kate was juggling bills when she landed a spot on a short but paid job competition at the Dallas bureau of Newslead, the worldwide wire service. She'd helped cover a devastating tornado and broke a national story about a missing baby boy. The competition had been ferocious but it led Chuck Laneer, a senior editor, to hire her last year as a national reporter at Newslead's world headquarters in Manhattan. Since then, she'd often led on coverage of major crimes and disasters across the country or around the world.

Throughout everything Kate had accepted that her life was an ongoing search for the truth about her sister and forgiveness.

A highway distance sign flashed by.

Kate was now less than forty-five minutes from the crash site.

She let out a long breath and pulled into a gas station in the tiny town of Field, British Columbia. She got fuel, used the restroom, bought a bouquet of fresh flowers and returned to the highway.

As she got closer to the site, her memories of that day twenty years ago grew stronger and…singing voices echoed.

Old MacDonald had a farm, E-I-E-I-O...

Kate and Vanessa were in the backseat. They were both wearing their necklaces. It was a happy time. Their foster father, Ned, a bus driver, was at the wheel, beside him, Norma, his wife, a secretary. They were on vacation, singing and marveling at how the mountains were so close to the road you could almost touch them as they formed sheer rock walls shooting straight up so far you couldn't see the top.

It got darker and cooler in the shadows of the mountains. Kate remembered Norma telling Ned to slow down each time they'd passed a road sign warning of falling rocks. She remembered that when they came to a great valley the car started making a noise, Ned saying how they'd stop in the next town so he could take a look at it.

They were about ten miles east of Golden, British Columbia, where the Kicking Horse River intertwines with the Trans-Canada Highway.

And on his farm he had a duck...

Suddenly Ned's swearing, turning the wheel... bang...*Norma's screaming...they're flying—how could that be—flying, spinning...off the road...the world is rolling upside down...the car's crashing into the river...sinking...everything's in slow motion...the windows breaking open...cold water rushing in...holding her breath...Ned and Norma screaming, struggling underwater...dark...the dome light's glow...the car's upside down...roof banging against the rocky riverbed... the strong current pushing the car...Kate unbuckles her seatbelt...unbuckles Vanessa's...grabbing Vanessa's hand...lungs bursting...pulling her out...they're out of the car swimming...nearing the surface...the current's sweeping them downriver...numbing her... her fingers loosening...Vanessa's slipping away...her hand rising from the water, then disappearing... VANESSA!*

It all happened here, right here.

Kate had stopped her rental on the shoulder, stood next to it and stared at the river, listening to its rush. It was here. She checked the photographs in the time-worn newspaper clippings, checked the highway's curve, the rock formations near the river—Three American Tourists Killed When Car Crashed Into River…

Kate didn't remember much of the aftermath. Images blurred by police, rescuers, flying back to Chicago with a young social worker who cried with her, the memorial services for Ned, Norma and Vanessa, a grief counselor and more foster homes.

And the nightmares.

Vanessa's hand.

They dragged the river where they could. They used

divers and dog teams, search groups and a helicopter, to scour the banks but found nothing after five days of searching. Vanessa's body may have been wedged in the rocks, they said. It may have been washed up and dragged into the wild by wolves, cougars or a bear. All were possibilities.

Kate was the lone survivor.

Why did I survive? Why me?

She squeezed the flower stems tight as she carefully made her way to the river's edge. One by one she dropped flowers into the flowing water, watching each of them twirl downstream.

Please forgive me, Vanessa. I'm so sorry I let you slip away. Why couldn't they find you? I have to know what happened. I can't go on like this. Are you dead? Are you here, somewhere? Or did you somehow survive? Where are you Vanessa? What happened?

Kate studied the river and scanned the vast forests and glorious mountains. She sat on the bank. It was beautiful, peaceful and spiritual. She didn't know how long she'd been there when her phone rang.

Surprised that she had service here, she looked at it, thinking it might be Nancy with Grace returning her call.

The number was for Newslead in Manhattan. She answered.

"Kate, Reeka at the office. Can you talk?"

"What is it?"

"The Associated Press has just moved a story out of Rampart, citing unnamed sources, saying that additional human remains have been found in what police suspect are multiple murders at a remote barn site. Kate, why didn't you alert us to this?"

"What?"

Kate's mind raced. *Reeka's nerve! More victims! Was Vanessa one?*

"Why didn't you advise me of this, Kate, given your involvement?"

"You wanted me fired for my *involvement*, Reeka."

"You're still a Newslead employee."

"But you wanted me fired. You said there was no story there."

"Obviously things have changed."

"What do you want from me?"

"This is poised to become a huge story and we can't let our competition beat us on it. I want you to tell me all you know so I can pass it to our bureau people in Rochester and Syracuse."

"No."

"What did you say?"

Kate hung up and stared at the river.

22

Calgary, Alberta

It was a mistake to hang up on Reeka Beck.

Probably a fatal one given Newslead's plan to cut staff, Kate thought while driving back to Calgary, still stinging from the call.

Damn, Reeka had a lot of gall. But it's no surprise. She resents me.

Maybe it was Reeka's queen-bee syndrome. Kate had encountered it before with women in other newsrooms. Or maybe it was because Reeka regarded her as a gutter-girl-slut, a lowly community college grad.

Well, to hell with her, calling the way she did to attack me. She had it coming and I'm too tired to think about her right now.

It was late.

Kate had driven across Alberta and halfway back in one day. She'd uncovered more about Vanessa's case and relived a nightmare. She was exhausted, anguished and now that more human remains had been found in Rampart, even more fearful that the woods around the barn had become Vanessa's grave.

Kate pushed the thought from her mind as she drove, noticing how fast the sky had darkened after the sun set in the mountains. Her loneliness grew in the twilight but it left her when she stopped at a diner in Banff. She'd managed to reach Grace before Nancy put her to bed. The sound of her daughter's voice as she told Kate about her day was soothing.

"I hope you can get me a present from Canada, Mom."

Later, while preparing to leave the diner, Kate received a text from Chuck, which launched a terse exchange.

We need to talk over the phone in the am.

OK. What time? she responded.

Eight. We'll call you.

We?

Reeka and Ben will be on the call.

This was serious. Ben Sussman was an executive editor.

I'm in Alberta. I'll send you my hotel number.

Alberta?

Yes.

Fine. That'll be 6 a.m. your time.

Kate drove the rest of the way to Calgary grappling with a million concerns. *You're tired. You're not thinking clearly.*

Besides, so much was out of her control.

At the hotel she'd put in a wake-up call then went to bed plagued with terrifying dreams of a woman burning alive in a blazing barn; a hand rising from the river; all to the melody of *E-I-E-I-O*, until a phone started ringing and ringing.

Someone should answer it. Why doesn't somebody get that phone?

Kate opened her eyes to a torpid fog and answered her wake-up call.

She showered, made strong coffee, got dressed, went online and scoured news sites for the latest on Rampart. The case was attracting national attention. Bloomberg, Reuters and the Associated Press had all moved new stories on the mystery surrounding the discovery in Rampart and speculation there were more victims.

Kate had checked the status of her morning return flight when her room phone rang.

It was Chuck, on speaker with Ben and Reeka.

They got right to it.

"There's a major news conference in Rampart tomorrow morning," Chuck said. "We're getting beat on this story. We need to own it. We'd like you to send us all you know on the case ASAP. We need an exclusive hook. Ray Stone will write a setup piece today and Michelle Martin from our Syracuse bureau will go to Rampart and cover the conference."

"No."

"No?" Chuck muttered something, then said, "Are you refusing?"

"Yes."

"Insubordination given your situation puts you on thin ice, Kate."

"Kate, Ben Sussman here. Why are you refusing?"

"I want the story."

"I understand your personal interest," Sussman said, "concerning your sister's tragedy, and our hearts go out to you. But, as you know, to put you on the story violates our policy. You'd be using your position for personal gain, which is what got you into trouble in the first place."

"What personal gain? Our job as journalists is to seek the truth. As far as my sister's concerned, that's what I'm doing, seeking the truth about her. I'd be serving readers."

"Kate, it's not that simple," Chuck said.

"Hear me out. You all know that we've had staff produce work, good work, in which they used their position for personal gain. Our feature writer in Atlanta wrote about her daughter's terminal illness and cracks in the insurance system. One of our financial writers did a first-person series about how his relatives were victims of subprime mortgages. I could give you other examples."

"You make a valid argument," Sussman said. "But your case is a bit more complicated."

"That's right," Reeka said. "Kate, the distinction with your case is that you broke the law and could still be charged for trespassing on a crime scene."

They had her against the ropes and had hammered her with the truth.

She didn't know what to say.

A long silence passed before Chuck said, "Kate?"

"It's funny," she said. "I'm nearly fired for using my position for what you deem 'personal gain,' when Newslead is leaning on me to use my position for its corporate gain. Do you see the irony in that?"

"The fact is, Kate," Reeka said, "the police could bring those charges back on you at any time."

Kate shut her eyes and felt Vanessa's hand slip from hers, saw it shooting up from the river, saw it disappearing.

"Yes," she said. "I'm guilty of trespassing on a crime scene and taking pictures, but I'll give you some context. For twenty years I've lived with the guilt of my sister's death. For twenty years I've lived with the fact that her body was never found. Then Rampart police call me, telling me they've found a necklace at a crime scene identical to one my sister had. Can you imagine for one second what goes through your mind? Yes, I was overwhelmed, yes, I broke the law. I'm human and that was my mistake, but keeping me off this story, especially now, will be your mistake, because no one is going to give more to it than me. I'll go full tilt for you. So you can keep me off the story, you can fire me for insubordination. I'll go to AP, Bloomberg and Reuters. Maybe they'll be interested in what I've found out on my own up here. Being journalists, I'm surprised you didn't ask."

Now it was the editors who went silent for a long moment.

"Stay near your phone," Chuck said. "We'll get back to you."

Kate hung up, cupped her hands to her face, then

got busy. She went online and sent Grace an email of a picture of bighorn sheep she'd seen in the mountains. She checked flights again. After she'd started packing, her room phone rang.

It was Chuck.

"You're on the story. Get to Syracuse tonight and touch base with the bureau and go with our bureau photographer to Rampart in the morning for the news conference."

"Okay."

"What can you give us that's exclusive?"

"That it appears that my sister may have survived her crash and was abducted from Canada to become a victim in Rampart. I have elements that point to that scenario."

Chuck took a second to absorb that.

"All right, I want you to file a setup piece that includes that exclusive angle."

"Do you want it first person?"

"No, write it news style and we'll attach a disclosure disclaimer to your piece, clearly stating your relationship. We'll do it with anything you write that's relevant to the case."

"All right."

"I want it by 5:00 p.m., New York time, today. Looks like you can fly from Calgary to Chicago with a connection to Syracuse. You can write on the plane and file from O'Hare, if you don't have Wi-Fi in the air. We'll cover all costs as you now are officially on assignment."

"Thank you, Chuck."

"If you screw up, Kate, it's your job."

"I know."

"And mine."

23

Rampart, New York

"I just finished reading your story, Kate. It's incredible."

Jay Raney, Newslead's chief photographer at the Syracuse bureau, pocketed his phone and introduced himself to Kate in her motel lobby. He was a soft-spoken man in his late thirties with a few-days-growth beard. As he helped her with her bags and led her to his Ford Escape, she contended with her overriding fear about her sister.

Were the newly discovered human remains Vanessa's?

Was today the day she'd find the truth?

They headed north on Interstate 81 for Rampart and that morning's news conference. After some small talk—they'd discovered they had mutual news friends in Ohio and California—things fell quiet and Kate worked as the miles rushed under them.

Her flight back had been smooth. She'd slept well and was energized after talking with Grace on the phone earlier, before Raney arrived. Now, with farmland flashing by her window, Kate concentrated on her laptop, starting with a message from Chuck.

Pickup of your story was very strong, he had said. Keep us out front.

Scrolling through the rest of her messages, Kate came to a new one from Elliott Searle, the retired Mountie.

With regard to the partial plate, look for an article in one of the Denver papers, within a month of TDM's disappearance. It mentions the plate.

Kate began searching the databases for the *Denver Post* and *Rocky Mountain News*. The *Rocky* had folded in 2009, but its stories were archived. Each paper had small wire items about Tara Dawn Mae and the search for a missing Canadian girl, but none mentioned the plate.

She responded to Searle. Can't find it. Maybe you're unclear. If you have the article, why not just give it to me?

At the time, the information in the article was leaked by US law enforcement and ruffled some feathers up here. The story's there. Keep looking. You have to find it.

It was frustrating that some cops were so weird that way. Kate knew they didn't want to be accused of giving out anything contained in case files but would point you to public information. She continued searching before asking Newslead's news library for help, just as her phone chimed with a text from Reeka. We'll need to see your story within an hour of the news conference ending. The sooner the better.

Kate rolled her eyes, replying with, Okay. Thank you.

After they'd arrived in Rampart, Raney drove them to the town hall where the news conference was to be held.

They got there twenty minutes before things were to start. The parking lot and street were filled with TV trucks and news cars from Watertown, Rochester and Syracuse; radio stations from Plattsburgh and Potsdam; newspapers from Ogdensburg and Massena.

"I bet AP, Reuters and Bloomberg have people here, maybe even the *Post* and *Daily News*, too." Raney grabbed his gear from the back.

Inside, they showed their credentials to a man at the reception area. He slid a clipboard to them.

"Sign in, then go to the right, end of the hall."

About two dozen news people, along with a dozen or so police types were in a large meeting room. TV cameras on tripods lined the back like a firing squad as operators made adjustments. Local reporters in folding chairs gossiped; others talked on phones or were making notes.

At the front of the room, four solemn-faced men took their places at a table heaped with recorders and microphones with station flags. To the right was a tack board bearing enlarged photographs of Carl Nelson, John Charles Pollard, Bethany Ann Wynn and Tara Dawn Mae, from the time she'd vanished.

Staring into Tara Dawn's face jolted Kate.

That's Vanessa up there. Now, after what I've

learned, I believe in my heart that's her. All these years...stop...you don't know that she died here...

As Kate grappled with her anguish and anger she spotted Detective Ed Brennan standing against the wall with his partner. Brennan gave her a slight nod and she tightened her hold on her pen.

"Is everybody ready?" One of the men at the table spoke, allowing for several reporters to approach them and switch on their recorders.

"Thank you for coming, especially those from out of town. I'm Captain Dan Kennedy, with the Rampart PD. We lead this investigation and we're supported by a number of agencies, some of which are here. To my far right, Lorne Baker, Riverview County Sheriff's Office, Max Insley, the New York State Police and to my left, Emmett Lang, with the FBI out of Syracuse. I'll read you a summary of the case, then we'll take a few questions."

"At this time, our investigation into the deaths at the state property known as the old burial grounds leads us to conclude that the individual known as Carl Nelson did not die in the fire at an abandoned barn, as first suspected. We believe that Nelson murdered Bethany Ann Wynn, after keeping her in captivity for three years. Nelson also murdered John Charles Pollard and staged the scene to make it appear as though he had taken his own life.

"Additional human remains have been found within proximity of the barn leading us to believe that Nelson may have killed other people. Work is under way to confirm the identity of those remains, and we're expanding the scene and bringing in more people for an extensive search of the area. We're going to scour every square inch of the property. Now, based on evidence found at the scene, we've reason to suspect that the case is linked to the disappearance of Tara Dawn Mae, who's been missing from Brooks, Alberta, Canada, for over fifteen years."

Soft gasps rippled among the reporters along with the hurried turning of notebook pages. Kate glanced at Tara Dawn's face, then at Brennan. It was more real, for now they were closer to talking officially about a link to Vanessa. Kate regained her concentration as Kennedy continued.

"We're working with the RCMP on this part of the investigation. Finally, we believe Carl Nelson is alive and at large using an assumed name. A warrant has been issued for his arrest for the murders of John Charles Pollard and Bethany Ann Wynn. Today, the FBI will place him on its Most Wanted list. Nelson should be considered dangerous. He should not be approached by the public. We're also appealing to anyone with any information concerning this case to call our tip line or their local police. Okay, we'll take a few questions."

Hands went up.

"Yes," Kennedy said, "Marissa, from the *Rampart Examiner*."

"Are you telling us that Nelson held one of his victims in captivity in that barn for fifteen years?"

"We know that, in the Canadian case, Tara Dawn Mae's been missing for that time. We know that Nelson's been in Rampart for ten years."

Kate's hand shot up, but she was passed over for a newspaper reporter from Rochester.

"Where was Nelson before that time?"

"That's under investigation."

Kate raised her hand, but Kennedy went to a reporter from Plattsburgh.

"Is the case connected to the abandoned insane asylum?"

"We're looking into that. I see lots of hands—next."

Again Kate tried but lost out to a TV reporter from Syracuse.

"Captain, how is it that Nelson, a computer technician and recluse, was able to keep prisoners at that barn for as long as a decade without anyone noticing?"

"The property was abandoned. We found evidence of confinement rooms concealed in a lower level. He stole small amounts of electricity undetected from the grid. Few people traveled that deep into the wooded area—in fact none to our knowledge, until the discovery of the fire. Next."

Kate's hand went up again, but the Bloomberg reporter got the question.

"You said you found confinement rooms. What was going on out there?"

"We don't know."

"It's rumored there was bondage, perhaps torture?"

"We don't know. We can only speculate that it was horrible. Next."

Kennedy looked directly at Kate and she started to speak, but he shifted his attention, taking another reporter's question. She knew what was happening and was tempted to raise her middle finger.

"Given that Nelson worked at the MRKT DataFlow Call Center, did you find Bethany Ann Wynn's financial records there?" a radio reporter from Ogdensburg asked. "And did Nelson have access to them? Is that how he selected his victims?"

"We're investigating that aspect."

Kate waved her notebook, tried to raise a question, but Moore continued.

"And, given Nelson's work, isn't it possible he could assume or steal anyone's identity?"

"Yes, it's possible, next question."

Kate waved her hand and again she was ignored.

"Did Nelson act alone?" the reporter from the Associated Press asked.

"It appears so, but we're early in the investigation."

Again, Kate raised her hand, and again Kennedy looked directly at her as he took a question from the reporter behind her from Reuters.

"To be clear on the victims, we have Bethany Ann Wynn and John Charles Pollard. So, two confirmed at this time, but you're confident that number will rise?"

"Correct."

"One more question," the Reuters guy said. "Any idea on Nelson's whereabouts?"

"Finding him is our priority, Jim." Kennedy shifted the subject. "You all know that the site remains closed, but because most of you asked about getting pictures of the scene we're arranging pool coverage, drawing names from the sign-in sheet. Okay, thank you, everyone, I think we'll wrap this—"

"Excuse me!" Kate stood. "Kate Page, Newslead. Captain, I think we need more than just five minutes here."

Kennedy's face tightened.

"What's your question?"

"Captain, how close are you to determining the identity of the recently discovered remains?"

"As I indicated at the outset, they're with the pathologist. These matters take time."

"Sir," Kate continued. "What factors led you to connect this case to the cold case of Tara Dawn Mae in Canada?"

"We're not prepared to discuss that at this time."

"Did you find evidence at the scene to make the connection?"

"We're not going to discuss evidence." Kennedy stared at Kate.

"What about Nelson? Can you put him in Canada at the time of Tara Dawn's disappearance?"

"We're not going to discuss that part of our investigation at this time. That's it for now, thank you, everyone."

As Kennedy stood to leave, Kate raised her voice above the shuffle of the closing press conference and news cameras were directed at her.

"Captain Kennedy, can you elaborate on how Tara Dawn Mae's case is tied to that of Vanessa Page of Chicago, who went missing after a car accident in Canada twenty years ago?"

Kennedy and the others halted. He took stock of the other investigators before answering.

"Ms. Page, we're aware of your interest and your story. I say, with the greatest respect and understanding, that we're not in a position to discuss all aspects of our investigation at this time. Thank you."

Reporters tried to get in last questions, but Kennedy waved them off as police officials gathered folders and left the room for a smaller glass-walled office adjoining it. The reporters immediately surrounded Kate and peppered her with questions under the glare of the TV cameras as the still photographers fired shot after shot.

"We read your story, Kate. Will you tell our listeners why you're convinced your sister's a victim here?"

"How did you learn your sister's case was tied to this one?"

"What did you discover in Canada about your sister's cold case and this one? Your story never said what Canadian authorities told you."

"How have the past twenty years been for you, Kate?"

She looked at Anita Moore, the reporter who'd asked the last one.

"They've been hard and I'd give anything to see my sister again."

At that point, Kate saw Brennan nodding at her from the doorway to the other officials in the glass-walled office. He mouthed the word *now.* She extricated herself from the press pack. Some reporters objected when Kate alone joined the cops in the office, for it appeared she was given journalistic preference.

"What's going on, Ed?" the reporter for the *Examiner* asked.

Brennan dismissed them and closed the door after he and Kate entered the office where Kennedy, who'd loosened his tie, was waiting with the others.

"Our hearts go out to you, Kate," Kennedy said. "We're sympathetic to your situation. We appreciate that you've helped us, but our hands are tied."

Kate said nothing, letting her resentment bubble as Kennedy continued.

"You have to let us do our job."

"I'm not stopping you."

"Kate, we know—" Kennedy stopped to see news cameras recording them on the other side of the glass. "Would someone shut the blinds? Now, Kate, we know where you've been, who you've talked to and what you've been doing."

"You're stating the obvious, since I wrote about it for Newslead."

"Yes, and I will thank you for keeping evidentiary details out of your story. That was important."

"I'm not stupid, Captain."

"I wasn't suggesting that, Kate. We're concerned about tipping off the suspect to everything we know. Our focus is finding Nelson and arresting him while we determine the scope of his crimes and identify the victims."

"And everything points to my sister being one of them."

"Yes, I'm afraid that's possible. We haven't identified the remains yet. Kate, you have to brace yourself for the possibility that she's a victim."

"That's what I've been doing all of my life, Captain. But if you know something that I don't, if those are Vanessa's remains that you found, then you tell me right now!"

"At this point, we don't know who the deceased is. But when the pathologist confirms the identity, we'll release the information." Kennedy paused. "Kate, we're urging you not to interfere, to back off."

"No. I'm not going to be the docile, grieving family member on the sidelines. I have a constitutional right to ask questions. I've lived with this all of my life. I've got a blood right to the truth. I'll never back off."

"We're asking you to exercise a little judgment here."

"Kate." Kennedy rubbed his chin. "Just to remind you, those charges against you can always be brought back."

"Are you threatening me?"

"No, but consider the ramifications. Kate, it's dangerous to get too close to a case, especially when it concerns a dangerous fugitive."

"He's right, Kate," Brennan said. "Nelson's at large, and you're involved in this. You should dial things down."

"No, I'm not backing off."

"All right," Kennedy said. "I think we're done here."

Leaving the town hall with Jay, Kate was stopped by reporters insisting on more comments. Kate kept them short, then headed with Raney to his SUV.

"AP's shooting still images for the pool," he said. "Bloomberg will send copy. We should go with the pack to Nelson's house, see what we can find there."

"Sure, but I have to file something first. Let's grab a coffee somewhere and I'll write."

At that moment, her phone rang.

"Kate, this is Nicky Green from the library. I found that news story from Denver you wanted, the one about a license plate and missing girl in Canada."

"Great. Can you send it to me?"

"Just did."

24

Rampart, New York

Three blocks from the town hall, Kate and Raney shared a booth in Sally's Diner.

Kate was anxious to read the old clipping from Denver, but her deadline was looming. She needed to file her story, and she was hungry.

While waiting for their food, they set up their laptops. Raney selected and adjusted images he'd shot at the news conference. Kate inserted an earpiece, plucked key quotes from her recorder, consulted her notes and wrote, her keyboard clicking softly as she tuned out the noise around her.

By the time the waitress set their burgers down—"My, you two are busy bees"—Kate was well into her story, stopping at each paragraph to take a bite. When she'd finished she'd filed seven hundred clean, solid words to Newslead, just under the deadline.

Raney was on the phone to the photo desk in New York. While he talked, Kate went to her email and the Colorado article. It was from the *Denver Star-Times*, a community weekly that had ceased publication nearly ten years ago. It was a short item:

> Police Probe Possible Denver Link to Missing Canadian Girl
> By Will Goodsill
>
> Denver detectives are investigating a possible local link to a ten-year-old Canadian girl who recently went missing from a truck stop in Alberta, Canada.
>
> Tara Dawn Mae vanished last week from the Grand Horizon Plaza, along the Trans-Canada Highway at Brooks, Alberta, about 100 miles east of Calgary.
>
> Canadian authorities gave Colorado law enforcement officials a list of partial license plates and descriptions of vehicles that were in the area at the time, with a request to verify them in relation to the Canadian case.
>
> "We're running them down where we can, eliminating possibilities. A few are promising leads, but it's a needle-in-a-haystack thing," a police source told the *Star-Times*.

A stamp-sized photo of Tara Dawn accompanied the article.

Kate reread the piece, drawn to the quote *"A few are promising leads."* Which few? What happened to them? Who was the source? Did Carl Nelson ever live in Denver?

I need to follow this, but it's going to take time.

Raney ended his call, then snapped his laptop shut.

"Ready to go, Kate?" He signaled the waitress for the checks.

A few minutes later, Raney pulled onto Knox Lane and rolled by Nelson's modest ranch-style bungalow with its tidy yard.

The situation was different from when Kate was last here. The entire property was sealed with yellow tape and Rampart officers had been posted to keep people out. The street was sprinkled with news vehicles. Nelson's neighbors were giving doorstep and sidewalk interviews, their faces etched with concern. Some held their children close.

Kate and Raney approached a man and woman in their thirties, who'd just finished talking to a TV crew on the sidewalk, two doors down from Nelson's house. The couple, Neil and Belinda Wilcox, agreed to have their picture taken and to talk about their missing neighbor.

"It shocks you to the core." Belinda cupped her hand to her cheek and stared at Nelson's house. "It's frightening. We had him in our home once."

"Really?" Kate took out her notebook. "Tell me about that?"

"Well, it sounds cliché," Neil started, "but Nelson kept to himself. He was a hermit."

"Yeah," Belinda added. "With his long hair and beard, he looked like one."

"Yeah, well, one day in winter," Neil continued, "he was clearing his driveway and I'd run out of gas for my snowblower. I asked him if I could borrow some. Well, I got telling him how my computer didn't work and he volunteered to fix it. It took him about two minutes, the guy's a genius."

"Another time," Belinda recalled, "I saw that he had like a ton of groceries in the back of his truck. I asked him if he was feeding an army, because we knew he lived alone. He was kind of startled and said he was donating a lot to a soup kitchen in Ogdensburg."

The Wilcoxes remembered little else that was noteworthy. Raney indicated an older man and woman across the street, walking a golden retriever, and they went to them.

Doris Stitz was a retired schoolteacher, and her husband, Harvey, was a retired mechanic. They lived at the corner of the street.

"We came down to see what all this fuss was today," Harvey said.

"We've been following the story in the news," Doris said. "And it's just getting worse and worse. It's so awful. You never expect this kind of thing in our quiet little town."

"Did you ever meet Nelson?"

"Once," Harvey said. "He seemed friendly enough, but it felt like it was forced. You got a sense that he wanted to be left alone."

"How so?"

"Just an air about him. It was last year. Boone, here, got off his leash and chased a squirrel into Nelson's backyard. I rang his doorbell and asked if I could go get my dog. Nelson just gave off this icy air, like he didn't appreciate being bothered, or want anybody on his property. Then he said I could go get Boone. I didn't notice anything back there. It was all very well kept, very neat. On my way out with Boone, Nelson looked at my ball cap, asked if I was a Broncos' fan. I said damn straight I am, then Nelson smiled and that was it."

"The Denver Broncos, the NFL football team?" Kate made a quick note.

"Yes."

"Did Nelson ever say if he lived in Denver?"

"Heck no, that was the extent of our conversation," Harvey said. "I don't think that guy ever really talked with anyone."

During the drive to the Syracuse airport, Kate updated her story. Along the way she called Grace, who was happy she'd be home later that night.

"Did you get me a present?"

"Sure did."

"What is it?"

"A surprise."

Kate then used the drive time to continue looking into the *Denver Star-Times* story. She needed to talk to Will Goodsill, the reporter. Maybe Goodsill could get in touch with his source, prompt him on what became of the "promising leads."

Online she found scores of listings for Goodsill across the country, a few in Denver, none for a Will Goodsill. She started making calls and leaving messages, knowing it was a long shot. The story was fifteen years old. Memories fade, people move and people die.

After Raney dropped Kate off at the airport she checked her bag, went through security and on to pre-boarding. At her gate, TV screens suspended throughout the area, were dialed to news networks with pictures of Carl Nelson flashing across them.

The Rampart case had exploded into a national story.

Again, Kate met the cold eyes that glared from the face of a fully bearded man with wild hair, in his forties.

Carl Nelson.

Is this the last face my sister saw?

This was her enemy.

If you killed my sister, then I'll find you. I swear to God, I'll find you.

Before boarding, Kate downloaded every fresh news story she could find so she could go through them during the flight.

On the plane, Kate studied the news reports. The TV items carried pictures of Nelson, accompanied by the pool images of the razed barn and investigators in white coveralls sifting the earth for human remains in a remote corner of the isolated property.

Network graphic headlines called the case:

Horror in Upstate NY

NY Body Farm

Hunt for a Monster

All day long Kate had struggled to push one supreme fear out of her mind, but now it hit her full force, the old agony tearing at her with renewed ferocity. She turned from the laptop to her window. Somewhere down there were either the ashes of her sister's prison or the remnants of her grave.

Oh, God, I don't know if I can do this.

Kate turned back to her monitor to see it filled

with Carl Nelson's face glowering at her above the new headline:

Face of Evil: Who Is Carl Nelson?

25

Gary, Indiana

The toilet ran on, the mattress sagged and brownish stains webbed down the cracked walls of the motel room at the city's fringe near the interstate.

The guest in Unit 14 didn't care.

The Slumber Breeze Inn's customers were chiefly addicts, hookers and deviants. But Unit 14 considered himself well above that stratum. What mattered was that the motel accepted cash while providing anonymity and indifference.

Working at two laptops on the room's desk, was Sorin Zurrn. But nobody—*nobody living*—knew him by that name, a name that resurrected undying pain for him. At this moment, he was Donald W.R. Fulmert, age thirty-two, a professional driver from Philadelphia, Pennsylvania.

In the darkness, his clean-shaven face and bald head glowed spectrally in the bluish light of his computer screens. He glimpsed himself in the room's fractured mirror, satisfied that he bore no resemblance to Carl Nelson.

That man had never really existed.

Zurrn had grown comfortable living in Nelson's skin, quietly tending to his collection over the years. But he'd never intended to reside there forever. He'd grown restless and proud of what he'd achieved.

But Rampart was such a small stage.

He deserved adoration for his accomplishments.

Although it was dangerous, he yearned for the world to be aware of his power; he ached for his life to be bigger, something grandiose and magnificent. He had to move on to the next stage of his evolution.

Over the past few years, he'd planned it all with such attention to detail, he thought, admiring the photographs of his new property. This would be his Asgard, his Valhalla; his Palace of Supreme Perfection. He could almost touch it, but it was still over a thousand miles and several states away, a vast expanse of isolated land.

The cost was unimportant.

Obtaining money was easy for him.

He knew the electronic security gaps with retailers and banks. Three months ago, he'd siphoned more than nine hundred thousand dollars in unmarked, nonsequential bills from cash advance kiosks at casinos in Las Vegas and Atlantic City. He had access to an eternity of credit cards and identities, enabling him to be anyone he needed to be, with access to just about anything.

And he could do it all without leaving a trace.

As he continued looking at pictures of his sweeping new property, envisioning how glorious his new kingdom would be, one of his laptops trilled with a message from Ashley.

He's so hot. Totally crushing on him! IDK! Help!

The pretty fourteen-year-old from Minnesota was breathless about a boy named Nick. Zurrn had been cultivating her online for the past six months, convincing her that he was Jenn, a sixteen-year-old girl from Milwaukee. He'd drilled deep into Ashley's life. He knew everything about her and her family—their home address, all their bank and credit card information, their medications, Ashley's grades, her habits and daily routine. He'd done a little work to get a feed off her phone and laptop so he could remotely watch her undetected.

He responded to her plea: Tell him, Ash! GTG! BFF!

BFF!

Best Friends Forever. Poor little Ashley might find out what forever really means, for Zurrn had her believing that Jenn's parents were taking her to the Mall of America soon.

Now, Ashley was dying to meet her BFF.

Wait, what's this?

In the corner of the room, a muted TV was tuned to an all-news channel. Images of the crime scene at a farm in Rampart, New York, appeared, prompting Zurrn to reach for the remote.

Carl Nelson's face filled the TV over a graphic that read, "Wanted by the FBI." As Zurrn listened, he went online, checking major news sites, devouring the breaking story.

What the hell's this?

In the past few days, he'd monitored the initial coverage of the Rampart story. As expected, early reports portrayed it as a local murder-suicide. Coverage was contained to the region. That's how it was designed and executed to play, with "Carl Nelson" and the woman dead, allowing Zurrn to disappear.

A perfect crime.

What happened?

Now, a woman named Kate Page was telling reporters of her search for her sister. A series of photos appeared from the cold case of a ten-year-old girl missing for fifteen years from Alberta, Canada.

"In my heart I feel my sister's case is linked to the Alberta case and these events in Rampart. I want to find the man who did this. I want to know what happened. I'd give anything to see her again."

Zurrn locked on to Kate Page, his face burning with contempt.

Long after the news ended, Zurrn sat motionless in the near dark, his neck muscles pulsating as he processed the news over the quiet hum of interstate traffic. Then loud music began throbbing from several rooms away, with the roll of drums hammering along the motel as if to signal war.

He went to one of the online news stories and examined the accompanying photo of Kate Page.

Who the hell're you? Do you think you're going to stop me? Me?

Zurrn put his hands together, steepled his fingers, touched them to his lips, his nostrils flaring. Then he shut off his computers, took them with him, got into his van and headed into the night. He drove along a stretch of strip malls, car washes and warehouses, coming to a Burger King with a twenty-four-hour drive-through.

After collecting his order, the aroma of onions and French fries filled the interior. As he threaded his way through a light industrial no-man's land, he took stock of his situation.

Where'd he screw up? He'd been careful. Yes, he'd made mistakes long ago when he was young, but time had buried them. He'd perfected his technique.

Calm down! So my perfect crime in Rampart was not so perfect. It doesn't matter what police think they know. I'll adjust. They can't touch me because I'll always have the upper hand. I'll always be in control.

He stopped at the gate of JBD 24-7 Mini-Storage. He inserted his card with the chip, then touched his code on the security keypad. The gate opened. He drove slowly through the facility's neat rows of garage-sized units. It was late, the grounds were deserted. When he found Number 84, he carefully backed the rear of his vehicle to the door, blocking the security cameras from clearly seeing inside.

He pressed the unit's password on the keypad, then inserted the key into the lock. Metal grumbled as he lifted the unit's steel door and switched on the light. It was clean and dry inside.

He closed the door.

In the unit's center, there was a large rectangle shape covered by a sound-absorbing tarpaulin. He pulled it back, revealing two oblong matching wooden crates, each large enough to hold a coffin. Each crate had a small, hinged inspection door, about the size of a hardcover book. His keys jingled as he unlocked the steel lock and opened the first one.

He dropped fast food into it, then locked the door.

Then he unlocked the second one, opened it and hesitated.

"Please! I'll be good, please! Please!" A soft voice rose from the darkness.

Ignoring it, he dropped the food and locked the door.

Then he sat in the corner and as he listened to the small movements of life coming from the boxes, he stared at them, thinking.

Thinking hard about what he was going to do.

26

Utica, New York

Lori Koller, an assistant at Essential Office Supply, set her fresh cup of orange tea on her desk and looked at her calendar.

Day by day. She sighed.

Ever since her husband, Luke, had died ten months ago, she'd struggled to carry on with their two little girls, the way he would've wanted. He was devoted to his family.

She glanced out the window of her building on Genesee Street.

Luke had been a construction worker. He was killed after falling ten stories at the site of a new apartment complex. But Lori hadn't received much in the way of compensation, because the investigation found that Luke routinely unhitched his safety harness. It complicated everything. Luke's life insurance policy was small. They had been planning to increase their coverage before he died.

After the funeral costs and the loss of Luke's income, debts started piling up. Friends helped by holding a small memorial banquet but in grappling with her grief, caring for the girls, who cried for their daddy, Lori had had a rough time. She got counseling for her and her daughters, sold their SUV, their van, Luke's tools, his boat and trailer, got a smaller car and paid down some bills.

Things were not easy and the hurting never went away, but day by day they were getting better, Lori thought, sipping her tea. She had gotten busy updating the monthly reports when her phone rang.

"Hey, it's me. Did you see today's *OD*?"

Her younger brother, Dylan, was a city bus driver, and, judging from the background noise, he was calling from the yard. Why would he ask if she'd read today's *Observer-Dispatch*?

"No. Why?"

"Go online now and look for the story about Rampart."

"I'm kinda busy."

"You have to do it, right now."

"Dylan."

"Right now, it'll only take a moment. I'll stay on the line to be sure you find it."

"All right." Her keyboard clicked. "You are such a pain." She went online to the newspaper's website, found the story and started reading.

"Did you find it?" Her brother was anxious.

"Shh!"

Lori read fast, and her attention shifted from the text to the images, particularly the photo of Carl Nelson.

"See the picture of the guy they're looking for?"

"Oh, my God!"

"It's him! That's the guy who bought your van."

"But he said he was from Cleveland and I don't think that's his name. I'd have to check the sales papers."

"Lori. I was there with you. That's him! You have to call the police line and tell them."

"I don't know, Dylan, this is all scary. It's all too much."

"You have to, Lori. Do it right now!"

After Dylan hung up, she looked at the article. At the bottom was the toll-free number of the police tip line. Lori took a few breaths then reread the story. What happened in Rampart was such a horrible thing. Then it occurred to her that she wouldn't want police to think she was somehow involved. Okay, okay, she'd do what any good citizen should do. Before she realized it, she'd dialed the number.

As the line rang in her ear she stared at the article and the photos, the search for human remains, then into the eyes of the man who had bought her family van.

27

New York City

Kate scrolled through news stories on her phone while sitting in the upholstered chair in the reception room of her daughter's dentist.

Still no confirmation out of Rampart on the ID of the remains.

Kate bit her lip to push away the fear.

It had been a day since she'd returned and in that time, between pursuing leads, she'd reconnected with her home life. While she'd only been away a couple of nights, it felt longer. Getting Grace to today's appointment gave her a sense of being a mom again.

Holding Grace's jacket in her lap, she traced the little hearts that were on the cuffs, thinking how lucky she was to have her. Grace was her rock, her anchor. She'd kept Kate sane through the years, just by being a kid.

Grace was practically the same age that Vanessa was when the accident happened. She even looked a little like her. Kate smiled and lifted her face to the opposite wall, which was plastered with snapshots of children showing mostly gap-toothed grins.

The display was called "Smiling Angels," and it propelled Kate back to: *her mother setting down a tray of fresh-baked chocolate-chip cookies, the kitchen smelling so yummy. "You can each have one, girls. I don't want you getting cavities." She and Vanessa each took one but split a second cookie when Mom wasn't looking...Vanessa laughing so hard.*

Kate suddenly thought of dental records and human remains.

"Hi, Mom!" Grace appeared, clutching her new free toothbrush, floss and toothpaste. "No cavities!"

"That's great, sweetie!"

"Mom, were you crying?" Grace tugged on her jacket as Kate helped.

"No, just a little tired from the plane." She blinked. "Let's get you back to school."

After taking Grace to school and signing her in, Kate got on the subway to Penn Station, then walked to Newslead. At her desk she again scanned the latest stories out of Rampart, checking to see if her competition had broken anything on Carl Nelson.

Nothing had surfaced.

The first message she checked was from Chuck.

Find something today to advance the story, keep us out front.

I'm working on it, Chuck.

Kate was still checking her messages when a new one arrived from Reeka.

Could you please come to my office?

Reeka had her face in her phone, texting, when Kate tapped softly on her open door. She'd noticed how small Reeka seemed behind her desk, as if it, or her position, was oversize for her.

"Please sit down." Reeka kept her face in her phone. Kate saw that the flat-screen TV in the corner was frozen on footage of the Rampart case. "So..." Reeka exhaled and put the phone down. "How'd things go for you?"

"Okay." Kate was guarded. "Considering everything."

"And how're you holding up, considering everything?"

"I'm okay."

"Your stories are solid."

"Thanks." Kate remained wary, the way a mongoose is wary of a cobra.

"But you do have the inside track."

"Excuse me?"

"I wanted to show you something." Reeka played the footage of Kate being interviewed at Rampart, then froze it. "You're aware of Newslead policy about reporters giving interviews to other press?"

"Yes."

"Reporters don't comment on the news without prior permission from a supervising editor. It's decided on a case-by-case basis. You needed prior permission."

"Reeka, what is this? You do know what this story's about? You're aware of what was agreed to in my covering the case with Chuck, Morris and Ben Sussman? You were part of it. I've been digging my ass off. You're aware of what I'm going through here, and how my 'inside track,' as you call it, my personal anguish, is being exploited by Newslead?"

"Of course. And I couldn't begin to imagine the heartache you're enduring, but I have to keep in mind what happened in London. That situation eroded our credibility and our integrity. I have to insure we do things by the book, Kate."

"This is not the same thing as what happened in London, Reeka, and you know that."

A knock sounded at the door and both women turned to see Sussman standing at it.

"There you are, Kate. I just wanted to say pickup rates on this story are sky-high. We understand how hard this must be personally for you, Kate. We're all praying for you, so whatever you need, you let us know."

"Thank you, Ben."

"Be assured, Newslead's behind you. By the way, I've heard through the grapevine *Good Morning America* and the *Today* show, are showing interest in having you on soon. So let's see how things go."

After Sussman left, Kate turned to Reeka.

"I'd like to get back to work."

Kate detoured to the restroom to check her face and contend with the corporate hypocrisy. *We're all praying for you. A few days ago they all wanted me fired. If I didn't love the job here—if Chuck didn't have my back I'd—calm down. Just calm down and stop thinking about yourself.*

Back in the newsroom, Kate was struck with an idea.

She went to the business section and the desk of Hugh Davidson, who reported on computer technology. Hugh was otherwise known as Newslead's Emperor Nerd. He was partial to bow ties and pastel shirts.

"Hey, Hugh, got a sec? I need your help."

He swiveled in his chair, crossed his arms.

"Shoot, Kate. I got five minutes before I have to go talk to some Apple honchos."

"You've written about hackers and the best of the best out there."

"That's correct. Nice that you're familiar with my work."

"You've got contacts in hackerdom, or whatever it's called."

"Correct."

"You know about my situation?"

"Yes, I also read your work."

"Do you think you could put me in touch with some of your hacker friends? I want to write a deep bio on Carl Nelson."

Hugh touched one finger to his lips.

"I do know of some entities in the cyber mists who're remarkably skilled and would be up to the challenge."

Kate's cell phone rang.

"Great. I've got to take this, Hugh."

"I'll put some feelers out there and get back to you."

Kate's phone rang a second time.

"Thanks, Hugh. Kate Page," she said into her phone.

"Hello. This is Will Goodsill in Denver. I got a call from a cousin who said you were trying to reach me."

"Yes, Will, thanks for calling. This concerns a story you wrote fifteen years ago for the *Denver Star-Times*, about a missing Canadian girl."

"So you said in your message. I looked you up and your current work. You're looking for a connection to Alberta, Denver and New York?"

"Exactly, yes." Kate was impressed. "Can you help me?"

"I'm a hoarder of files and notebooks, but we had some flooding a few years back, so I can't say if I've still got everything from that time. I remember that story, and I did some digging on it myself. I'll have to look to see if it survived and get back to you, Kate."

28

Rampart, New York

Lori Koller, the woman on the phone from Utica, was uneasy.

"You're certain you sold your van to the man in the photograph, Carl Nelson?" asked Ed.

"Yes. Only he said his name was John Feeney from Rochester. But I swear that's him in the picture. Please don't give out my name."

"No, ma'am. Now, you posted your van on a buy-and-sell site. He responded, paid cash, and this was four months ago?"

"Yes."

"How did he take the van away? Did he have a friend with him?"

"No, he had a pickup truck pulling a trailer."

"Okay, good. Now, I've got your contact information. Someone's going to be in touch with you real soon."

"Who?"

"Likely someone from the Utica police, or state

police or the FBI. They'll take a statement from you and we're going to need the VIN and—"

"The VIN?"

"It's the Vehicle Identification Number. It'll be on your papers. We'll need your documents to verify the registration history for the vehicle. We'll also want all your maintenance records, showing what kind of tires you had on the vehicle. Do you still have the records, or the name of the shop where you had your van serviced?"

"I do."

"Do you have a recent photo of the van?"

"The one I used on the site."

"Can you send it to me?"

"Yes."

"Okay, someone will be in touch shortly."

"Please don't give my name to the public. I'm a little scared."

"No, ma'am."

After hanging up, Brennan called Utica police, the state police, the FBI and then he alerted his lieutenant.

"This one's good," Brennan told him before he began submitting details of the lead into the case data file.

Since the news conference and public appeal, the investigators had received more than one hundred tips, but most of the callers were vague: *"I think it's my new neighbor. He's creepy."* Or, *"I met this guy at a bar, who said he knew a guy, who thinks he knows where Carl Nelson is, but I can't remember the bar—I was pretty loaded."*

The Utica lead was different. It was solid and could be supported by official records. It held the potential to be physical evidence that would stand up in court. It also fit with the theory that Nelson had used a second vehicle to leave the area. At the scene, they'd found tire impressions that didn't come from his pickup truck or the car belonging to the teens who'd discovered the fire.

It would be a major break if we could match the impressions with the Utica van. Once the information was verified, details about the van and its link to the case would be submitted to regional, state and national crime databases, like the National Crime Information Center and Violent Criminal Apprehension Program. Bulletins for the van would go to every law enforcement agency in the country.

An email arrived from Lori Koller containing photos of the van. Brennan was reviewing them when Dickson returned to the office after following up on the search warrants executed at the MRKT DataFlow Call Center.

"Not much there. I talked to one coworker, Mark Rupp, who swears he saw Nelson online at work looking at real estate websites and taking notes. But the preliminary search of Nelson's computer found nothing, so that one dead-ended."

The warrants also included Nelson's personnel file, where Dickson had followed up.

"We dug up his CV and it's just what we figured," he said. "Ten years ago when they hired him, the company's background check determined Nelson was clean. Nelson said he was from Houston. Turns out he never lived at the address he gave and we now suspect the references he gave were bogus. He likely answered the checks himself. As for activity on his credit card, banking and phone records, we've still got nothing. Ed, this guy's invisible."

"Maybe not for long—take a look. A woman in Utica just called. She's certain she sold her van to Nelson a few months ago."

The detectives studied the photos on Brennan's monitor. Several views of a silver Chevy 2013 Class B camper van.

"Bit by bit we're gaining on him, Paul. Bit by bit."

29

Rampart, New York

Magnified images of death reflected on Morten's glasses.

Staring into his twenty-four-inch monitor, the pathologist was thankful he'd persuaded the town and county to buy the scanning electron microscope. The unit took up one corner of his small lab across the hall from the cooler and the autopsy room at Rampart General. He was using it to search for microscopic clues into the cause and manner of death of the third victim whose remains were found at the scene.

The deceased was a female.

Her identity was still unknown, but since the case had gained a greater profile—Field of Screams, one New York City paper called it—Compton was confident that it was only a matter of time before they had confirmation, because now he had more help.

Radiographs of the deceased's teeth had been sent electronically to the chief forensic odontologist at the New York State Police lab in Albany. The FBI was also assisting in accelerating DNA analysis for comparison through its CODIS system with forensic DNA evidence from other criminal investigations across the country and around the world. The FBI was also comparing the deceased's DNA with the sample provided by Kate Page.

While awaiting word on identification, Compton continued his investigation with the scanning electron microscope. It was unusual for a small jurisdiction like Rampart to have such a piece of equipment. The price tag of a new Swiss-made model was $250,000, but Compton got a second-hand version for next to nothing through a contact at MIT.

The green light to buy it was part of the agreement by the locals to convince Compton not to accept a job offer in Arizona. He'd also taken a course on how to operate the equipment. And recently, he'd attended a conference in Chicago that included a workshop on how to use the technology to analyze markings of bones found at crime scenes.

The unit's magnification power was stunning. The image on the screen of bones looked otherworldly, but to Compton it was evidence. He'd already concluded that the deceased was approximately five feet four inches or five feet three inches in height. Twenty-three to thirty years of age. The cause, manner and time of death remained a challenge because of the condition of the remains.

When the remains were removed, the forensic investigators working on the immediate scene sifted the soil and used metal detectors to determine if bullets were fired into the body, or if a knife, or identifying jewelry, or any other evidence was present.

The body had been found in a makeshift grave in

bramble, leaving much of it exposed to air, which had an impact on the rate of decomposition. Little skin was left, much of it like leather. Some of the bones were no longer enfleshed or connected by ligaments, which meant they'd been displaced. At first Compton theorized that a combination of decomposition and animal disturbance accounted for the displacement, but the scanning electron microscope pointed him to something chilling.

Further analysis revealed that the body had, in fact, been dismembered, postmortem.

He'd found marks left on the bones, marks indicating cutting.

With the higher magnification he was able to study the striations formed by the cutting teeth of the saw. The marks were unique in the push and pull strokes. This could point to a specific saw used. Compton was making notes for the report he would send to the FBI for its Firearms/Toolmarks Unit (FTU). The Bureau's analysts could compare the marks and use their expertise and tool databases to point to the model and make of the saw used.

It would be a lead.

Compton removed his glasses, rubbed his tired eyes and reflected on the case. The killer had dismembered the victim after death and placed the remains in a shallow grave like pieces of a puzzle awaiting assembly.

Field of Screams is not that far off the mark.

We've got something evil at work.

Compton's phone rang.

"Morton, Colin Hawkley in Albany."

"Hey, Colin."

"Got an ID on your female deceased, are you ready to take it down?'

As Compton reached for his pen he stared at his monitor. The magnified images were about to become more than bones. Soon they'd have a name; soon they'd be someone's daughter or someone's wife or someone's sister.

They'd be a life to be mourned.

30

New York City

A scream pierced the air.

It was followed with squeals of delight rising from crowds at the Children's Zoo in Central Park where Kate had taken Grace.

This was one of their favorite places to go. Kate had even brought Grace here for her birthday a couple of months ago.

Now, it was after school and Kate had finished at Newslead, but she was anxious to hear back from sources and checked her phone often. There was nothing new from Goodsill in Denver on a link to Alberta and nothing from Davidson on reaching out to hackers. Looming over everything was Kate's agitation while awaiting identification of the third victim at Rampart.

The fear that it could be Vanessa gnawed at her in ruthless juxtaposition to the park's calming beauty, the trees arching over the sidewalk portrait sketchers, the vendors, and the young street artists creating huge iridescent soap bubbles. And there was Grace's favorite, the musical clock tower with its animal band that circled while striking a classical tune every half hour.

Sometimes the songs were seasonal, like "April Showers" in spring or "Jingle Bells" in December.

"Look, Mom, they're starting!" Grace pointed.

The musicians began playing the nursery rhyme, "Three Blind Mice," with the hippo on the fiddle leading the elephant, the goat and the others. As the animals danced and Grace sang along, Kate's phone rang. She took the call while keeping her eyes on her daughter.

"Kate, it's Ed Brennan in Rampart."

"Yes."

"We've confirmed the identity of the third victim."

In the moment before Brennan said another word, Kate gripped her phone and held her breath. Her world moved in slow motion—the penguin banging the drum, the bear tapping the tambourine. All sound suddenly deadened as if she was underwater, *again, struggling to breathe.*

"Kate? Did you hear me?" Brennan repeated. "It's not your sister."

"Yes." She took a breath, sat on the nearest bench, dug out her pen and pad, looking at Grace as the clock played on. "Yes, can you give me the name and details?"

"We're putting out a news release within the hour."

"Can't you tell me anything now?"

"We're playing things pretty tight."

"Are you any closer to finding Nelson, any leads?"

"Kate."

"But you're still looking for more victims, right?"

"I can't discuss anything further. Watch for the release."

The call ended, leaving Kate stunned.

Now, another family is going to be devastated. If it's not Vanessa, then where is she? How many more bodies will they find?

Kate sat there, wondering. And as the clock's tune played she recalled its haunting words.

They all ran after the farmer's wife, who cut off their tails with a carving knife. Did you ever see such a sight in your life?

Grace ran to her.

"Mom, can I get a drink?"

"Sure, then let's go home."

In the cab, Kate alerted Newslead that she'd have a story coming on the third victim. Less than a minute later, Reeka called.

"We're going to need something with an exclusive peg, Kate."

"I don't even have a name yet, Reeka. I'll do what I can."

Kate exhaled and shook her head slowly. When the cab got to their neighborhood, Kate and Grace picked up soup, salads and sandwiches from the corner deli for their supper. By the time they got home, the news release had been posted on the Rampart PD's website. As they ate, Kate looked into the pretty, smiling face of the victim, then read the information.

She was Mandy Marie Bryce, aged twenty-six, from Charlotte, North Carolina, a dental assistant who'd been missing for four years. She was last seen at Virginia Beach, Virginia, walking from a restaurant to her hotel where she'd been attending a conference.

Rampart PD's release provided few other details, so Kate went online, pulling older articles from the Virginia and Charlotte newspapers, gleaning data from them. She soon learned that Mandy had a little brother with Down syndrome and that she'd volunteered with many groups. She was engaged to a carpenter, who'd been cleared as a suspect, and had organized searches for Mandy in Virginia. To help their case, police had pinpointed Mandy's last known whereabouts and released her last text to her boyfriend and his response.

Probably my imagination, but I think I'm being followed.

Go into the first store or bar and call a cab.

Mandy had never answered and her boyfriend had called Virginia police.

Investigators soon determined that Mandy's hotel room key was never used after she'd texted her boyfriend. Records showed no activity on her phone, bank and credit cards at any point after her last text. Mandy had vanished. *Until four years later, when her remains were found in a shallow grave near a barn in New York.*

She compared Mandy's case to what had happened to the first victim, Bethany Ann Wynn, aged nineteen when she went missing. Bethany was last seen leaving her part-time job at a mall. She was waiting for a bus to her home in suburban Hartford, Connecticut. Both cases were miles apart but seemed to fit a pattern: young women who'd vanished while alone in vulnerable places.

Kate's heart skipped a beat when she felt a hand on her lap.

"Mom, can I have some cookies?"

She smiled at Grace.

"Just one. Then brush your teeth and reach back, like the dentist said."

Kate sighed, then resumed reading.

It appeared that both Bethany and Mandy had been stalked. Was there a connection to their financial records and the data center where Nelson worked? What was his real name? Did he have a tie to Denver, or was everything circumstantial? Kate needed to do a lot more digging but it had to wait, because right now she had to pull a story together.

In the older news articles she saw that from time to time, Mandy's mother, Judy Bryce, had spoken to the *Charlotte Observer.*

The keys on Kate's keyboard clicked and within a minute she had a listing in Charlotte and called it, hoping that Brennan had notified the family. The line rang five times before a man answered.

"Hello, my name's Kate Page. I'm a reporter with Newslead, the wire service in New York."

"Yes." His tone was neutral.

"Would it be possible to speak with a relative of Mandy Marie Bryce? It concerns the news release issued a short time ago by police in Rampart, New York. I take it you're aware of it?"

"Yes, we're aware."

"Would you be a relative, sir?"

"Me? No, you want Judy. I'm a friend of the family, hang on."

The sound of a hand over the phone's mouthpiece and muffled words about a reporter in New York.

"I'm Judy Bryce, Mandy's mother."

"My condolences for your loss, Mrs. Bryce," Kate said, repeating her introduction and explanation for calling before requesting Mrs. Bryce reflect on her daughter for her news story.

"My Mandy was a selfless angel who always put everyone's needs before hers."

Kate underlined those words in her notes. As she continued talking with Judy, the older woman said her devotion to her faith had helped her deal with her daughter's tragedy.

"It may sound funny, even cold, but when she first went missing, I knew in my heart that I'd never see her again."

"How did you know?"

"I can't explain it, but a mother just knows, or maybe God let me know. When Mandy was ten, she took a bad fall down the stairs. In the hospital, seeing her in the bed, I had this powerful, crystalline feeling that I was going to outlive her. I just knew it. I—I—I'm sorry." Judy stopped to choke back a sob. Kate overheard her say something to the man at her end that she was okay to go on. Then she came back to Kate. "Deep in my heart I just knew that when Mandy disappeared, I'd lost her forever. The pain will never go away, but I'm at peace with it now. We're making arrangements to bring her home."

Struggling with her own emotions, Kate opened up to Judy about her personal connection to the story, about Vanessa and how she couldn't give up her feeling that she was somehow still alive. After listening, Judy gave Kate advice.

"Trust your heart. It's telling you there's hope. Hang on to that."

The woman's unexpected compassion for Kate, when she was the one who'd intruded on her pain, was somehow therapeutic. Kate then asked if Mandy had any ties to Bethany Ann Wynn in Hartford, or Carl Nelson or Vanessa, or Alberta or Denver?

There were no links, Judy said.

After hanging up Kate sat alone in the kitchen with her elbows on the table and her face in her hands, as if to stem the emotion draining from her. Calls to the bereaved were never easy. They always cost Kate a piece of her soul.

Get to work.

Kate marshaled all of her concentration and threw herself into writing her story as fast as she could. She didn't think there was much of an exclusive angle to it but didn't care. It brought Mandy Marie Bryce to life, letting readers know what the world had lost. Kate looked at Mandy's picture and, for a moment, smiled back at her.

She pressed Send and filed her story.

Then Kate joined Grace, who was on the sofa watching a movie about puppies. She put her arm around her and for a moment tried not to think about missing women, shallow graves and monsters.

"Ouch, Mom, you're scrunching me too tight!"

"Sorry, honey."

As Kate's mind raced back to…*the mountains, the river, Vanessa's hand—letting go*…her cell phone vibrated. Thinking it was likely Reeka with some problem with her story, she was inclined to ignore it. But the area code was for Colorado and she answered.

"Hi, Kate, Will Goodsill in Denver."

"Yes, hi, Will."

"I found something in my notes that may help you."

31

Lost River State Forest, Minnesota

"You come up here for the birding?"

Zurrn didn't expect the attendant pumping gas into his van to start a conversation. He was in Pine Mills, a village that skirted the state forest near the Canadian border.

The forest was known for bird-watching.

It was dusk. Bishop's General Store and Gas, where he'd stopped, was the only sign of life. The attendant, "Ferg," according to the smudged name patch on his shirt, was chatty.

"That's right," Zurrn said to his side-view mirror.

"I figured." Ferg clamped on his toothpick as the smell of gasoline wafted while the flow hummed. "I see by your plate you're from Delaware. Folks that come that far, usually—"

A sudden muffled sound from inside the van caught Ferg's attention. Cupping his free hand to his temple, he drew his face to the tinted window.

"You got a dog in there, or something?"

Zurrn eyed him then caught the flash of a turn signal. A car was approaching the service station from the highway. It bore the emergency light bar of a police unit.

"No." He kept his voice soft. "My wife's trying to get some sleep."

Oh, Ferg mouthed. "Okay." After finishing the fill-up, he replaced the nozzle quietly and took care tightening the van's gas cap.

"That'll be forty-five," Ferg whispered. "Want me to check the oil?"

Zurrn held three twenties out the window.

"Nope. Keep the change." He started the engine.

"Thank you, sir! Want a receipt?"

"Nope."

As a Klassen County sheriff's white patrol car wheeled up to the pumps, Zurrn slipped the transmission into Drive and eased away.

That was close.

Watching Bishop's General Store and Gas shrink in his mirror, Zurrn then glanced over his shoulder, his attention flicking to the enlarged storage area he'd built under the van's master bed. The sleeping pills were wearing off. Not to worry, it wasn't much farther.

That little scene back there underscored the need to be vigilant.

Now that he was at war, now that his struggle was national news, mistakes could not be made. He glanced at the newspaper on the passenger seat, folded to the latest article on Rampart. There were photos of the farm with insets of the victims and that reporter, Kate Page, the one who'd begged and pleaded to know more about her sister.

There was a sidebar story about Page and her painful, unrelenting search for her sister. The story praised her as "heroic, brave, courageous and smart."

Your reverence is misplaced.

Zurrn seized the paper and looked at her face with contempt before tossing it aside. She was a moth, circling mindlessly in his brilliance. He was on the edge of immortality, of achieving something monumental.

You have no understanding of who I am.

Or what I am.

As twilight yielded to the dark he searched the dense woods, unearthing the pieces of his life. His mother had come to America to live with relatives when she was a student from Bulgaria, or Romania, or Serbia. He was never sure. She drank a lot and told him different stories. She may have been a Gypsy. She became an US citizen, working as a nurse until she became a drug addict and lost her job. Her life was far from the American dream. When Frank, the paramedic she'd married, realized that Zurrn was not his son but the bastard of one of her many affairs, he walked out on them.

Zurrn stared into the darkness ahead and admitted what he was.

I am the result of a whore's barter for drugs.

He had no idea who his father was. Zurrn grew up poor, friendless and with a love-hate relationship with his mother. As a child, he had an ungainly limp, which he'd had surgically corrected as an adult. His mother was protective of him during her periods of lucidity, feeding him the promise of a better life, telling him he was exceptional.

"You're not like other kids, Sorin. You're destined for greatness."

His teachers had found that his IQ was the highest of any student they had taught and that he had an eidetic memory. But Zurrn was ostracized and bullied at school. He would hide away alone after classes in one of the labs, building new computers from discarded ones.

His mother struggled to pay the rent on their cold, ramshackle home but was hostage to her addiction between jobs cleaning hotel rooms or serving fast food, leaving them to rely on charity. One day a boy teased Zurrn because of his shirt.

Hey, why're you wearing that rag, Hopalong? My mom donated it to a church. How'd you get it? You steal it?

Others soon gathered round and started poking Zurrn.

Know what I heard? A bigger boy grinned. *I heard your old lady gives blow jobs for dope, anywhere and anytime!*

Zurrn burned with shame.

Limping away, he tore off the shirt and threw it in a Dumpster before he got home and sought refuge in his collection. Ever since a class trip to the Chicago Botanic Garden, he'd started collecting butterflies. He began by stealing several exotic ones from the Garden, putting them under his shirt, feeling his prisoners flapping against his chest near his heart. He was enamored with their beauty and, later, the whole process of chasing and capturing specimens in parks.

He soon became expert with his killing jar where he imprisoned each catch. He'd watch his beauties flutter themselves to death or die slowly in captivity. Sometimes he'd pinch the thorax to stun them. After death, he took great care spreading their wings, pinning them, mounting them and soaking up their poetry.

My pretty dead things.

They didn't leave you to buy drugs and get stoned in the bathroom. They didn't bring home strange men stinking of alcohol.

They didn't humiliate you.

They were his to own, his to possess, his to control.

He held the power of life and death over them.

He was never alone when he was with his collection. They were individual works of art, so beautiful. Unlike the ugliness he'd endured at every turn. Every day with each indignity he suffered, his anger grew, evolving into a quiet rage.

He remembered walking home one afternoon and seeing his mother searching through the trash cans along their street. At that moment he saw a pack of neighborhood teenage girls swarm her, mock her, slap her and rip apart her plastic bags, scattering her soda and beer cans. Mortified, Zurrn stayed out of sight. Then he ran off, his tears and fury nearly blinding him with shame for not defending his mother.

And shame because of her.

Tonya Plesivsky was the girl who'd led the attack. He knew where she lived and that she had a beloved dog, Pepper. That night, Zurrn lay awake seething. A week later, MISSING flyers went up in the neighborhood for Tonya's dog. Pet lovers were sympathetic. One day Tonya even stopped Zurrn on the street near Ben Bailey Park.

Have you seen Pepper, Sorin? This is serious. I'm worried.

She had a lot of nerve, after what she'd done to his mother.

No, he had lied.

Of course, he knew where Pepper was and he considered sending the mutt's head to her with a note—"I'm missing you in hell"—before dismissing the plan. He was happy knowing that she would never see her precious Pepper again. At the same time, as much as he loathed Tonya, he saw how fear became her, how pretty she was in her anguish. His power over her enthralled him and he fantasized about what he'd do to her, about seeing a MISSING poster with Tonya's face on it.

The van's headlights raked the woods and gravel popped under the tires as Zurrn turned onto an abandoned forestry road. He knew this area, he'd been here before. As the van toddled along the old rutted path, soft groaning and cries rose from the back.

"Don't worry. Not much longer," he said aloud.

That incident with Tonya was the catalyst that had put him on the path of what was truly his life's work as a collector. First, he earned scholarships to college and studied computer design. That didn't last long before he drifted across the country trying this and trying that, before jumping from one computer job to another. During this time, he grappled with his animosity toward his mother, growing distant and out of touch. Only she knew where he was—he'd allow her that much—but he rarely responded to her letters or calls.

Perhaps out of guilt, but more out of curiosity, he monitored the online editions of the Chicago newspapers. He was living in Denver when he saw his mother's death notice in the *Chicago Tribune*.

His mother's church had placed the notice.

He contacted the church, then returned to Chicago to quietly arrange for her funeral. But he couldn't bear to attend. Instead, he'd watched from a distance as they buried her, along with his past.

After her death he returned to Colorado and began severing all ties with his mother and the family name. She had no estate. She had nothing. He ignored or tossed into the trash any records or correspondence linking him to Chicago and the Zurrn name.

At this time he used his expertise to take on a new identity.

He was reborn and started a new life, off the grid.

He was invisible.

Still, he longed for the only joy he'd known through his collection. And he recalled how much he had enjoyed Tonya's anguish. That's when his metamorphosis happened. He was traveling when he was seized with a compulsion to start a new collection, a special one that rivaled anything the world had known.

He was nervous and made tiny errors in the early days when he captured his first specimen.

But it was a success.

A work of art.

He cherished it because he owned it.

Over the years he acquired other pretty specimens, enhancing his collection. He became expert at finding them, hunting them and keeping them for as long as he wanted. Each new capture enthralled him, so much so that he would press himself against their cell to feel the panic in their hearts beat against him. Oh, how he loved it.

Flutterings in the kill jar.

Most specimens were cooperative and loyal, but some would fall ill, harm themselves or try to escape. *Escape was treasonous—it meant disloyalty. It was a wish to abandon him, like his father abandoned him; to break a promise and walk away from parental responsibility.*

It meant that over the years it was necessary to discard and replace them. It broke his heart, but that's how it was. The posters of the missing online, with terms such as "last seen," and "disappeared without a trace" stood as testament to his refined skills as a collector.

My glory.

And no one ever knew.

Yes, other enthusiasts would occasionally surface in the news but only because they'd failed. Some across the country and around the world had kept their work going for years, as well, but they were defeated because of mistakes.

Never let a specimen escape.

True, Rampart didn't go according to Zurrn's plan. He'd intended for the case to be closed with the death of "Carl Nelson." Sure, he could've ended things in the house rather than the barn. But the fire and staging of the specimen were stylistic touches he couldn't resist. Still, the discovery by police wasn't a setback.

It was a challenge.

Maybe I'll go public like the Zodiac and the Ripper.

Zurrn would carry on creating his new garden paradise. But he'd have to make further adjustments along the way. At this moment, he was grappling with keeping the last of his remaining specimens. For years his plan was to start over with all new prospects to capture. But he'd grown partial to some of his specimens and decided to keep them.

And now, with the situation brewing in Rampart and all that business with that reporter, he realized that this was a game changer. This was his chance to showcase his mastery to the world. And the only way to do it was to sacrifice his treasures.

It had to be done. He was at war.

Time to get started.

He brought the van to a stop on a soft, earthen patch alongside a fast-flowing stream. Crickets chirped and starlight glimmered on the water. Isolated. No one around for miles.

No one to hear a thing. Perfect. History will be made, right here.

He stepped from the van wearing high-quality night-vision goggles. They provided him with brilliant, sharp images in the darkness as he worked.

First, he maneuvered the heavy-duty handcart used for moving vending machines and removed the wooden crates, positioning them on the ground.

Then he set out his instruments.

Next, he set up the stands for the studio photography lights, aligning them just so. Then he stood there addressing the questions:

Which one, and how?

A soft cry rose from one of the boxes.

"Please."

32

New York City

After Kate got Grace to bed she made fresh coffee and called Goodsill back so they could work on the Colorado link to the abduction in Alberta.

Could this lead me to Carl Nelson and information about Vanessa?

Kate needed to follow this through.

"Good news, I found my old files," Goodsill said over the phone. "Fifteen years is a long time but when I read over my notes, it all came back to me, and I found some interesting stuff. I just sent it to you."

Kate set her phone to speaker, turned the volume low then started downloading the attachments of scanned documents arriving in her in-box.

"Strange thing is," Goodsill went on, "that clipping you found is the only story that I wrote on the case, but I put in a lot of time on it."

"What do you mean?" The documents blossoming on Kate's screen were crumpled, torn and stained bills, invoices, along with other records. "I don't understand what I'm looking at here. Walk me through everything"

Goodsill took Kate to the beginning. His cousin was married to a Denver detective, Ned Eckles, and the two men got to talking at a family gathering. Goodsill had learned that Ned was looking into a query from Canadian police to run down a partial plate possibly connected to an abduction.

Ned's supervisors said that the plate info was so vague it could've applied to about twenty-five other states, meaning that without something more specific, they didn't want him investing much time in the check. Using the vehicle description and the plate's partial sequence, Ned had the records people do an analysis and they came up with five possibilities for Denver.

"Ned ran them all down, made personal visits and questioned the vehicle owners. Four were easily ruled out. And although he'd ruled out the fifth, Ned told me the vehicle owner gave him a bad vibe."

"You're talking about this Jerome Fell."

Kate looked at her monitor and saw notes for Jerome Fell, aged 30, of 2909 Falstaff Street, Denver. Goodsill had scanned in Fell's driver's license with a photo of a clean-shaven man with an expression of indifference staring from it. She touched her fingers to the lower part of his face, covering it and visualizing him with a beard. He could resemble Carl Nelson. She couldn't be sure. There was a time difference of at least fifteen years.

"Yes. Ned had said that before he visited Fell he already knew from US border people that Fell had been to Canada around the time of the abduction and that he'd returned through Eastport, Idaho. But Fell was never detained at the border and never searched."

"Why?"

"Border people claimed that they never had any alerts about a van and partial plate, at that time. That's something the Canadians disputed."

"But Ned met with Fell?"

"Yes."

"And had a bad vibe about him, yet he still ruled him out? Why?"

"When Ned questioned Fell cold, about his whereabouts for that time period, Fell acknowledged right off that he'd been to Canada on vacation. He said he'd been in British Columbia but not Alberta and even showed Ned motel receipts to prove it."

"So then what?"

"Ned cleared him, but something about Fell niggled at him. Ned told me later that Fell seemed unusually well prepared, almost as if he were expecting to account for his travels for that period. Still, Ned's supervisors, citing the partial-plate business, were satisfied and pulled Ned away to other investigations."

"Was that the end of it?"

"Not quite. Ned was still bothered by Fell and not long after that suggested I do some quiet digging on him."

"What'd you do?"

"I never talked to Fell. I didn't want him to get suspicious. I talked to his neighbors, kept an eye on his place. I learned that he was a computer expert, a contractor, that he lived alone, kept to himself and kept up his property. See the pictures. He had a tidy little bungalow with a garage."

"What did you find out?"

"Not much, but I figured that if this guy had kidnapped a Canadian girl and was living in Denver, this would be a huge story, so before letting it go, I decided to do a trash hit."

"You stole his garbage from the curb?"

"Yup, I think I did it about six times under cover of night. You ever do that, Kate?"

"A few times."

"Dirty, messy work, but the Supreme Court says it's not an invasion of privacy once it's on the street," Goodsill said. "You can find out a lot by going through people's garbage. At first, there was nothing that stood out in Fell's trash."

"Did you find anything suggesting that Jerome Fell was an alias?"

"No."

"You've seen the pictures of Carl Nelson. Do you think Nelson and Fell are the same person?"

"Well, fifteen years is a long time, but I thought about that when I saw the stories out of New York and I got to thinking that it sure is possible."

"Did you find anything with the name Carl Nelson, or anything linking him to Rampart? I don't see it in the samples you sent me, in the ones I've opened so far."

"I'm afraid not. A lot of junk food wrappers, empty take-out containers, pizza boxes, some bills for cable, for utilities, all to Jerome Fell, or J. Fell. A few items of mail for neighbors sent to his address. I saw that he was not kind. Instead of giving them to his neighbors he opened them and tossed them. It's all there. I've got more coming your way, maybe forty in all."

"I'm not surprised you didn't find anything. I know it's possible he could've missed something. But I think he would've been careful not to miss anything. You think he would've used a shredder."

"That's what I thought, too. Maybe he shredded stuff, maybe he burned stuff, but all in all, I found nothing unusual and dropped it. Then my wife noticed something, I'd missed—a couple things actually."

"What?"

"See attachment number sixteen, the stained receipt for a bracelet kit, a Spirograph set, a bead art kit and a colored pencil set?"

"My wife thought those are items or toys you'd buy for a young girl, especially one who might be bored."

Kate's concentration sharpened on that point and she agreed.

"Then my wife noticed another one. That's number twenty-two, a small ripped receipt from a drugstore for sanitary napkins and whatnot, excuse me, but see?"

Kate moved her mouse to number twenty-two and opened it.

"Yes."

"Now, I looked into this and most American girls get their period when they turn twelve or so, and this Canadian girl, who could've been your sister, was about ten when she was abducted, right?"

"Actually, my sister would've been closer to eleven and a half."

"Those two factors were kind of disturbing, but I said to my wife, Fell could've had a girlfriend, who had a daughter, you know? There could be explanations. Besides there are privacy issues and I was thinking, how do I challenge him? So I gave it some thought over the next few weeks, thinking the best thing to do was talk to Ned."

"What happened?"

"Ned suffered a heart attack and stroke. That was a big scare for my family and it took me away from things for a while. By the time I went back to check on Fell a month or so later, he'd moved away. I couldn't get a new address for him."

"What about the Realtors, neighbors, his employer, the post office?"

"I tried them all, Kate, and got nothing. It was like he'd vanished."

Kate sat there staring at the items on her monitor. Several moments of silence passed before she thanked Goodsill and hung up.

For the next hour or so, Kate clicked on every attachment, examining each one for clues, anything Goodsill missed. But he'd been thorough. He'd done everything that she would've done and as she clicked from item to item, she considered herself lucky he'd helped her.

When Kate came to pictures of Jerome Fell's house, her thoughts darkened.

Was Vanessa held captive here? Was Fell actually Carl Nelson? Or was she chasing another mirage?

Kate pulled up the FBI photo of a Nelson Wanted poster and positioned it next to the Jerome Fell's Colorado driver's license. There was about fifteen years of time between the two images. Kate placed her notebook against her monitor so that only the eyes and top of the head of each photo were visible.

Are his eyes the same?

In both cases they had the icy veneer of a deep-seated resentment. Definitely a guy who wouldn't return your misdirected mail, Kate thought before looking at the miscellaneous attachments again, the invoices, the bills and what appeared to be a misdirected invoice or note.

What's this?

Something from Chicago about a burial site of Krasimira Zurrn.

What could that be? Who is Krasimira Zurrn?

She'd check that out later. It was 3:45 a.m. She had to get to bed.

33

Rampart, New York

A large dry-erase board stood at one end of the Investigative Unit of the Rampart Police Department.

Ed studied it over the rim of his mug as he took another hit of black coffee. His concentration shifted to Carl Nelson's photo.

Inch by inch, we're getting closer to you.

Tire impressions found at the scene were made by 10-ply radials, LT245/75R16, load range E. The same tires were on the silver Chevy 2013 Class B camper van that Carl Nelson bought in Utica. *We can place that van at the scene. Now we have to locate that van.*

So far, nothing had surfaced from the alerts.

Brennan rubbed his eyes. He'd been up much of the night, padding through the house, watching over his wife and son, contending with the weight of the case.

What're we missing?

He took another hit of coffee while reviewing the board. He stood among the half-dozen empty desks. All the unit's detectives had been assigned to the case.

They were out following leads.

Rampart headed the task force, supported by Riverview County, the state police, the FBI and other agencies. The case was divided into several parts. Rampart and the county had most local aspects arising from Carl Nelson. The FBI had the fugitive element. State and the FBI had the crime scene, which was still being processed. Other components crossed jurisdictions, depending on expertise and resources.

There was an update on the necklace from the manufacturer via the FBI. The model in question was no longer made and sold. During the period it was marketed, 600,000 units were sold in the US and another 700,000 units were sold globally. The maker said engraving names on the charms was common and examination of the damaged piece and the comparison piece, obtained from Kate Page, showed that both were made by the company. But insofar as to the two pieces being the exact two pieces Kate's mother had bought, the finding was inconclusive.

Brennan continued to survey the board.

All work to date was up there: the pictures, names of the victims, case numbers, color arrows and the latest notes showing if warrants had been issued. There were summaries of areas canvassed, neighbors to be reinterviewed and security cameras to be checked or rechecked.

So far, eighty-three tips had been followed, prioritized or closed.

And nothing ever came of that coworker who claims he saw Carl online looking at real estate and taking notes. That one's eating at me.

The FBI's Behavioral Science Unit was developing a profile of the suspect, looking at motivation, methodology and the psychology of his actions and personality.

Brennan turned from the board. Dickson had just ended a call with the FBI.

"Well, it's official," Dickson said. "That was the FBI's Cyber Crime team. They've been working with the Secret Service and two forensic teams at the Data-Flow Call Center."

"Did Nelson compromise their system?"

"Big-time. He devised and installed some type of software that allowed him to siphon everything from the company's payment processing network. He stole Social Security numbers, PINs, addresses, telephone numbers, bank and credit card information."

"How many people are we talking?"

"Forty million."

Brennan ran his hand over his face.

"The company's working with the FBI to issue a news release," Dickson said. "All retailers and all card-holders will be alerted. Customers will be advised to destroy their cards, retailers will issue new ones."

"Small comfort knowing Nelson has everything."

"He's one smart prick, Ed."

"Maybe, but sooner or later, he'll make a mistake."

Brennan's phone rang.

"Ed, it's Mitch, you'd better come out to the scene."

As they drove to the old burial grounds Brennan grappled with his frustrations. That these crimes had been going on for years in his backyard sickened him and he sought assurance in a mantra for investigators.

The suspect has to be lucky at every turn. We need to get lucky once.

So far, Nelson's victims were helping with their killer's undoing. Look at Pollard, who'd kept his dog tags in his boot so no one would yank them from his neck if he got assaulted. That thwarted Nelson's attempt to stage a murder-suicide. Then the message left by Tara Dawn Mae, and there was the angel charm necklace and its inconclusive link to Kate Page. Everyone on the task force was going all out on this case.

We just need a lead, a solid lead. Entrance to the site through the old cemetery road remained sealed and more Riverview deputies had been posted at other points of the expanded perimeter. The increased magnitude of the case was made manifest by the police encampment that had arisen next to the ruins of the barn.

A mobile double-wide trailer, which served as the command post, had been hauled in on a flatbed and placed near the edge of the property among lines of trucks. An array of equipment, lights, generators, tents and canopies dotted the vast property.

Exhaustive ground searches had been conducted. More dogs were used, along with infrared technology. More aerial photographs were taken. Vapor detectors were brought in. A tube connected to the device was inserted into the ground to detect gasses from decomposition.

The entire scene was gridded and sectioned off with string and flags, like an archaeological dig. Forensic archaeologists from universities in Rochester and Syracuse had been requested to join the FBI and state police forensic experts to help.

Section by section, teams undertook the slow, systematic process of removing segments of soil in four-to six-inch layers. Meticulously they sifted it through screens to search for evidence of human remains.

Brennan and Dickson met Mitch Komerick inside the command post. He pulled off the hood on his white coveralls, slipped off his face mask and bent over a large table with unfurled maps.

"What've we got, Mitch?" Brennan leaned over the map with him.

Komerick took a pencil and used the eraser end to tap the primary map of the scene.

"More remains."

"One more victim?"

"Not one. Twelve."

Brennan's stomach tensed.

"Twelve?"

Komerick tapped several neatly penciled squares on the map.

"We've confirmed human remains, here, here, here and here. We're just getting started. Ed, this could be one of the biggest cases we've ever seen."

34

New York City

Kate made her way through the crush at Penn Station.

She'd become accustomed to the subway, the urine-scented platforms, the whoosh of foul, inbound air, crowds jostling at the doors, the smells of perfume and the body odor. She was relieved to find a seat. Within seconds, her car was crammed to capacity.

As her train thundered from the station she took out her phone and read stories on Rampart by the Associated Press, Reuters and Bloomberg. Then she read the story she'd filed and was satisfied that Newslead's reporting was strongest.

We're still ahead of the competition.

When Kate finished reading, she gazed out her window into the rolling darkness. As tunnel lights flashed by and her car rocked, she grappled with the turmoil broiling inside her.

Twelve more victims.

She could no longer fend off the facts and fears that crept from the darkest fringes to crush her.

Twelve more victims. Surely, Vanessa's among the dead.

It's over. Carl Nelson, or whoever he was, had won. The rhythmic clacking of the train hammered it home. Her hope, if it ever really lived, was dead. Her dream of seeing her sister again had slipped away…the way Vanessa's hand had slipped from hers twenty years ago in the icy mountain river.

Kate shut her eyes.

Tears rolled down her face as the train's steel wheels grinded against steel tracks creating a high-pitched scream.

On the way to her building, Kate picked up a pizza, then collected Grace from Nancy's apartment.

"I saw the latest news." Nancy had lowered her voice to Kate when Grace was down the hall, out of earshot. "It's terrible. How much worse can it get?"

Kate shrugged.

At home Grace bit into her pizza and, between chews, told Kate about a new boy at school who was annoying all the girls. But Kate's attention had drifted. Being with her daughter, Kate felt spears of sunshine piercing her battle-weary heart and tried desperately to hang on to the moment.

"Mom, are you listening?"

"Sorry, sweetie."

"I said his name is Devon and all he wants to do is kiss you. Yech!"

After their supper Kate went through the motions of their evening routine, cleaning up, then homework for Grace before any computer or TV time. All the while Kate was unable to emerge from the numbness that had filled her. Once she got Grace to bed, she dimmed the lights, opened a bottle of wine and tuned her TV to news channels.

As she listened to commentators and watched footage of the Rampart scene over and over, she became enveloped with loss and the bitter realization that she'd been a fool to dream she'd find Vanessa. For a time she'd convinced herself that she was not only on the trail to the truth about what had happened to Vanessa, but closer to finding her alive and well.

I believed with all my heart I'd have my sister back. Kate continued to watch the white-suited forensic experts conducting their work on what was a killing field.

Twelve more victims.

Her phone rang.

"Kate, it's Nancy."

"Hey."

"I've been watching the news coverage and I'm worried about you. Are you okay?"

"No, to be honest, not really."

"I'll be right over."

Maybe it was her nursing background but upon arriving, Nancy seemed to know what to do. She turned Kate's TV off, turned the lights up, put away the wine and made tea.

"All the fight's gone out of you, Kate."

She struggled to explain to Nancy how she'd felt defeated in the face of the cruel reality that the monster she was pursuing had killed fifteen people.

"It's like the earth shifted under my feet."

Nancy thought for a moment before she took Kate's hands in hers.

"You listen to me." Nancy stared hard into her eyes. "You're not going to curl into a ball and give up. You're going to pull through this. I guarantee it."

"You guarantee it?"

"Look back on your life. You've faced every hardship I can think of and you've endured. You have a right to the truth and there's no way you're going to let this creep stop you. It's not in your DNA, Kate. Do you hear me?"

Nancy squeezed Kate's hands hard.

"Do you hear me?"

Before she realized it Kate was nodding slowly and her concentration went to a file folder on the table nearby and a photo of Nelson.

"You know I'm right, Kate."

Kate continued nodding, bigger nods with more confidence. *Yes, Nancy is right.* Kate's eyes were welded to Carl Nelson's. *No way are you going to get away with this, you evil son of a bitch. If my sister's dead, or I can't find her, then I'll find you.*

35

Lost River State Forest, Minnesota

There it is!

Deep within the thick woods of tamarack and black spruce there were flashes of gray throat and gray breast, of yellow belly.

Careful.

Dan Whitmore was a patient bird-watcher who knew not to be in a hurry to raise the binoculars to his eyes, or to page through the guidebook to identify his subject.

It could vanish on you.

Experience had taught him to focus on the bird, study its shape, its bill, its colors and markings. If the situation allowed, he'd lift his binoculars in a smooth, practiced motion while never losing sight of the bird. Then, when it winged away, he'd consult the book to identify it.

Dan watched for several minutes before finally looking through his binoculars. He was rewarded with a long, gorgeous view before the bird took flight.

"That was a Great Crested Flycatcher." Dan turned

to his partner, Vivian Chambers, who'd flipped through the guide and nodded.

"Yes, it had beautiful primaries."

"That's six more today, Viv."

Dan noted the sighting, confident he'd hit five hundred on his life list by the time their trip ended.

"Let's go over there," Vivian said, "near the edge of that bog. It looks like a great spot for owls."

Dan, a doctor, had retired from his family practice in Omaha fifteen years ago. He and Vivian, a retired elementary school principal, lived alone in the same condo complex. Each had lost a spouse and after meeting through one of Omaha's birder clubs they'd become partners.

They'd gone out on many group outings but for the past five years, upon discovering how much they'd enjoyed each other's company, they'd traveled alone together to different parts of the country to look at birds. Birding had given them a sense of order, and their relationship had helped them survive some of the hardest times of their lives. Their mutual understanding and respect for what they'd both endured had grown into a nurturing, healing kind of love. They counted their blessings and birds as they journeyed along the back roads together.

This section of the park bordered Manitoba and was the most isolated. It was dense with white cedar, jack pine and aspen trees. There were thickets of willow and alder. The hiking trails were rugged, but Dan and Vivian often ventured wherever the birds led them. As they neared the fringes of the peat bog, Vivian grabbed Dan's arm and stopped.

"Listen," she said.

Birdsong filtered through the distant trees.

"Tzeet. Kip. Tzeet kip."

It repeated in a harsh, sputtering series.

"That's a kingbird. I recognize that from my CDs," Dan said.

"Eastern or Western?"

"Could be either, given our location."

Dan scanned the forest for any telltale signs but saw nothing. After giving it a full five minutes, he tried again, this time with the binoculars, zeroing in on the area most likely to be the bird's location.

"Anything?" Vivian said from behind her binoculars.

"Nothing." As he lowered his glasses he glimpsed a low pale flash but lost it. "Wait," he repositioned his binoculars.

"Something?"

"I think." Dan hesitated, unable to find it again. "Actually, I think we've got company. I think I saw someone waving to us. I lost them."

"Let's get closer, say hello and compare lists."

Stepping carefully through the thick woodland, they forged their way closer to the beginnings of the bog and to what Dan had reasoned was the spot where he'd last seen the person waving.

"There's nothing here. Let's take a break."

A large fallen alder tree served as a natural bench seat big enough for both of them. He reached for his water bottle and Vivian pulled a small towel from her backpack. She was using it to pad her face when she froze.

Dan followed her gaze, which was locked on a sight in a clearing some twenty feet away.

At first he thought that what they were seeing was a trick of light and shadow.

Dan couldn't believe it—it couldn't be real.

Without realizing it, he stood.

He'd closed his eyes but the image burned before him, refusing to leave until Vivian started screaming.

36

Lost River State Forest, Minnesota

The textbooks, *Tactical Investigation*, *Deductive Assessment* and *Scene Work*, bounced with the course binder on the passenger seat of Klassen County deputy Cal Meckler's patrol car.

Since his girlfriend was visiting her sister in Wisconsin he'd decided he would put in a few hours of study when his shift ended. *Gotta keep working on the dream.* He sipped coffee as he drove, reviewing his life plan to leave Klassen County for the Minneapolis PD, make detective, then ultimately go to the FBI.

He was twenty-three and policing for the county was fine, for now. But, as his old man used to say each day after working the farm in Moss Valley, a man needs to keep looking down the road.

Meckler's shift was nearly over and he was on his way to Blake Fossom's place to issue a summons for noise. Blake liked to party, play his heavy metal and tune up his Harleys, all at the same time, something his neighbors didn't exactly embrace.

As the Dodge pickup rusting on cinder blocks came

into view, the signpost for the Fossom property, Meckler's radio crackled with a call for his unit.

"Seventy-five. From LR, a couple of birders reported a ten-sixty-two that the COs are verifying as a ten-ninety-one."

Catching the subtle emotion in the dispatcher's voice, Meckler sat up. The conservation officers had a corpse that was a homicide at Lost River State Forest.

This takes priority over Blake Fossom.

Meckler keyed his microphone.

"Seventy-five. Ten-four, Julie. I'm fifteen from the gate."

"Copy. Brian will meet you there and take you in, Cal."

Meckler hit his siren and lights and sped toward the state park.

Klassen County didn't see many murders and he didn't want to screw this up as the first responding officer for the county. He went through a mental checklist of what he'd need to do. Then he advised his dispatcher to alert Ned Sloan, the investigator for Klassen County, the agents in Rennerton with the state's Bureau of Criminal Apprehension. They'd also need the BCA forensic team, and the medical examiner to dispatch somebody out of Ramsay.

"Because it's close to the reservation we should also alert the FBI's resident agent in Bemidji."

"Already on it, Cal."

Brian Fahey, an officer with the park, wasted no time when Meckler arrived at the gate. He gave him a quick wave, threw his SUV into gear and began leading him to the scene. Meckler killed his siren but kept his emergency lights going, in keeping with procedure.

Fahey led him along the park's main dirt roads for a couple of miles before his brake lights brightened. He stopped, left the road and cut into the dense woods. They swayed along an ancient logger's trail overgrown with scrub and brushwood. The smells of pine and spruce filled Meckler's car. The light had dimmed because the treetops formed a natural canopy blocking the sun. Meckler's emergency lights splashed red and blue onto the trees, creating a dreamlike air.

For several miles the undergrowth scraped along the undercarriage, while leafy branches slapped and tugged at the sides of their vehicles. The *snap-crack* of their progress echoed. Meckler caught a glimpse of chrome and recognized a second wildlife SUV ahead at a clearing.

They pulled up behind it.

Meckler checked in with his dispatcher, then began logging the date, time and details in his notebook before stepping out to confer with Fahey and Ashlee Danser, Fahey's partner, who'd been waiting at the scene. The trio huddled out of earshot of the vehicles and Meckler nodded to man and woman in the back seat of Danser's SUV.

"Those are the people who made the find?"

"Yes, bird-watchers, Dan Whitmore and Vivian Chambers, retired couple from Omaha."

Danser's face was taut, as if she were grappling with something.

"Okay," Meckler said. "I'll get a statement from them. Where's the scene?"

"That way, go about fifty yards through the woods."

Danser pointed. "You won't miss it. I flagged it with some yellow scene tape. It's really bad, Cal, really bad. I just glanced, I couldn't bear looking."

"So you walked into the crime scene?" Meckler made notes. "I don't see any other tape to cordon the area."

"There's nobody else around, Cal."

"We can't risk other hikers happening on it. We need to protect the scene. I'll get my tape from my trunk. Can you guys use it and yours to form a perimeter to seal the whole scene?"

"Sure, Cal," Fahey said.

"I'll need you to show me the path you took in, Ashlee, but first I'll talk to our witnesses." Meckler walked to the SUV.

The elderly woman was sitting in the back with her elbows on her knees, holding her face in her hands while the man rubbed her shoulders.

"Excuse me, Mr. Whitmore, Ms. Chambers. I know this is a difficult time. I'm Deputy Cal Meckler with the Klassen County Sheriff's Office. Could you please tell me how you came upon the discovery?"

"Oh, my God, it's horrible! It's just—" Vivian stifled a sob.

"We've already told the young officer there everything," Whitmore said. "I'm sorry, I forget her name."

"I know, and my apologies, but you'll have to talk to a number of other investigators before we're done. And we'll need to verify your identification. It's all part of the procedure, given the gravity of the events here."

"We were just looking at birds!" Vivian said to no one. "Just looking for owls and a kingbird when we found it! Dear lord!"

"Take it easy, Viv. Have some more water." Whitmore passed her a bottle, then turned to Meckler. "Son, as a doctor, I've seen a lot of terrible things. I was a medic in Vietnam and I saw every kind of battle wound you can imagine, but what we saw in there exceeds comprehension. I…tried to clear away—I…tried…to see if there were any signs of life—even though I knew there were none. I still—I'm sorry."

Whitmore looked toward the scene, dragged the back of his dirt-stained hand across his mouth, regained his composure and recounted the discovery.

Afterward, Meckler went to his trunk. He slipped on shoe covers, tugged on latex gloves, got his camera, his notebook and followed the same line Ashlee Danser had taken into the scene. The air was pleasant with birdsong as he followed a widened pathway into the forest. Parts of the underbrush were flattened, indicating a vehicle had passed through.

He stopped to take several photos before moving on.

Soon he saw the foot-long yellow strip of tape affixed to a tree branch and lifting in the breeze as if beckoning—*or daring*—him to continue. He stepped toward the clearing and the fallen tree where Vivian Chambers had been sitting a short time ago.

He scanned the area but saw nothing.

Then he heard the drone of flies and stopped dead.

It was under the dappled light.

The victim was a white female.

In his short time as a deputy Meckler had seen the results of most tragedies—people who'd died in wrecks, fires, drownings; suicides by gunshots or hangings.

He'd experienced the toll and the aftermath up close.

But this was different from any death he'd ever seen.

It was as if some malevolent force had ripped its way into this world from a nether region to break down all that we know as human.

As he stared at the scene gooseflesh rose on his arms. The tiny hairs at the back of his neck stood up and all the saliva in his mouth evaporated.

Two bare and pale human hands were jutting from the earth, exposed down to the forearms. The hands were about three feet apart, as if the owner had raised them from underground, breaking the earth's surface in a macabre cheer.

Dirt had been clawed frantically from around the head with a tree branch, as the doctor had described.

The mouth was agape.

Clusters of insects were feasting inside.

Flies encrusted her face.

The eyes were wide-open in a frozen silent scream as if still imploring Meckler to save her.

37

Lost River State Forest, Minnesota

Several hours after the bird-watchers had made their grisly discovery, a Minnesota State Patrol helicopter thumped over the scene.

Lester Pratt watched from his Ford as he finished off the coffee his wife had made for him, then resealed the cup on his Thermos with a snap. He resumed studying the images on his laptop. The chopper was transmitting live video as it photographed the site, determining the size and boundaries of the crime scene.

Because the primary crime scene was in the state forest and Klassen County had few resources, it was decided that the state's Bureau of Criminal Apprehension would lead the investigation with support from local agencies and the FBI.

"Ever see one like this, Les?" Ben Koehler, Pratt's partner, was concentrating on his phone and photos of the victim and the scene they'd taken when they'd first arrived.

Pratt was a seasoned cop partial to the Vikings and Springsteen. He was near retirement. As a BCA agent Pratt had led or worked on nearly one hundred homicides. He peered over his bifocals at his laptop to make a small sketch in his case notebook.

"No," he said without looking away. "Not like this."

At that point Klassen County deputy Cal Meckler was approaching Pratt's vehicle, prompting Koehler to smile.

"Jeez, that kid must've roped off a twenty-mile perimeter," Koehler said as Meckler stepped up to Pratt's side.

"We've cordoned the scene." Meckler wiped his brow. "Is there anything else I can help you with?"

"Thank you," Pratt said. "We'll need help with the canvas. But we'll take that up at the meeting after we've learned more from our forensic people to help guide us in what we're looking for."

"And when and where will that meeting take place?"

"Likely tomorrow morning in Rennerton."

"Thank you, sir. I'll be there, willing to help, even if I'm off duty."

"We appreciate that, son."

"I'll search the roadside leading to the scene for anything tossed."

"The canine team already went through it but go ahead if you want."

After the deputy left, Koehler shook his head, amused.

"He's a keener, Les."

"Nothing wrong with that."

Pratt had been keen himself, especially after he was shot in the leg after he'd stopped a speeding car near

Duluth when he was a greenhorn state trooper. While he was recovering, he decided to become a detective.

Then you blink, twenty-five years go by, and you're confronted with this.

Pratt's stomach twisted again at the gruesome pictures of the victim's hands and head.

No, he'd never seen anything like this.

The thing that hit home: Pratt's two daughters were about the same age as this young woman.

We've got to find the animal that did this, he thought, glancing toward the wooded area where the crime scene people were working. Pratt was counting on them to find something to guide him.

They were very good.

A little deeper into the woods from where Pratt and Koehler's vehicle was parked, Staci Anderson, coordinator for the BCA's Crime Scene Team, glanced at the sky, hoping the weather would hold.

Outdoor scenes were tough—rain could wash away trace evidence.

Anderson took stock of her team, clothed in white coveralls, shoe covers, latex gloves. They were forensic scientists, expert in their disciplines such as chemistry, biology, latent prints, firearms and trace analysis. They worked well with the group that came up from Midwest Medical Examiner's Office in Ramsey.

All members knew their jobs. They worked quietly, efficiently.

Anderson and her team were devotees of the exchange theory of forensics, which held that with every scene the killer leaves a trace of something and leaves with something from it.

It'd been a long day already, Anderson thought, reviewing the work done and the work ahead. They'd taken great care removing all the soil from around the body. It would be sifted for trace and other analysis. They were meticulous about collecting samples of vegetation and soil for study and later comparison. The trees and nearby brush and shrubs were examined for hair, thread, fibers, other materials or broken branches, anything indicative of a struggle.

They scrutinized the area for traces of phlegm, saliva, seminal fluid and other biological material, knowing that it was susceptible to rapid destruction by the elements. Additionally, they searched for shell casings, knives, anything that may have been used as a weapon.

It would be dark soon. That's when they'd prepare a solution of water, sodium perborate, sodium carbonate and luminol to spray on the area in a process known as chemical luminescence, to detect blood. If the solution contacted blood it would react glowing blue under ultraviolet light.

They painstakingly identified foot and tire impressions, first eliminating those of the witnesses, local law enforcement and any known service vehicles. Fortunately, the scene was pristine in that regard. They photographed and made casts of the impressions they found for further analysis and comparison.

Things were going well, Anderson thought, as she collected her tablet and left the scene. She followed the flagged path of entry and exit to update Pratt, who got out of his vehicle when he saw her.

"Where're we at, Staci?"

"The ME says they'll be ready to transport the body before dark for an autopsy in Ramsey."

Pratt nodded.

"We'll do our spraying for blood then."

"What about time frame on death? How long was she there?"

"Hard to pinpoint, we'll defer to the ME. But the way things look, with insects, status of decomposition, et cetera, I estimate less than a week, maybe even three or four days, hard to say."

"All right."

"Once we can analyze the tire impressions we may have a suspect vehicle for you."

"That would be good."

"One other thing." Anderson cued some clear photographs on her tablet. "Take a look."

They were very tight, clear pictures of marble-sized, circular impressions in soft soil in a grouping of three in a triangular shape.

"What's that?"

"We're fairly certain these are impressions of a tripod. Now, given this is bird-watching country, they could've been made by birders."

"Right."

"They could've also been made by the killer."

"Are you saying he may have recorded this?"

Anderson nodded.

38

New York City

Sirens echoed in the night when Kate got out of the cab at 6th Avenue near Times Square and walked along West 46th Street.

A few hours ago, Hugh Davidson had called her at home, excited that he'd arranged a meeting with a computer network security expert who was an ex-contractor with the CIA and the NSA.

"We have to meet him tonight," Hugh said. "We're lucky. These people rarely step out of the shadows. Our guy's been involved in some nefarious projects."

The bar where they'd arranged to meet was slivered between the Cafe Ocho and Samantha's Hair Salon. Kate arrived early and stayed outside to scan the street for people coming and going. There was nothing unusual, just another night in Manhattan after spending a frustrating, fruitless day following leads.

This meeting with Hugh's contact could be something.

Now, while waiting on the street for him, Kate used her phone to check on the competition. She read the latest Associated Press story on Rampart, a situational piece containing no real news. It emphasized the challenges of identifying the staggering number of new victims. *It's only a matter of time before they identify my sister.* Kate pushed the thought aside and stood firm, drawing on Nancy's encouragement to never give up her fight to learn the truth about Vanessa.

That's why she'd come down here tonight. Plus, she was still on the story. She followed her personal rule to avoid taking the subway after dark. Having been alone much of her life, she knew how to take care of herself. When it came to meeting news sources who were strangers, especially those with questionable backgrounds, she kept her guard up.

My name and face are out there, along with a lot of freaky people.

Twenty minutes and still no sign of Hugh. Kate texted him. *Maybe he's in the bar already?* When she didn't get a response, she went in.

Live piano music was playing above the laughter of the after-work crowd blending with the conversations of the night crowd. As the TVs above the bar flashed with sports and news, Kate searched for Hugh.

It was futile.

Fortunately a booth nearby was emptying and she moved fast to claim it. A server cleared the table, Kate ordered a diet cola, then her phone vibrated with a text from Hugh.

A pipe burst in my bldg. I'm flooded. Can't make it. Sorry.

Darn, Hugh. How will I know him?

He'll know you.

What's his name? Appearance?

I've never seen him before.

What!?!

He goes by Viper.

Seriously?

Yes. Sorry, Kate. I have to go. Good luck.

Great. Shaking her head, she set her phone on the table.

Her drink came with a bowl of peanuts. She munched on a few as she took inventory in a bid to spot her source. The place was packed with Manhattan white-collar types. She noticed a man nearby warming a stool at the bar. Tie loosened, he was stealing glimpses of her while pretending to watch the TV overhead.

What? Now he was grinning and offering Kate little waves.

He couldn't be Viper. No chance.

She turned away, sipped her drink and checked the time on her phone.

Viper was half an hour late.

This was starting to feel like a washout.

Well, she still hadn't exhausted the Denver angle. She had more work to do following up on the information Will Goodsill had sent her. Maybe there was a link to Nelson and who he really was. She consoled herself with the belief that the Colorado case still held promise, before she glanced at one of the TVs showing a news report on Rampart.

A sudden wave of sadness rolled over her. For the first time she realized that she'd have to think about planning a funeral for Vanessa.

Kate shut her eyes tight for a second.

How much more of this I can take?

"Kate Page?"

A man in his twenties—early twenties—materialized at her table.

"Yes."

"I'm a friend of Hugh Davidson's. We were to meet."

The stranger was about six feet tall with a medium build. He had dark, slicked-back hair cut short, a stubbled goatee and stud in his left lobe. He was wearing a polo shirt under his leather jacket.

"I suppose I should ask you your code name."

He started to grin, nodding to himself.

"Viper. But you can call me Erich."

"All right, have a seat, Erich."

As he removed his jacket, Kate noticed small tattoos on his toned arms.

"May I get you something?" A waitress set down a coaster.

"Tomato juice with ice."

After the server left Kate asked why he'd ordered the juice.

"Are you under twenty-one, Erich?"

"I'm twenty-two." His eyes went to Kate's phone. "May I?"

She pushed it his way and he inspected it without touching it.

"What was that all about?" Kate asked.

"Nothing." He shrugged. "I have an interest in the types of phones people use."

"You're twenty-two, and Hugh says you did some work for the CIA and NSA. Is that true?"

"Yes."

"What kind of work?"

"Network security."

"What exactly did you do?"

"I can't discuss that."

"Figures. Oh, Hugh couldn't make it because—"

"I know why."

"Who are you working for now?"

"I'm freelancing here and there. I do okay."

After Erich's juice arrived, Kate waited until the server had left.

"Okay, then," she said. "Hugh told you why I need help."

"You're trying to find Carl Nelson, the guy the FBI's looking for."

"Yes. Are you willing to help me, to help me confidentially?"

Erich nodded.

"Hugh told you that neither I, nor Newslead, can pay you?"

"Not a problem," he said.

Kate sipped her drink, heartened to have help.

"All right, so what can you do, how does this work, because I can't tell you how badly I want to find this guy."

"It's about your sister."

"That. Yes. And all the other victims."

Erich looked off at nothing. "I'll give you an overview, how's that?"

"Yes."

"For starters, I'll tell you what's going on. The FBI will have secured IP addresses of every computer Nelson's had access to."

"Home and work?"

"Right, cell phones, laptops. They'll look at his online history, with every site he's visited, every email he's sent, every online transaction. They'll get warrants or subpoena the networks he's been on.

"Sounds exhaustive."

"It'll likely be useless and the FBI knows this, given Nelson's line of work and his mind-set."

"What do you mean?"

"I've been following the case. He's supposedly a network security expert. He'll know some tricks of the trade, and he's already attempted to cover his tracks. So he's likely taken steps not to leave any digital trail."

"Oh."

"Additionally, if he never touches a computer and goes off the grid, he's gone. Then it becomes the proverbial needle-in-a-haystack search, leaving police to rely on traditional evidence like fingerprints, license plates, DNA and eyewitness sighting, or anticipating and leveraging who he might physically contact."

"Right." Kate's heart sank.

"However, I don't think that's the case with Carl Nelson."

"What do you mean?"

"Look, he's stolen access to private financial data

for some forty million people, which is child's play, by the way."

"For you, maybe."

"My guess is Carl's going to use that data while he's on the run."

"What if he doesn't? What if he stays off the grid and uses cash?"

"It's possible, but today there are places that won't take cash, increasing the chances that he'd use one of his stolen digital identities."

"If that's true, then how would you know who, what or when?"

"There are some protocols I could run."

"I see. Okay."

"Look, I have to go," Erich said. "I'll work on this, I'll keep in touch."

"Wait, I'll give you my cell phone and email—"

"I don't need any of that." He smiled.

"Or course," she said. "Before you go, tell me something. Why agree to help? Is this sport for you?"

"Sport?"

He looked into his glass of tomato juice.

"No, a few years ago a friend of mind, who was quite troubled and naive, had been lured over time by an online predator who eventually raped her. She committed suicide. I was a pallbearer."

"Oh, God."

"Police couldn't find the man responsible, so I looked for him with a vengeance. In my zeal, I attacked a few places, intruded—guess you'd call it hacking. But I found him."

Erich nodded and finished his juice. Kate suddenly noticed that he'd been drinking it with the napkin wrapped around the glass so he wouldn't leave any fingerprints. He pulled on his jacket to leave.

"You got this?"

"Yes. Wait. Erich, what happened? You found the creep, what happened to him?"

"He's dead."

39

New York City

The morning after her meeting with Erich, Kate got to the newsroom around nine-thirty.

Something about this "Viper" character disturbed her.

Implying that he'd been involved in someone's death as an act of vengeance had left her feeling uneasy. So did the way he held his glass, as if being careful not to leave fingerprints. It prompted her to head straight for the business section.

She found Hugh at his desk, wearing a pale blue shirt and bow tie. He was putting his jacket on a hanger when he saw her.

"Kate, I'm sorry I stood you up last night. My apartment's a disaster. So how'd it go with Viper? Did he show up?"

"Yes. What's the story with him tracking down an online predator who assaulted his friend and then died?"

"Oh, that."

"Yes, that. Did Viper have something to do with his death?"

"Yes. Let me buy you a coffee and explain."

Downstairs in the building's food court Kate recounted her meeting. Then Hugh told her how he'd first found Viper through industry sources when he wrote a series on corporate cyber security.

"He's kind of a ghost," Hugh said. "After his friend's suicide, he used his skill to track her rapist. Turned out the bad guy was a computer expert, contracted with the NSA. Viper broke several laws infiltrating supposedly impenetrable systems to secure damning evidence against the guy."

"Then what?"

"Viper alerted the FBI, provided them with everything. When they went to arrest the man, he led them on a wild high-speed chase through Virginia that ended with his car wrapped around a tree and his death."

"Wow."

"Later the CIA and the NSA reached out to Viper to work for them."

"He's that good?"

"He's that good. Did he agree to help you?"

"Yes."

"Count yourself lucky."

Back at her desk Kate's coffee was kicking in.

Having Viper on her side had spurred her to continue her own investigation on Nelson. She returned to the Alberta-Colorado angle, reexamining all the old documents that Goodsill had sent her from his trash grab fifteen years ago. The circumstances concerning the initial Denver suspect, Jerome Fell, niggled at her. The one document that seemed to be a misdirected notice regarding a burial site in Chicago of Krasimira Zurrn puzzled her. The page in the attachment was torn, creased and stained from the trash.

She couldn't find an address on it for anyone in Colorado.

Kate began flipping through her notes but was interrupted by the ping of a message from Reeka.

Reuters just moved this. How did we miss it? I'm at the airport heading to Atlanta. Get on it and keep us posted.

Kate, are you OK to get on it? asked Chuck, whom Reeka had copied on the message.

Reuters had an exclusive, short breaking-news item that said Rampart police had confirmed the identities of four of the twelve recently discovered victims and were poised to release their names.

Kate's stomach twisted as her sister's face blurred before her eyes.

Vanessa could be one of them. It could all end here.

Her fingers shook over her keyboard as she moved to respond. She stopped, took a breath, regained her composure, then typed her answer to Reeka and Chuck.

I can handle it. I'm on it.

Before she knew it, she was on the phone to Brennan in Rampart, pushing aside the betrayal of his promise to keep her updated on identities.

"Brennan," he answered.

"Kate Page. Reuters says you've identified four more victims."

A long silence followed until Kate broke it.

"Ed, is my sister one of them?" Her voice quivered.

"No. She's not."

"You tell me right now. I deserve to know."

"She's not, Kate."

"You're certain."

"We have your DNA. Remember, you volunteered it?"

Kate swallowed hard, briefly relieved. But her heart broke for the families of the dead.

"Okay." She collected herself. "Are there any new developments in the case?"

"No. Work continues on the investigation."

"I want the four new names for a story."

"Give me twenty minutes. We're wrapping up notifying the families."

Half an hour later Brennan emailed Kate a news release that was going out in fifteen minutes. It was succinct, with few details, identifying the four victims as: Camila Castillo, twenty-four, missing from Mesa, Arizona, for six years. Kathy Shepherd, nineteen, disappeared from Greensboro, North Carolina, three years ago. Tiffany Osborn, twenty-five, vanished after going to a movie in Lexington, Kentucky, five years ago. Valerie Stride, twenty, had been missing from her suburban home in Orlando, Florida, for three years.

Kate looked into their young faces in the accompanying photographs, their bright smiles and eyes filled with hope. Her heart ached for them, for the horrors they must've suffered. The magnitude of evil was crushing.

Four more victims identified.

Eight more to go. Eight more chances for Vanessa to be one.

Who knows how many more victims they'll unearth?

A chill shot through her as she concentrated on her story. The desk wanted her copy ASAP. She set out working with the news library assembling and detailing the circumstances of each case. Once she felt she had enough information, she sought numbers for relatives of the women, then steeled herself for the anguish of calling the four families in mourning.

The next hour passed with a quick succession of heart-wrenching interviews. Most of the families wanted to talk, wanted to share their grief, starting with Tiffany Osborn's father in Kentucky. "You know, Tiff came to me in a dream last week and said, 'Everything's going to be okay, Dad.'" Kate then reached Kathy Shepherd's mother in North Carolina. "It's just not real," she told Kate. "It never was. I still expect my little girl to walk through the door."

Camila Castillo's brother was a trucker and Kate reached him on the road near Tulsa. "I'm flying to New York in the morning. We're going to bring Cammy home, to rest in peace where she grew up. I hope they catch the guy who did this so he can rot in hell." The last person Kate reached was Valerie Stride's dad, a retired marine in Orlando. "Who would do this kind of thing? Can anyone tell me?"

In each case, Kate had asked relatives if they knew of any connection between their loved one and Carl

Nelson, or Rampart, or Tara Dawn Mae, or Canada, or Denver, or Vanessa's necklace. In each case, the answer was no.

The calls were anguishing and Kate carried the pain of the families as she wrote. After she filed her story she went to the restroom and splashed water on her face as the words of Valerie Stride's father echoed.

Who would do this kind of thing?

His question resonated with her as she went back to her desk and stared at Carl Nelson's Wanted poster on the FBI's website.

You. You did this.

Kate resumed her research with renewed fervor. Again she scrutinized the material from Colorado, focusing on the notice from Chicago dealing with the burial site for Krasimira Zurrn. Kate dug into Newslead's databases, making notes as she searched public records for Illinois, Cook County and Chicago. *There has to be something here.* She collected her files and headed for Chuck's office, tapping on the door frame.

"Come in," he said. "Just read your story. Nice work."

"Can we talk?"

Kate opened her file folder and began explaining her gut feeling about Krasimira Zurrn and the link to Jerome Fell in Denver.

"Just hear me out, Chuck. Let me connect the dots."

They knew that Nelson was an obvious name changer who'd faked his death. Investigators admitted to not knowing his true identity. In Rampart she'd found a neighbor who made reference to Nelson's familiarity with Denver. The Alberta abduction of Tara Dawn Mae, with its ties to her sister, had a potential

Denver link through a license plate to Jerome Fell. One Denver detective considered Fell a possible suspect in the abduction. Fell admitted he'd been in Canada at the time Tara vanished.

"Now. Look. Fell bears a resemblance to Nelson," Kate showed Chuck the photo she had. "And, like Nelson, Fell was a computer expert who lived alone. However, according to neighbor interviews and documents Goodsill obtained at the time, there are unsubstantiated indications that Fell may have had a girl on his property whose age would fit with Tara's."

Then she explained the record for Krasimira Zurrn.

"Where're you going with this, Kate?"

"Chicago."

40

Saint Paul, Minnesota

The state's main crime lab was housed in the Bureau of Criminal Apprehension's headquarters, a three-story brick-and-glass building on Maryland Avenue. Displayed in the atrium was a large steel-and-stained-glass sculpture known as "Exquisite Corpse."

Staci Anderson considered the eye-catching artwork a beautiful metaphor for uniting the crime-solving work done in the complex. She drew heavily on its inspiration today as she worked, for she was feeling the pressure of this new case on all fronts.

It had been twenty-four hours since her crime scene team had returned from the grisly homicide in Lost River State Forest. Today she'd learned that it had been given priority status. The BCA state lab also functioned as one of the FBI's regional mitochondrial DNA labs and Anderson was told there was a "federal push" to expedite the case, given its ritualistic nature.

The lab was already grappling with a backlog, but the team set aside all other ongoing work to undertake analysis of the evidence they'd collected at Lost River.

Anderson's husband, an engineering contractor, was not pleased when she'd called him to say she'd miss dinner and would be late getting home. Again.

"It means you have to take Chloe to the mall tonight to get a birthday present for her friend's party tomorrow," she told him.

"Me? But I'm meeting the guys to watch the game at Stan's tonight."

"I'm sorry. See if Taylor can sit when you get back from the mall, then catch up with the guys."

"Yeah, I'll do that. You're putting in a lot of OT these days."

It was true.

But when she measured her personal guilt against the agony of the victims and their families, it was easy to concentrate on her job. She was good at it and was often called upon to coordinate investigations.

Anderson held a master's degree in microbiology from the University of Illinois and degrees in science and chemistry from the University of Wisconsin. She was one of the section's strongest scientists when it came to presenting court testimony and was being considered for a senior supervisory post.

Today she'd been working steadily at her station on the hair sample taken from the victim's scalp, which included the root. With the first level, microscopic examination, she was studying shaft characteristics, scale patterns, color, length and many other aspects before extracting the DNA, which could conclusively prove identity.

DNA analysis involved many time-consuming steps.

Extraction usually took a day. Then there was quantitation and amplification, usually another day. They were followed by an instrument run that could take half a day. The procedure then called for a rigorous cover-to-cover review of her work by another section scientist, which could take up to a week. Once that was completed the results could be submitted for comparison to state and federal databases like the FBI's CODIS databank, a variety of state and national missing persons networks, and new systems holding the DNA of victims of major crimes.

After working for several hours amid the white countertops and neat array of equipment, Anderson collected her tablet and left her station. She needed to check the status of work under way by scientists in other sections who were examining items from Lost River.

Glancing at her screen, Anderson continually insured that the team had taken care with the proper collection and disposition of the evidence. Each piece had been stored separately in proper containers, marked with its position, location, description and the name of the analyst responsible for it. Anderson checked that each item had been photographed before it was removed from the scene.

Janice Foley, expert in biological fluids, was handling what they believed to be blood. She'd scraped some dried traces. Where she couldn't scrape, she'd moistened a gauze pad with distilled water. Foley was also analyzing a discarded fast-food take-out cup and straw for traces of saliva. She didn't find much else at the scene in the way of substances.

"We didn't find any indication of urine, feces or vomit," Foley said.

"Yes, we've noted that."

"I've got no semen traces near the body or at the scene."

"Okay." Anderson made a note on her tablet. "We'll send a reminder to the ME in Ramsey to take a vaginal swab while he's conducting the autopsy. I know they know, but it's our job. Keep me posted, Janice."

Anderson moved on to Heather Wick, who was responsible for trace evidence. Wick was studying the fibers, fabric and additional hair she'd collected at the scene near the impressions.

"I've got some hemp, some cotton, nylon polyester, chips of treated wood." Wick was bent over her microscope. "And I'm looking at thread counts and fiber twists before I can be conclusive."

"When will you have that additional hair ready for me?"

"Shouldn't be much longer, then you can start extracting."

"Sounds good, Heather, thanks."

Travis Shaw was one of the country's best analysts when it came to tracks and footprints. Tire impressions filled his large computer monitor when Anderson approached him for an update. Head nodding to the music flowing through his earbuds, he was the youngest scientist on the team. Anderson tapped his shoulder and he tugged at his plugs, music ticking from them after they'd fallen to his shoulders.

"What about the tripod theory, Trav?"

"I agree one hundred percent. The impressions and the positioning with the buried body are consistent with recording, photographs, video or both."

"But?"

"As we've said, this is bird-watching country. A birder could've set up there. Still, soil conditions match what we've got on the foot and tire impressions. Take a look."

Shaw clicked on an array of enlarged tire tracks in the dirt.

"I got great images and casts of everything. I'm still analyzing the tire impressions, but we've ruled out police or park vehicles. I'm confident, given the conditions of the soil that captured the impressions and the soil that entombed the victim, these impressions are from our suspect vehicle. You know, weather wear, timing, all concern the same time period."

"Good."

"As with my earlier analysis, again, given soil depth, estimated vehicle weight and tread, we're looking for a heavy-duty pickup, utility or a van, as the suspect's vehicle. I've still got work to do on damage, wear, then I'll start going through the directories to confirm tire type and model."

"Okay."

Shaw clicked on images of foot and shoe impressions. "Like with the tires, I ruled out all other potential shoe impressions—our witnesses, the first responding officers."

"Good."

"Got some awesome ones here. The soil was very moldable—it worked to our advantage."

"I see that."

"The victim was buried without shoes, so these are her foot impressions. Now here—" he clicked "—it looks like a male size-twelve boot. I'm still working on it. And here, another set of smaller impressions from footwear from a female. Again, in both cases, I still have to study characteristic properties, tread wear and look for shoe type and model."

"What do you think?"

"My preliminary take? I think there were three people at this crime scene. Two women and one man."

"And if we only have one victim that means two people connected to this woman's murder are still at large, and I don't know if anyone's stated the obvious."

"What's that?"

"This is one of the most horrific scenes we've ever had."

41

Ramsey, Minnesota

The unidentified victim's naked corpse lay on a stainless-steel tray in one of the autopsy rooms of the Midwest Medical Examiner's Office in Ramsey.

Female. White. Five feet four inches. One hundred twenty pounds. Age between twenty-four and twenty-eight.

Her open, lifeless eyes stared up into the brilliant LED exam light.

What dreams did they hold? Did she have a good life? Pathologist Dr. Garry Weaver wondered before he and Monica Ozmek, who was assisting, resumed their work.

Weaver and Ozmek had conducted many autopsies over the years.

They'd grown accustomed to the coolness of the autopsy room with its smells of ammonia and formaldehyde. They knew the egg-like odor of organs, their meaty shades of red and pink. They were familiar with the *pop* sound when the calvarium was removed, opening the skull to reveal the brain and dura. Weaver made the usual primary Y incision across the chest as they worked their way through the external and internal examination of the body.

They'd photographed it, weighed it, measured it and x-rayed it.

Their job was to determine the manner, cause, time and classification of death, as well as positively confirm the victim's identification. Weaver was confident about manner and cause, but identification would be a challenge.

"The dermis of the victim's fingertips has been disfigured, likely due to being subjected to a caustic substance," he said.

"Yes, I noted that when we were bagging the hands after we'd removed the body from the ground."

"This tattoo may help."

Weaver's rubber-gloved right hand pointed a finger at the left upper neck and the tattoo of a small heart with wings.

"It should."

"Did you submit the dental chart to the databases?"

"Yes."

"And we also have a shot if Anderson's team down in Saint Paul gets a hit through DNA—Monica? Are you all right?"

He saw that, behind her plastic shield, her face had saddened.

"Yes, let's continue."

Weaver hesitated before resuming.

Bearing in mind that his assistant seemed to be struggling with her composure, he maintained his clinical, professional distance as he found the facts to support his findings. The victim had been buried and as a result she had suffocated. There was thorax compression, but death by asphyxiation was a result of occlusion of the respiratory tract.

For a moment, before they'd concluded, Weaver considered the sensations of the victim's last moments of being buried alive. She would have felt the crushing pressure of the soil. The pain of it pressing on her, on her organs, would have numbed her, but she would've still been able to think as she slowly became entombed. The soil would've grown warm around her face. Reflexively, she would've clenched her mouth shut, but eventually she'd have been forced to inhale soil, which, in combination with the earth encasing her, led to death.

He was at his computer writing his report after they had finished when Ozmek came into his office and sat in the chair near him.

She contemplated the frosty can of diet soda from the vending machine that she held in her hands.

Weaver stopped.

"Want to talk about it?"

She stared deep into the framed painting of the sun setting on the Caribbean Sea that Weaver had on the wall next to his degrees.

"I don't know, Garry."

"What don't you know?"

"We go way back, don't we?"

"Sure, way back to before the ME's office was at the Mercy and the morgue was in the basement, remember that?"

"Sure." She took a hit of her soda and swallowed. "But the thing is, we've seen it all—the fires, the car wrecks, stabbings, shootings, drownings, hypothermia, suicides, just about everything you can think of."

"Right."

"But this. I mean she was buried alive. We both know what she would've gone through."

"Yes, but it would've been short, a minute or two, if that's any comfort."

"It isn't. What I cannot comprehend is why someone would take her life with such vile, calculating malevolence."

Weaver nodded.

"This one just pierced me. It just—" She shook her head.

Weaver patted her hand.

"Let's move on getting our findings to BCA, submit everything to every possible database, so we can help catch her killer."

42

Chicago

As the jetliner approached O'Hare International Airport, Kate took in Chicago's sprawl and skyline, knowing that time was ticking down on the inevitable.

Sooner or later Vanessa would be identified as one of Nelson's victims, but Kate couldn't sit back and do nothing.

She had to find him.

During her flight from JFK, she'd reviewed key aspects of the story. It took some convincing, but Chuck, who was a hard-core old-school reporter, had approved the trip. He'd agreed that if they struck out on her hunch about Nelson's links to Chicago, Denver and the Alberta abduction, they struck out.

"That's the way it goes. With this story we have to roll the dice," he'd said, behind his steepled fingers. "We'll put in the legwork and see where this leads. We're not going to risk having a competitor beat us. You're sure you're okay to go?"

"I'm sure, Chuck. I need to do this."

"All right. I'll alert our Chicago bureau. Call on

them if you need anything, like a shooter if you find something."

"I will."

"I'll give you a couple of days. Good luck."

Before she left headquarters she'd put in more research with the news library, then she went to Davidson. Viper had not given her a way to contact him. She needed Hugh to reach out to him through his sources.

"I will, Kate. But you know that he might not respond."

Now, as the jet's flaps groaned, Kate turned her thoughts from the window to her files, rereading the document dealing with the Chicago burial site for Krasimira Zurrn.

Who was she?

Kate concentrated on the newest information she'd uncovered: A death notice that appeared in the *Chicago Tribune* in 1998.

> Krasimira Anna Zurrn, 53 years old, died Oct. 12, 1998. Beloved mother of Sorin Zurrn. Visitation on Tuesday 10:00 a.m. until Mass 11:00 a.m. at Glorious Martyrs and Saints Church, Belmont. Interment Service 2:00 p.m. at New Jenny Park Cemetery, 9200 Kimball.

After landing Kate made calls while waiting in line for her rental car. She could've had someone from the bureau pick her up, but she needed to do this on her own.

The funeral home that had handled Zurrn's service was no longer in business. Kate's calls to the Glorious Martyrs and Saints Church for help reaching the dead woman's son, Sorin Zurrn, had not been returned. But Kate's earlier search of archived public records had yielded a nugget of information: In 1998, Krasimira Zurrn lived at 6168 Craddick Street. Kate entered the address in the GPS of her rented Nissan Altima before leaving O'Hare.

Merging with traffic on the Kennedy Expressway, Kate experienced the familiar rush of self-doubt that usually plagued her whenever she embarked on a difficult assignment.

This time her stomach tensed.

Oh, God, what am I doing here? This is likely a waste of time, my way of avoiding the truth—that Vanessa is dead in Rampart or died twenty years ago in the river, and that somehow someone found her necklace and it made its way to New York and... Stop it! Just stop it and work!

She took the Kimball Avenue exit.

Craddick Street was on the Northwest Side of Chicago. It fell between the areas of Avondale and Belmont Gardens in a neighborhood known as New Jenny Park, which had a large Polish and Eastern European population. According to the park's history, the name arose from the phonetic sound of Nee-WOE-Jenny, thought to be the Polish word for *peace*.

Kate agreed with her research—this was a solid blue-collar community. Meat shops, bakeries, grocery stores and cafés sprinkled the business district. The streets were lined with modest bungalows on small lots, a playground here and there.

She found the Zurrn house at the fringe of the neighborhood, where freshly painted homes with neat lawns stood next to those with overgrown yards and boarded-up windows laced with graffiti.

Kate shut off the car.

The motor ticked down as she studied the compact wood-frame house, sneaking a few quick pictures with her phone. The small front yard was overtaken with weeds. A couple of panels of the vinyl siding had warped and bent out from the walls. Shingles curled or were missing from the roof, and the chimney had gaps where the mortar had eroded and blown away.

The place stood as a tired headstone to hope, she thought as she knocked on the door. Flyers overwhelmed the mailbox. No one responded. A dog barked far off in the distance. A siren faded. Kate knocked again and pressed her ear to the door.

Nothing.

She took out a business card, jotted a request for the residents to call her cell phone ASAP, wedged it in the frame, turned and tapped her notebook to her leg. Of course different people had lived in the house over the years, but she was hopeful someone might remember Krasimira Zurrn and her son, Sorin.

Bright patches of blue and yellow flashed from the backyard of the house across the street. Kate would try the neighbors.

The house across the street had a lush manicured lawn, a thriving flower garden. The brick bungalow, with its gleaming windows, gave off a pleasant soapy smell as Kate walked along the driveway.

"Hello!" she called as she approached the back.

A man and woman were on their knees working in the small jungle that was their vegetable garden. The man wore a ball cap. The woman wore a large straw hat. They were gathering berries into a plastic bowl.

"Can I help you?" The man got to his feet, eyeing her carefully.

"I'm Kate Page, a reporter with Newslead." Kate fished her Newslead photo ID from her bag and showed it to him.

"You come here from New York?"

"Yes, I'm researching the history of Krasimira and Sorin Zurrn, who used to live across the street. I was wondering if I could talk to you about them."

"Krasimira Zurrn?" the old man repeated. "Why come from New York?"

"Well, we're looking at family history for a story."

"What kind of story?"

"A crime story."

The woman stood and spoke a long stream in what Kate thought was Polish to the man, who debated with her in Polish before answering Kate.

"Krasimira Zurrn died a long time ago," he said.

"I know. Did you live here then? Did you know her?"

"I remember that one." His eyes glinted.

The woman spoke in Polish again and the old man waved her off.

"Yes. This Zurrn woman, she had problems."

"What kind of problems?" Kate took out her notebook.

"Are you going to write my name down in your story?"

"I don't know your name, unless you want to give it to me?"

"I don't care. Stan Popek, eighty-three, retired welder. My wife is Magda."

"I don't want my name in the paper." Magda Popek waved her hand.

"Okay," Kate said. "Just Stan. How do you spell Popek?"

"P-o-p-e-k."

"Got it."

"This Zurrn—" Popek nodded at the house "—she was a nurse, but then she took drugs. She had men coming and going. That's how she paid her rent. This was very bad for the boy."

"What can you tell me about Sorin, her son?"

"He was strange."

"What'd you mean?"

"He always played by himself. He had no friends. He had a bad limp. He was a sad boy. Always running after butterflies and working on electrical things in his basement."

"Did you ever talk to him?"

"A little bit. I used to give him old tools because I felt sorry for him. He was pretty smart about computers. Once he showed me in their garage how he built one using parts from others. It worked really well. I think he was very intelligent."

"Do you know where Sorin lives now?"

Popek stuck out his bottom lip, shook his head, then turned to his wife and said something in Polish before returning to Kate.

"No, it's been too long."

"Do you know if the people living in the Zurrn place now might know?"

"Nobody's there now. The landlord's trying to rent it. Lots of people have lived there since the Zurrns."

"Do you know the landlord?"

"Tabor something."

"Lipinski," Magda Popek said. "Tabor Lipinski, he's rented it for years."

"Do you have number for him?"

"No," Magda said. "He's a nasty, greedy man."

Kate made some notes.

"Did Sorin Zurrn have any brothers, sisters or any other relatives?"

Popek shook his head.

"You say he had no friends, not even one?"

"Never saw him with other kids."

"Did he belong to Scouts or any clubs? Did he work after school?"

"No, nothing like that."

"What school would he have gone to? What high school?"

"Thornwood High School. It's not too far. I can draw you a map."

Kate asked a few more questions before thanking Popek and exchanging contact information.

"You know, he had a mean side," Popek said.

"How so?"

"He never went to his mother's funeral."

"Did you go?"

"Yes, we both did. She was our neighbor. But there were less than ten people and Sorin, who was a grown man, was not one of them."

"That's sad."

"It's worse than sad. His mother committed suicide and they say he never showed up when they buried her. That's cold-blooded."

43

Chicago

Kate climbed the front steps of Thornwood High School, a classic three-story redbrick-and-yellow-stone building.

She went to the central office lobby and reported to the security desk, as the admin staffer had advised when she'd called ahead with her request for help to contact a former student.

It had been nearly fifteen minutes since Kate arrived at the counter where she now stood watching Officer Fred Jenkins, according to his nameplate. He'd already called the school official she was to meet, searched her bag and run a metal-detecting wand over her. He was now meticulously entering her driver's license number into his computer.

As Jenkins slowly double-checked the number, Kate's attention went to the security rules posted on a board under the flags and portrait photos of the president, governor, mayor and principal, spelled out in plain language for all to see. No guns, no knives, no weapons of any sort, no gang colors, no gang clothing, no fighting, no bullying and so on and so on.

"Here you go, ma'am." Jenkins passed her a visitor's pass. "I'll keep your license, then exchange it for the pass on your way out."

As she clipped the pass to her blazer pocket the door squeaked open.

"Kate Page?"

A woman in her late forties had entered.

"Yes."

"I'm Donna Lee with the Alumni Association. Welcome to Thornwood, please come this way."

They went down a hallway lined with lockers. The air smelled of floor polish, perfume and cologne, with traces of the gymnasium and body odor. They passed glass trophy cases and banners heralding the championships and glory captured over the years by the Thornwood Thunderbolts: basketball, wrestling, swim, track, football and other teams.

"I understand you're looking for information on a former grad?" Donna asked as they walked.

"Yes, I was hoping the Alumni Association could help me."

"And you're a reporter?"

"Yes." Kate gave her a business card. "I'm doing some biographical research for a story."

"I see. This way, to the right."

They proceeded down another hallway.

"We're fortunate. Not every high school has an Alumni Association on-site. We're very well supported here," Donna said. "Thornwood's enrollment is about seventeen hundred students. Our alumni include two vice presidents, a governor, a Supreme Court justice, a number of actors, writers, professional athletes and successful business people."

And how many murderers, Kate wondered as Donna continued.

"The school opened in 1927, so we're talking about the histories of a hundred-and-thirty-thousand dead and living students."

"You have files on all of them?"

"A while back we digitalized everybody, so we have a pretty comprehensive database. Our listings vary from student to student, and we adhere to a strict privacy policy. Here we are."

The alumni office had a table with two large desks at the far end of the room. A bank of file cabinets stood against one wall next to shelves with yearbooks going back to the 1920s. A section of one wall was plastered with reunion photos, people with babies and people in landmark locations around the world, as well as cards and notes thanking the association.

A woman at one desk with a sweater draped over her shoulders removed her glasses and stood.

"This is Yolanda White, our director. This is Kate Page from Newslead in New York."

"Welcome, Kate." Yolanda extended her hand. "The admin office said that you're looking for a particular former student?"

"Yes."

Kate put her bag on the table, took out the death notice for Krasimira Zurrn and tapped the name Sorin.

"I'm trying to locate her son, Sorin. They lived on Craddick Street."

Yolanda replaced her glasses, studied the notice then sat at the keyboard of her computer.

"And do you have his age?"

Kate used the age police had given for Carl Nelson. "About forty-five."

"So, Class of Eighty-Eight." Yolanda began typing and within a few seconds her computer chimed. "Yes, Sorin Zurrn, graduated in eighty-eight."

Donna selected a yearbook, flipped through it and showed Kate Sorin Zurrn's high school photo. Kate's pulse quickened as she stared at it. For her gut told her this was Carl Nelson, then she thought, no. It was Jerome Fell from Denver. Then she accepted that it could be anybody.

"Is this the man you're looking for?" Donna pointed to a listing.

"It is. Would you have a contact address for him?"

"I'm afraid that's private," Yolanda said.

"Wait," Donna said. "We have to see if he's registered first."

"Registered?"

"If he's registered to the Alumni Association, we'll have his current information and we can send him a message to see if he's okay to release it to you."

"No," Kate said. "I need to contact him directly. It's complicated."

Yolanda's keyboard clicked.

"It doesn't matter, he's not listed."

"Do you have any other information on him?" Kate asked.

"That would be it," Donna said. "I'm sorry."

"Hold on. We could go to our coordinators," Yolanda suggested.

"Coordinators?"

"Alumni executives who are knowledgeable for a

graduating year." Yolanda's keyboard clicked. Then a speakerphone clicked on and a line started ringing. "They usually graduated that year and worked on the yearbook." The line was answered on the third ring.

"Hello," a woman answered.

"Hey, Cindy, it's Yolanda at the association. We got you on speaker."

"What's up?"

"Got a reporter here, Kate Page from Newslead in New York. She's doing research asking about Sorin Zurrn."

"Sorin Zurrn, Sorin Zurrn. Kind of a nerd, geek kid with a limp?"

"Yes," Kate said. "Hi, Cindy, Kate Page here. What can you tell me about him?"

"Gosh, he really kept to himself. Quiet, weird guy as I recall. He was in my history class. We had Mr. Deacon. Sorin got picked on a lot. I think his mother had psychological problems."

"Do you happen to know how we can get a message to him? I mean, do you know in general where he's living right now?"

"No, sorry. I think he left town. I think his mother died some years ago."

"Did he have any friends, Cindy?" Kate asked.

"No. He was a pretty sad case. Hold on, I think there was one person, Gwen Garcia, she was an eighty-eight, too. She used to hang with Tonya Plesivsky. They tormented Sorin quite a bit. I think Gwen had a change of heart and tried to be friends with him after the incident. I know Gwen—she's Gwen Vollick, now lives in Koz Park. Let me give her a call, see if she'll talk to you."

Cindy hung up before Kate had a chance to ask her to elaborate on "the incident." She asked Donna and Yolanda but neither recalled. They had graduated from Thornwood in the early eighties. Yolanda flipped through the yearbook to Tonya Plesivsky's picture for Kate.

Tonya was pretty and, judging from the long list of clubs and societies she'd belonged to, she must've been popular, too. While they waited Kate asked Yolanda to submit the names Carl Nelson, Jerome Fell, Tara Mae—or Tara Dawn Mae—and Vanessa Page into the school data banks. There were quite a few Vanessas, Jeromes, Carls, Taras, Nelsons and Pages but nothing that fit. Then the office phone rang. It was Cindy calling back. Yolanda put her on speaker.

"Hi there. I reached Gwen and she said she really didn't want to talk about Sorin or Tonya. She said she'd always felt bad about teasing Sorin, but they were just stupid kids. Gwen figured you were writing a story about bullying and didn't want her name used. She said the whole thing is still sad for her."

"I understand, Cindy," Kate said.

"Sorry, wish I could help you."

"There's one thing. Can you tell me about the incident and how it led Gwen to change?"

A silence filled the air.

"Tonya was one of Gwen's best friends and she died."

"I'm so sorry. What happened?"

"She died when she was fifteen. She was looking for her dog."

44

Chicago

After leaving Thornwood High School, Kate sat at the wheel of her rental car making notes while struggling to put together the pieces of information she'd gleaned about Sorin Zurrn.

Am I any closer to finding him?

The women of the Alumni Association had been friendly and helpful, but they wouldn't give her addresses, emails or phone numbers. She'd sensed an undercurrent of unease at having a reporter asking questions about former students.

After looking over her notes, Kate tried, yet again, to find any address information for Sorin Zurrn in Chicago. Again she struck out. She then searched for Tonya Plesivsky's family and caught her breath.

An Ivan Plesivsky came up on Craddick Street.

Two blocks from the Zurrn home.

He has to be a relative.

Newslead subscribed to an array of online information databases that allowed reporters to conduct extensive searches through any device they used. Kate ran the Plesivsky name through the databases for the Chicago papers, an obit or news item, anything on Tonya's death.

A story in the *Sun-Times* came up. It was short with no byline.

Girl Dies after Fall in Park

A fifteen-year-old girl from the Northwest Side died Saturday night after she fell in Ben Bailey Park while looking for her lost dog, officials said.

Medical crews responded to a 911 call at around 3:35 p.m. Saturday that reported a girl with a traumatic head injury was found by joggers at the base of a stone stairway. The joggers administered CPR until paramedics arrived and transported the girl, identified as Tonya Plesivsky of Craddick Street, to Verger Green Memorial, where she was pronounced dead.

"This is not real. I can't believe it," Ivan Plesivsky, the girl's father, told the *Sun-Times*.

It appears that the girl tripped and fell, striking her head on the stone steps, according to parks officials and Chicago police.

A small photo of Tonya holding her dog, Pepper, accompanied the article.

That's so sad. She was such a young girl. But this was the girl who would "torment" Sorin. Why did her friend Gwen stop bullying him? I suppose it could be expected in the wake of Tonya's death. But how bad was it if, after all these years, Gwen refused to talk about it? And would any of this have any connection to Jerome Fell in Denver, or Carl Nelson, or Vanessa, or anything? Kate shook her head. *Sure it's a long shot, but that's what I'm here to do, take a long shot.*

The white picket fence protecting the islands of dirt and tufts of browned grass of the Plesivskys' front yard was missing a few pickets. The next thing Kate noticed was that the front of the wood frame bungalow had a wheelchair ramp. She glimpsed sheets and shirts flapping on a clothesline in the backyard as she went to the front door and knocked.

Kate heard movement, then voices. A moment later the door cracked open, releasing the smell of cigarettes as a woman, her face creased with a taut frown, greeted her.

"We're not buying anything, thank you." She started closing the door.

"Wait, please! I'm a reporter from New York. I need your help."

The door stopped.

Kate held up her ID. "Kate Page with Newslead."

"She says she's a reporter!" The woman shouted to someone else in the house, which prompted a muffled response before the woman turned back to Kate: "What do you want?"

"I'm researching some neighborhood history that involves Tonya Plesivsky. Would you be a relative?"

A cloud of pain passed over the woman.

"Tonya was our daughter."

Kate let a moment of respect pass.

"May I talk to you a little bit?"

"Wait."

The woman left Kate at the door. She heard subdued voices before she returned and invited Kate inside. Now the cigarette smell mingled with onions and something evocative of a hospital as they went to a small living room where a man in a wheelchair muted *Wheel of Fortune* on a large-screen TV.

He had thin white hair, glasses and white stubble. He wore a flannel shirt and work pants that looked like shorts. His legs were missing below his knees. He gestured to the sofa and Kate sat.

"Why're you writing an article about our daughter?"

Kate took out her notebook.

"I'm sorry. I'll explain," she said. "First, I should get your name, you're Ivan Plesivsky?"

"Yes, and my wife, Elena. Do you have a card or something?"

Kate gave him a card.

"Would you like a coffee or soda?" Elena asked.

"I don't want to trouble you."

"No trouble."

"Black coffee would be fine."

"So?" Ivan leaned forward in his chair. "Answer my question."

"I'm researching the background of Sorin Zurrn for a story. He may have some connection to some crimes. Or he may not."

"What kind of crimes?"

"Computer crimes, cyber theft, maybe harming people physically, but we're not sure."

"Doesn't surprise me." Ivan grunted. "He was odd."

"I understand Tonya and Sorin went to Thornwood High and knew each other. And since you were neighbors, I was hoping you'd tell me what you remember of the Zurrn family."

The man looked long and hard at Kate before turning to the mantel holding framed photographs of Tonya with Pepper. Then he removed his glasses and ran his hand over his face.

"You're aware of what happened to our daughter?" Elena asked from the doorway.

"Yes, and I'm terribly sorry."

"It's very painful for us to think about that time," Elena added as a kettle in the kitchen came to a boil.

Ivan replaced his glasses, sat straighter as if steeling himself.

"We didn't know the Zurrns," he said. "We weren't friends. We knew his mother was a slut and her boy was odd. Some kind of computer whiz who chased butterflies all day, or something. We didn't bother with them."

Elena set a mug of coffee with a Cubs logo on the table before Kate.

"Didn't Tonya and Sorin have difficulties with each other?"

Elena and Ivan exchanged glances, telegraphing to Kate that she'd shifted matters to an uncomfortable level.

"That was so long ago," Elena said. "Why bring this up?"

"I need to know as much about Sorin as possible for the story."

"We were aware of the rumors," Ivan said.

"What rumors?"

"That Tonya and her friends sometimes teased the Zurrn boy. And maybe his mother a little bit."

"His mother?"

"Look," Ivan said. "They were kids in high school. Hell, who doesn't get teased at school?"

"Tonya was very popular at school," Elena said.

"That's right," Ivan agreed. "She had a bit of a following. Was it right for her to tease Sorin? No, but that's what goes on in high school. Besides—" His chin suddenly crumpled and he froze a heaving sob as he turned to the photo shrine of his daughter.

Elena stood, put her hands on his shoulders and, as if sensing what was coming, turned to Kate.

"Maybe you should go."

Surprised, Kate was at a loss. In the moment she'd hesitated, Ivan found his composure.

"No, stay. I want her to hear this. All of it."

"Ivan," his wife cautioned him.

"Listen." Ivan stared at Kate, his jaw muscles pulsating. "Whatever sins our little girl may have committed as a child, she paid for them. I paid for them." He glanced to his wife. "We paid for them."

"I'm not sure I understand."

"What happened with Tonya is why I'm in this chair."

Kate glanced at Elena, then back at Ivan.

"Pepper was Tonya's dog," Ivan started. "When he was lost, Tonya was beside herself, putting up posters, looking everywhere. When she fell in the park our world stopped turning. You can't imagine our pain at losing our angel, our only child. It hurt so much. But we had to go on. For Tonya. So I went back to work thinking I was coping with it, thinking I was strong, but I wasn't. I was a shell."

"What work did you do?" Kate asked.

"I was a utility lineman. After Tonya was gone, the silence of her room, seeing her things and knowing she was never coming back…God. I started drinking. One day I was doing maintenance work on a substation. Something went wrong and I got electrocuted. I lived, but I lost my legs below the knee. I tried to sue, but the court said because of the level of alcohol in my blood at the time, I was at fault. Go figure. I'm mourning my daughter and I'm at fault. Anyway, I got a tiny compensation and pension. We barely survive."

"I'm so sorry it's been so hard for you."

Ivan looked off at the photographs.

"Every day, it feels like it happened yesterday. I miss her so much. She was so pretty, wasn't she, Elena?"

"She was."

"I think of what she'd look like now, that she'd have children, our grandchildren, and how you would spoil them and how happy we'd be."

Elena patted Ivan's shoulders and Kate said nothing.

Ivan inhaled a loud, deep breath.

"And then it happened," he said.

"Excuse me?" Kate was confused.

"Then, one by one, the years passed and we started to cope with losing Tonya. We were holding strong, then that Zurrn woman, that psychotic—"

"What happened?"

"She came to our house one night, banging on the door. She was a mess, drunk, crying. She'd been living alone for years. We knew she was the neighborhood whore, with men coming and going, that she took drugs."

"What did she want?"

"It was about two in the morning. She was drunk or high. She was nearly incoherent, but she starts telling us that she's been haunted by her fear that her son, Sorin, pushed Tonya down the stairs that day at the park."

"What?"

"We didn't know what to do with her. There she was on our kitchen floor in a heap of self-pity going on about missing her boy, who had grown and was long gone. She was going on about her wasted life and that she needed to go back to her homeland, wherever that was."

"What did you think about her fear that Sorin killed Tonya?"

"We didn't put any stock in her drunken mutterings. Later I talked to a cop about it. He said without evidence, witnesses or a verifiable admission of guilt, there was nothing we could do. It wouldn't bring Tonya back. Then a few weeks later the Zurrn woman killed herself."

45

Chicago

Kate drove away from the Plesivsky home excited and depleted.

The new information she'd picked up on Sorin Zurrn had alarmed her.

But can I put any credence in the ramblings of a drunken, suicidal drug addict who accuses her fifteen-year-old son of murder?

These thoughts, along with those of Sorin's upbringing, his intelligence, his strangeness, the bullying, along with the invoice dealing with Krasimira Zurrn's burial site, spun in Kate's head as she stopped at a red light.

It had been a long, exhausting day. She'd forgotten about the time difference, had missed lunch and was getting hungry. She had to get a room, recharge, assess things and plan her next steps. The closest hotels looked sketchy to her. She kept driving until she came to a Days Inn suggested by her GPS.

After checking in, she took a hot shower then called home, talked to Grace and heard about her day.

"That new boy, Devon, asked me if he could kiss me."

"Oh, my. What did you tell him?"

"I said no way! That's gross! I could get his germs on me!"

Kate laughed. The sound of her daughter's voice was comforting. After the call Kate walked to the Burger King across the street to get supper. *Fast food, cheap hotels, pressure, deadlines and only the fear of failure to keep you company. Such is the life of a national reporter.*

After eating in her room, Kate set up her tablet and worked, first checking for any new stories out of Rampart. Her stomach began to tighten a little in anticipation of what she might find. There were a few news features, but nothing new had surfaced.

No new identifications.

Kate took a hit of her bottled water and continued. She saw Davidson's message saying that he'd reached out to Viper through his sources with a request that he contact Kate.

Nothing, so far.

While Kate had gained some momentum from what she'd uncovered about Sorin Zurrn, admittedly, it was a tenuous thread linking the Zurrns to the document found in Jerome Fell's Denver garbage to the Alberta abduction, Vanessa and Carl Nelson.

Kate sent a message to Chuck and Reeka.

"I've found new, disturbing information on Sorin Zurrn. I believe we're on the right track, but I need to keep digging, to tie it all together."

After sending the message she made notes on what she still needed to do: ask Chicago police for the reports on the deaths of Tonya Plesivsky and Krasimira

Zurrn; check for coroner's reports; check the Cook County Clerk of the Circuit Court in case Krasimira Zurrn had a will. Above all, she needed to follow the burial site document, so she'd check to see if another company assumed the business of the original funeral home. She'd also go to the cemetery administration office and keep trying the Glorious Martyrs and Saints Church, pressing on all fronts for more help.

Kate was tired and decided to rest her eyes.

Sooner or later I'll shake something loose, she thought while growing drowsy. Doubt crept up on her again as she considered what she was trying to do, connect Carl Nelson to Alberta, Denver and Chicago. It was like the rhyme about the lady who swallowed the fly, then the spider to catch the fly, then the bird to catch the spider, then the cat…how did it end?

She dies in the end.

Kate jolted awake when her cell phone rang.

In her torpor she saw the hotel room, rain streaking across the window in the night before remembering where she was and fumbling for her phone.

"Is this Kate Page, the reporter with Newslead?"

"Yes." She sat up rubbing her temple.

"This is Ritchie Lipinski. You left your card in the door of my house on Craddick Street requesting I call you. What's this about?"

"I'm doing some biographical research for a story on a person who lived there long ago."

"What kind of story?"

"A news story. We're trying to locate a former resident, actually."

"The name?"

"Zurrn, Sorin Zurrn."

A moment passed. Kate knew landlords, knew that Lipinski was weighing the pros and cons of talking to her.

"The story would have no reflection on the property," Kate assured him.

"Would you mention that it's a nice place and that my father and I are trying to rent it?"

"That's possible. By the way, is your father Tabor?"

"Yes, he retired, I'm his son and I manage our properties."

"Do you recall the Zurrns?"

"Most definitely."

"Would you talk to me about them?"

"I'm at the house now. If you could be here in the next half hour, I'll talk to you."

46

Chicago

The hotel parking lot was not well lit as Kate, bent against the rain, hurried to her car.

How long did I sleep?

Wiping water from her face, she keyed 6168 Craddick Street into her GPS. As she wheeled out, the thought crossed her mind to contact Newslead's Chicago bureau to request a photographer meet her there.

No, there's no time.

Kate put her wipers on high speed. Lightning flashed and thunder grumbled as she navigated across New Jenny Park to the address. This could be the house of a killer, the place where his mother committed suicide, she thought.

And I'm going there alone to meet a stranger on a night like this.

Kate repositioned her grip on the wheel.

Maybe it's a risk—but I can't lose this chance to get inside the house.

She could handle herself. She'd taken firearms courses, although she detested guns and never carried one. She'd taken self-defense courses. She had a can of pepper spray and a personal alarm in her bag.

She always took precautions.

She arrived at the house to see a late-model Cadillac parked in the driveway.

Kate eased up behind it, then took a photo of the car with her phone, then another, zooming in on the license plate. Then she sent them to Chuck and Reeka along with a message.

Going to meet Ritchie Lipinski, owner of the Zurrns' house on 6168 Craddick Street. This is his car and plate. FYI, going alone. If I don't send you an OK within one hour call Chicago PD.

She pulled up the hood of her jacket, hurried to the door and knocked. Lights were on inside. Thunder rolled then there was movement inside and the door opened.

"You must be Kate. I'm Ritchie."

The man extended his hand. As Kate shook it, hers disappeared in his. He held it firmly for half a second longer than she liked. He was in his fifties, about six-two, with an expensive suit, tie loosened. His long blondish hair was slicked back accentuating his clean-shaven pockmarked face. A scar meandered from the right side of his lower lip, disappearing under his chin, which moved with his rapid gum-chewing as his intense eyes took a walk all over Kate.

"Let me take your wet coat," he said.

"That's fine."

Ritchie's eyebrows went up a notch at her refusal.

"Suit yourself there, Kate." He turned and cast a

hand over the empty house. Naked walls, naked hardwood floors. It smelled musty and looked as if it could use a good cleaning, maybe some paint. "I'd offer you a drink or something, but I've got nothing. I just came by to give the place a quick look, check the wiring and plumbing, see what kind of shape it's in before we rent again, or sell it, or tear it down. I don't know. This way."

The floorboards moaned and his strong cologne trailed as he led her to the kitchen, where there was a table and four chairs.

"At least we can sit and talk here."

He pulled out a chair for her but remained standing, leaning against the sink with his arms folded. Before Kate got out her notebook, she positioned her pepper spray can in her bag so it was on the top, easy to reach without Ritchie seeing.

"What can you tell me about the Zurrns?"

He looked at the ceiling, chewing.

"That takes me back a few years. The woman was nuts, so was her kid. But they never gave us any trouble and she was always on time with the rent, until the day she hung herself in her bedroom closet."

"She hung herself."

Ritchie nodded, still chewing.

"I found her. Dad sent me to check on her when she was late with the rent. It was awful…and the smell. I tell you, I had nightmares."

"Did she leave a note?"

Ritchie shook his head.

"Nope, nothing. She was living alone. Her kid was grown, long gone. She used scarves, tied her scarves together. Sad."

"Any indication why she did it?"

"Drugs, booze, who knows? We all knew she was hooking, but there was never any trouble. She told Dad that they were her boyfriends. Look, I never knew the woman and my dad didn't know her. And neither of us were her johns, if that's what you're thinking."

"I wasn't thinking that."

His gum snapped.

"So what can you tell me about her son, Sorin?"

"Him?"

Ritchie looked off at the walls as if reading a memory there.

"Creepy."

"What do you mean?"

"I'll show you."

"Show me what?"

"In the basement, come on. You have to see this."

He walked to a door leading from the back just off the kitchen.

"Follow me." The door stuck and he jerked it open.

Kate hesitated.

"Come on," he said, and tugged the chain switch for the light. "You want to know about the kid, you should see this."

She tossed her notebook in her bag and collected it. As she reached the top of the stairs she felt inside her bag, sliding her fingers around the canister. A disagreeable, damp, cold smell wafted up as she followed him down the creaking staircase.

It was dim and unfinished.

Pipes, cables and ductwork were tucked into the joists of the main floor. Spiderwebs swayed in the breeze Ritchie made as he passed. Empty crates and boxes were piled into one corner. Somewhere water was dripping. Kate heard scratching as a large shadow zoomed across the floor.

Was that a rat?

"Over here." Ritchie stood by a heavy wooden door with a large steel lock. "There's a crawl space in there, but I don't let renters use it."

Keys jingled and he inserted one in the lock. It clicked and he opened it. He pulled on the door, swinging it, scraping it across the floor. No light reached inside the crawl space. It was black.

Keys jingled again and Ritchie selected a penlight from his key ring, crouched and entered. "In here. You won't believe this."

Kate froze.

Should I follow him in there?

She checked her grip on her pepper spray and twined her fingers with her keys in the spiked position. Then she followed him in. He'd lowered himself to a squatting position in a corner and began raking his flashlight across the crawl space.

"See?"

Kate saw a row of cinder blocks stacked to make a small room. Steel circles were anchored in the wall.

"I found this after they moved out. My dad said it didn't exist before they moved in. Her kid did this. I thought it was for a dog, or something. Looks like a little jail cell—what do you think?"

Brilliant light flashed as Kate took a picture.

She had to take several more because her hands were shaking.

47

Pine Mills, Minnesota

Something's going to break.

Klassen County deputy Cal Meckler held on to that belief. He had to, because this case had been troubling him ever since he'd first responded to the scene in Lost River.

The images of the victim—her hands rising from the earth—haunted him. But he didn't tell his girlfriend that when she'd returned.

"Is it true, Cal? Was she buried alive? Did you see her?"

Some of the TV stations in the Twin Cities had called it one of the most gruesome crimes in Northern Minnesota. The Bureau of Criminal Apprehension had taken the lead with support from the FBI. They'd also pulled in more resources and detectives from Rennerton, Tall Wolf River and Haldersly.

It was a big investigation and Meckler had taken pride in how the BCA and FBI agents had commended him for his "solid, by-the-book protection of the scene." But after that he was assigned to canvass designated rural areas with the other deputies.

Meckler wanted to do more to help.

But that was all BCA had asked of the county.

For the past few days he'd visited the homes of people who lived on the southwestern edge of Lost River State Forest. One by one he tried to find out if anyone had seen anything that could help—any strange vehicles, anything that seemed out of place or out of the ordinary.

He knew these people. They were the kind of people who'd drive into a snowstorm looking to help stranded travelers; they were the kind of people who turned off their cell phones in church. If you visited them, they walked you to your car when they said goodbye and insisted you take something home with you, a slice of homemade pie or at least the recipe.

That something so hideous had happened so near shook them.

When Meckler told them, some of the moms and dads shouted for their kids in the yard to stay closer to the house. "A murder in the woods, there? No kidding? Hope you catch the guy." Others tried hard to be helpful, scratching their heads. "No, I didn't see or hear anything, Cal, but if I think of something, I'll let you know." Most would look to the forest pensively in a way that told him that if they said they didn't see anything, it was the truth.

And always, before he left, they'd shift the subject, almost in a respectful, funereal fashion. "How do you think the Vikes are going to do, Cal?" or "How's your car running, there, Cal?"

That's how it had gone.

He'd pretty much visited everybody on the list attached to his clipboard. The addresses and Meckler's responses for them would be collected into a digital map the BCA analysts had created as part of the investigation. For now, he decided to go to Bishop's General Store and Gas, get a coffee and say hi. Meckler hadn't been by since the murder. He'd expected that Bishop's would be on his list of places to canvass but was told that Rennerton detectives would canvass all businesses in the area.

But what do those guys know about the folks out here around Pine Mills? They don't know how to talk to Fergus Tibble.

Ferg hadn't been quite the same since a car he was working under five years ago slipped off the jack and nearly crushed him.

Sure, he could still do his job, and eighty-year-old Agnes Bishop had been letting him run the store since her husband Wilson died. But sometimes Ferg was slow remembering stuff and you had to prompt him.

Maybe those Rennerton guys did that. They were detectives, after all, Meckler thought after parking his car at the side of the store.

Transom bells jingled when he entered, taking in the smells of motor oil, coffee, butter tarts and fresh bread. Agnes let the local churches sell baked goods at the store.

The place looked empty. He glanced down the small aisles stocked with cereals, canned beans, soups and condiments. The floorboards creaked as he walked by the chip racks and the coolers filled with milk and soft drinks.

"Ferg!"

A door in a back room closed and a man appeared wiping his hands on a towel. He wore a khaki work shirt with "Ferg" on his name patch and dirty jeans. He had a salt-and-pepper stubble, and Meckler figured he was in his early fifties. He knew Ferg had no kids and lived alone.

"Hey there, Cal, haven't seen you in a while."

"Been busy, got any coffee left?"

"You bet." Ferg went behind the counter to the coffeemaker and started pouring some into a take-out cup. "So, are they getting anywhere with this murder, Cal? Are they gonna find who did it?"

"They're working on it."

Ferg set the coffee on the counter. Meckler blew softly on the surface before sipping it.

"Got any sugar?'

Ferg reached into a box by the coffeemaker, tossed a couple of small packets on the counter.

"Two Rennerton cops talked to me yesterday, asked me if I saw or remembered anything unusual, or 'out of character for the community' was how they put it."

"And?"

Ferg shook his head.

"I didn't see anything. You know how it is. Same old, same old here, the same old regular customers, a few travelers and the bird-watchers come through."

"So nothing at all?"

Meckler shook the sugar packets as Ferg shook his head.

"Not even a little thing that you might remember? Think hard, Ferg."

Ferg scratched his whiskers.

"How little are we talking, Cal?"

"Small enough to make a memory. Don't think it has to be some foaming-at-the-mouth crazy with a sign that says I'm a Killer, Ferg, but any little thing that you might remember that stands out. It could help."

Ferg folded his arms, lowered his head and thought.

"Well come to think of it there was this one guy, out-of-state plate. He had a van, nice-looking van and he was a big tipper."

"Okay, is that all?"

"Well, when I was filling him I heard a noise in the back."

Meckler stared hard at Ferg.

"You heard a noise in the back? What kind of noise?"

"Kinda like a faint muffled moan. I asked the driver if he had a dog in the back and I tried to look inside through his side window."

"What you see?"

"Nothing, the reflection blocked me."

"What did the guy say?"

"The driver said his wife was in the back trying to sleep, so that was it. I was real quiet after that and he gave me a fifteen-buck tip. That's why I remember."

"Did he have any other passengers?"

"None that I could tell."

"Did you tell the Rennerton cops about this?"

"Never thought of it until just now."

Meckler pulled out his notebook, checked his watch.

"What do you remember about the driver—can you describe him?"

"He was a white guy, I'd say about forties, bald, had sunglasses on."

"Wait. Did Rennerton review your security cameras?"

"They tried to, but they're broken. I've been meaning to ask Mrs. Bishop if we can get a new system."

Meckler rolled his eyes.

"Your system's not broken, Ferg. I showed you the problem about two weeks ago. Let me get back there."

Ferg stepped clear as Meckler came around the counter and looked at the lower shelf, exhaling in frustration at the monitor, which was a black screen.

"Ferg, I showed you how to fix this."

Meckler squatted to the lower shelf before the DVR, which looked like a DVD player. He pulled the system out, and studied the web of wires and cables running between the DVR and the monitor, which recorded everything seen by the camera in the store and the camera at the pumps. He tightened a cable for the monitor's input. The monitor came to life, sectioned, splitting the screen into two, one with live images of the store, the other with images of the pump.

"See?" Meckler said. "The monitor cable came loose."

"Oh."

"Darn it, Ferg."

The image inside was fuzzy and the image outside was too dark.

"Ferg, you have to clean the inside camera lens. It's way too dusty. You need to get up there—" Meckler nodded to the camera in the corner near the ceiling "—and clean it with a soft cloth." Then Meckler pointed to the controls for the outside camera. "Look, I told you the light changes outside and you have to set the camera to the auto brightness setting, here, so it adjusts to the changing light conditions. You got it?"

"Yup. Auto bright for outside. Clean the lens inside and check the cable."

"Good, now it still recorded, so let's see if there's anything here. Is that okay with you?"

"Oh, yes, anything to help."

"Now we need to know what day that was, the day that you got your big tip from our van."

"Well, I remember Molly dropped some bread just before he came so that had to be Monday, around noon or so."

"I'll enter the date and the approximate time, so the recording takes us to there."

"Sounds good."

Images of activity at the pumps appeared. Vehicles came and went with Ferg pumping gas, checking oil or cleaning windshields. But this time they were so bright they were difficult to distinguish, like staring into the sun at silhouettes.

"Wait, go back," Ferg said. "There! That's him! I recognize the shape."

A van rolled up to the pumps, but it was all in shadow.

"I don't think we're going to get a plate out of that," Meckler said.

"Let it play a bit, I think something happened after the van."

Soon after, the distinct silhouette of a police car rolled up to the pumps in the opposite direction as the van was leaving.

"That's you, Cal."

"I'll be darned."

"And you got a dash-mounted camera, right?"

Meckler nodded.

"If you had it on," Ferg said. "You would've got a better shot of the guy."

48

Edina, Minnesota

OMG, this is totally stupid!

Ashley Ostermelle slammed her bedroom door and fell onto her bed. She hated book reports—*loathed and despised them! They should be banned from the universe!*

Ashley swiped the stupid textbooks from her bed and they thudded to the floor.

"We can do without the drama up there, young lady!"

There should be some sort of United Nations law about what cruel punishment it is to make fourteen-year-old girls do reports on stupid books written by dead old English guys!

Why was her mother being so unreasonable?

Would someone please tell her why?

To order her to redo her essay or she wouldn't be allowed to go to Courtney's party was *just plain mean.* She'd worked hard on this thing. Still, her mother said that she'd missed the point, that she hadn't addressed the questions about the book's characters, about themes, about applying them to life today.

You can't be serious, Mother! I did my best! It's Charles Dickens! He's been dead, like for a million years, so why should I care about Great Expectations*?*

Great expectations.

That must be code for what parents have for their children.

Her mother was a nurse. Her father was a carpenter who built houses. They were both perfectionists and Ashley felt they wanted her to be perfect, too.

The perfect child with the perfect grades to get into the perfect school and have the perfect life.

Well, guess what, Mother? I'm not perfect. Maybe I'll end up being a crazy old lady like that Miss Havisham, living like a ghost in my gross bug-filled old house with my rotting wedding dress. Miss Havisham was dumb. You don't let your life stop after a big disappointment. You have to keep going or you end up like a dead thing stuck in the past.

Wait a minute.

That's it, that's a theme about a character you can apply to your life.

No. No. It won't work. How do I write that so it sounds all scholarly? I don't know. This is so hard!

"You stay off your phone and get to work, Ashley!"

"I am working on it! Stop torturing me!"

Ashley's phone chirped with a message, then another, then another.

Something was going on. It started with Breen. She had news about "an incident" she'd witnessed at school today. Nick Patterson, the boy Ashley was secretly in love with had just asked Shawna Cano for a date.

No! No! No! My life's over!

Breen was telling everyone that it happened after school while they were waiting for the bus and Nick just walked up alone to a group where Shawna and Breen were and asked Shawna if she wanted to maybe go to McDonald's or something sometime with him or whatever, and if not, he was cool with that, and how Shawna, who really liked him, said sure that would be fun and how Nick walked away smiling his dreamy smile. Everyone was now saying how that had to be the most romantic, bravest thing for Nick to do, right out there in front of everybody.

Ashley stuffed her face in her pillow.

Her life had been reduced to crap.

How did this happen?

It had to have been that day Nick had walked near her when she was at her locker with Madison and Madison was saying "Don't move," because Nick was standing three feet behind her talking to Brendan. Ashley wanted Madison to take a picture of him that close to her, he was so hot. Then Ashley thought of that horrible pimple she had on her forehead and began rummaging through her bag for her makeup. That's when her books and stuff splashed on the floor and when she got down to pick stuff up, Nick just backed away still talking to Brendan.

Like I didn't even exist!

Oh, my God. My life is ruined. I'm going to die. I need help. I need guidance. Still gripping her phone, Ashley texted Jenn.

OMFG where are you I need you!

It'd been several days since she last heard from her older and wiser friend from Milwaukee. And now she could really use help from an experienced woman of the world.

Like an answered prayer, Ashley's phone chirped.

Sorry, been mega busy with stuff. I'm here, I'm here, what's up?

In a series of desperate texts, Ashley told Jenn everything.

Don't worry. It'll be okay. I'll get you through this.

Thanks, I needed to hear that.

BTW. Remember how my parents want to visit the Mall of America?

Yes.

I think it's going to happen really soon. We should meet.

Definitely!!! Yes I soooo want to meet you!!!

It'll be awesome, just me and you!

AH I can't wait!

Me neither ahh!!

49

Quantico, Virginia

Carly Salvito settled into her desk at the FBI's Violent Criminal Apprehension Program and got ready for the new case coming her way.

The word out of the morning meeting was that a bad one had emerged out of Region 3, the Midwest.

She logged onto her computer, then took in her unit, the soft murmur of conversations and the clicking of keyboards as some forty crime analysts worked at solving crimes. The program, known as ViCAP, maintained the largest investigative database of major violent crime cases in the US.

Salvito's unit collected and analyzed information about homicides, sexual assaults, missing persons and unidentified human remains, searching for links among cases that were scattered across the country.

ViCAP was headquartered within Critical Incident Response Group—the CIRG building—at the FBI Academy about forty miles southwest of Washington, DC, nestled in an expanse of Virginia forest.

Salvito had come a long way from Queens, where

she'd been a detective with the NYPD, before becoming an FBI crime analyst with ViCAP.

Like most CAs, she was devoted to the program and its ability to connect cases and catch criminals. Given her background, she was good at assuring detectives that the information they submitted, particularly their holdback information, which only they and their suspect knew, was zealously guarded by the FBI analysts.

"I know your holdback is your case. I've been there," Salvito would tell them. "We follow your instructions to the letter. No other agency sees your holdback without your say-so."

Before Salvito scrolled through her files, she opened her can of cold diet cola. She preferred cold soda in the morning to coffee. As she took a sip her computer pinged.

This is it. Here we go.

The new case came via Minnesota out of the state's Bureau of Criminal Apprehension in Saint Paul. Salvito keyed in her security codes to the file. It had been submitted by BCA Agent Lester Pratt. She went first to the Details of Discovery section, showing the date that a homicide victim was found in Lost River State Forest, near the Canadian border.

She'd been buried alive.

The body belonged to an unidentified white female, five feet four inches, one hundred twenty pounds, age between twenty-four and twenty-eight. Her fingertips had been disfigured, likely with acid. Still, Minnesota had submitted them to the national fingerprint database.

Good, they were smart to do that. It could be a signature.

The victim also had a tattoo of a small heart with wings on the left upper neck. That was submitted to databases for missing persons. They'd also submitted a dental chart. DNA from the crime scene had been submitted to CODIS and other databanks. Given the backlog at CODIS, results might take a while, but sometimes people were lucky.

No evidence of sexual assault.

Salvito reflected for a moment before continuing. There was a lot of other detail to review but like most CAs, she then went right to the evidentiary mode, key fact evidence.

In this one, the critical piece of evidence was the tire impressions at the scene belonging to the suspect's vehicle. No other tracks or impressions were detected at that scene, aside from foot impressions believed to belong to the victim and the suspect. In the case of the suspect, it was believed he wore a size-twelve boot.

The holdback was the belief the suspect recorded the crime, arising from impressions from a tripod that were found in soil in which conditions were consistent with the time frame for the tire and foot impressions.

Okay, we'll just lock that away.

The tire impressions were made by 10-ply radials, LT245/75R16, load range E. The file included photos of casts, enlarged to show tread wear and other characteristics.

This is good. This is pretty unique. It's a solid identifier.

Salvito took a deep breath, let it out slowly, then, using the tire evidence, ran a comparison with other similar cases in the system for the region and states she was responsible for. She was in Region 1, and the states that fell to her were South Carolina, Maryland, New Jersey and New York.

Starting with South Carolina, she entered codes and information about the tires. In a few seconds the response was negative. Then she tried Maryland and found nothing. New Jersey yielded no response, as well.

Last one, New York.

She keyed in the information, hit Enter and within seconds a file was found. She opened it.

Goodness, this file's huge, with numerous victims and details.

She went to the key fact evidence.

There was a necklace with a guardian angel charm.

And tire impressions.

The tire impressions were made by 10-ply radials, LT245/75R16, load range E, the same as with Minnesota.

Bingo! Salvito clapped her hands. *Gotcha!*

The file had been submitted by Detective Ed Brennan, Rampart PD.

Salvito reached for her phone.

50

Rampart, New York

Driving home from the hospital in the morning, Ed saw his wife and son in the rearview mirror, asleep in the backseat.

Marie had her arm around Cody.

He'd had a seizure in the night, one that lasted fifteen minutes, which was normal for him. To be safe, they'd taken him to the emergency room. The episode was all part of Cody's condition and had passed, the doctor said. He was fine. Take him home.

Stopped at a light, Brennan rubbed his tired eyes.

He hadn't been sleeping. His frustration with the case had been keeping him up most nights because no matter how hard everyone was working, they had nothing new to help them find Carl Nelson.

Putting Nelson on the FBI's Ten Most Wanted had yielded tips from news reports, but none were concrete. And nothing had arisen in the search for the van.

The FBI's Cyber Crime team had picked up what appeared to be a trail of Nelson's old internet activity but it went cold. He was good at covering his tracks.

The warrants they'd executed had not led anywhere. The information they'd developed from the victims they'd identified so far had not generated any hits with local, state, national and international crime databases.

The Mounties in Canada hadn't uncovered any new, solid evidence tying the Tara Dawn Mae message they'd found carved in the barn's ruins to the Alberta abduction. The necklace element was still circumstantial. Yes, there were theories but nothing harder than that, so far. It could have made its way to the crime scene any number of ways. Still, the Tara Dawn Mae message was troubling.

In town, nothing significant had emerged from interviewing Nelson's neighbors and coworkers.

No new evidence had been discovered at the primary crime scene, although the forensic work there was far from finished. Thankfully, they hadn't found any new graves.

They still had eight homicide victims they were trying to identify.

The conditions of the remains continued to make identifications difficult. Not every case offered distinguishable attributes, like fingerprints, usable dental charts, tattoos, medical implants, clothing or jewelry. And DNA extraction for comparison was also a time-consuming challenge. Confirming identities of the victims was critical to the investigation.

Any one of these cases could lead us to Nelson. We just need a break.

Marie pulled him from his thoughts to immediate matters.

"Stop at the store. We're out of bread and milk."

Millard's Corner Store was four blocks from their

house. Brennan went in, selected a quart of milk from the cooler then went to the bread aisle. As he reached for a loaf his cell phone rang. The number was blocked.

"Hello."

"Detective Ed Brennan with Rampart PD?"

"Yes, who's calling?"

"Carly Salvito with the FBI's Violent Criminal Apprehension Program in Quantico, Virginia."

It took a moment for Brennan to focus on the significance.

"ViCAP?"

"Yes, sir. You recently submitted a case to us." Salvito recited a twelve-character number.

"I don't have the number with me, but we did submit to ViCAP."

"Sir, we have a very strong case-to-case link concerning your homicides in Rampart, New York, and another jurisdiction."

"What's the other jurisdiction?"

"Minnesota. A recent homicide in Lost River State Forest."

Brennan moved to set the milk down, wedged his phone to his ear with his shoulder, fished out his notebook and started writing.

"Can you tell me what the strong link is? How recent is this case?"

"That's not our procedure. As you know we respect everyone's key fact evidence. What I can do right now is give you the contact information for the investigator on the Lost River case so you can talk to each other. Let me know when you're ready to copy."

"I'm ready."

* * *

Across the country in Rennerton, Minnesota, BCA agent Lester Pratt, an early riser, was alone in his kitchen making scrambled eggs when his cell phone went off for the second time that morning.

In consideration of his wife, who wouldn't be up for another two hours, he'd kept his phone on vibrate.

"Pratt."

"Lester Pratt with the Bureau of Criminal Apprehension?"

"Yup."

"Ed Brennan, Rampart PD, Rampart, New York. ViCAP in Quantico gave me your number."

"They just alerted me to a hit saying I should expect a call."

After talking for nearly twenty minutes the two investigators agreed that their cases were linked through the tire impressions and other aspects. The next step was to share more evidence to find common links that would lead them to the killer.

Less than an hour later, Brennan had showered, eaten a bagel and was at his desk in the Investigative Unit of the Rampart Police Department.

There was no sign of Dickson. Most of the detectives were out. Brennan glanced at the case status board, the faces of the victims, the facts and the numbers: a total of fifteen victims, eight of them still unidentified. They'd now pursued more than one hundred local tips.

But ViCAP had come through, he thought as he went to his lieutenant's office and knocked on the door. Steve Kilborn was on his phone and held up a finger to Brennan before he ended his call.

"Something's up, Ed, I see it in your face. This good or bad?"

"Good."

After Brennan updated him, both men went to the captain's office and briefed him. After listening, Kennedy cupped one hand over his mouth and thought for a moment.

"All right. We can't lose time on this," Kennedy said. "Ed, you and Dickson get on the next plane to Minnesota and start working with BCA. I'll alert the Chief, the county, state and the FBI. We'll expand the task force. None of this leaks out! We can't let the suspect know we're this close."

After Brennan had collected his files onto a secure, encrypted USB key he went home to pack.

It was a huge break, but it came with a huge price.

Another unidentified victim.

Who is she? And will her death help us stop this monster?

51

Chicago

A lake-driven wind pressed dead leaves against the black granite headstone in New Jenny Park Cemetery.

Kate brushed them away and read the engraving:

Krasimira Anna Zurrn
Born June 29, 1945. Died October 12, 1998.
Beloved Mother of Sorin.

Tragedy upon tragedy, she thought. A drug-addicted prostitute takes her life because she believed her son had killed a schoolmate. That son is regarded by all who remember him as weird and creepy, a fact hammered home by what Kate saw in the crawl space of their basement last night.

"He built a wooden box in there, looked like a coffin," Ritchie Lipinski, the landlord, had said. "I pulled it out, took it to the landfill. I don't know what the hell that freak was into."

Ritchie hadn't given Kate any problems. In fact,

he'd let her take photographs and had promised to find ones he'd taken of the box.

In her hotel room later, she was tormented by images of the crawl space, Sorin Zurrn's history and her growing belief that it was all tied to Rampart.

And Vanessa.

Kate was getting closer to the truth about Carl Nelson. She could feel it in her gut, but she needed more than a feeling.

Earlier that morning, her phone had rung with a call from an administrator with the Glorious Martyrs and Saints Church who'd agreed to meet her. Since the cemetery was on the way, Kate stopped to see Krasimira Zurrn's grave site and take photos.

She checked her phone. It was time to go.

The church wasn't far. Its twin tower facade soared over the neighborhood. It was more than a century old, built in the Romanesque style with beautiful stained glass windows. After parking, Kate went by the ornate wooden doors, taking the sidewalk leading to the office in the rear, as instructed, and pushed the button for the bell.

A short woman came to the door. She had Cleopatra bangs and large black-framed glasses hanging from a chain around her neck.

"Kate Page, here to see Joan DiPaulo."

"Yes, I'm Joan. Come in."

The smaller woman took Kate down a hallway smelling of candle wax, linen and incense. They came to an austere office. A crucifix on the plain white wall looked down on the desk, computer, phone and file cabinet. The woman indicated a wooden chair for Kate.

"Now, my apologies for not getting back to you," Joan said. "We don't have regular hours at this office."

"That's fine, I understand."

"In your call you said you're doing some genealogical work?"

"I'm looking into the history of a family."

"Your family?"

"No."

"Oh, are you with an estate lawyer? Do you have a letter?"

"No." Kate put her Newslead identification on the table.

The woman slid on her glasses and studied it.

"A reporter?" The warmth in her voice evaporated. "You shouldn't have misrepresented yourself to me on the phone."

"I didn't. I said I wanted to research a family history. And here I've identified myself to you."

"I'm sorry." She handed the ID back to Kate. "I can't help you. Church policy forbids me from disclosing the private information of parishioners."

"I understand, but please let me explain the background."

"I'm sorry, Ms. Page. I'm unable to help you."

Kate didn't move.

Something had triggered a sense of injustice—an eruption of internal anger at how the church bureaucracy that had gone out of its way to protect criminal priests was now stopping her cold in trying to find a murderer and the truth about her sister.

"I'm a Catholic, Joan."

"Excuse me?"

"Maybe I'm not a good Catholic, but our parents had us baptized."

"I don't see what that's got to do with this. Now, as I've said—"

"Please, let me put all my cards on the table and tell you why I need your help."

"I'm sorry, I don't have the time."

"This is extremely important. It's information you should know."

Joan sighed.

"Please, ma'am."

"Be brief."

Kate began with her own tragedy, her lifelong search for the truth about Vanessa, then fast-forwarding to the discovery of her necklace at Rampart, the horrors there, the message and links to the Alberta abduction, the Denver suspect, which brought her to Chicago and her work on the Zurrns. Kate unfolded a photocopy of Krasimira Zurrn's obituary from the newspaper. "I need any information you could help me with on this family."

Joan read the clipping, shaking her head.

"I'm sorry, but I cannot help you."

Kate struggled to keep control.

"Does your computer have access to the internet?"

"Yes, but I see no reason to continue this."

"Please, one more thing. Then I'll leave. Go to this website." Kate jotted an address on her notebook and turned it to her.

"Please. Go to this site. It's important and it won't take long. Please."

Joan went to the site. Soon her breathing quickened as she clicked on stories about the Rampart case.

The faces of the victims who'd been identified stared back at her.

"I'd like you to remember those faces," Kate said, "because in not helping me you're helping the man who murdered these women. So later tonight when you lay your head on your pillow, just consider who we really protect and who we hurt when we serve bureaucracy without question. I'm sure a new face will emerge soon and when it does, I'll send you her picture. We know the killer will be especially grateful to the church, which could have done something to stop him but chose not to. Thanks for your time, Joan."

Kate stood to leave.

"Wait."

Kate turned.

"I don't appreciate your insinuating that I'm a champion of evil."

"It was directed at the institution. I'm sorry, but I have an emotional connection to all of this and—I'm—"

"Kate, tell me what you're looking for."

"I'm just trying to locate family members and thought the church might have records."

"We'll keep this confidential?"

"Like the seal of the confessional."

Joan thought a bit longer, consulted the obituary before typing on her keyboard. Within seconds it beeped. Kate was unable to see what she was reading on her monitor. A long moment, heavy with anticipation, passed before Joan typed another command and the printer came to life. She reached for the single sheet, read it, then turned it facedown.

"Krasimira Zurrn was a member of this parish and

her card shows that she'd listed her son, Sorin, as next of kin. At the time of her death it appears we had him listed at this address."

She slid the page to Kate, whose heart sank as she read "1388 Vista Verde, San Diego."

"Is that the only address you have for him? There's a notation."

Joan DiPaulo took the page back, drew it to her face and lifted her glasses to study it. "Yes, so there is." Joan then typed. Again the printer came to life with another sheet.

"Here you go. It appears Krasimira Zurrn had updated the information. This was the address we had for her son. We have no other information."

A sudden pulse of victory thudded in Kate's chest.

The address: *2909 Falstaff Street, Denver, Colorado.*

Kate had a vague memory of shaking Joan DiPaulo's hand and thanking her before she was standing in the parking lot, fumbling through her bag for her phone.

She had a plane to catch.

She texted Chuck to call her, then drove to the hotel to check out. Before heading to O'Hare she tried calling him but got his voice mail. Her heart raced as she wove through traffic along the Kennedy Expressway. After returning the rental, she got in line for a check-in kiosk to get her boarding pass. While waiting she scrolled the dozens of photos on her phone while growing anxious that she hadn't heard from Chuck.

She was contemplating calling Reeka when her phone rang.

"Kate Page."

"It's Chuck—"

"Good, Chuck, listen I'm at O'Hare heading home. I can put big pieces of the puzzle together. Huge creepy pieces, I think our guy killed a fifteen-year-old girl when they were in school together—"

"Kate—"

"Chuck, listen, his mother committed suicide believing he was a murderer. I can confirm Jerome Fell, a key suspect in the Alberta abduction was Sorin Zurrn. We just need to confirm Fell is Carl Nelson—I know we can—"

"Kate—"

"In his teens he built a confinement room and kept a coffin in it—"

"Kate, he's in Minnesota."

"What?"

"Don't fly back. I want you to get on the next plane to Minneapolis and get up north to a place called Pine Mills near the Lost River State Forest. We'll get a photog to meet up with you. I want you to write up your Chicago stuff on the flight and help with our coverage in Minnesota."

"I don't understand, what's happening?"

"Our Minneapolis bureau got a tip that some birdwatchers found the body of a white female in the forest and that investigators have evidence tying the murder to Rampart. We hear they're planning a major press conference up there with Rampart cops, FBI. The story's getting bigger."

Kate froze.

"Excuse me, miss, are you using that machine?"

Kate turned to an older man with a ball cap, then

stepped away, keeping her phone to her ear and swallowing.

She thought of Vanessa.

"Chuck, did they identify the victim?"

"No, nothing like that so far. Sorry. Kate, can you handle this?"

"I'll get on the next plane to Minneapolis."

52

Albany, New York

All right, here we go again.

Constance Baylick set out on another day of searching the regional, state and national data banks holding DNA profiles to determine if any new ones added to the system matched hers.

Maybe this time.

She'd been assigned to lead on DNA analysis of profiles collected thus far from the Rampart investigation to help with identification or links to other crimes.

Constance was a new hire of the New York State Police Forensic Investigation Center, part of the state police crime lab in Albany. She'd graduated among the top in her class at University of California, Davis, where she'd studied molecular cell biology. She was still working on her PhD. She knew her stuff.

Constance slipped on her headphones to listen to "Born This Way." Mother Monster helped her concentrate as she set out to work.

She had full authority to access CODIS, all affiliated databases and networks. She received all the newsletters, alerts and bulletins and was well aware of the backlogs.

Sometimes you pray and sometimes you get lucky.

She started by running her routine checks, locally, then with the New York State DNA Databank, then the regional systems.

Then she went into the National DNA Index System, known as NDIS, which held profiles of convicted criminals, people arrested or detained, unidentified human remains, missing persons and the relatives of missing persons. It was common for police agencies across the country to regularly search their profiles against new ones added to the system.

As expected, nothing new so far.

Constance continued clicking through the system. The song had nearly ended when Constance froze.

Ping. Ping. Two hits. *Holy cow!*

Constance yanked off her headphones, the music ticking at her neck as she checked the identifier number of the submitting agency: Minnesota Bureau of Criminal Apprehension. She entered her security code and downloaded the profiles.

These were two distinct forensic hits that the system had identified as possible matches with profiles she'd submitted from the Rampart case.

Constance immediately began working to verify that the two Minnesota profiles matched two from Rampart. She scrutinized and tested the genetic markers—alleles—comparing them to the first one until she had it.

Okay. Looks like a definite match here.

She went to the second.

It was trickier. It drifted into pedigree and familial

searches that required all alleles to match. But Constance knew that the target and candidate profiles could contain a different number of alleles, as was the case here.

What we have here is a partial DNA match. But it's strong enough to confirm identity. One person in the Minnesota case and a person in the Rampart case are in the same family.

Constance would swear on it under oath in court if she had to.

She began writing her preliminary report for her supervisor to send to the investigators in Rampart and Minnesota.

53

Pine Mills, Minnesota

After landing in Minneapolis, Kate got on a regional flight to Grand Forks, North Dakota.

Ninety minutes later, when she arrived in the Grand Forks terminal she saw a tall man with white hair and a friendly face holding a piece of cardboard with "Kate Page" scrawled in black marker.

She went to him.

"I'm Kate Page."

"Hi, Kate. Lund Sanner, freelance with Newslead. All set? We've got a two-hour drive ahead of us."

Along the way Kate worked on her Chicago story. After she'd sent it to New York she called home to Nancy and then spoke with Grace for fifteen minutes before she had to go.

"I'll be back in a few days. I miss you like crazy, sweetie," Kate said.

Kate then bombarded Rampart Detective Ed Brennan again with calls, texts and emails. Again, she received no response. She tried his partner, Paul Dickson. Nothing. It was futile, leaving her frustrated and uneasy.

Something's happened with this murder. Maybe they got a break?

The sun was setting when they got to Pine Mills, which was at the edge of Lost River State Forest near the Canadian border. Sanner had had the foresight to reserve two rooms at the Timberline Motel.

"You're lucky," the clerk said. "Everybody around here's booked up, mostly with newspeople from all over. Folks say it's got something to do with that murder. Do you guys know anything?"

"There's a press conference in the morning in the community hall. We'll all know more after that," Sanner said.

Kate was exhausted but agreed to have dinner with Sanner at Greta's Homestyle Restaurant across the street. Over club sandwiches Sanner told Kate he'd retired from the *Pioneer Press* after thirty years as a news photographer. He had a cabin near Thief River Falls, not far from here. Kate told him a bit about herself, then Sanner spoke up.

"Kate, when I got the call for this assignment I did some reading on the New York case," he said. "You've got a connection to all of this."

Kate nodded and told him the story.

"I saw that you were pretty intense during the drive," he said. "And I didn't want to interrupt you."

"I'm sorry, Lund, that was rude of me."

"No, no apologies. I understand. That was work. I hope things go well for you tomorrow, Kate, all things considered."

Alone in her room, Kate switched off the lights, stood at her window and stared into the night and at the stars.

What am I doing? My life is moving at a thousand miles an hour. I should be home holding Grace. But I'm so close, so close I can feel it.

She got into bed and as sleep came, she thought of the victim in Lost River.

Up here, amid the isolation rolling with fields, lakes, rivers and forests.

Such a lonely place to die.

Then she thought of Vanessa and cried.

The Pine Mills Community Hall was a sturdy stone-and-wood structure built by volunteers in the 1930s.

Police vehicles and scores of news vans, some from Minneapolis and Winnipeg, jammed the parking lot. Satellite trucks from the major networks had their antennae extended. Radio news cars lined the street in front of the hall. A deputy at the entrance checked and recorded press IDs.

Rows of folding chairs had been set up in the main room before a long table, with TV monitors on stands posted at each end and a large board, covered with large sheets of paper. A heap of recorders and microphones with station flags rose at the center of the table as reporters settled into spots while taking calls from their desks. Kate estimated upward of seventy news types were there.

Metal clanked as TV crews erected tripods, called for cables and batteries to be ferried from satellite trucks. Harried cell phone calls were made to editors, patched through to booths and networks. Data about birds, dishes, coordinates, feeds, airtime and sound tests were exchanged. Overgroomed TV reporters checked their hair, teeth, earpieces, mikes and helped with white balances by holding notebooks before cameras.

"Right, so how many known homicide victims? Sixteen now?" a TV reporter, his hand cupped to one ear, repeated into his camera. "Right. Fifteen in New York. One here, right. Sixteen and we're going live through New York."

As Sanner caught up and reminisced with other news photographers, Kate searched the men in suits and jackets lining the walls near the side and back, hoping to see Brennan or Dickson or at least some official she knew from Rampart.

She felt a tap on her shoulder before hearing her name.

She turned to see Brennan.

"Ed, I've been trying to reach you."

"Come with me."

"But—" She indicated the news conference was about to start.

"You won't miss anything. Come with me."

Kate left a trail of "Who's that?" and "What's that about?" and "She looks familiar..." from the few reporters who'd noticed she was being pulled aside in advance of a national press conference.

Brennan took her to a small office at the rear, crowded with several other FBI, state and county investigators. She looked at the grim faces watching her.

"What's going on, Ed?"

"Kate, please sit down."

Pierced by the sudden fear that it was over, she caught her breath.

"Kate, we're going to identify two victims arising from the forest scene."

"But you only found one?"

"The homicide victim has been identified and we'll release that name momentarily. The identity of a second person has also been confirmed. In both cases we used expedited DNA analysis."

Kate stared at him.

"Kate, one is your sister, Vanessa. There is no doubt. We've confirmed it by using the DNA you provided through analysis with the biological material found at the scene."

"What?"

"It's true."

"Are you saying—" Kate swallowed "—my sister's dead?"

"No, we're confirming that she was at the scene. We don't know her whereabouts. We don't know if she's still alive or has been hurt, but, until very recently, she was alive and at that scene."

Kate cupped her hands over her mouth as she absorbed the news, her mind reeling, her thoughts rocketing through the years of pain.

"Both names will be released with pictures and information," Brennan said. "Kate, are you hearing me?"

She nodded.

"Kate, Emmett Lang with the FBI. We met in Rampart."

Kate had a vague memory.

"We know this is a lot to take in," Lang said. "The evidence strongly points to a live prisoner situation, although we can't rule out an accomplice. We expect our suspect will be watching the news. We walk a fine line between public safety and protecting an investigation. We're criticized no matter what we do. In this case, given a safety concern, we're going to release a lot of information as part of a public appeal. We have other solid information that we can't disclose but we're pursuing. We believe we're very close to Carl Nelson."

As Kate stared at Lang, at Brennan, at the others, something deep inside detonated a lifetime of pent-up anguish and anger. Kate did all she could to control it, to use it as a weapon, for she realized now more than ever, she was now truly in a battle for Vanessa's life.

And they were losing time.

"His name's Sorin Zurrn. He grew up in Chicago. His mother committed suicide because she believed he murdered a classmate."

The investigators exchanged glances of disbelief.

"Kate, where did you learn this?" Brennan asked.

As she quickly related the results of her trip to Chicago and the links of Zurrn to Jerome Fell in Denver, Fell's link to the Tara Dawn Mae abduction in Alberta with its ties to Vanessa and Rampart through a message in the ruins and the necklace, FBI agents took notes.

"Everything about Zurrn will be in the story I'm filing today. That will be my statement to you."

Some of the investigators huddled and in hushed tones compared Kate's information to their own confidential aspects of the case. A few had started making calls, when a knock sounded at the door.

"Excuse me, but the networks want to start, something about satellite time and going live."

Kate returned to her seat in the hall.

The press conference was led by George Varden,

the FBI's Special Agent in Charge of Minnesota, who introduced state, local officials and those from New York.

As it began, Kate slipped into a surreal state, struggling to do her job while the painful truth about her little sister was unveiled before her.

Enlarged photos of Carl Nelson, age-progressed images of Vanessa and photos of a white woman in her twenties appeared alongside locator maps and timelines as Varden summarized the Minnesota aspect of the investigation, then its link to Rampart, New York. He outlined key points of the case, how bird-watchers had discovered the scene a few miles from here in Lost River State Forest. He reviewed matters chronologically with dates and locations but would not discuss vital, key fact aspects.

He acknowledged that the case now had sixteen homicide victims, many of whom had yet to be identified.

"Evidence leads us to believe that the individual known as Carl Nelson is our leading suspect in these crimes. Let me stress that this investigation is ongoing, and we continue to pursue a number of leads," Varden said before identifying the Lost River victim.

"Brittany Ellen Sykes, aged twenty-four, who was reported missing while walking to her home in Tulsa, Oklahoma, nine years ago, has been identified as yet another homicide victim in this case.

"We also found evidence that Vanessa Page, believed to be a kidnap victim of Carl Nelson, was also present at the scene and may be a prisoner in a hostage situation. Because of our concern for her safety, we'll be releasing more information in our effort to locate her and Carl Nelson."

As Varden outlined Vanessa's case, whispers rippled among the reporters. Cell phones began vibrating. Some reporters took hushed calls while shooting glances to Kate.

Then the monitors came to life with footage of a van at Bishop's General Store and Gas.

"The van is a silver Chevy 2013 Class B camper van. We've provided photos to you. We're looking for that van."

The driver, owing to glare and angles of light, was in silhouette behind the wheel.

"We believe the driver is Carl Nelson. We'll provide this video along with other pictures to you. The scene has been released. We'll have people there and we ask that you be respectful of it. Now, we're asking anyone with any information about this case to contact us. We'll take your questions."

For the next fifty minutes Varden and other investigators took a rapid succession of questions that covered nearly every element of the case. During that time, Kate was passed notes and received messages requesting interviews, including those from the major news networks.

She didn't respond to them. She had her own work to do first.

When the conference ended Kate and Lund hurried to his SUV and they drove to the scene.

"How are you holding up, Kate?" Sanner asked.

"I don't know. I'm numb. I just need to focus on my story, update it and get it filed after we get to the scene."

It was a half-hour drive to the state forest gate. From there it took another thirty minutes, following the trail marked by fluorescent tags conservation officers had put up to guide the press.

"Much of this area's inaccessible," Sanner said as they cut through the thick forest and stretches of fields, peat bog, streams, thickets and wetland. "A birder's paradise."

A number of news trucks had already arrived at the scene before them. Klassen County deputies were directing press to the site, which was accessible by foot.

The sounds of breezes fingering through trees carrying birdsong gave the site a funereal air. The scene was small, with a clean, hollowed-out hole in the earth. The excavated and sifted soil was piled neatly next to it. Other news crews worked quietly, respectfully around the scene, recording it from different angles.

Sanner took a number of shots as Kate made notes.

No one spoke. There was little to say, until Sanner took Kate aside.

"I'm going up in a charter with a Minneapolis TV station to get aerial shots. I can drop you at the motel, or leave you here to get a ride back."

"Leave me, Lund. I'll write my story here and catch up with you at the motel."

Before Sanner left, he showed Kate a shot he had taken of her. It was a head and shoulders of her at the press conference, a beautiful crisp shot that captured the anguish written in her face as she studied the enlarged photo of Vanessa.

"You're part of the story, Kate. New York was watching the live coverage and asked me to get that shot. Sorry."

Kate understood.

After Sanner left she walked farther into the woods, found a private spot on lush grass in the shade of a tree and took out her laptop. Her fingers were shaking as she held them over the keypad. She bit back on her emotions and forced herself into her zone to write fast, clean copy.

After proofing, then filing her story to New York, she sat motionless, listening to the birds, trying hard not to think, for if she thought about it all, she knew she'd crack and break. She didn't know how much time had passed before her phone rang.

"How are you doing, Kate?" asked Chuck.

"The best I can," she responded.

"I can't imagine how hard this must be. We're all praying for your sister."

"Thank you, Chuck."

"Outstanding work. Every Newslead subscriber wants your story. Every competitor wants to interview you. You're cleared by HQ to grant interviews, if you're up to it."

"Not yet, I'm still a bit shaky."

"Whatever you want to do on that front is fine, especially if you think it will help find your sister. We've got the Tulsa bureau talking to the family of Brittany Ellen Sykes. I've told them to ask about links to your sister, but you know from your experience what the chances are."

"Yes, thanks, Chuck."

"Our thoughts are with you. I hope like hell they catch the bastard soon. Safe travels home."

Kate got to her feet and walked back to the scene.

With each step she embraced the fact her sister

was here. Across time, across the continent, against all hope, *Vanessa had survived and was here! And she was alive!*

The realization jolted her back to the icy mountain river, feeling Vanessa's little hand as it slipped from hers. Now, by the grace of God, Kate felt it inching closer, inching back, giving her a second chance to seize Vanessa and never let go.

54

Hennepin County, Minnesota

The large property stood alone on the edge of a new subdivision.

A rusting metal fence protected several dozen wrecks in one corner. Next to it, there was an oversize garage and a big house. Trees and bramble lined the acreage. The nearest neighbor was a quarter mile away.

At one time, this was a rural auto salvage business. A few years after the owner died, it was rented to a numbered company, controlled, through a complex network of shell companies, by Sorin Zurrn.

Now dust rose in the wake of Zurrn's pickup truck as it cut along the dirt road that twisted across the rutted fields. He savored the isolation as he parked the truck at the rear of the house and hoisted two bags of groceries from the cab.

Inside he pulled out a wrapped chicken sandwich, a bag of potato chips, an apple and a bottle of water. He whistled as he trotted down the creaky basement stairs. In the faint light he went to a dank, cinder-block room that was about eight square feet. It was sealed with a reinforced steel-mesh door that was secured with a lock.

As he approached, something inside moved.

"Give me your bucket," Zurrn said.

He unlocked a smaller door within the main one and the woman inside passed Zurrn a metal waste bucket. Its contents made a liquid swishing sound. He emptied it in the floor drain, then uncoiled a hose, washed the contents down and rinsed the bucket before returning it to the cell.

He was still holding the hose.

"Look at you!" he said. "Get those clothes off, time to shower!"

The woman removed her soiled clothes. Zurrn unlocked and opened the steel mesh door. As he sprayed her naked body with the hose, water gurgled out the slat of the sloped floor and snaked to the drain. He passed her soap and shampoo. She immediately washed herself, as if this was a ritual. Zurrn rinsed her, then tossed her a towel and dry clothes. As she dressed he set her food inside, then shut the door, hard.

It rattled, shaking cinder blocks around the door frame.

He locked the door and tossed the hose aside, leaned against the cage-like front of the cell and watched her eat.

Still a glorious specimen.

"We're only staying here for a little while before we move on," he said. "You'll love the new place. It's breathtaking. Like you." His fingers traced the steel mesh as he watched the woman for a long moment. "Well," he said, "excuse me, I have work to do."

Zurrn went outside to the large garage, unlocked the side entrance door and entered. The air was heavy with smells of rubber, oil and gas. A dozen vehicles—cars, official-looking service trucks and vans—were partially covered with tarpaulins. The van he'd bought in Utica, New York, was among them. The storage shelves lining one wall held an array of tools, equipment, new computer and IT components stacked in unopened boxes. Another area contained racks of clothing and uniforms of all types. It resembled the wardrobe department of a film production company.

Over the years, he'd established several properties like this across the country. His "depots," he called them. Satisfied that he had enough resources to be anyone he needed to be or make any key adjustments he needed to continue his collection work, he returned to the house.

He had converted the dining room to his war room by placing a large table in the center. He leaned over it to study the pictures, maps and property records of the new Palace of Supreme Perfection that awaited him on a remote and vast expanse of land. Admiring the detail and effort he'd invested over the years, Zurrn closed his eyes and inhaled the dream that was within his grasp.

Then he sat in a musty sofa chair, kept perfectly still and contemplated his situation. He considered the news stories and that reporter. *Kate Page, prattling on. "My sister, my sister." Kate Page is a brainless moth blindly flicking about in my brilliance, an annoyance of no consequence.* Like the police, she'd never know the truth. Nobody would, because it no longer existed. *Haven't I established my superiority? Soon,*

I'll assume my rightful place among the immortals, like Jack the Ripper and the Zodiac.

They'll revere me throughout the ages.

Zurrn shifted his thoughts.

Recently he'd made some difficult choices on which specimens to terminate and which to keep as he rebuilt his collection. With a heavy heart he went to one of his laptops and replayed a video—a video he'd shared with a very select group who appreciated his art.

Oh, those expressive eyes, the sheer terror, evocative of my butterflies fluttering themselves to death in the kill jar. My pretty things, you make me tingle all over.

But it was all for the best. He needed to collect fresh specimens.

Time for a treat, a little reward.

Time for Jenn to send Ashley a text.

Hey bestie what's up?

Nothing. What's up with you?

I'm in Minnesota.

OMFG NO WAY SERIOUSLY?!?!

With my parents visiting kin in the country near Twin Cities.

OMG so close!

We have to meet at the mall real soon!

OMG YES!!!

Okay I'll let you know deets tomorrow!

YES PLEASE!!!

Then we can really talk. Will you be there?

Easy. I'll get away! OMG OMG YEAH!!!

55

Bloomington, Minnesota

I have a weird question lol don't judge. Have you ever kissed a dead person?

Why would she ask that?

The next morning, Ashley Ostermelle was confused. *Was Jenn joking?*

Um, no?? Have you??

My grandma died 4 days ago. They made me kiss her corpse at the wake. It was nasty.

Aw sorry to hear that.

She was sick. It's why we came to Minnesota. I meant to tell you.

But that's really sad, I feel bad.

Thanks. I didn't really know her.

Still sad.

Mom needs a funeral dress we'll be at the mall at noon. We can finally meet in person!!

Yes!

Meet you at the Apple Store at noon.

Ashley's plan was to go to the school nurse, tell her she was sick and needed to go home. They'd call her mom, but no one would be home to check on her. Then she'd head to the mall. If she got caught she'd say she was getting Mom a present for her birthday, which was next month.

That would lessen any punishment.

Ashley knew how to work the system.

By midmorning it had all worked smoothly. Upon leaving her school, she hopped a bus to the mall.

Riding across the city, she grew excited. She'd snuck off to the mall a couple times before with friends, but this was different. She was adventuring on her own, to meet a friend with whom she'd bonded.

Jenn knew way more about boys than she did and Ashley ached to get her advice on Nick and other stuff. Jenn had tried drugs, gotten drunk and done other things—*like kissed a dead person*—while Ashley lived her boring little suburban life in Edina, home of the walking dead.

Just shoot me.

* * *

A little over an hour after she'd left school Ashley was in the Mall of America standing outside the Apple Store.

It was 12:10 p.m. and she sent Jenn a message.

I'm here. Where are you?

As the minutes passed Ashley studied the streams of shoppers, looking for one who resembled the picture Jenn had sent of herself.

She was so pretty.

Bad news, was the response.

Thinking she'd been stood up, Ashley's heart sank.

What's up? Are you coming?

Mom made me wait in the car in the parking lot with my sick aunt.

Okay, I'll wait for you.

Mom may get her dress and then we'll leave, sorry.

Oh.

Everyone's still sad about Grandma's death.

I understand.

You could come to the car & we could talk?

Ashley hesitated.

Parking garages were kind of creepy. In the time she took to think, Jenn sent another message.

This could be our only chance to meet, Ash.

Ashley caught her bottom lip between her teeth. It made sense and since she'd already cut classes and come this far.

Okay, where are you?

West lot. P4 West Arizona level. I can see the main door.

See you soon.

Ashley consulted the mall's maps and cut across the mammoth complex to the doors to P4 West Arizona. The cool, cement-like smell hit her when she left the mall for the parking lot. Waiting in the garage at the doors, she sent Jenn a message. Few other people were around.

OK. I'm here.

I think I see you, what are you wearing?

A yellow top and pink jacket.

I'll tap the horn and flash the lights.

Ashley stared out at the lake of cars and vans.

A horn sounded, lights flashed, drawing her to a white SUV.

I see you!

I'll leave the passenger door open for you.

Ashley was nervous walking to Jenn's car. There were so many creeps but she told herself it was okay. She knew Jenn. They'd had many deep conversations. They were best friends and Ashley was excited about meeting.

I need to talk to her!

As Ashley approached the SUV's open door she was hopeful that Jenn would get out so she wouldn't be forced to talk in front of her aunt. *That would be weird.* Ashley glanced around.

The SUV was parked between a van and pickup truck. She inched toward the open door and gasped when she looked inside.

An ugly old woman was behind the wheel. Her arm shot out with the speed of a cobra, seized Ashley's jacket and yanked her into the vehicle.

A damp cloth covered Ashley's face, smothering weak cries until her eyes rolled back and everything went dark.

56

Hennepin County, Minnesota

The woman in the basement cell couldn't stop trembling in her cold, wet prison, shaking at the horrors she'd witnessed and the horrors to come.

I watched Brittany die. I saw them all die. I saw what he did.

Tears rolled down her face.

He's going to kill me next. He's killed all the others. I'm the last one.

She'd welcome death, because for most of her waking moments she felt like she already was dead. Years of captivity had shredded her sanity—her life was a never-ending nightmare. She couldn't go on. But each day a small voice rose from a buried corner of her heart urging her not to give up. It was a positive force reaching into her darkness to save her, imploring her to keep fighting. She had to keep fighting.

You're the only one left. You have to live to tell the world what he did.

Brushing at her tears, she searched the floor until she found her rusted nail, stood and resumed scraping it against the stone wall. He had called her his prettiest one, his favorite, and promised that he'd keep her forever. But she'd learned never to believe anything he said.

He was a liar.

He had always called her Eve, but deep inside at the core of her being, she'd never accepted that name. She had other names.

She scraped and scratched.

I am Tara Dawn Mae. My name used to be—

She stopped to remember her other name before Tara Dawn.

Next, she scratched a V into the wall.

It's Vanessa.

This is how she'd survived each day, by clinging to the faraway lives that she'd once lived. On the edges of her memory she remembered people calling her Vanessa. Those were the happiest times. She felt the purest, strongest kind of love. A bond she felt would never, ever, be broken. She remembered having a mom, a dad, a big sister, then came a sudden sadness and visits with relatives and strangers.

Those memories were like distant stars.

Those memories ended in violent, watery darkness.

Her next life began when she was rescued on a riverbank by her new mother and father. Her memories of that time were clouded. She recalled asking questions about her foster parents and her sister, then crying and crying, as the Maes told her that her life had changed, that God had wanted them to rescue her and be her new mother and father.

They'd taken her to live with them on their farm, where they called her Tara Dawn. She had a dog, kittens and she played with horses. She recalled the eternal flatland and the big sky, going to school and learning. Her new mother and father had given her a new life before Carl took her away.

Back then, he'd called himself Jerome before he changed his name to Carl. He made her tell him everything about her life. She was only eleven years old, but he'd forced her to tell him everything she could remember. Then he'd told her that he'd been sent by a secret government agency to save her from evil people who were planning to kill her, like they'd killed her parents and big sister in the car crash. He said that for her own safety he'd have to change her name and keep her hidden away because evil agents would be looking for them. Then one day he showed her some kind of papers that he claimed were official court documents and said, "You belong to me now."

He'd always kept her locked up in a jail. He'd feed her, give her a bucket for a toilet, a tub to wash, toiletries and clean clothes. He'd bring her books and magazines. Sometimes he'd let her listen to a radio, or he'd give her a TV that didn't get many channels. Over the years she'd lost track of time, forgot how old she was. She'd try to calculate her age by the dates of the magazines.

There was no hope of escape.

This was her life.

Sometimes Carl would sit outside her jail and watch her. Sometimes he'd come inside, chain her and do things to her. Sometimes, he talked to her about how beautiful she was and how she was his most treasured specimen. A few, rare times, he'd taken her outside the barn for short walks in the woods for fresh air, telling her he was going to be collecting new specimens. That's what he called them.

Sometimes he'd make her watch what he did to the new ones.

Carl was a monster.

Because of the things he did to her and the other girls he'd captured.

Their screams haunted her.

Vanessa scraped at the wall with renewed fear. So much had happened recently. They'd left the barn. *Why?* For a new home, Carl said, a better one. She never trusted him. He'd put them in boxes that were like coffins. He drove and drove all over.

Now they were here.

Why did he bring me here? Is he going to kill me here?

As she scratched at the wall, shaping letters of her real name, fine particles of stone sprinkled from mortar between the cinder blocks.

Something bad was coming, she could feel it in her bones.

Time was running out.

I don't want to die!

Becoming frantic, Vanessa scraped and scraped until she grew hysterical and was on the verge of screaming. She pounded her palms against the cinder block and froze.

It moved! One of those heavy blocks moved!

In her frenzy she'd somehow caused it to shift a fraction of an inch. How could that be? She bent over and examined the mortar. Much of it had eroded. She ran her fingers along the gap-filled seam, causing more mortar to fall. Recalling how the door frame holding the steel mesh of her cell had rattled when Carl locked it, she studied the mortar and seams of the blocks supporting the door frame.

Jabbing her rusty nail into the mortar, she discovered that it crumbled. Faint light passed through the gaps. Very little mortar remained to hold the blocks in place. She pushed hard on them and they shifted.

If I could push out the ones framing the door it might give way.

Wait.

Is Carl here?

She was convinced he'd left. The floor above hadn't creaked for more than an hour. No rush of water through the pipes. Certain she was alone, she began pushing and shoving the blocks, moving them a fraction of an inch at a time.

Minutes went by and her effort grew difficult then futile because she'd moved the blocks to such an angle, the door had wedged.

Nothing would move now.

Carl would see this. *Escape attempts are forbidden!* He'd reinforce the door, then he'd punish her.

Think!

She got down on the floor, on her back and, using her legs, pressed her feet against the blocks and heaved with all of her strength. The blocks moved. Grunting under the strain, she kept it up, shifting them to the point of teetering.

Vanessa stood and slammed her shoulder against the steel mesh.

Gritting her teeth, she slammed again and again until the steel door collapsed outward and she fell on it, as a few of the cinder blocks toppled with rocky thunder and a dust cloud.

I did it! I'm out!

Stunned, she got to her feet, breathing fast. Her pant leg had torn, her thigh was bleeding. Her forehead and arm were bleeding, too. But she felt no pain as adrenaline pumped through her.

She hurried to the first basement window—it was secured with bars. All of the windows were sealed. She'd have to take the stairs. Casting about for a weapon, she went to a workbench, found a ruler-sized piece of steel and hurried up the stairs. At the top, she pressed her back to the wall, held her breath and listened.

Nothing.

She moved down the hall. The floorboards cried out with loud telltale squeak-creaks as she arrived in the kitchen. She unlocked the door and stepped outside, finding herself at the back of the house.

Her skin came alive in the sunlight and fresh air.

Thank you, God! Thank you!

She ran down the dirt driveway.

Not knowing when Carl would return she kept close to the ditch. *Is he chasing me?* She kept checking over her shoulder and saw nothing. It took several minutes before she'd cleared the long dirt road on the property and came to a paved ribbon of country road.

Looking left, she saw the distant rooftops of a subdivision.

That way's help! That way's life!

She put her steel bar in her back pocket and ran down the empty road, struggling to grasp what had happened, scanning the horizon for a car, a truck, someone walking or on a bicycle, anyone to help. The emptiness of the region was underscored by the slap of her feet on the pavement, her hard breathing and the twitter of birds as she recited what she needed to tell police.

I escaped! My name's Vanessa! I used to be Tara Dawn from Alberta! He killed them all!

As she neared the subdivision, chrome glinted on the road ahead. In the distance a lone car was approaching.

Be careful. Carl drives a van. I know what it looks like.

Vanessa hid in the bushes as she studied the car.

Not a van. A white SUV!

Her heart nearly bursting, Vanessa rushed to the middle of the road, waving her arms over her head for the vehicle to stop.

Please, please, please!

The vehicle slowed to stop. The woman behind the wheel looked worried and moved to open the passenger door.

Vanessa ran to it, barely able to think—her years of imprisonment, the horrors of her life, all blazing before her to embrace her resurrection.

"Oh, God, help me! Please! I escaped. My name's Vanessa. He kill—"

In the next nanosecond her brain overloaded at the heart-stopping realization that the woman in the car looked wrong because her body was wrong, her hands were too big, because she was Carl dressed as a woman and he was now reaching for her. At the same time muffled screams came from the rear, a teenage girl sitting up, her hands and mouth bound, while she'd managed to nearly remove the tape from her legs.

Carl's big hand seized Vanessa's wrist.

Instinctively Vanessa stepped back and, with her free hand, reached into her pocket for her steel bar and screamed at the new prisoner.

"Run for your life! Out this door!"

With the blinding speed of a frightened bird the young girl flew over the front seat to the open door as Vanessa smashed Carl's head with steel, enabling the teen to scurry out the door.

"Run for help!"

The groggy teen staggered, then ran fast, but Vanessa was locked in Carl's grip. She hit him repeatedly with the bar, but her blows landed more on the curls of his grotesque wig. He'd managed to drag her into the front, managed to close and lock the doors as they struggled.

Within a minute he'd overpowered her.

Her sobs mingled with his savage grunts and the peel of duct tape as he secured her and hefted her like a roped steer into the backseat.

He turned and glared at her.

Under the twisted wig, his face was a hideous riot of smeared makeup, sweat, snot and rage at Vanessa for what she'd done.

The teenage girl was gone. Not a trace of her.

Vanessa whispered a prayer for her.

57

Greater Minneapolis, Minnesota

Twenty-five minutes after landing, Kate watched Minneapolis blurring by her window as Pete Driscoll, a reporter with Newslead's Minneapolis bureau, pushed his Jeep Wrangler over the limit.

The bureau had been tipped to the failed abduction of a teenage girl, which had happened earlier that afternoon. Law enforcement sources suspected the fugitive abductor was Carl Nelson.

"The information we have is spotty," Driscoll said. "The girl got away, ran for help to a house in Blue Jay Creek. I've got a name and an address."

"That's where we're going now?"

"Yeah. They've taken the girl away. I think she's fourteen. They're not releasing her name but we can talk to the person who helped her, a woman by the name of Evelyn Hines."

"Good, okay."

"We've got a shooter heading there, too. But we have to move. If I've got the name, you can bet the competition's onto it, too."

Kate had been wrapping up her story in Pine Mills when New York called her with the news out of Minneapolis. She'd called Ed Brennan. He wouldn't confirm or deny anything but suggested she get to Minneapolis ASAP.

She got the first plane she could.

Kate's stomach lifted as Driscoll sailed along the expressways. The whole time he made calls and sent messages to sources with his hands-free, voice-activated system. Kate called her sources with the FBI and other agencies, pressing them for more information.

The Bungalows of Blue Jay Creek was a new subdivision at the edge of Hennepin County. Evelyn Hines lived at 104 Apple Blossom Trail. They were relieved that no news or police vehicles were parked out front when they arrived. Kate rang the bell and a woman in her early seventies answered.

She looked at Kate, then Driscoll.

"Yes?"

"Are you Evelyn Hines?" Kate asked.

"Yes."

"I'm Kate Page, this is Pete Driscoll. We're reporters with Newslead the newswire service." Kate held up her ID. "May we talk to you, please? It's about a teenage girl. We understand you helped her?"

Worry clouded Evelyn's face as she considered the request.

"It's terrible, but it's true," she said. "The paramedics took the girl and the police just left. I saw something on the TV news. I suppose this is what you'd call a big story. Come in."

Driscoll took Kate aside and tapped his phone.

"Kate, we just got word, there's police activity near here. You take the interview, I'll check it out. Our photographer is on her way."

Driscoll left and Kate joined Evelyn, walking through her neat-as-a-pin home to the backyard.

"Thank you for agreeing to talk to me, Mrs. Hines." Kate took out her notebook and recorder. "Can you tell me about yourself and what happened?"

"Well, like I told the police, I've been living here on my own since my husband passed away three years ago. My daughter and grandson live in California. I volunteer at the hospital and I keep busy with my garden."

"It's beautiful," Kate said.

"Thank you. The azaleas, daylilies and rosebushes are coming along. I'm thinking of adding a fountain and a gazebo, to make things more calming, more serene."

"So what happened today?"

"I was working out here when I heard a faint cry in the distance." She indicated the vast fields behind the fence of her property. "It was high-pitched, I thought it might be a dog, or something. Then I saw a person running toward me, shouting, 'Help! Help!'"

"What did you do?"

"At first, I wasn't sure what to do. I saw what turned out to be a young girl running and shouting for help. She was running in an odd way, with her hands together. I thought it was a trick, or kids playing, but her tone was one of genuine fear, so I opened my gate."

"Then what happened?"

"The girl was sobbing. Her jacket and shirt were torn, streaked with grime. Her hair was frazzled. What

I thought was a necklace turned out to be tape she'd clawed from around her mouth. Her hands were bound with tape. I was scared for her. 'Dear God,' I said. 'What happened to you?' She begged me to call 911."

"What else do you remember?"

"I got her inside. She was delirious, clinging to me, afraid she was being chased, but there was no one. I cut away the tape. Police took that."

"What did she tell you?"

"She said her name was Ashley. That she was fourteen. That she lived in Edina. Then she was nearly incoherent, saying things like, 'She was my friend, but he's a man, a freak! He tried to abduct me—then he took another woman, she saved me! Her name's Vanessa!'"

Kate froze.

"Are you certain that she said the name Vanessa?"

"Oh, yes."

"Did she say where the man and Vanessa went?"

"No, just that he took the woman Vanessa, that she'd saved her, is what she told me."

Kate struggled to process what she'd just heard.

Maintaining a hold on her composure, on her incredulity, she continued asking Evelyn questions until Casey Mulvane, the photographer, arrived. After quick introductions, Casey took over, quickly, professionally, getting shots of Evelyn in her backyard by her open gate, looking at the field. The whole time Kate contended with the tectonic shift of her emotions.

We're close, so close to Vanessa.

Later, in Casey's car, they sped through the neighborhood.

"Look, those are the TV networks." Casey pointed

to at least three helicopters circling over a distant acreage, a wrecking yard and a cluster of buildings. "It's crazy there!"

After traveling a half mile down an empty rural road they came to the entrance, blocked with yellow tape and by clusters of police vehicles. Dozens of news cars and trucks had gathered there with a steady stream of new arrivals. There were more press here than Kate had seen in Pine Mills. Down the long driveway, near the house, were forensic trucks and other emergency vehicles. Investigators and technicians were working among the various buildings. News cameras were aimed at the activity, reporters were making calls. Others were trying in vain to squeeze more information from police at the cordon.

After Casey parked they found Pete Driscoll, who took them aside.

"Okay, this is what I know from calling my sources and a buddy in Homicide that I spotted in there." Driscoll flipped through his notes.

"Homicide?" Kate repeated.

"I don't think they've found any victims in there, Kate. After the girl got away, and the 911 call, they started to canvass the area and found this place abandoned. They found the van in the garage, that 2013 silver Chevy Class B camper, the one sought in the murders in Rampart, New York. The VIN matched."

"Anything else?"

"They found a small cell in the basement that appears as if someone broke out of it."

Kate stood there, absorbing every word as Driscoll continued.

"At this point, they think this started at the Mall of

America, where the teen was supposed to meet an online friend who turned out to be the abductor. We've got people from our bureau there. Anyway, they're pretty sure it's Nelson, the guy behind the sixteen murders from New York."

"This is wild," Casey said. "I need my long lens and tripod to get shots of the house."

"Excuse me? You're Kate Page, with Newslead?"

She turned, nodding.

"Phil Topley, producer with NBC. Would you give us a few minutes for an on-camera interview concerning your search for your sister?"

"Hi, Kate." A woman shouldered in with a card. "Kelly Vanmeer, FOX. We'd like to talk to you for a live interview."

Within minutes, Kate was besieged with requests by national and local news organizations. Amid the chaos, the emotional upheaval and her exhaustion, she found a point of crystalline clarity.

My sister was here, in this area, a few hours ago, saving a girl's life. Vanessa's alive and fighting. I've got to help her. I've got to keep the pressure on Zurrn. My God, he's going to kill her anyway. My silence would only help him. I have to scream for Vanessa!

One by one Kate granted all interviews, telling the world everything she knew about Vanessa, about Sorin Zurrn, Jerome Fell, Carl Nelson. She offered condolences for all of his victims. She found the strength to keep it together, for this was a battle and Vanessa's life was at stake.

You don't get this one. We know who you are; we know what you are and we're going to stop you!

58

Somewhere in the United States

After driving more than four hundred miles, Sorin Zurrn's body was still tight with rage.

When he'd finally stopped at a cast-off, godforsaken motel called The Slumbering Timbers, he nearly lost it with the clerk, who took too long to respond to the desk bell. Something to do with his hearing, he'd apologized when he'd emerged from the back, cigar in the corner of his mouth. Pleased to have a guest, he attempted to make amends after glancing through the window at Zurrn's vehicle as he registered.

"Betcha you don't get many complaints in your line of work."

Zurrn stared at the clerk long enough to make him uncomfortable. Then he tossed cash onto the counter to cover the night and snatched his key.

In his room Zurrn set up his laptops and started to work.

He had to think, but it was hard to concentrate in the wake of the day's events. He removed his thick-framed glasses, wig and goatee, then took a shower. Under the needles of hot water, he pounded his fists to the side of his head.

After showering, he dressed and walked across the empty parking lot. He'd parked in a remote, dimly lit section that bordered on a wooded area. His vehicle stood alone, hidden in the shadows. He glanced back at the motel. No one else was in sight. His keys jingled as he went to the passenger side of the black van with tinted glass and a small silver cross affixed to each rear window. Signs on the front doors read Vitalee & Denridder Mortuary Services.

A low rumble sounded as he rolled open the side door.

The rear interior was filled with heavy tarp. He threw it back to a reveal a steel casket, secured with a chain and lock. The lock clicked as he opened it and raised the top half of the two-piece lid.

In the darkness, the whites of Vanessa's eyes glowed as she looked up.

Her mouth was taped.

Her hands and ankles were bound.

"You know what you did, don't you?"

She stared at him.

"Answer me!"

Vanessa blinked, tears filled her eyes and she nodded.

"You broke the cardinal rule! I was in the process of cultivating a new specimen, *and you destroyed that, too*!"

Vanessa sobbed.

"After all of our time together, after all I've done for you, you betray me!"

He dropped the lid. Secured the chains then returned to his room.

Energized by his visit with his most cherished specimen, Zurrn resumed work on his laptops, reviewing details, making preparations, activating stages that needed activating.

Near him, the motel TV flickered with the latest on the breaking news out of Minnesota and its connection to the case in Rampart, New York. The case was a lead story across the country. He viewed a special report with caution, concern and a sense of pride.

Carl Nelson was the most wanted man in America.

Variations of his appearance were displayed on the screen.

Zurrn had no concerns. Few people paid attention and he changed his disguises constantly.

"The suspect known as Carl Nelson is believed to be responsible for the murders of sixteen people, possibly more, according to the FBI..."

Photos of the identified victims with locator maps and timelines of their disappearances filled the screen.

My beautiful specimens. Zurrn marveled at his collection.

The story zigzagged with images from the Lost River State Forest to Minneapolis and the Mall of America, then the property in a corner of Hennepin County. There was a range of long shots and aerial footage of the house and garage at Hennepin.

"...sources tell us that a fourteen-year-old girl from suburban Minneapolis was lured to a meeting with an online friend at the Mall of America. That friend turned out to be the wanted suspect, and after abducting the teen and driving to this remote property, they came upon another female victim who'd escaped. In the chaos that ensued, the teen says the woman helped her escape to tell her story. However, police sources tell us, the woman was recaptured by the suspect and remains missing…"

Zurrn turned the volume up for the next segment of the report.

"…this story continues to evolve with one remarkable development after another. Sources tell us that police believe the escaped woman is Vanessa Page, also known as Tara Dawn Mae, a girl missing for fifteen years from Alberta, Canada. Now, one of the reporters covering this story is Vanessa's sister, Kate Page, with Newslead. Kate has been on a lifelong pursuit to learn the truth behind her sister's disappearance, a story that reaches back to a tragic car crash in the Canadian Rockies. The tragedy, which Kate Page survived, led her on a journalistic investigation that has recently resulted in several stunning revelations…"

Kate Page appeared on the screen.

"…Kate Page reports today for Newslead that Carl Nelson had resided in Denver under the name Jerome Fell when he'd abducted Tara Dawn Mae. Prior to that, Fell was actually Sorin Zurrn, who grew up in Chicago…"

Zurrn froze.

Images swam on the screen, images of the life he'd buried, images of Zurrn as a teen, then images of his mother, of their home in Chicago, his school, his mother's grave, and the park where Tonya Plesivsky died.

Zurrn stared at Kate Page.

How dare she trespass on my pain!

Then came something about the FBI, the RCMP and warrants. There were images of police forensic units at addresses in Chicago, in Denver, in Alberta.

Zurrn groaned with rage and anguish as he glared at Kate Page.

She'd ripped open an ancient wound.

How dare she do this?

The camera tightened on the reporter as she stared into it.

"Now the world knows the truth about Sorin Zurrn. Now I know the truth about my brave, beautiful sister, Vanessa. For too long there's been too much fear and pain. We love you, Vanessa. We're coming for you."

Zurrn slammed his fists on the table.

"I'll show you pain! I'll show the whole world!"

59

Rampart, New York

Ashley Ostermelle is texting while walking from the Apple Store west through the Mall of America. She stops to check the directory before she exits. Now she enters the garage at P4 West Arizona, stops to text, then the picture goes fuzzy and she disappears from view.

Frustrated, Ed clicked and replayed the security camera footage, hoping to find something different.

How many times have I seen this?

The FBI had determined that Sorin Zurrn had breached the mall's stand-alone system. He'd managed to obscure the security cameras recording in the areas where he'd been active. Brennan had examined the footage and the rest of the case over and over, searching for anything he may have missed.

Come on. There's got to be something.

Time was hammering against them.

Zurrn had Vanessa Page and was likely preparing to kill her.

If he hasn't done it already.

Every detective on the case was going flat out, but after Minneapolis they'd made little progress in picking up Zurrn's trail.

I know I'm missing something that twigged with me earlier.

Whatever it was, it was gone.

Brennan left his desk to freshen his coffee. It had been four days since the Minneapolis break. He'd gotten home late last night and was up before dawn this morning to get back at it. The weight of the case was enormous. The task force was now having case status calls twice a day and had grown to include investigators from Chicago, Minnesota, Colorado and more from Canada. It had gained more profile—most network newscasts had led with it for the past few days and the press calls were nonstop.

Returning to his desk, Brennan reviewed the major points again. They'd found no trace of Ashley's phone. Zurrn must've removed the battery and tossed it. The FBI worked with the family's service provider and had gotten Ashley's exchange of texts from the phone and her tablet, hoping to get a lead to Milwaukee, if that was in fact where Zurrn had been operating. But that line of investigation soon dead-ended.

He was good at covering his tracks, but we've got him on the run and as we get closer he makes mistakes.

Forensic teams were still processing Zurrn's complex in Hennepin County, and everyone was optimistic it would yield something to tell them where he was headed. In the garage they'd found twelve vehicles, including the SUV used to abduct Ashley and the Chevy van linked to Rampart and the Lost River State Forest. They'd also found an array of commercial and service vehicles, like an ambulance, an armored car and a utility truck. Trouble was, they didn't know which vehicle was missing or if he had others stashed elsewhere in the country.

Zurrn was a brilliant planner.

No one who knew the area and the auto-wrecking yard would have been suspicious if they saw a trailer hauling vehicles to the property.

Investigators got lucky when they managed to lift some latents at the property. They'd capitalized on Kate Page's journalistic digging. Her work into Zurrn's past had impressed most of the investigators. The FBI and Chicago PD made a full-court press executing warrants on Zurrn. They'd learned that he had done a stint with the Illinois National Guard, which enabled the FBI to confirm his fingerprints with those found at the property.

Here in Rampart, forensic teams were still working at the scene. Everyone was grateful that they hadn't found more victims as they continued their efforts to identify those whose remains had been unearthed.

Brennan looked at the files on his desk, which obstructed the framed photographs of his wife and son. He looked at the case board at the end of the room. He knew what Zurrn had done. He knew where he'd been.

We need to know where he's going to be.

There had to be something he'd missed. Something he'd overlooked. There had to be a pattern, a puzzle piece.

Brennan looked at the map with its pins flagging locations, events, victims and time lines before he sat at his computer and scrolled through the folders and databases.

Wait.

He glanced at the map, then the computer folders, concentrating on the one holding interviews with Zurrn/Nelson's coworkers at the data center.

Who was that guy? Rupp. Mark Rupp.

Brennan clicked on the interview they'd conducted, reading fast, searching for the section where Rupp had recalled seeing Carl Nelson sitting at a coworker's terminal.

What was it Rupp saw?

...Carl was looking at a real estate page and making notes. Looked like he was interested in some property...seriously interested...he thought that no one saw him, but I saw him and I saw what he was looking at.

Brennan kept reading while shooting glances at the map, feeling his heart beat faster.

It was a coworker's terminal! That's why we missed it! This could be it! I think I know where Zurrn's going!

60

New York City

Kate stared at her screen in the newsroom struggling to forge a clear thought on what she should do next.

Since returning yesterday from Minnesota, she'd been pulled in a thousand directions. Reeka and Chuck wanted her to break more stories—Newslead needed to stay out front. Other news organizations wanted interviews. Grace was feeling the stress, too. She'd seen the TV reports, and kids at school talked about the case. She hugged Kate more often, tighter and for longer stretches.

Eclipsing everything was Kate's agony over Vanessa.

She had been alive and free only to be recaptured by Zurrn. Where is she? Each passing minute increases the odds that he'll kill her, if he hasn't already.

Kate's phone rang, the display showing an area code she didn't immediately recognize.

"Kate Page, Newslead."

"Hi, Kate, this is Sheri Young in Tilley, Alberta. We talked when you were here."

"Yes, hi, Sheri."

"You said to call if anything came up on Tara's, well, your sister's, case?"

"Yes."

"This will sound strange, but a raccoon burrowed into one of the upstairs rooms at Eileen and Norbert's place. It used to be a sewing room."

"Okay…"

"When they started to make repairs, they found something in the wall, a short journal that Fiona Mae had kept in the days after Barton died. We think you should see it before we pass it to the RCMP."

Within an hour Sheri had scanned some two dozen pages and sent them to Kate. Fiona's entries were neatly written in blue ink.

> We were camping near the Kicking Horse River in BC. The beauty of the place always helped us deal with the pain of losing our baby. Incredulously, during a moment of sublime peace, Barton spotted a child struggling in the river—a little girl. He got in the water and pulled her clear.
>
> She was alive, terrified and didn't speak. We put her in our trailer, and kept her warm and safe until she slept. All through the night we gazed at the stars, and this little angel, thinking this was a heavenly sign.

Fiona detailed how in the morning they'd learned about the horrible crash, the deaths, and the search, miles upstream.

> God forgive me, I know we should have informed the authorities that we'd found the child,

but our hearts were conflicted. We'd learned on the radio news that her parents were dead. We were convinced she needed a family and we were forever aching for a child. Barton and I believed that this was ordained by God. Suddenly, we felt whole again at having a child with us to love. We decided to keep her and name her Tara Dawn. In the early days, she'd told what she could of her turbulent, tragic history. Over time she stopped asking questions about her new situation, as she was accustomed to moving from home to home. But I confess, it tore me to pieces when she cried for her sister.

Instinctively, in the core of our souls, we knew what we did was wrong. We found comfort at church where we were bathed in God's blessing and compassion, for *He knew and He understood*, that we did what we did with profound love in our hearts. We had rescued an angel who rescued us.

Fiona wrote how she and Barton had devised the idea to portray Tara Dawn as being a child they'd adopted from a distant relative in the US. Fiona went on to say how happy Tara Dawn had become living a healthy life in a loving home.

Then came the day she disappeared. When it was clear she was truly gone I was struck with a lightning bolt of horror. We were being punished for what we did. It was too late to tell the truth. The burden of our guilt added to our loss. We felt shame in God's eyes. Our second child was gone, leaving us to live in agony and the pain of our sin. I fear it is too much to bear.

From there Fiona's entries trailed, to brief notations of the weather and her disposition. "Sunny, cloudy. So alone today. I can't go on."

After she'd finished reading the journal, Kate left the newsroom and walked around the block, absorbing the new information. For fifteen years she'd ached to know what had happened to Vanessa.

Now I know.

Kate was angry at the Maes, yet understanding. They'd never harmed Vanessa. They'd loved her. But what they had done was wrong.

She returned to the Newslead building.

In the elevator, Kate felt that the truth had somehow brought her another step closer to her sister. At her desk she sent a message to Chuck and Reeka.

I've got a new story coming, an exclusive— Kate stopped herself to consider what she was typing next; something that she would normally write if she were writing about strangers. She swallowed, blinked quickly and typed it anyway, adding to her note: And this one's a real heartbreaker, people will eat it up.

61

New York City

"Don't be nervous, it'll be a conversation about your sister's situation. I like your jacket."

Betty Lynne, who was filling in for a vacationing host of the *Today* show, smiled as she readied Kate for her live interview, which was less than a minute away.

Kate's last story about Vanessa had received major play across the country. While there were no developments on Zurrn, she knew that keeping the case in the spotlight kept the pressure on him.

During the commercial break, Kate checked her phone quickly for messages. Then she took in the lights, the cameras, the sets and the crew. The show was produced at Rockefeller Center in a ground-floor street-side studio. Through the glass windows she saw the audience lining the sidewalk, waving signs and cheering to get on camera.

Surveying the river of strange faces, Kate felt a ping of concern—*Zurrn could be among them.* But she dismissed it as unlikely. Besides, every audience member in the plaza had been subjected to a security check. Kate's attention shifted back to the set.

I have to concentrate. My sister's life is at stake.

Theme music played; a crew member gave a count-down.

"And we're back." Betty Lynne looked into the camera and read from a prompter. "In the terrible wake of the recently discovered horrific crimes in Upstate New York and Minnesota, the manhunt for Sorin Zurrn has gripped the nation.

"So far, police have linked Zurrn to sixteen murders making him one of the worst serial killers in American history."

Photos of Zurrn appeared on-screen as she continued.

"The FBI has confirmed that Zurrn, a computer engineering expert, who kidnapped Vanessa Page some fifteen years ago, is on the run with her. The fear for her safety is unimaginable, especially for her sister, Kate Page.

"Kate is a reporter based here in New York, but her connection to the case is remarkable, reaching back to when she and her little sister Vanessa, were orphaned by tragedy twenty years ago.

"Kate joins us now to tell us their incredible story."

The cameras moved to a two-shot of Betty and Kate.

"Thank you for being with us. Our thoughts and prayers are for your sister Vanessa's safe return."

"Thank you. And I want to offer my condolences to the families and the friends of the other victims for the excruciating anguish they're enduring."

"Absolutely, our prayers go to them, as well." Betty

Lynne paused respectfully, glanced at the notes on her lap. "Kate, tell us about your earliest memories of your sister, Vanessa."

As she remembered their childhood, a montage of photographs showing them as little girls came up on the screen.

"They were our happiest times—birthdays, Christmases, family trips, just being together." Kate recalled moments with Vanessa and their mom and dad leading to the point when her mother gave her and Vanessa each a necklace with a guardian angel charm. Brennan had cleared Kate to talk about it and a photograph of a necklace appeared on the screen. "That's not it, but we each got one like it."

"That necklace was a key link to this case, but we're jumping ahead," Betty Lynne said. "Tragically, it was shortly after your mother gave you the guardian angels that your parents were killed in a hotel fire and you and Vanessa were orphaned. How old were you?"

"I was seven and Vanessa was four." Kate touched the corners of her eyes. "That was so hard for us. After it happened we lived with relatives, then in foster homes."

"And it was while you were with foster parents on a trip to the Canadian Rockies that you lost Vanessa and your foster parents in that terrible crash. That must've been horrible for you. What do you remember of that time?"

Those tragic moments were part of the fabric of Kate's being. She recounted details as if she were experiencing them up to the moment Vanessa's hand slipped from hers; how she'd coped with years of having to accept that Vanessa had drowned and was gone forever.

"But deep down you didn't accept it. You'd always believed that somehow, some way, your sister survived," Betty Lynne said. "And you never gave up looking for her."

"No, because her body was never found. In my heart I always felt that she'd survived and I started searching for her. It was one of the reasons I became a reporter. If she survived, I was going to find her. I looked for her in the faces of strangers on the street. I did everything I could to find her."

Age-progressed photos of Vanessa on missing persons posters, social media pages and other online sites appeared on the screen.

"It turned out you were right and your work paid off, when your sister's necklace surfaced at the crime scene in Rampart, New York, and later the FBI used your DNA to compare with DNA found at one of the crime scenes to prove Vanessa had been there so she couldn't have drowned in the river."

"Yes."

"Okay, we're going to take a short break and when we return, Kate will tell us how she broke this case wide-open and put the FBI on Sorin Zurrn's trail."

Theme music played; a crew member counted them out and Betty Lynne touched Kate's shoulder.

"You're doing great, Kate, thank you."

As Betty Lynne turned for a makeup adjustment, Kate checked her phone, which she'd kept on silent mode. The show had wanted her to switch it off, but she'd insisted on keeping it on for any developments in the case. Kate scrolled through several supportive messages from former colleagues in Ohio. Others were from people at Newslead. Her brow creased when she came upon one that she didn't recognize.

I'm watching you. I have information about the case. I'll be in touch.

A little uneasy, Kate took a breath as a shadow crossed in front of her.

"I'm just going to neaten your hair, Kate." The makeup woman used the end of a comb to shift a few fallen strands. "There."

Music played and the break ended.

As they resumed, Kate told Betty Lynne how discoveries at Rampart led her to the case of Tara Dawn Mae, the little girl who'd vanished from a truck stop at Brooks, Alberta, Canada.

"What did you learn when you went to Canada?"

As Kate related the history of Fiona and Barton Mae, pictures of Tara Dawn were put up next to those of Vanessa, including one where both were wearing the necklace, which had been enlarged in separate photos.

"Unbelievable," Betty Lynne said. "And a few years later, tragedy struck again when Tara Dawn vanished from the highway truck stop near the Maes' farm?"

"Yes."

"And your relentless journalistic digging yielded the lead that pointed to Jerome Fell in Denver, who turned out to be Sorin Zurrn from Chicago, who was living as Carl Nelson in Rampart, New York, and was behind the crimes there, and in Minnesota, according to the FBI."

"Yes."

"Can you tell our viewers how you did that?"

As Kate elaborated, she saw a studio crew member flagging Betty Lynne to the time remaining.

"Kate, before we close, do you have anything that you'd like to say?"

"Yes, my sister has been in captivity for at least fifteen years. During that time, she transformed from a girl to a woman. I cannot imagine her nightmare existence. We're asking if anyone knows anything about this case to call police. Sorin Zurrn, if you're watching me now..."

Kate's composure slipped and the camera moved in for a closer shot.

"Sorin, if you're watching...before you met Vanessa, she'd already suffered more than any child should have to bear. I've discovered some things about your life. I know that you suffered, too. You've already shown the world by what you've done just how smart you are. Show everyone how powerful you really are by giving Vanessa her life back." Tears rolled down Kate's face. "Please, I'm begging you, Sorin."

The show closed the segment in silence and went to commercial.

"Thank you, Kate." Betty Lynne blinked back tears as crew members came to Kate. One started unclipping her microphone while the makeup woman passed her a tissue.

"That was extremely moving, Kate. Thank you for being on our show," one of the senior producers said. "We'll have someone go with you to the car, if you like."

Before leaving the studio Kate stopped off at a restroom, splashed water on her face. Then she took out her phone and responded to her anonymous message.

Who are you? What information do you have?

An assistant walked Kate to the street where a driver opened the rear door of a polished black sedan. The car service was waiting to take her to Newslead, as had been arranged. Kate got in and buckled up.

As the car pulled into Midtown traffic Kate's phone rang. It was Grace.

"Hi, sweetie."

"I saw you on TV, Mom. It made me sad."

"It made me sad, too."

"But maybe it will help us find Aunt Vanessa."

"That's what we're praying for. Now, hurry up. Don't be late for school. We'll get a pizza tonight if you want, or we can ask Nancy if she'd like to go out somewhere nice with us."

"Okay, I'll ask her. I love you, bye."

"Love you too, bye."

After the call, Kate searched her messages for a response from her anonymous tipster. There were many messages from friends who'd seen her on *Today.* Chuck wrote: You did great! While Reeka said: It looked good but not once did they say you worked for Newslead. Kate also received interview requests from *USA Today*, the *Wall Street Journal* and *ABC News*, but nothing from the anonymous messenger.

She searched news sites for updates on the case. Nothing was happening. Watching Manhattan roll by, Kate rested her head on the high-backed seat. These past few days of her life had been a surreal blur. But she couldn't stop. She had to go full tilt until she found Vanessa.

One way or another I will find you, I swear.

"Miss?"

Kate surfaced from her thoughts to the sounds of the street. They'd arrived. The car was parked in front of the building where Newslead was headquartered. The driver was holding the car door open for her.

"Yes, sorry." She reached into her bag and her wallet. She put a twenty in the driver's hand.

Kate stepped toward the entrance but stopped upon seeing a man staring at her. His back was against the building. He had short, slicked-back hair, a stubbled beard, dark glasses and an untucked denim shirt under his leather jacket.

"Viper? I mean, Erich?"

"There's something you need to see. Let's go."

62

New York City

"Yes, I messaged you anonymously when you were on the show," Erich told Kate as they stood in line for a booth.

"Why so cryptic? You scared me."

"I had to get your attention and I had to be careful."

"What do I need to see, Erich?"

"Wait till we sit down."

They had walked three blocks east to the Wyoming Diner, a classic eatery wrapped in battered chrome-and-blue trim. TVs were suspended at each end of the dining room, where every booth and stool was taken. The midmorning breakfast crowd was still thick with commuters from Penn Station. Ten minutes passed before a spot opened up. Erich ordered whole wheat toast and tomato juice, Kate got a bagel and water.

She welcomed the din of the busy diner. It made it hard to hear and insured a measure of privacy as Erich leaned to Kate.

"Are you familiar with shock sites?"

"That's where freaks and people with fetishes post gross stuff online."

"The content is obscene, vulgar and so graphic it's often illegal."

"There're some notorious ones," Kate said.

Two women at a booth nearby were looking at them and talking. They were too far away to hear through the noise but seemed interested in Kate.

"Some of these sites have their own subcultures," Erich said. "And in some cases the sites are gateways to others that are far worse."

"What're you getting at?"

"I found something alarming on one of them."

As Erich reached for his phone, a woman materialized at their table. She looked to be in her midfifties.

"Excuse me," she said to Kate, who, as she turned to the woman, accidentally knocked her bag from her seat to the floor.

"I'll get that for you," Erich leaned over and reached under the table to retrieve Kate's bag.

"Yes?" Kate said to the woman.

"My friend couldn't help but notice—" the woman nodded to one of the TVs "—but weren't you just on the *Today* show? You're looking for your long-lost sister who's caught up in the big serial killer case?"

"Yes."

"We just want you to know that we're praying for you and your sister."

"Thank you. That's very kind."

"Would you mind—" the woman waved over her friend "—if we got our picture taken with you?"

"I don't think it would be appropria—"

"Please, it'll just be a sec, here." She passed her

phone to Erich. "I'm sure this nice young man would take it for us?"

The two women got up close to Kate and Erich took the picture. The women thanked them and left. When Kate and Erich were alone again, Erich brought out his phone.

"So what is it?" Kate asked. "What did you find?"

"There's a site, hidden under layers of others, that purports to host videos of actual amputations, decapitations, cruelties of anything you can imagine."

Kate said nothing.

"Lately there's been a lot of hype about a series of postings called 'Scenes from the Kill Jar.' A kill jar is used in the collection of insects, like butterflies—"

"Butterflies?"

"Kate, it looks like Zurrn has been posting video recordings of some of his murders and tortures of women."

Their food arrived. Kate glanced at Erich's glass, nearly glowing red with tomato juice.

"Kate, you asked me to help you. I know these are some of the most graphic images you could ever view, but do you want to see them? I have about six minutes. It's hard to tell, but I think he made your sister watch his work."

Kate hesitated as her mind reeled. As a journalist she'd seen horrible things. And as a journalist it was her job to gather and see all the facts for her work. As Vanessa's sister, Kate accepted that if she was to understand what she'd endured, looking at the video was something she must do.

I'm sure Zurrn never gave her the chance to look away.

Kate stared at Erich's phone and the earphones he held out.

"Okay."

Erich cued up the video, set the volume and passed his phone to Kate. The clarity, sharpness and sound were extremely high quality. Tears filled her eyes as she realized what she was seeing, hearing and feeling. By the time it ended she was drained and overwhelmed with violation and outrage.

"Pretty bad," Erich said.

Kate swallowed and brushed at her tears before pushing her food aside.

"I can make you a copy to have for your research."

Kate nodded.

"Kate, I know this is disturbing but it's a good thing. It's a key lead. I've arranged for copies and information to be sent to every police agency on the task force looking for Zurrn. You can bet the FBI is searching for the trail to Zurrn. And there are protocols I can run to try to track Zurrn down. It brings us a step closer to him."

"It also brings my sister closer to death."

63

Somewhere in the United States

Vanessa rocked gently in and out of consciousness, lost in a black chasm of dull, lethargic awareness.

She was on the floor of a moving vehicle, feeling the drone of its wheels, the rhythmic sway of its suspension. She was under a tarp.

No longer in the box—the casket.

I'm groggy. Carl drugged me. He drugs me whenever he's transferring me—or preparing something bad—so I can't resist.

Where are we? What's he doing?

The vehicle jerked, triggering a sudden heavy clank of metal. Like tools and equipment.

Oh, God, this is it!

Vanessa's mind swirled with fear and emotion. She had no sense of direction, no sense of time. How many days has it been since she'd escaped and was recaptured? Maybe she was sleeping, dreaming?

Why did he take me out of the casket? Where's the casket?

Fear swelled inside her until she forced herself to

become calm, to relax, to find her favorite memories and hang on to them.

I'm in a park on a swing with my big sister. Mom and Dad are pushing us and my tummy tickles like I'm flying—it feels so good I scream.

The vehicle slowed to a crawl.

The road under the wheels had become soft, silent, like well-kept grass.

Where are we?

Calm washed over her in waves—the drugs—she wanted to sleep. *No, don't sleep. Be aware. Try to escape.* But her head was so heavy.

They stopped.

The transmission shifted, the motor switched off.

A slight sway and a door opened, then air rushed in as other doors were opened. Tools knocked together. *He's moving things, equipment, grunting as he lifts things, then humming as he works nearby.*

In the quiet she heard crickets and nothing else.

"Okay," Carl said. "I think we're ready."

A moment later the tarp was pulled away and Carl's hands slipped under her as he lifted her, and in an instant she saw what awaited her. A steel casket, its lid yawning, was positioned atop an open grave on a casket-lowering device. As Carl carried her to it, her screams were stifled by tape he'd put around her mouth. She struggled in vain as he placed her in the coffin and secured her inside with chains. He taped her wrists, fastened clips to her fingers and something to her body.

"Listen to me—shh-shh—listen. I'm going to remove the tape from your mouth so you can breathe easier, okay? No more noise or the tape goes back. Nod if you agree."

She nodded. He removed the tape and she drank in fresh air.

"Please, Carl," she whispered. "Don't do this, please!"

"Shh-shh. I've customized this. I've installed an oxygen tank with a meter, a ventilator to keep your carbon dioxide level low. You'll have a light and instructions. Once I set things in motion, you'll have a little more than four hours, if you don't struggle and use up oxygen quickly. Do you understand?"

No, she didn't understand. How could she understand his cruelty?

"Do you understand?"

She gave him a weak, terrified nod.

"Good. I'm sorry but it's all for the best. You really were my favorite." He looked at her, absorbing her. "I chose this specific spot because of its history. In a few hours you and I will be the most famous people on earth. You'll be immortalized. People will realize who I really am and they will revere me."

Carl shut the lid and darkness swallowed Vanessa.

She felt the scrape of the chains as he locked them. She heard him turn the crank handle, release the brake, then the gears began clicking on the device as the casket descended slowly into the grave.

Several moments later it ceased with a soft thud.

Then came the sound of dirt raining on the lid. It was steady before it faded, grew muffled, then died away.

64

New York City

Is my sister dead?

The question hammered at Kate as she showered.

It had been a week since Minneapolis and nothing on Vanessa's location had surfaced. No leads on where she was, nothing but the anguish of knowing that for a burning moment she had been alive and free to save a young girl before Zurrn clawed her back into hell.

After Kate got dressed she got Grace off to school. Nancy, who'd been a saint through all of this, would pick her up and take her to a sleepover at her friend Hayley's because Kate planned to work late.

On the subway, Kate was haunted by the images from the shock site videos. Brennan had assured her that the FBI and other police agencies on the task force were going all out trying to track them, but so far they had nothing.

At the office she got coffee, went to her desk and started working. It wasn't long before Reeka was standing next to her, nose in her phone, thumbs blurring as she worked on the daily news sked.

"What've you got for today?"

"Nothing concrete, following up on a few things."

"We need news on the story, Kate."

"I know."

"We've had absolutely nothing in the past few days. Subscribers are getting weary of recaps and situationals. We need to break something."

"Don't you think I know that?"

Nearby, conversations trailed off and heads turned to them.

"No one on this planet wants that more than me, Reeka!"

A long moment of silence passed before Chuck joined Reeka at Kate's desk.

"Is everything all right here?"

Chuck's attention went from Kate to Reeka and back again.

Kate stared at her monitor, said nothing.

"Kate," Chuck said, "I know these past few days have been hell for you. I've got every bureau looking into Vanessa's case. You know that."

Kate nodded.

"And if you need time off, you've got it. You know that, too."

Kate covered her face with her hands to salvage her composure.

"I will see this through," she said. "I'll keep working."

Chuck let a few seconds pass to melt the tension.

"All right," he said. "It's obvious you'll give us a story when you have one." Then he looked at Reeka as he said, "I don't think we need to ask you for it."

* * *

Kate spent the rest of the morning going through her messages. She was still getting a steady stream from her *Today* show appearance, things like:

We're praying for you and your sister.

Such a tragic story. God bless you.

My brother's got a hunting dog who could find your sister.

Aliens took your sister.

I'm psychic and your sister's a spirit now.

Saw you on TV; you're clearly a bitch who is doing this to make a name for yourself.

Kate kept working, contacting people she'd talked to in Rampart, in Chicago, in Minnesota, in Denver and Alberta. She called her sources with missing persons agencies and she searched databases. When her stomach rumbled, she got a sandwich at the deli downstairs and ate at her desk.

Nothing was emerging.

Commentators on the network news shows speculated that Zurrn had committed a murder-suicide and that it was only a matter of time before he was found. Others believed Zurrn would succumb to being the most wanted fugitive in the country and make a mistake. There were those who were convinced Zurrn would attempt to grab the spotlight in some disturbing fashion.

Despite the national media attention, despite all the tips to the task force, nothing new had surfaced, at least nothing that the investigators were willing to discuss. Kate had a vague feeling that something was happening but no matter how she tried, she couldn't nail it down.

Nobody was talking.

By the time she lifted her head from her desk it was early evening and most of the day-side staff had gone. The smaller night crew was working quietly. As darkness fell, Kate went to the windows and studied the lights of Midtown Manhattan.

Exhausted, frustrated and fearful, Kate felt a lump rising in her throat with a mounting sense of defeat. She had to accept that Zurrn was going to kill Vanessa, if he hadn't done it already.

That was how this was going to end. Kate would never see her sister.

I had her and she slipped away from me again.

She ached to see Vanessa, to hold her, to comfort her, to tell her how much she loved her and that everything would be okay. They probably wouldn't even recognize each other, but that wouldn't matter because they'd know the bond that had survived.

Somewhere in the skyline's glimmering lights Kate found hope.

What am I doing? I can't give up. There's no proof of anything. After all she's been through Vanessa hasn't given up! I've got to keep fighting to find her!

Kate returned to her desk, intending to call Brennan and push him hard for information.

As she reached for her phone it rang.

The number was blocked.

"Newslead, Kate Page."

Kate heard nothing.

"Hello," she said, "this is Kate Page at Newslead."

"I saw you on TV."

The caller's voice was robotic, monotone as if coming from a voice changer or electronic synthesizer.

Her thoughts raced.

Was this a joke? Was this Erich being cryptic again?

"Who is this?"

"Are you at a computer? Check your email and the link I've sent you."

Wedging the phone to her ear with her shoulder, Kate typed quickly, moved her mouse, found a new email and froze upon reading the subject line: Final Scene from The Kill Jar.

"Did you find it? Open the link."

Holding her breath, Kate clicked on the link. It went to a live feed of a woman, her eyes wide with terror.

"Say goodbye to your sister. I put her in her grave so you and the world can watch her die."

65

New York City

No, this can't be real!

Kate was rooted in shock.

The woman's face—*Vanessa's face*—was creased with terror. Her lips were moving, *like she's praying.* Her upper body filled Kate's monitor. At the bottom of the frame graphics of meters flashed while measuring her blood and heart rates; the level of carbon dioxide; the remaining amount of oxygen. A digital clock counted down the hours, minutes and seconds, left on Vanessa's life.

Kate's hands were trembling when she called 911.

"Police operator, what's your emergency?"

"I need to report a woman buried alive in a coffin! She doesn't have much time—"

"What is your name and location, ma'am?"

"Kate Page, 470 West 33rd Street, Newslead."

"Where's the woman buried, what's the location?"

"I don't know! It's online with a live feed!"

"Online? Do you have a web address?"

"It's—hang on—it's 'ScenesFromTheKillJar,' all one word."

The operator repeated it twice as Kate heard the rapid clicking of a keyboard.

"You've got to track it, find her!" Kate said. "She's running out of time! I'm a reporter with Newslead. This is the Sorin Zurrn case. Someone called me two minutes ago, telling me about the live video. I think it's Zurrn. Alert Detective Ed Brennan, with the Rampart police department, the FBI, the task force!"

"Stay on the line."

"Hurry, she's got three hours and fifty-five minutes left!"

Two night editors were drawn to Kate's desk.

"What the hell? Is this real?" Brad Davis stared at her screen.

Kate nodded big nods, knowing that Davis, who handled copy from reporters in crisis spots around the world, had one of the quickest minds at Newslead. He turned to Phil Keelor, the junior editor.

"Call our twenty-four-hour IT people. We're going to need all the help we can get," Davis said. "I'll call Chuck to alert the honchos. We've got to move fast."

"Okay, Kate?" the operator said.

"Yes!"

"We've got people on the way to you."

Within the first hour the newsroom had filled with uniformed NYPD officers, detectives, FBI agents and investigators from several other federal agencies. They'd set up quickly in the newsroom. They were monitoring Kate's phone in case Zurrn called again. Someone had a trauma doctor on speakerphone. He was studying the meters that appeared to be connected to Vanessa. Kate could hear him.

"If those meters are genuine, her signs are way up. Her stress is causing her to use more oxygen, which could reduce her time. Her carbon dioxide level is three percent, if it climbs to four or higher, we're in trouble. And you've got to hope that the box doesn't collapse under the weight and pressure of all the dirt."

Chuck, Reeka, along with executive editors Rhett Lerner and Dianne Watson arrived. Newslead's chief legal counsel, Tischa Goldman, was on the line to advise them on releasing any information police may need to help locate Vanessa.

As word spread, other news staff arrived to offer help, but most everyone huddled in small groups at terminals transfixed by what was playing out before their eyes. Kate couldn't stop trembling, or praying, as she watched the seconds blazing by.

Glimpsing at her framed photo of Grace, Kate called Nancy and told her what was happening.

"I know," Nancy said, "it's been on TV with a breaking news bulletin."

Kate needed to know Grace was okay.

"I'll go down and check on her," Nancy said. Ten minutes later, she called back to say that Grace was fine.

As a precaution, Kate pulled one of the NYPD officers aside and requested that, given the fact Zurrn had called her, they send someone to her building to check on her daughter's welfare.

When Kate returned to her desk, her line rang. She looked at an FBI agent wearing headphones and waited for him to nod before she answered.

"You're seeing what's happening online, Kate?" the caller asked.

It was Erich. Kate indicated to the agent that the caller was a friend.

"Yes, Zurrn called me."

"He called?"

"We're sure it was him. He wants the world to see him kill Vanessa."

"He's getting attention."

"We've got the NYPD, the FBI and I don't know how many others, trying to locate her. Tell me the truth, Erich, can we find her?"

He didn't answer.

"Erich, will we find her?"

"It depends."

"On what?"

"How good he really is at hiding his tracks."

"That's not what I need to hear right now."

"You got people working on it. I'll work on it and I'll get my friends to work on it. Everyone's trying to pinpoint the source of the feed and Vanessa's location."

"Hurry!"

As the first hour became the second, the press picked up the situation via social media. The *New York Times*, Reuters, NBC, CNN, the Associated Press and several other news organizations called Newslead for interviews.

"All our efforts are concentrated on the safety of Vanessa Page, whom we consider a member of the Newslead family," Dianne Watson said in an issued statement.

Strained calm permeated the newsroom as the second hour passed with investigators working with other experts across the city and across the country. Several blocks south in Manhattan, near the Brooklyn Bridge, a team of analysts had been put on Vanessa's case at the NYPD's Real Time Crime Center, which was located in a windowless room on a midlevel floor of One Police Plaza. The team used every high-tech resource in trying to trace the live stream to Vanessa's location.

The FBI, with experts in combating cyber-based terrorism, had activated cyber squads at the New York Field Office in FBI headquarters. They were also working with other federal agencies, including the Department of Defense and Homeland Security. They soon determined that the person who'd called Kate had used a disposable phone. The call had been made in the greater New York City area, but that was all they had so far.

In the urgent life-and-death effort to track the video feed to Vanessa, analysts had made emergency requests for data to several dozen service providers. The companies had twenty-four-hour hotlines with lawyers on duty. All cooperated immediately without requiring subpoenas or warrants.

"The challenge is," an FBI agent explained, "our suspect has masked and encrypted the signal. It's bouncing off satellites and towers all over Canada, Mexico and everywhere in the US. He's even using Russian and Chinese-based IP addresses. It's complex and it's a fast-moving target."

"So what do you do?" Lerner asked.

"We keep working, exercising different strategies."

"We've got a little over two hours left."

In a far corner, Reeka was lobbying Dianne and Chuck for Newslead to put out its own story.

"I don't know," Watson said, "there's some ambiguity here."

"The case is already public," Reeka said. "We've already issued a statement. It's news. We owe it to subscribers to cover it."

Watson turned to Chuck. "What do you think?"

"All valid points. We'll get someone other than Kate to do a straight-up news piece."

At her desk, Kate stared at Vanessa's image, her heart breaking again and again with each second that passed.

This can't be real. It can't be happening all over again.

First underwater, now underground, Vanessa was slipping away before her eyes.

Please, don't let this happen again.

Kate pressed her hand tenderly to her monitor, aching to hold her little sister one last time.

Where are you?

A commotion rose across the newsroom among several FBI agents.

"New Jersey! Central New Jersey, north of Trenton!" someone shouted.

Kate stood and searched the crowd for meaning, her heart rising.

"They've isolated it to a location just outside of Hopewell, New Jersey!" someone else shouted to cheers.

Ellie Ridder, a Newslead reporter and Sal Perez, a photographer, rushed to Kate.

"That's a ninety-minute drive, Kate," Sal said. "Let's go!"

66

New Jersey

Darkness.

Vanessa had been devoured by absolute darkness.

The air was heavy. The suffocating stillness overwhelmed her. The only sound of life was the thumping blood rush in her ears from her beating heart.

Buried alive! I've been buried alive like Brittany!

Screaming sobs exploded from her.

Don't let me die! Please, God, I don't want to die here!

She kicked her feet and pounded her bound hands against her coffin's lid before she realized it and stopped.

Stay calm! You're using up air!

It took several jagged breaths before she got a semblance of control, sniffling and brushing at her tears. The air was hotter. She was sweating as she gradually slowed her breathing.

She didn't know how much time had passed, how

long she'd been entombed. She flinched when a light came on.

Blinking her eyes to adjust, she saw soft, blue-tinted LED lights directed at her and from behind her overhead. She gasped as the illumination defined her horrible claustrophobic space.

Midway down above her waist, suspended from the lid, she saw the line of small glowing screens with active level bars and numbers. Cables meandered from the monitors to the clips Carl had attached to her fingers. Farther down, at her feet, she saw the cylinder shape of the oxygen tank. In the row of screens, the one to the extreme right was the largest.

It came to life with text scrolling slowly.

"I hope you're comfortable. The world is watching you, thousands of people, as each second ticks down. It'll grow to millions around the planet, for this is a global death and viewers will be riveted. Especially since I've installed the meters to monitor your vital signs, the amount of oxygen remaining, and the clock, which is calibrated to my precise calculation on how much time you'll have to live. Each one is identified for you. Remember, the more you panic, struggle or flutter, the more you'll deplete your oxygen. You're six feet down. The casket is steel, but it's cheap steel and it's possible it could be defeated by the tonnage of earth above you. It's pointless to struggle against it. No one can hear you and no one will ever find you. I hope you'll forgive me because I wanted to take you with me to my new base of operation to be part of my new collection. It's going to be glorious. But you interfered and betrayed me and must suffer the penalty.

I'll miss you terribly. Of all my specimens, you were my favorite. Goodbye."

Vanessa's heart slammed against her rib cage. Her scream sent the level bars on the monitors soaring as tears blurred her eyes.

No, please no! Oh, God, somebody help me!

At that moment she detected a light sensation—*something moving*—atop her midsection, a gentle pressure. *What's that?* She raised her head, then her hands to block the light directed at her, so she could better see. A curtain of fine dirt was leaking from the coffin lid at the seam between the upper and lower doors.

No! No, no, no!

Vanessa gasped and tried not to think but was suddenly haunted by the screams—the horrible screams—of all the girls Carl had killed before her.

Now it's my turn! Now it's me!

Her panicked mind reeled, pulled her back to another life, to a moment of absolute joy as she was enveloped by brilliant sunlight. She was floating and floating. She saw her mother—her real mother's smiling face, then her father's. Then she heard their laughter as she ran in the park with her big sister—*Kate!*

Yes, her name was Kate!

Suddenly, the sunlight is gone, her parents are gone, and now Vanessa is underwater, cold, black rushing water, and Kate's hand is pulling her...saving her...please save me, Kate!

A sharp metallic, crackling sound filled the casket. Vanessa felt the vibration as a corner buckled.

More dirt was now trickling in at her feet and mid-section.

The clock was showing that she had one hour and fifty minutes to live.

67

Hopewell, New Jersey

The gleaming white walls of the Lincoln Tunnel rushed by Kate's front passenger window.

Sal Perez guided his Dodge Journey SUV under the Hudson River and into New Jersey. After passing through the tollgate and barreling south on I-95, he tossed a worn notebook to Ellie Ridder in the backseat.

He'd already passed her his two portable police scanners.

"Ellie, tune into the frequencies for the New Jersey State Police for the Troop C—they cover Mercer County, where Hopewell is."

"I don't see it."

"Go to the *N* tab for New Jersey."

Ellie snapped through pages while Kate checked online for updates and the minutes and seconds ticked down on Vanessa.

"Okay, got it!"

"Good, program them in like I showed you, then go online and get the frequency for Mercer County. You should get local paramedics, fire, everybody."

Fear had numbed Kate's fingertips as she watched her messages for news of a location. She took some comfort that she was with Perez and Ridder. Sal and Ellie both had reported in Iraq and Afghanistan, while at home they'd covered tornadoes, floods, wildfires and major shootings.

As they put miles behind them, the scanners crackled to life with dispatches of cross talk from emergency responders in and surrounding Hopewell. Sal pushed his SUV hard, weaving through traffic to pass news vans from New York.

"Looks like everybody's headed to Hopewell," Sal said after he'd passed the third one.

"It's déjà vu," Ellie said.

"What'd you mean?"

"Hopewell. You don't know about Hopewell, New Jersey, Sal?"

"I'm drawing a blank."

"You remember Charles Lindbergh, the first person to fly solo across the Atlantic?"

"Yeah."

"Well in 1932, his baby boy was kidnapped from his home in Hopewell, New Jersey, for ransom. After Lindbergh paid fifty thousand, the baby's body was found in a wooded area south of Hopewell. At that time, it was the biggest story in the world."

"Oh, right. They executed the guy who did it."

Ellie touched Kate's shoulder.

"I'm sorry to bring this up, Kate."

"It's history. It's true. I know that and I was thinking maybe Zurrn was trying to emulate the Lindbergh case. But none of this seems real to me right now—I'm sorry. Please go faster, Sal."

The scanner's transmissions concerned the positioning of work crews around the town. As Kate turned to the window to search the night, a loud ringing sounded in the SUV and Sal answered his hands-free phone, boosting the volume.

"It's Chuck, how far are you from Hopewell, Sal?"

He glanced at his GPS.

"Twenty, twenty-five minutes, Chuck. What've you got?"

"Here's the latest. They haven't pinpointed the site but they believe they're close to locking in. What they're doing is using every local government crew, and every available contractor to trailer backhoes to the compass points surrounding Hopewell, to get ready to move. They've got a medical helicopter standing by and the trauma team at Viola Memorial in Newark is on alert. The medical experts said her signs are deteriorating and she's down to thirty minutes."

As the highway markers streaked under them and the miles passed, Kate clenched her eyes shut and whispered a prayer. It might've been five minutes, maybe longer, before Ellie shouted.

"They've got something!" She cranked the crackling dispatches.

"Yes," Chuck said, "the FBI here are nodding! They've got a crew there and they've started digging!"

"Its north, about one and a half miles on Wertsville Road!" Ellie said.

Sal entered the information into his GPS and accelerated. Kate's knuckles whitened as she clasped her hands together. Within ten minutes they were cutting through town. Sal threaded around other work crews, their lights flashing as they hauled equipment. Overhead the air vibrated with the thump of police and news helicopters.

"Oh, no!" Ellie held out a scanner. "Listen!"

"...got down about four feet—found an opened metal toolbox—he left some kind of transmission device inside and a note that says—'Ha-ha! Try again! Ticktock!'..."

Kate's heart sank. *Oh, God, oh, God, no!*

The phone line to Chuck and the scanners crackled with a somber silence. Then there was soft background noise from Chuck's end.

"They're baffled here. They've just got a call from Detective Brennan in Rampart strongly suggesting the site could be in Montana."

"Montana! What the—how does Brennan know that?" Kate was losing it. "What's going on, Chuck?"

"No wait, Kate!" Chuck was optimistic. "Others here are still insisting that the signal's coming from Hopewell."

Kate's cell phone rang.

"It's Erich. My friends are following this online, Kate."

"Where is she?"

"Hopewell—it's Hopewell!"

Two New Jersey State Trooper cars shot by their SUV in the opposite direction, sirens wailing, lights wig-wagging.

"Did you see that?" Sal's head whipped around. "Something's up!"

"Another signal!" Ellie said. "South!"

"Yes!" Chuck said. "We've got it here! They're saying the Hopewell-Princeton Road!"

Sal wheeled the SUV around. Above them the

choppers banked south, as well. As the SUV's motor growled Ellie relayed the radio dispatches.

"They're pinpointing it, Sal. The area is one mile south from the road's junction with 518. Old Mount Rose Road comes into play. I don't believe this!"

"What?" Kate turned to Ellie. "What is it?"

"It's the same spot where they found the Lindbergh baby!"

Backhoe contractor "Big Ben" Pickett, got his Case 590 into position at a patch of disturbed earth they'd identified as the site in the woods some forty yards from the road.

Pickett had moved fast when he got the call at home from the township and the background nearly two hours ago. Posting him on the south side was smart. They were practically on the site when they confirmed the location.

With some twenty-five years in the business, Pickett lived on his machine. He could open this hole up in about four minutes, "like digging into mashed potatoes," he told the troopers. They were working with the FBI agent and firefighter waving him into position, while a state police K-9 unit barked at the ground.

Portable light towers were rolled in to illuminate the scene.

As he worked, Pickett was deaf to helicopters overhead, the sirens of arriving emergency vehicles and the growing stream of news media. Troopers stretched crime scene tape at the road to keep the press back.

Lights from the cameras glowed and flashed on Pickett.

His engine roared as his bucket bit into the soft

earth, scooping out over a foot of dirt. Firefighters used ground-penetrating locators and probe poles, feeling for a container, before waving Pickett to remove another layer. The process was completed again and again, quickly, efficiently until the poles hit a solid object at the depth of nearly six feet.

Firefighters waved for Pickett to stop. Ladders were lowered and crews cleared off the dirt, revealing a casket with chains sealing the lid. Industrial bolt cutters and other high-powered rescue tools were passed to the firefighters, who immediately opened the lid and looked down.

Vanessa Page was inside, barely conscious.

She offered a weak smile.

Firefighters transferred her to a spine board, secured an oxygen mask to her face and initiated a flow stream before they hefted her from her grave to hurry her toward the open clamshell doors of the waiting medical helicopter.

Kate jumped from Sal's SUV before he brought it to a stop and flew to the police line where other news people were gathered, recording events as they unfolded. News camera operators zoomed in tight on Vanessa's rescue.

"She's alive!" one of them shouted.

Unable to bear it, Kate lifted the tape and, before state troopers and deputies could react, ran to Vanessa.

Kate's heart was nearly bursting as she ran over the rugged terrain to the clearing as rescuers carrying Vanessa neared the helicopter. The deafening beating of the rotors made it impossible to hear but couldn't stop her from screaming Vanessa's name.

The men carrying her were stunned when Kate appeared, shouting at the top of her lungs.

"I'm her sister! I'm her family!" Then taking Vanessa's hand and shouting to her, "I'm your sister! Kate! I'm your family! You're not alone anymore!" Kate squeezed Vanessa's hand and then she felt her squeeze back, so hard.

They found each other's eyes and peace in the roaring chaos.

Strong hands gripped Kate's shoulders as deputies and troopers pulled her back and paramedics secured Vanessa, closed the chopper's door and lifted off. Its blinking lights disappeared into the night.

As they escorted Kate back to the tape, she explained over and over who she was and why she did what she did.

"I'm her sister! I have to be with her!"

"We know who you are, Kate," one of the troopers said. "They're going to Viola in Newark. We'll take you there now so you can be with her."

At the tape, nearly fifty reporters and photographers blocked the path to the police vehicles. They jostled amid the crush as the pack demanded Kate give a statement.

She agreed.

Amid the glare and subdued confusion Kate battled to collect herself, with adrenaline coursing through her and her heart racing.

"I thank God, and everyone else who helped, that we found my sister alive. To the families who've lost loved ones in this horrible nightmare, you have our prayers. To Sorin Zurrn, it's over for you because my sister fought back and stopped you. You lose. It's time to surrender."

68

Newark, New Jersey

When Kate arrived at Viola Memorial Hospital, they wouldn't let her see Vanessa.

"She's been sedated," the doctor told her in the emergency reception area. "She's asleep."

"How is she?"

"In some shock, malnourished, dehydrated, but her signs are good—she needs rest." He uncollared his stethoscope. "She asked about you."

Kate's heart lifted.

"I have to be at her side. I don't want to leave her alone."

The doctor's focus shifted to survey the people who'd gathered behind Kate—the FBI agents, state police, senior hospital administration.

"We have an active investigation," one of the agents said. "We're attempting to locate a dangerous fugitive. Your patient is our witness and we need to talk to her."

"Yes, I respect that, but I think in this case allowing a family member to be in the room may prove beneficial to her recovery," the doctor said.

"As long as one of our people remains present at all times," the agent said. "And, a police officer remains posted outside the door."

First, they took Kate to an office where she signed papers for Vanessa. Then she called home.

"You found her! Thank heaven! It's wonderful news!" Nancy said through tears as Kate told her that she'd be spending the night at the hospital and asked her to get Grace off to school in the morning. Nancy said that with two NYPD officers in the building and more on the street, she felt safe, "even with that monster on the loose!"

Kate then contacted Chuck to give him an update and a quote for Newslead's story. News outlets were requesting interviews, he said. Kate gave him a statement thanking everyone while pleading for privacy and time so that she and her sister could reconcile their lives.

A nurse took Kate to an elevator.

When it stopped, the nurse's soft-soled shoes squeaked as they walked along the polished floor. Kate noticed the antiseptic smell in the hallway, then saw the Newark police officer in a chair outside Vanessa's room.

The officer nodded.

"You may go in if you like." The nurse smiled, pushing the door open.

Kate froze.

Is it really over? Twenty lost years compressed into this moment. The sister I've carried alive in my heart for two decades is now a few feet from me!

She took a deep breath and entered, absorbing the

soft, calming light, the hum and tick of the room's air system. The FBI agent in a chair at the foot of the bed indicated the empty chair next to Vanessa.

Kate studied her sister as if gazing upon a miracle. An IV was attached to one arm. An air tube looped under her nose. There were small bloodied scratches on her cheeks and forehead, and her long hair shot out on the pillow in an unkempt panic. Underneath it all, Kate saw a dignified, enduring beauty in the woman she had become.

And as she looked at her, anger bubbled in her gut at all that Zurrn had stolen from Vanessa—her milestones, the things she'd missed. Her first kiss, high school, her first boyfriend, her prom, college, birthdays, Christmas, her sense of family.

Family.

Suddenly memories blazed before Kate like a shooting star, brilliant images of them together as children, up until the horrible crash that tore them apart. She gasped, exploding in heaving sobs she fought to subdue as she reached for her sister's hand, slowly, painstakingly entwining her fingers with hers, and held tight.

Kate fell asleep in the chair holding on to Vanessa.

In the morning sunlight filled the room.

Kate woke and saw the FBI agent at the door talking quietly with the police officer. Vanessa was awake staring at the ceiling.

"Hi." Kate smiled.

Vanessa turned to her and said nothing.

"I'm your big sister, Kate. Kate Page."

Vanessa swallowed and stared blankly at her, as

if afraid. Then her eyes went round the room and her face congested with confusion.

"It's okay. You're in a hospital in Newark, New Jersey. You're free and you're safe. Police are here watching over you. He can't hurt you anymore."

Vanessa's eyes came back to Kate's and searched them, across oceans of pain to a distant time.

"You're Vanessa Page," Kate said. "Our mother's name was Judy. Our dad was Raymond, but everyone called him Ray."

Vanessa said nothing but listened.

"We were a happy family. We lived in a house in a nice neighborhood near Washington, DC. We had dolls. You called yours Molly the Dolly. We had a yard and a tire swing where we played. You liked blowing soap bubbles, remember?"

Vanessa blinked a few times.

"Then Mom and Dad died and we were so sad. We had to live with relatives, then we lived in foster homes all over the country." Kate reached for a tissue. "Then we were on a vacation driving in the mountains in Canada when our car crashed and went upside down into the river. Our foster parents were killed. I had your hand and tried to pull you out, but you slipped away and ever since that moment I've searched for you everywhere. Do you remember these parts of your life, Vanessa?"

A long moment went by before she slowly began nodding.

"Mostly I remember you," Vanessa said.

"Oh..." Kate's voice broke and as she slid her arms around Vanessa, she felt her sister's arms around her, holding her with all of her strength. In that moment Kate's heart flooded with a bittersweet sensation of mourning what they'd lost and celebrating what they'd found. Then Kate noticed the agent and two nurses watching from the door and she started telling Vanessa what was going to happen.

"The people here are going to help you heal. You're with people who love you and will care for you. I'll be here every second I can."

Vanessa nodded.

"The police need to talk to you about Sorin Zurrn, the man who held you. We know he had lots of names, but that's his real name. The police need to know things, like how he hurt you and the others, who he knew, and if he talked about where he might be going, anything to help them find him."

"Find him?"

Fear rose in her eyes.

"It's okay, Vanessa, you're safe. Police are here." Kate looked at her and repeated, "I know this is hard to understand, but you're safe. You're with me now."

Vanessa blinked several times then Kate reached for her phone.

"I have a little girl, Grace. You're her aunt."

Kate showed her a picture.

"She looks like you," Vanessa said.

"That's funny because I think she looks like you."

Kate smiled, glanced at the FBI agent and continued. "Okay, Vanessa, police will need you to help them. They'll need you to remember everything and to be strong, just like you were when you helped that girl get away."

* * *

Kate went home but spent most of the next several days at the hospital.

In that time, Vanessa talked privately in her room with FBI agents from the task force, telling them everything she could about her time in captivity.

For her part, Kate, in a press conference held at the FBI's Field Office in Manhattan, continued offering condolences to the families of Zurrn's victims, her thanks for the avalanche of messages supporting her sister and a plea for the public to help find Zurrn. And at Reeka's insistence, Kate also spoke with Newslead reporters for an exclusive feature on the rescue.

The hunt for Zurrn, the "most wanted man in America," remained one of the nation's leading news stories. Across the country and in Canada, the press dug deep at the tentacles of the case that reached into their communities.

Speculation on Zurrn's whereabouts, his life, his crimes and motive, fueled debate, theories and rumors on national network discussion panels. Zurrn's evocation of the Lindbergh baby kidnapping case, his near-successful attempt to broadcast a murder-in-progress live online, was chilling. His ability to outsmart detectives while being, what one pundit called, "an invisible chameleon," made Sorin Zurrn one of the most intelligent and dangerous killers of the past century, according to a strident expert on one cable news talk show.

The FBI, state police in New Jersey and New York, Newark police and the NYPD, continued taking every precaution. They'd mounted an ongoing police presence at Kate's building, and Kate was routinely driven by law enforcement from Manhattan to her hospital visits.

Newslead, the State of New Jersey and the FBI's Office for Victim Assistance, insured that Vanessa was given the best medical care at the hospital. She received treatment from a psychiatrist expert in helping people with their recovery after being long-term hostages or prisoners.

In the first days, Vanessa's sessions had gone well. The doctor had insisted that she not see or read news reports of her case, so that she could process the enormity of her experience at her own pace without creating additional stress. The psychiatrist saw Kate as a therapeutic source of comfort for Vanessa and encouraged her hospital visits. Kate brought photos of their early life together and they soon began talking about how they would build Vanessa's new life.

Little by little the healing had begun.

Over those days, Kate received a message from Erich—Happy you got your sister back. But she thought it odd that she hadn't heard from Ed Brennan.

Then on the seventh day after Vanessa's rescue, Kate was at home helping Grace with her homework when her phone rang.

"Kate, this is Brennan."

"Ed, I was wondering why I haven't heard from you."

"We've been working and we've got something."

"What is it?"

"Nobody outside the task force knows what I'm going to tell you, but after all you and your sister have been through, I owe you."

"Tell me."

"You can't breathe a word to anyone. We put in a lot of hard work on this."

"I swear."

"We've got him."

"What, when, where?"

"The other side of the country, we're locked on to him. It'll be all over and you'll be hearing about it real soon."

69

Near Miles City, Montana

The wind rolled in waves over the vast grasslands, tumbling into the coulees and raking the cottonwood grove where Brennan lay hidden from view.

Face clenched behind mounted, high-powered binoculars, he studied the ranch house and outbuildings rising from the plain over a mile away.

This is where Sorin Zurrn's going to be today.

Through his earpiece Brennan listened to whispered spurts of encrypted transmissions over walkie-talkies.

No movement or activity.

The FBI's Hostage Rescue Team controlled the inner perimeter.

They'd set up lookout posts while sharpshooters and assault team members were concealed in spots surrounding the house. They were backed up by an FBI unit from Salt Lake City and tactical teams from across Montana. They held positions at the outer perimeter, where Brennan and other task force members waited.

Flying above them, silent and unseen, a small remotely controlled surveillance drone sent live images of the isolated region to the FBI's command post four miles away in a building where the Montana Department of Transportation kept snowplows.

Brennan had been at his perimeter position for ten hours now, confident that the investigation was solid.

This is Zurrn's property. He'll be here. Everything fits.

They'd connected all the dots going back to Carl Nelson's coworker Mark Rupp, who'd glimpsed Nelson looking at a real estate page and making notes more than a year ago. It turned out Nelson had used an absent coworker's computer, which had been sold later as surplus with other equipment to an out-of-state office supply warehouse.

It was a challenge, but the FBI moved fast and located the unit in Beltsville, Maryland. Examining it, they recovered and extracted the information, like browser history, that led to a real estate sale in Custer County, Montana. Executing warrants, the FBI determined that Zurrn had used a network of aliases and numbered companies to purchase the property under the name Wallace Cordell. When the FBI showed Zurrn's photos to the agent on the deal she was incredulous. "Yes, that sort of looks like him! But Wallace Cordell had red hair and thick sideburns. My Lord! You're telling me this is the man on the news?"

The agent said the deal had closed a few months ago and all that was left was for Cordell/Zurrn to take possession very soon. In fact, she'd already left the keys for him in a lockbox. The agent gave the FBI the date Cordell was to arrive to take possession.

"He assured me he'd be there at any time on that date. I was going to drop by after he called me to congratulate him and pick up the lockbox."

The sprawling property was in a windswept region of farms and ranches. It had been owned by a doomsday cult. Records and plans obtained by the FBI showed that the group had constructed a well-maintained underground bunker, "with a large number of sealable, dorm-like chambers," to prepare for a predicted Armageddon in 2012. But when the prophesy failed, followers left and the ranch was put up for sale.

It was ideal for Zurrn.

In the days before Zurrn's possession date, the FBI executed warrants to search it and confirm it was empty, that no victims or prisoners were being held there. They also checked it for hidden cameras or security measures Zurrn may have surreptitiously installed.

Then the FBI questioned Hub Arness, who owned the neighboring property. Hub, who'd always kept an eye on the place, said there'd been no recent activity. But a couple years back there was some regular trouble. "These ex-cult types still trekked out there and sometimes vandalized the property," Hub said.

Zurrn's return date and the task force's swift investigation led to the execution of more warrants and their arrest strategy. The Hostage Rescue Team flew from Quantico, Virginia, and, so not to attract attention, landed about 165 miles away at the Gillette-Campbell County Airport in Gillette, Wyoming.

Then, in an undisclosed location in Montana, the team and equipment were transferred to state and county service trucks. Under cover of night, they embedded at key points on the property while other tactical units, including members of the task force, took up positions in the outer perimeter where they'd been waiting since the predawn hours.

Now, as sunset neared, the radio crackled with a dispatch from the command post.

"Head's up. Eyes in the sky have activity."

Brennan tensed.

"We've got a van approaching from the east."

Dust clouds rose in the distance as a lone vehicle rolled along the dirt road to the property. It was headed to the ranch house.

"Hold your positions."

Brennan dragged the back of his hand across his mouth as he watched through his binoculars.

"Hold."

The van slowed, then braked. Nothing happened. From what Brennan could see, there was only the driver in the front. Judging from the shadow silhouette, the driver was doing something behind the wheel.

"Maintain positions."

The driver's door opened and a male got out and began walking to the rear of the van.

"Go! Go! Go! Go!"

Heavily armed tactical members rushed from their covers with weapons drawn on the driver, instantly putting him facedown on the dirt.

"What the—don't kill me!"

As the driver was handcuffed a tactical team member fished through his pants for a wallet and ID. According to his Montana driver's license, the man was Marshall Chang, aged thirty-two from Billings, where he worked for Big Sky Rapid Courier.

"What're you doing here, Mr. Chang?" an agent asked.

"I'm delivering to Wallace Cordell. This is my last one of the day."

"Did you speak with Cordell today?"

"No."

"Do you know his whereabouts?"

"No. I don't know the guy. This is my first time to this place."

"What sort of delivery are you making?"

"I don't know, it says 'parts.'"

"Parts for what?" The agent turned to another. "Let's take a look."

Weapons at the ready, team members opened the van's rear doors to a large wooden crate. They pried off the lid to find it lined with heavy plastic. The first agent pulled at the plastic, then suddenly recoiled.

"Whoa!"

The agent backed into the second agent, who moved forward to look.

"What the hell?"

Others crowded, peered inside to a mass of severed arms, legs, torsos and heads with sinewy tendons. One agent grabbed the lid and read the shipping label, which was stamped "Urgent Express."

"Look at this." He pointed to the shipper's address. "Studio Quality Body Parts Discount Movie Props, Burbank, California—they're fake! This is for us! He expected us to find this place and be waiting today!"

70

New York City

Across the country, Kate was in her apartment when her phone rang. The number displayed was for the NYPD.

"Hello?"

"Hi, this is Officer Morello with the NYPD, calling for Kate Page."

"I'm Kate."

"Ms. Page, as you know, Newark PD has informed us that they're unable to transport you to the hospital. I've been assigned to be your ride."

"I never heard from Newark."

"They said they'd called you."

"No, I didn't get a call."

"Must've been a screwup. Sorry about that, ma'am, but can I pick you up in twenty-minutes?"

That was earlier than usual. Kate hesitated. Days ago, Newark police and the FBI's Office for Victim Assistance had indicated to Kate that, for security reasons, the job of ferrying her to and from the hospital might be shared by various police agencies.

"Ma'am, I'm sorry for any inconvenience, but I got court duty in the morning and—"

"No, it's fine."

"Good. Just so you know I won't be in uniform. My sarge said this is plainclothes duty."

"I'll be in front of my building in twenty minutes."

Officer Morello thanked Kate and recited her address.

"That's it."

Kate alerted Nancy that she was leaving a bit early, then hurried getting herself ready. Fifteen minutes later she was downstairs standing in front of her building. Uniformed officers were no longer in sight. They'd only been posted to the street during the first days after Vanessa's rescue. Kate didn't mind because it reinforced Brennan's call, that they'd found Zurrn somewhere far off. *Was it Colorado?* Kate watched the traffic until a shining black Chevy sedan stopped in front. The driver dropped the passenger window and leaned out.

"Excuse me, are you Kate Page?"

"Yes."

"Officer Morello. I called."

"Hi." Kate stepped to the unmarked cruiser.

As Morello got out and opened the rear door Kate heard radio dispatches spilling out. Morello was in his forties, had a thick black mustache, thick dark hair and glasses. He wore a dark blue houndstooth sport coat, light blue shirt and dark pants.

"Watch your head," he cautioned as she got in.

She glimpsed the butt of a gun peeking from his shoulder holster as he closed the door, then walked around to get behind the wheel.

The car was not as nice as the Newark and FBI cars that had come for her over the past week. The air was musty, the seats torn and patched with tape. A scarred Plexiglas shield divided the rear and front seats, but the sliding gap was open so they could talk.

"You could ride in the front with me if you like," Morello said into the rearview mirror, "but our policy dictates that you ride back there for your safety."

"Better stick to the policy." Kate smiled. "Thanks for doing this."

"No problem, ma'am."

As they pulled away Kate asked the usual question.

"Have you heard of any breaks finding Zurrn?"

"Me? Naw, they don't keep grunts like me in the loop."

"Just thought I'd ask."

"No problem, you just take it easy back there."

As he wheeled into Manhattan traffic, Kate's thoughts went to Brennan's confidential tip. He'd left her on pins and needles ever since he'd told her they'd found Zurrn. She fell into her habit of checking her phone for news, searching the competition and regional wires.

Nothing.

She called Brennan and again it went straight to his voice mail.

Kate took a breath, smiling as she considered Vanessa. It had only been a week, but the psychiatrist said she was making remarkable progress and soon Kate could bring Grace to meet her. Thinking of their new future together as a family, Kate took in her surroundings and realized they were on 125th Street and had just passed Amsterdam Avenue.

"Excuse me." Kate moved to the divider. "I think

you're going east—this is the wrong way. We should be getting on the West Side Highway, for the Lincoln Tunnel, that's the way everybody goes."

Morello didn't respond.

"Officer, you're going the wrong way."

Morello ignored her.

Kate sat forward and thrust her face toward his shoulder. "Officer!"

Morello said nothing.

As Kate puzzled over her situation a terrible unease hit her like a cobra's strike. Staring hard at Morello's neck, Kate noticed for the first time how a stubbly ridge of shaved hair crept below what should have been his hairline.

He's wearing a wig.

She questioned if his mustache was real, then the pieces—*Morello's call, switching drivers, coming early, going the wrong way*—and in an awful instant, realization exploded.

Oh, God, Morello is Sorin Zurrn!

Kate's pulse soared.

This is how it happened to the others! He just reaches into your world and takes you into his!

Kate had regarded his victims as young, inexperienced, vulnerable, easy prey, like Vanessa. Now, he proved that none of Kate's street smarts or her gut instincts mattered.

Think! You have to think!

She still had her phone, her lifeline. She forced herself to be calm.

"Okay," she said. "I'm sorry. Maybe you know a better way. Guess I'm tense today."

Her hand trembled as secretly she reached for her

phone. Fearing he'd hear the emergency dispatcher, Kate started to text an emergency message to Nancy to call 911. But her blood turned to ice.

Her phone was dead.

She met Zurrn's eyes in the rearview mirror.

"You're fluttering, Kate."

Zurrn held up his phone.

"As a collector, I took care of everything. I hacked your phone long ago. I just fried it."

The saliva in Kate's mouth evaporated.

"You told everyone it was over for me, didn't you?" he said. "I had astounding plans, but you destroyed them! You exhumed the name I buried and shamed me! Now I have nothing—*except you*!"

Kate tried her door handle.

It was gone, so was the other one. There was no escape.

She tried waving to people in other cars for help.

Zurrn activated the siren and emergency lights, to insure she looked like a disturbed person under arrest.

"We'll start over, together!" he said. "You're a magnificent specimen! The rarest, most glorious! No one will ever find you! And you can't conceive of the wonders I will show you—*of what I'm going to do to you*!"

Kate undid her seat belt, repositioned her body and began kicking at the rear windshield.

"Beautiful," Zurrn said as he reached for something. "Flutter away, Kate. You know—" Zurrn strained, now gripping something that looked like a large electric razor "—in time, you'll come to love me."

He quickly lifted himself, extended his reach and

pressed the device against Kate's neck. It crackled, instantly overwhelming her neuromuscular system, disorienting her until she collapsed.

71

New York City

At that moment, in a loft in the Midtown neighborhood of Hell's Kitchen, a distinct alarm sounded on one of Erich's computers.

The trip wire! Kate's in trouble. Her phone suddenly went dead.

Immediately he rushed to his desk and began entering commands, taking him to the surveillance security cameras of the store across the street that also captured the entrance to Kate's building. Erich had breached the feed. With rapid stop-action, he reversed footage until Kate emerged, stepping into a vehicle.

Holy cow, that has to be him!

Erich made a screen grab photo of the suspect, then the vehicle, an older Chevy Impala, the kind used as unmarked cars by the NYPD.

I knew he'd try something.

In his gut, Erich had feared Zurrn would come for Kate.

Her increasingly high profile, her public anger toward Zurrn, had concerned Erich. He'd secretly cloned

Kate's phone and replaced it unnoticed when she'd dropped her bag in the restaurant after her *Today* show appearance. He'd installed in Kate's phone new ultra-secret "infect" software developed for the NSA and CIA. The software instantly infiltrated and tracked any phone that attempted to hack or destroy a protected phone, in this case: Kate's. The software first defeated, without detection, any security installed on the intruder's phone, then infected it with a stealth tracking program. The instant Zurrn killed Kate's phone, he'd triggered Erich's trip wire alarm, allowing him to instantly pinpoint Zurrn's phone and track his location without his knowledge.

"Gotcha!" Erich said aloud to his computers.

With a few key strokes he was looking at a geo-map showing the location, direction and speed of Zurrn's vehicle.

Erich called 911.

The emergency operator passed Erich's call to the NYPD's Real Time Crime Center at One Police Plaza in Lower Manhattan.

Immediately, crime analysts at the center, working at rows of computers before a large two-story array of flat video panels known as the data wall, used every high-tech resource they had. They tapped into large displays of detailed city maps and live feeds of surveillance cameras throughout the city.

Within ninety seconds of Erich's call they'd located Zurrn's car.

"He's leaving 125th and is starting southbound on FDR Drive," one analyst told the responding team.

"Keep this off the air!" Lieutenant Walt Mercer,

the center's duty commander, had taken charge of the unfolding situation. "Get all available unmarked units into position. No lights, no sirens!"

The analysts used one of the center's geocode maps to locate on-duty unmarked units in precincts along FDR south, the 25th, the 23rd, the 19th and 17th.

Dispatchers made urgent cell-phone calls and sent encrypted messages to detectives and officers whose units were closest. Several unmarked cruisers began roaring toward the expressway.

In the Upper East Side, Detective Vinnie Cerito, of the 19th Precinct, had completed a burglary beef at a clothing store near E 63rd Street and 1st Avenue.

He was working alone. Ruiz, his temporary partner, had booked off with a toothache. Cerito didn't care. It was better when he was alone because he was on edge. It'd been a month since he'd returned to duty from stress leave.

Maybe it's too early after what happened to Quinn. But I couldn't take another minute sitting at home watching TV, picking at the scab of my life.

Cerito had believed that being an NYPD detective was the best a cop could ask for. He and Quinn had lived the job, they'd put in the time. They'd climbed a million stairs, knocked on a million doors, dealt with every terrified, arrogant, snotty, idiotic citizen and criminal that dwelled here, only to see the courts let evildoers go; only to see that no one cared and good cops ended up like Quinn: shot in the head.

It was a night like this five months ago. They pull over an SUV wanted in a domestic and—bam—

the driver shoots Quinn in the head. He dies on the street in Cerito's arms. The suspect gets away, leaving Cerito to question everything.

To hell with it. Cerito had to keep going, had to push it aside tonight.

Now, he considered picking up some Chinese takeout when he got a message on his phone.

A dangerous homicide suspect abducted a woman after posing as a detective, is driving a black 2012 Chevy Impala, southbound on FDR. Take a position on the eastbound on-ramp to the 59th Street Bridge and await further instructions. No siren, no lights.

Cerito wheeled his Ford to the bridge, three blocks away, his stomach churning as he bit back on his rising anger. This call tore at his wound.

Whoever this A-hole is, he better pray he doesn't come my way.

Kate lay on the backseat, every muscle vibrating.

The initial pain of her body stiffening was wearing off, but she was still quivering.

Watching lights streak by, she struggled to grasp what had transpired…Detective Morello had come to drive her to the hospital…no, not Morello…not a detective… Zurrn!

Fear billowed in her.

He'd shocked her with a stun gun…she remembered… she was in Zurrn's car now, sensing they were still in the city speeding along an expressway, but she didn't know where.

Oh, God, think. Think!

She considered sitting up and looking but rejected the idea.

Better to remain quiet, let him think that she was still unconscious.

It gave her the advantage of surprise.

She looked at the plastic dividing shield. The sliding portion for the gap remained open.

Get ready! Wait for the right time and get ready!

At the center, analysts updated Lieutenant Mercer that the suspect had left FDR for 63rd.

"Where's everybody?" Mercer glared at the center's geocode map. "We need to get people into position to box him!"

They continued tracking the suspect's vehicle entering the on-ramp for the 59th Street Bridge to Queens. But not enough units were in place to choke the ramp for a proper takedown, not with a hostage situation.

"What about that one?" Mercer pointed to a unit on the map. "Bring him into play."

At that moment, Cerito's cell phone rang. It was a dispatcher from the Real Time Crime Center, confirming that he was now live in the hot zone.

"Target vehicle to pass you in seconds, five…four…three…"

Cerito had been idling on a shoulder. When Zurrn's dark Chevy Impala passed him he slid the transmission into Drive.

"Got a visual! I'm on him!"

"You are to follow unseen and await further orders."

* * *

Mercer was satisfied. Now they could execute a proper takedown.

The center had alerted the 114th and 108th precincts in Queens. Mercer instructed them to seal the bridge's off-ramp with all available units, marked, unmarked, so that the suspect would have no place to go. The unmarked unit following him would help box him. With enough manpower they could swarm the target car and reduce the risk to the hostage and the traffic.

That way we keep it off the bridge.

It would all be over in about three minutes.

One car was between Zurrn and Cerito as they proceeded along the approach for the upper level. Two narrow eastbound lanes bordered by concrete barriers flowed under the intricate webbing of arched steel trusses. They were in the right lane.

Cerito adjusted his grip on the wheel.

No way is this guy getting outta this!

In Zurrn's car Kate knew from the steelwork rolling by that they were on one of the major bridges.

Zurrn would be concentrating on driving.

This is my chance!

She whispered a prayer, took a breath, sprang up, shot her hands through the divider's open gap and clawed at Zurrn's face. Startled, he swerved, scraping against the barrier as he fought with her. Horns sounded, the car behind Zurrn veered around him into the left lane.

* * *

Cerito was now directly behind them.

Witnessing the struggle, Cerito accelerated until he was flanking Zurrn. Cerito hit his lights and siren, flagging Zurrn to stop. Zurrn's response was to crank his wheel left, slamming his Chevy against the side of Cerito's Ford, jolting him and detonating the cop's rage.

"You freakin' motherfu—!"

Something inside Cerito exploded—for Quinn, for all of Cerito's bitterness and pent-up anger. Adrenaline surged through him. He mashed the pedal to the floor, pushing the Ford half a length ahead of Zurrn, then he cut him off, forcing the Chevy into the concrete barrier.

Kate fell back into the seat.

Metal crunched, sparks cascaded as Cerito's fury, and the Ford's momentum forced the Chevy to jounce up the concrete barrier.

Kate screamed.

The sky, city lights and the East River flashed in a surreal montage as the Chevy sailed over the barrier. Her stomach lurched as she rolled and the car hung in the air for a sickening second before dropping upside down twenty feet, crashing onto the pavement of the single outer roadway of the lower deck, landing on its roof in the path of a VW Jetta.

The impact hurled Kate against the roof, her eyes frantic as the oncoming Jetta braked, skidded and slammed into the Chevy's rear quarter, plowing it through the steel wire fence, over the edge until the car's front half teetered in the air over the East River 130 feet below.

Metal crumpled as the car seesawed at the precipice.

The collision knocked Kate's head, jarring her teeth. Blood flowed from her injuries. Dazed, she tried to escape but was locked inside.

Zurrn was unconscious, his bloodied face buried in a deployed air bag.

Horns were blaring, people were shouting, calling for Kate.

"Don't move!" a man's voice boomed. "We'll get you out!"

A crowd gathered. Cerito had climbed to the lower level and radioed for help. Amid the chaos, construction workers emerged with tools, a rope. Working fast while others helped hold the car, one man used a special hammer to break open the rear windshield. They got a rope around Kate and under her arms.

"Climb out!"

As she clambered, something clamped onto her ankle.

Zurrn had seized her. Metal creaked loudly because his sudden movements had tipped the car's balance and it began slipping.

"We can't hold it!" the men felt the car's rear half rising.

"Come on! It's starting to fall!"

Kate kicked Zurrn's head, shook herself free and scrambled through the broken windshield as the Chevy, with Zurrn inside, plummeted nose first into the East River.

The construction workers pulled Kate to the bridge

and safety. There, she joined the others staring in disbelief at Zurrn's car, headlights glowing, then fading in the water as it sank.

Amid the noise and confusion, Kate trembled through her blood and tears as she watched the lights of the police and news choppers and the emergency boats. On the bridge, witnesses shared images and video they'd captured of the crash and plunge.

Sirens wailed. Traffic was frozen. Police had closed the bridge.

Someone had draped a blanket around Kate and was talking to her, but she couldn't hear them. Her ears rang with one thought:

It's over, it's over, it's over.

Epilogue

Soft breezes carried the giant iridescent soap bubble skyward and over Central Park's treetops before it popped.

A warm memory floated over Kate as she, Grace and Vanessa watched the street artist create another swirly sphere.

It's like when Vanessa made bubbles in our backyard. Now we've got another new memory.

It had been six weeks since Vanessa's rescue and they'd been taking her recovery day by day. Kate was still shaky from her close call with Zurrn and had taken a leave from Newslead. Together, they were working through the healing process as they moved on with their new lives.

The new bubble lifted off, Kate's phone rang and she answered it.

"Kate, it's Ed Brennan."

Since the search for Zurrn had ended she'd only heard from him a few times.

"Hi, Ed."

"How are you two doing?"

"A step at a time, you know."

"Listen, I'm in Manhattan meeting with the FBI.

I would like to see you and Vanessa, give you an update. Would that be okay?"

"Sure. Say, three at my place?"

"See you then."

Later on the subway home, Kate wondered about the update. After Zurrn's death, Brennan had been working steadily with the task force tying up loose ends of the case in Rampart, New Jersey, Chicago, Minnesota, Colorado and Alberta.

Sorin Zurrn was definitely dead.

Of that, Kate was certain. Divers had retrieved his corpse from the car and she'd insisted on seeing his autopsy photos. He had no family to claim him so the city took over disposal. His body was put in a pine coffin and buried on Hart Island by convicts from Rikers Island who were tasked with such work. There was no marker to draw twisted fans to the grave of one of the nation's most notorious murderers.

They'd found more remains at the barn site near Rampart, so the known number of people Zurrn had killed, including the Chicago schoolgirl who'd taunted his mother, was twenty-one. The identities of twenty had been confirmed. Across the country in the cities and towns where his victims had lived, people held candlelight memorial services, set up foundations, charities and scholarships.

Starting in Minnesota, with the state patrol, various groups in other states planned to honor Vanessa and Kate as heroes for saving lives because their actions had helped locate and stop Sorin Zurrn. Vanessa and Kate agreed to participate in a Minneapolis award ceremony in three months where Ashley Ostermelle, the teen Vanessa had freed, would be present to thank her.

All of the events were valid, positive steps in Vanessa's path to recovery. But one of the most significant aspects of her healing was Grace, her niece, Vanessa's psychiatrist had said.

Two weeks after her rescue, Vanessa had requested Kate bring Grace to the hospital so that they could meet for the first time, something the psychiatrist supported. Prior to that day, the psychiatrist talked to Grace, to let her know that it was okay to be nervous, even a little scared, but it would be all right.

Their first meeting involved lots of hugging and joyful tears.

Afterward, the psychiatrist told Vanessa and Kate that because Grace mirrored their ages during the tragedies of their young lives, she would be something of a therapeutic anchor for them, a strong focal point for their healing and a reflection of the unbreakable bond of their love. Understanding that would help them move on, would help them put the past in its proper place, to reach through the worst moments of their lives to connect with the best, and hang on.

After three weeks in the hospital, Vanessa had been discharged to live with her and Grace.

Kate had given her sister her own room. Initially there were rough moments with nightmares, anxiety attacks, fears of trust, of things not being safe. Gradually, those episodes diminished. The psychiatrist had said that Vanessa had emotional scars and that some would take longer than others to heal.

Nancy, with her nursing background, was a godsend to Vanessa, helping her adjust. Some days Kate and Vanessa would pore over old pictures of them. Eventually Kate arranged for a tutor to help Vanessa as an early step to help rebuild her life and Vanessa talked about maybe finding some sort of a job.

Since Zurrn's death Kate and Vanessa had declined the wave of interview requests, but they agreed to representation by a firm to help them consider which of the numerous book and movie deal offers they'd received was the best way to tell their story.

And it was during those early weeks that Erich called to see how they were recovering. Kate invited him over and he arrived bearing two small gift-wrapped boxes topped with pretty bows. Inside were new cell phones for Kate and Vanessa.

"They're the very best on the market," he said.

"No spy stuff installed?" Kate asked.

"They're as private as they can be." He winked.

"Thank you, Erich." Kate hugged him. "For all that you did."

"You've got my number, so don't be a stranger, Kate."

It was two forty-five when they got home.

Some twenty minutes later, Brennan got there.

"I got tied up with the FBI," he said at the door.

Nancy had taken Grace to her apartment. Kate directed him to the sofa where Vanessa greeted him with a hug. They'd met before when Brennan had questioned her at the hospital and she liked him.

"So, what's the update, Ed?" Kate asked, offering him coffee, which he declined.

"Since I was the first to talk to you when the case

surfaced, I wanted to be the first to tell you that it's closed."

"Thank God," Kate said.

"The reason it took so long is that we had to work with the US Attorney to be sure that no other person was criminally connected to Zurrn, that he'd acted alone when he'd committed his crimes. That took time."

"What if other victims are found?"

"If that happens, those cases will be investigated individually, of course. They're done searching the Rampart scene. It looks like there was nothing more in Minnesota, and he never got started in Montana. So for our purposes, the case has been cleared."

Vanessa was nodding but not smiling. She'd clasped her hands together so tightly her knuckles had whitened.

"That's not the only reason I'm here."

"What else is there?" Kate asked.

"This." Brennan reached into his pocket for a small box, passing it to Kate. "These are yours and I'm happy to return them to you."

Kate opened the box to two tiny guardian angel necklaces, with their names engraved.

One charm was battered and charred, the other was glistening.

* * * * *

Acknowledgments

Throughout history we've seen horrific cases around the world of real abductions where people have been held captive before their rescue or escape.

Those who survived their ordeals are true heroes.

Those who didn't must never be forgotten.

Full Tilt is a work of fiction about two sisters separated by tragedies. In telling their story, I took liberty with geography, police procedure, jurisdiction and technology, so please bear that in mind. I would also like you to bear in mind that if you thought this was a good story, it's because I benefited from the help of many people. I would like to thank the following for their hard work and support:

My thanks to Amy Moore-Benson, Emily Ohanjanians and the incredible editorial, marketing, sales and PR teams at Harlequin and MIRA Books in Toronto, New York and around the world.

Wendy Dudley, as always, made this story better.

Very special thanks to Barbara, Laura and Michael.

It's important you know that in getting this book to you, I also relied on the generosity of many people, too many to thank individually here. I am indebted to everyone in all stages of production, the sales representatives, librarians and booksellers for putting my work in your hands.

This brings me to what I hold to be the most critical part of the entire enterprise: you, the reader. This aspect has become something of a creed for me, one that bears repeating with each book.

Thank you very much for your time for without you, a book remains an untold tale. Thank you for setting your life on pause and taking the journey. I deeply appreciate my audience around the world and those who've been with me since the beginning who keep in touch. Thank you all for your very kind words. I hope you enjoyed the ride and will check out my earlier books while watching for my next one. I welcome your feedback. Drop by at (www.rickmofina.com), subscribe to my newsletter and send me a note.

Rick Mofina

http://www.facebook.com/rickmofina
http://twitter.com/RickMofina

New York Times Bestselling Author

CARLA NEGGERS

In snowy Swift River Valley, unexpected romance is just around the corner...

Heather Sloan has landed her dream job—the renovation of Vic Scarlatti's stately country home overlooking the icy waters of Echo Lake in Knights Bridge, Massachusetts. It's the perfect project for the family business, but for once, Heather is in charge.

Diplomatic Security Service agent Brody Hancock left Knights Bridge at eighteen, barely avoiding arrest and the wrath of Heather's brothers. Returning to help Vic, a retired diplomat and friend, Brody runs into Heather at every turn. Seeing her again has affected him more than he wants to admit. But Heather is wary of Brody's sudden interest in her, and she suspects there's more to his homecoming than he's letting on…

Set against the scenic backdrop of a New England winter, Echo Lake *is a captivating tale of family, friends and the possibility of new love.*

Available now, wherever books are sold!

Be sure to connect with us at:

Harlequin.com/Newsletters

Facebook.com/HarlequinBooks

Twitter.com/HarlequinBooks

www.MIRABooks.com

MCN1743